UNCOILED LIES

*Secrets from the grave can come
back to haunt you.*

D.I. Gus McGuire Book 2

By

Liz Mistry

PUBLICATIONS

i

This edition published in 2019

By

PUBLICATIONS

Murder Book Publications

First Published in 2017 by BHB

PRINT ISBN: 978-1-9161835-5-1

DI Gus McGuire Series:

Unquiet Souls
Uncoiled Lies
Untainted Blood
Uncommon Cruelty
Unspoken Truths
Unseen Evil
Unbound Ties

DS Nikki Parekh series:

Last Request
Broken Silence
Dark Memories

Praise for Liz Mistry

'I have great admiration for Mistry's skill, this is one of the best crime thrillers I've read in ages.'

'Absolutely fantastic read.'

'Simply unputdownable.'

'Devoured in two days.'

DEDICATION

To Nilesh, Ravi, Kasi and Jimi with all my love

xxx

PROLOGUE
Then
November 5th

The Catherine wheel sizzled and whirred, before crescendoing to a screech that had Sadia clambering onto the sofa. Her hands gripped the back and her eyes blazed in excitement. The stained-glass panes rattled as she pressed her nose against them, searching the sky for the floral shower that should have accompanied the firework. The sky remained dark. Disappointed, Sadia's mouth drooped, but, as she turned to slide from the sofa, an orange flicker appeared outside. With a frown, she rubbed a clear circle onto the steamed-up window. Strange sputtering sounds, followed by a low hum, drifted through the darkness. It sounded like the distressed 'moos' of cattle on their way to slaughter.

Then, the meaty smell of overdone barbecue seeped through the rotting wooden window frames, making her retch. With the fingers of one hand pinching her nostrils and the other kneading the sofa cushions, she stared, all trace of excitement replaced by horror, at the ball of flames outside her gate.

The distorted human form weaved from side to side; a ghastly puppet, arms flailing against the flames. Suddenly, a sharp pop rent the air and blue sparks burst from the eye sockets. The puppet fell to the floor, melting like a grotesque ice lolly before her eyes.

She screamed and dived off the sofa landing on her knees before the coffee table. Her skinny arms reached up to cover her head and, as she lay there, she heard the sounds of sirens approach.

Her father's strong arms lifted her up and crushed her against his chest. The rough fabric of his jacket was soaked in the fetid stench of burnt flesh and petrol. The girl struggled, pulling away, lashing out blindly at imaginary flames.

'*Beti, beti!* It's okay. It's me.' Her father gently cupped her cheeks and pulled her head to his until their foreheads met. 'Shh, Shhh. It's all over now. Finished.'

Sadia breathed deeply, hiccupped and fell against him, sobbing. He held her, rhythmically smoothing her long dark hair. When her cries faded to the occasional hiccup, he glanced at his wife, who stood by the door, arms folded tightly round her chest. Her face was strained and her fragile body trembled. His smile was sad as he held his hand out to her. She pushed away from the doorframe and approached him, pulling her dupatta over her hair as she walked. For long seconds they looked at each other, each understanding that protecting their daughter was the priority. Bowing her head, she joined her daughter in his embrace.

He cradled Sadia's head against his shoulder, protecting her from the scene outside, as he and his wife watched the paramedics work on the burnt lump that had been Millie Green. Firemen, no longer needed, loitered nearby, their helmets respectfully removed. Sadia pulled away from her father and, despite his pleas not to, peered outside. At the very back of the crowd was Millie's daughter, Jessica. A tear rolled down Sadia's cheek as she watched Jessica struggle to reach her mother, her cry a mewing monotone.

Behind her, Jessica's half-brother, Shahid, yelled at the police officer. His pleading words so loud they almost rattled the brittle window pane. 'Let me have her. I'll look after Jess. She's my sister.'

Jessica twisted round and spat in his face.

'I'm not going with you,' she shouted, kicking him in the shins. 'You fucking bastard! *You* did this! *You* burnt me mam! You and your fuckin' dad.'

Sadia felt her father's hands firm on her shoulder as they watched a police officer, aided by a lady in a heavy coat, pull Jessica towards a police car. Shahid lifted his arm and, with his sleeve, wiped the spit from his face. As the car drove off his final words drifted through the Hussain's window and hung in the air. 'I didn't burn your mam, Jess! I didn't!'

With a sigh, Sadia's dad guided his family through to the hallway. Stopping at the bottom of the stairs, he knelt before Sadia. 'I've got to go to work now, *beti,* okay?'

Sadia sniffed and nodded, 'Yes, *Bapa,* I know.'

He ruffled her hair and turned to speak to her mother. 'You two go straight upstairs and have a shower. Get out of those smelly clothes and put them in a bin bag – we'll chuck them tomorrow.' He looked directly at his wife and his tone changed. 'You *will* do this now, won't you, Amina?'

Sadia, puzzled, looked to each parent in turn. Her mother avoided her husband's eyes and nodded.

A loud knock on the door startled them, then a male voice yelled through the letter box, 'DS Hussain, sarg says we need you outside.'

Hussain pushed Sadia towards her mother. 'Go now.'

Sadia slid her small hand into her mother's and together they walked upstairs.

Running his fingers through his hair, Hussain replied, 'I'm coming, I'm coming!' and, with a single backward glance at his wife and child, he shrugged his overcoat on and left the house to join the rest of his team.

CHAPTER 1
Leeds Road

Halfway up Leeds Road, past the Sikh gurudwara, Pakeezah Halal Food Depot and half a dozen Asian Restaurants, Shahid Khan's club, The Delius, stood back from the road with a car park fronting it. It had once been an enormous single-storey sandstone hardware store owned by a Sikh family. When the parents retired, after years of working thirteen and fourteen hour days to send their kids to medical school, they found they had over-educated their family and done themselves out of someone to take over their family business.

When Shahid took the opportunity to buy it, he had immediately added an upper level to house his office and the administrative side of his various businesses. The Delius became one of his legitimate concerns. Securing the area behind the club with huge metal fences, he had reduced the risk of trouble making its way into the club and of guilty parties disappearing into the labyrinth of terraced streets that could provide cover all the way up to the Thornbury roundabout through the mainly Pakistani-owned residential area. Near the building stood a canvas-covered deck with gas heaters and picnic tables for the smokers. He made sure to keep in good relations with the long-established neighbouring communities. Especially as when his father died and his step-mother moved back to Pakistan he and his stepbrother Imtiaz had remained in the family's four-storey terraced house, on Upper Rushton Road.

Inside The Delius, the bass beat bounced against the walls drowning out the singer and the rest of the band. Thursday

5

night was fifteen-and-overs night, yet still an assortment of manufactured mood lifters circulated the dance floor. The scent of less than subtly shared spliffs drifting in through the open fire-door, added to the edgy, adrenaline-fuelled atmosphere

In the mosh pit skanky girls in too few clothes shrieked, making odd little darts into the pit only to turn and run back to their friends, giggling like the teenagers they were. Only a few of the less flighty girls braved the centre. Boys wearing tight jeans that skittered down their arses pronouncing their trendiness alongside their support of Calvin Klein jerked and jolted their pointy limbs at right angles in an effort to inflict maximum damage on their best mates: 'What happens in the mosh stays in the mosh.'

Tonight it looked like the bouncers' job would be easy. Doors were shut and none of the troublemakers or gang factions had made an appearance. Keeping an eye on the mosh pit involved nothing more than Imtiaz sending a cursory glance at regular intervals and keeping a full ice bucket and first aid kit on the ready for the odd few daft enough to risk endless slagging for being a 'soft dick'.

Imtiaz Khan worked the bar and still managed to oversee the rest of the club through carefully positioned mirrors that revealed activities in even the darkest corners. His best skill, though, was an uncanny ability to detect trouble from the unlikeliest sources. The hench Eastern European, talking to the young woman at the end of the bar looked more of a 'trouble certainty' than any of the mosh pit lads. Although he recognised the woman, Imti was sure he'd not seen the bloke before – he'd definitely have remembered him with his closely cropped hair and the distinctive snake tattoo slithering down his neck, as well as the prison tattoos; one on his eyelid, the other just under his eye. Imti's mate Petrov had warned him to look out for those tatts; said they were a symbol of a notorious Polish gang known as the Grypsers. Petrov was shit-scared of anyone who wore them and said they were toxic. Imti made a mental note to double check with the bouncers later. Find out if they'd seen the man before.

The girl had been propping up the bar with an orange juice since around 7pm. The bouncers had clearly allowed the bloke in early. That would have been fine, except Imti had seen the way the girl had tensed when he'd slid into the bar stool next to her and the sudden flash of fear that had flickered across her face. A quick glance at the clock told him that it was nearly time to usher the younger kids out. He raised both arms, fingers splayed to signify ten more minutes to the DJ. The DJ's distorted voice broke over the thrashing bass, 'Ten minutes mosh time left, kids.'

The kids groaned, making Imti smile. He loved these Thursday nights and insisted on providing this 'youth club facility' despite Shahid's moans that they never made any profit. Imti knew that it would pay off in the long run. When they turned eighteen, they'd be back, spending real money.

As he poured a Diet Pepsi at the other end of the bar, he flicked the switch to focus the CCTV on the Eastern European. This would alert his brother Shahid, who was in the upstairs office with a bank of TVs in front of him. Imti edged his way up to that end of the bar and, using the unobtrusive panel behind the till, buzzed the bouncers who edged their way from their various stations to the bar.

Despite the pounding beat, Imti could hear the couple arguing in Polish. Their voices were loud, with the man making the majority of the noise. The man jumped off the bar stool, his aggressive posture putting Imti on alert as he towered over the woman. She'd begun to climb down from her bar stool when Imti saw the man's fist hammering into her cheek, knocking her into a sideways sprawl. One leg tangled in the stool and her head bounced off the floor. On Imti's nod, four of the bouncers grabbed the man. His head flung back and his mouth stretched into a snarl of dental decay. Imti watched as the man's skull swung, with force, towards his biggest bouncer, Jai. Jai twisted round, taking a glancing blow to the shoulder which he followed through with an upward thrust that caught the hulk under the chin.

The kids from the mosh pit swarmed over. Imti could see from their eyes that they were feral with adrenalin and the promise of blood. Their phones, held high, were set to record. Jeers of 'Fight! Fight! Fight!' took on momentum as the crowd jostled forward. Imti signalled to the DJ to cut the music and raised his voice. 'Right you lot, time to head off. Phones off or I'll confiscate them. Go on, off you go.'

He turned back and saw Jai still struggling. Two more bouncers joined the fray. Snake tattoo man's thick muscled arms strained against the bouncers' hold as they dragged him through the back door, chucking him into the empty alley.

Action over, the teenagers, grumbling in low voices, lowered their phones and, with good-natured high fives, left the premises through the front doors where their dad taxis awaited.

Flicking the CCTV control to focus on the back alley, Imti watched as the man, both arms stretched out to either side, palms upward in a 'what the fuck?' gesture, kicked the door. Baring his teeth, he dropped into a boxer's stance and punched the door in a series of jabs, before hoiking up a glob of phlegm and ejecting it onto the paintwork. He looked directly into the camera and raised his middle finger before swaggering off into the dark.

Nice, thought Imti, jumping over the bar, and approaching the woman. She'd been helped to her feet by two girls wearing startlingly white makeup, punctuated by black lipstick and eyeliner. He grinned at them, 'Thanks, girls. I've got it from here.'

Grabbing two clean tea towels, he dumped a handful of crushed ice in each and gave her one for her cheek, which was beginning to bruise, whilst he held the other at the back of her head.

'You need an ambulance?'

She shook her head, grimacing as she prodded her cheek. Then, in a clear but accented voice she said, 'No. When I get home my mother will look after me and...' She jerked her head towards the back exit, 'my brothers will look after him.'

Despite her nonchalant head jerk, Imti thought she didn't look convinced. To be honest, he didn't blame her. The guy was a thug... and a big one at that. Her brothers would have to be huge to stand a chance against that brute. Hiding his scepticism, he said, 'Just hold on. I'll get Jai to drop you back home.'

He walked over to the bar to buzz Jai, but by the time he'd turned back, all that was left was a blast of chill air as the fire exit slammed shut behind her. Imti lifted his eyes to the TV screen and saw her outside in the alley. She stopped to pull her coat on before, with a glance towards the shadows on her right, she began to run in the opposite direction from her earlier companion.

CHAPTER 2
Lilycroft Allotments

The uneven earth was dotted with sludge-filled holes. Strewn amongst the filth, were empty spray cans, discarded condoms, used syringes and… the woman's body.

Her hair trailed like long rats' tails through the sludge. She resembled a discarded doll wantonly tossed aside. Streaks of mascara marbled her face, giving her the look of a painted Celt. A silk scarf was pulled tight enough to cut into her neck and her mouth gaped like a gargoyle revealing insufficient oral hygiene and the caries born of a drug habit.

She wore the uniform of her trade – halter T-shirt, fake leather jacket, short denim skirt and stiletto sandals. Whoever had killed her had scrunched her skirt up to her waist and prised open her skinny, pock marked legs to reveal the wine bottle thrust, neck first, up her vagina.

Jessica's pulse pumped as she stared at the body. Then, she shoved her fist in her mouth to stifle the anguished scream that clawed for release at her chest. She shivered uncontrollably, searching the dark shadows for movement. Slowly, she backed down the alley, closer to the street lights. Hands shaking, she fumbled in her jeans pocket for her phone. Cursing her trembling fingers, she finally managed to dial 999 and blurt out the details before tears coursed down her cheeks. Wrapping her arms round her body, she squatted in a frozen huddle, her gaze focused on the shape halfway down the alley. The shape that had been her friend. She twisted toward the fence and, half falling into the weeds, she vomited until her throat nipped and her stomach muscles protested.

CHAPTER 3
Marriners Drive

Detective Inspector Gus McGuire hardly registered the insistent whining at the door.

He was rapidly losing awareness of his surroundings. Every nerve vibrated, as her hair tickled him. His entire body was on fire. First his thighs, then his belly and his chest, before she worked her way up until, finally, it fell curtaining their heads in dark satin, their tongues thrusting, plundering as they kissed.

Gently… tantalisingly, she raised her hips and, taking her time, brought herself down taking his erection inside her. He groaned against her open mouth as she moved with a lazy languor. Reaching up, he pulled her to him and caught one tight dark nipple between his lips. His tongue rasped over it and, when she groaned, he nipped very gently and then moved to the other breast. He sighed, enjoying the building sensation in his stomach as she clenched her muscles around him. As their breathing quickened, the whining at the door increased, punctuated by a few pitiful yelps. Gus moaned against her lips as she teased him with a slower rhythm.

The harsh ringing of his phone stilled them. Sadia's head jerked up. Still panting, her body slick with sweat, she glanced from the phone to Gus and back again, before sliding off him with a sigh.

Gus' erection rapidly diminished. 'Bloody Hell! Why now?'

Sadia giggled and flung herself full length onto the bed beside him. 'Probably divine intervention, to stop the poor Muslim girl from sinning.'

Gus slapping her gently on the arse, leaned over her prone body to grab the phone. 'A bit bloody late for *that,* my girl.'

She pouted and, standing up, padded over to let the still whinging dog in.

Gus took a moment to admire the perfection of her bottom and her long hair that skirted her buttocks, before, with regret, lifting the receiver at the exact same moment as Bingo launched himself past Sadia and landed right on his crotch. Gus' 'Yeah?' became a strangulated yelp.

'You alright, sir?' came the voice from the phone.

Glaring as Sadia, with a smile, lifted a struggling Bingo from his lap, Gus said, 'Just the dog, Harry. What's up?'

'There's been another one.'

'Shit.' Gus caught Sadia's eye and she put Bingo down and sat next to him, her face immediately transformed from relaxed flushed lover to focussed, alert police officer as Harry continued.

'Same as t'other two, sir.'

'Fuck!' Gus transferred the phone to his other hand and scratched his stomach. The last thing he'd wanted was a third dead prostitute on his hands. The damn vultures would be out in force yelling 'serial killer' and citing Bradford's existing reputation with The Yorkshire Ripper and The Crossbow Cannibal. Gus didn't need them lending gravitas to these killings. Especially when he felt his team hadn't made much progress on the first two murders. The press had already been eager to slate them for not apprehending anyone and quick to imply their slow progress was due to lack of concern because of the women's employment. His lips tightened as he listened.

'But that's not all...'

Gus could hear the hesitancy in Harry's tone. 'Spit it out, Harry.' He heard the other man take a deep breath before speaking.

'She's not one of Shahid Khan's this time. 'Barely able to contain his excitement the desk sergeant's voice rose. 'She's Bazza Green's.'

'Tit for tat?' asked Gus frowning

Harry hesitated, 'No, no I don't think so. Not heard about trouble between those two for ages'

'Hmm.' Gus wasn't convinced. Khan and Green had been enemies for years. He knew there was always trouble brewing between them. 'Whereabouts?' he asked, already getting out of bed.

'Lilycroft allotments. Shall I contact DS Hussain? DS Cooper's already on her way.'

Gus glanced at Sadia and winked. 'It's okay, Harry, I'll contact Hussain.'

He slammed the phone down and rested his head momentarily against the wall before saying, 'Fuck! Fuck! Fuck!'

Sadia, already pulling on her bra and knickers, threw Gus his trousers. 'Another girl?'

'Yep. Bazza Green's this time, down by the Lilycroft allotments.'

Dragging her hair back into a ponytail and, with practised speed, pulling her clothes back on, Sadia grimaced. 'He's a sleazy little bastard isn't he?'

'Hmm.' Gus pulled his jumper over his head and looked at Sadia. 'But so is Shahid Khan. Only difference is, Khan's a more polished kind of scum. They're both pimps, both in the business of screwing working girls.'

'Don't start, Gus. I know *exactly* what Shahid is, but Imti's not like that.'

Gus shrugged. 'I know you've got a soft spot for Imti but you need to be careful. What would your dad say if he knew you still saw them?'

Sadia thrust her chin out, hands on hips. 'You're using my *dad* as leverage, Gus… really?'

With an apologetic grimace, he dropped a kiss on her forehead, clicked his fingers for the dog and headed downstairs to the kitchen. 'Come on Bingo. Go do your business in the pooey grass.'

With a raised eyebrow, Sadia followed, shaking her head from side to side as she stepped from the bottom step. 'Distraction tactics? Shame on you, Gus, and what's with the *pooey grass*? You out of your mind? Who the hell says "pooey grass"?'

Realising that her joking hid her underlying anger, Gus avoided eye contact and opened the back door for Bingo. He was right to express his concern about her being friends with Shahid Khan's brother Imti. On a number of levels their friendship was ill-advised. On the other hand, Gus knew by now that confronting Sadia about it was just going to make her dig her heels in even more. With a sigh he watched Bingo scamper round in circles before heading over to a small square of grass in the corner of the garden. Linking arms with her by the back door, Gus nodded to the dog. 'I put in that little square of grass especially for him to do his doings on when I first got him. Took me ages to train him not to crap all over, but look, he learned. Now I only need to pooper scooper that area.' He risked a glance at Sadia and was pleased to see her face relax. Despite Bingo's dislike of Sadia, he knew she thought the dog was sweet. He squeezed her arm and grinned at her.

Unlinking her arm from his, she grinned back. 'Okay, okay, I admit it's cute, but the truth is Bingo *is* a bit of a passion killer *and* he *hates* me.'

Gus grabbed his over-sized fisherman's coat from the chair and whistled for Bingo.

'He's not used to you, that's all. He'll get used to you.'

Bingo, paws skittering over the lino, ran past Sadia, snarling as he went.

She sighed, 'I bloody hope so.'

Taking advantage of her change in mood, Gus dropped a kiss on the top of her head and walked over to take two mini Irn Bru bottles from the fridge. Thrusting them into the pocket of his jacket, he locked up and then walked through the hallway saying over his shoulder, 'Stay Bingo, stay.'

Stopping only to slip his trainers on, he opened the front door and waited for Sadia to shrug her coat and shoes on, before, together, they walked outside.

Their cars were lined up in the drive of his detached house. Gus got into his and poked his head out the window. 'You coming with me, Sad?'

'God, no! Last thing I need is us arriving together and my dad finding out.'

Gus tutted. 'Wish you'd just man up and tell him, Sadia. What's the worst he can do?'

Sadia pointed her key towards her car and waited till it beeped open. 'You don't want to know' And, with a tiny wave, she headed towards her vehicle and climbed in.

Wishing life was a bit simpler Gus watched her start up her car, and then, with a careless wave and an unnecessary rev, she was off. It's a pity, thought Gus, following her at a more sedate pace, that her dad is also the boss.

CHAPTER 4
The Delius, Leeds Road

'Pick up for fuck's sake!' Shahid Khan paced the floor in front of his desk, phone tight to his ear. When the number he'd dialled went to voicemail yet again, he turned and flung it, scattering the paperwork from his desk onto the floor. With a growl, he kicked the chair that stood nearby. Anger reverberated through every muscle and laboured pants wracked his body as he tried to control himself. Why wasn't she picking up? She'd promised him she'd phone at nine. What was she playing at? Shahid didn't know who he was most angry with – her for letting him down or himself for caring so fucking much. He'd vowed never to let a woman have the sort of hold on him that Millie Green had once had on his dad. When she'd dumped him, and who could blame her after the way he treated her, his dad had been devastated and now here he was dangling on the end of the phone like an idiot. He took a deep breath, bit his lip and reminded himself that Trixie wasn't like Millie and he was certainly nothing like his dad, but still the anger bubbled in his chest. He knew he'd have to do something about it before he exploded.

'Fuck!' He spat the word into the empty room and strode over to the annex in the corner where his punch bag hung – a hulk of malevolent shiny black leather, dangling in ominous silence, lit by a single spotlight casting its shadow over the real oak floor. Not bothering with the boxing gloves that lay on a shelf beside his weights, he thumped a bare-fisted one-two-one rhythm into the bag making it swing widely, forcing him to jump on the balls of his toes to avoid being hit on the rebound… again… faster.

After two minutes of pummelling, he was panting, sweat dripping from his brow. He stopped to catch his breath, relaxed his shoulders and looked at his bloodied knuckles. How many times had his trainer told him always to use the gloves? He flexed his fists, savouring the stinging stretch that made more blood ooze over his hands and gather in the creases between his fingers. Breathing steadier, he walked to the sink, flicked the cold tap on and watched as the water splashed his blood in abstract patterns onto the pristine ceramic – like one of the paint blot paintings Imti used to bring home from school when he was a kid. He smiled remembering how, in the absence of his dad's loving presence and, with his step-mum's indifference like a weight on his shoulders, he'd hugged the boy and carefully pinned Imti's proud offerings all over the kitchen. He'd lost his sister years ago, but he wasn't going to lose his baby brother – not a bloody chance!

Now, Imti was all grown up and managing the club, like he'd been born into it. His smile faded and once more his thoughts turned to Trixie. He could think of only one reason for her not picking up. But she'd promised him she wouldn't. That she'd stall Bazza. He hated feeling out of control, but, more than that, he hated the thought that maybe Bazza had one up on him.

He took a deep breath and grabbing two hand towels, he wrapped them round his fists. After a quick glance in the mirror, he walked back to his desk, flung himself into the swivel chair and cast a cursory glance over the bank of TVs which were positioned on the wall opposite his desk. This was his power station. He could work at his desk and a single glance allowed him an overview of the club without him having to move a muscle. Putting Trixie out of his mind for the moment, Shahid assessed the activity in the club. It wasn't as busy as he'd have liked, but, then again, it was a Thursday and the weekend trade normally more than made up for a mid-week lull. After the earlier hassle with the Polish brute, things seemed quiet. He'd seen the girl slip out the fire exit when Imti went to get Jai. He'd also seen Imti's face when he'd turned and she was gone. He smiled. Imti liked the girl. It was written all over him. He'd never been able to hide anything from Shahid. Shahid could read the boy like a book. He frowned, then reached for his phone and pumped in a number. 'Jai, get someone to find out where that Polish bint lives will you?'

Nothing was too much trouble for Imti. Nothing at all.

Still unsettled, he re-checked his phone for calls or texts. Nothing! Where the hell was she? He'd made her promise not to go to Bazza's tonight. Not tonight of all nights. Why the fuck couldn't she just walk away from him? It wasn't as if he couldn't exert bit of influence on her behalf. After all, he and Bazza had a lot of history together.

He pumped her number into his phone again, but, like before, it rung out. Shahid glanced at his PC for the time. Getting on for 11pm. Where the hell was she? His phone vibrated in his hand and he nearly dropped it in his eagerness to answer. 'Imti' flashed on the screen and his heart sank. Glancing at the TVs, he located Imti behind the bar, phone to his ear, aimlessly wiping the bar down. Shahid's smile was tight when he spoke. 'I'll be down in a minute, Imti.'

He listened as Imti moaned on about how they'd be late and how he hated being late. Fuck's sake, the boy was a real old woman at times. Cutting over his brother's whining, Shahid said, 'I know, I know, we're late. We'll get there when we get there. God, Imti, Birmingham's only a couple of hours' drive. Call Uncle Majid and explain we've been held up. He'll understand. He knows we've got a business to run. Get the bags in the car.'

Imti looked up at the camera and Shahid thrummed an impatient rhythm on his desk when he saw his brother's frown. Imti mouthed the words, 'Get a fucking move on' to the screen and then grabbing a sheet of paper, he turned to Jai who'd just sat down on a bar stool opposite him. Shahid smiled and shook his head. Poor Jai. Looked like he was in for yet another lecture on the dos and don'ts of running The Delius for the weekend.

CHAPTER 5
Lilycroft allotments

Emerging from the car, Gus rubbed his hands together. It was cold enough to freeze the balls off a snowman. Stuffing his hands back into his pockets, he studied the scene.

A row of terraced houses stood behind a high wooden fence, separating them from the alleyway skirting the allotments. The houses were brightly lit, the occupants no doubt wakened by the police activity outside. At some of the upstairs windows family groups were silhouetted against faint landing lights as they watched the scene below. Gus grimaced, feeling sorry for them. Whilst enjoying the excitement of the moment, they would soon become angered by the police's insistent questions, frustrated by the relentless journalists and scared of the unknown murderer.

Gus knew that in the summer these allotments were a focus for all sorts of community activities. By day, kids played in the nearby park after school. The local mosque was as well attended as the Ring O' Bells pub, and both served the diverse needs of the community. Each allotment proudly grew a masala of Asian and English vegetables. Now, with autumn turning to winter, there were only drifting leaves and wind-blown trees casting jagged shadows over the area.

After dark, the locals left the fenced-in allotments with their maze of interlinking paths to the night scavengers. Dense shadows provided enough cover for punters to grind against disinterested, stoned prostitutes, who remained upright solely by virtue of leaning against the wooden panels. Dealers, too, enjoyed private meetings, seen only by vagrants too pissed to bear witness to their dirty deals. Drug paraphernalia sprawled among the weeds; a detritus of bent cutlery and used syringes. Like most cities, Bradford's dregs came to life at dusk, hidden, in the main, until some brutal act lifted them out of the darkness and into the spotlight.

Gus sighed and pulled a Wee Bru from one pocket and his anti-depressants from another. Watching the police officers beavering under the artificial light, he popped two pills into his mouth, undid the lid from his drink and slugged straight from the bottle.

Detective Sergeant Alice Cooper approached, dressed from head to toe in black, her scarf coiled a zillion times round her neck, her coat dwarfing her.

'No sign of the press yet then, Al?' he asked.

'No, not yet. Thank God!' she peered from beneath her black beanie. 'The longer *they* stay away the better. Bloody parasites, especially that smarmy git Jez Hopkins. Two faced bastard – can't trust him an inch.'

'Thought you had a thing going with him?'

'Duh? Only till I realised he was more interested in that drugs bust in Keighley than the finer workings of my mind.'

Gus grinned. 'What have we got?'

'Victim's called Trixie – no surname so far. Runaway, according to her flatmate, who, coincidentally, found her. Apparently, Trixie's mentioned Bridlington in the past. Maybe she came from there. I'll get Missing Persons onto it.'

Gus nodded, turning as Sadia approached. She'd set off before him but had clearly decided to do a detour to avoid wagging tongues, 'About bloody time, too.'

Alice jumped lightly on the spot, flapping her arms, presumably to keep warm. 'Ignore Mr Grumpy, he's only just arrived himself.' She rubbed her gloved hands together before continuing, 'Come on. The scene's just down here.' Shoulders hunched, she led them down a semi-lit side path that took them to the cordoned off area and out of eyeshot of the houses.

Before following, Gus pulled his jacket closely round him, partly to harness heat, but mostly to minimise the risk of contamination from the less than salubrious surroundings.

Before they'd taken half a dozen steps into the alley, Sadia stopped abruptly. 'Shit I've stood in something... and it's squishy.'

Gus smirked. She'd put on new shoes earlier because before they'd gotten distracted they'd intended to go out. She'd be well pissed off.

The path opened onto a rough surprisingly large open area, bordered by a hotchpotch of wooden panelling that divided the individual allotments. Each fence was tall, some had coiled barbed wire at the top and a few had illegally placed broken bottles sunk into a thin layer of cement at the top. Huge padlocks hung from the gates and Gus noted some walls were reinforced by criss-crossed iron bars. He shrugged. He couldn't blame the owners for taking extreme security measures, but he wondered just how successfully they deterred unwanted visitors. In his experience the more visible your deterrent the more your premises appealed. Probably assumed there would be rich pickings inside in the form of lawn mowers and tools. The bottom corner of the square was sectioned off. Crime scene blocks were positioned at frequent intervals between the outer and inner cordons. The harsh lights made the shape of the body visible. Alice nodded towards a figure standing twenty yards to their right with a police-issue blanket draped over her shoulders, slender arms holding it together under her chin.

The girl stared straight ahead, seemingly paralysed, as she watched the activity.

'She found the body and phoned it in,' said Alice.

Gus nodded and looked at the girl, whose eyes never wavered from the crumpled body that lay unmoving on the floor.

'I tried to move her up to one of the cars but she got hysterical, so I left her there. She seems calmer, now.'

'She a user, Alice?'

Alice shrugged. 'Didn't see any tracks on her arms, so maybe not.'

He nodded towards the body. 'What about her?'

'Don't know, didn't get too close. We're still waiting for the pa–'

'Halloo all!' came a cheery voice from behind them. 'Ah, it's you, Angus laddie. Good to see you.'

Gus closed his eyes and mumbled *'Shit!'*, before turning with a forced smile to greet the huge man who lumbered over, swinging his medical case by his side. Gus would have preferred almost any other pathologist to his dad. As he watched the older man approach, he said in a strangled voice, 'What the *fuck* is he wearing?'

'Looks like a kilt to me, Gus.' Alice raised one hand to her brow in an exaggerated manner and peered through the gloom. 'Yep, definitely a kilt.'

When the pathologist, kilt undulating jauntily, reached them, Alice turned to him and said, 'Well, don't *you* look handsome, Doc?'

Gus snorted as the man's already ruddy face glowed even pinker at the compliment.

'Ah, the lovely Alice,' Dr McGuire said smiling. 'Always ready with a compliment and the good grace to make an old man feel welcome.' He pursed his mouth and glowered at Gus who stood, shoulders slumped with a grudging half-smile on his face.

'As you can see, Alice, I was at my Scottish country dance club when I got the call.' He turned to Sadia and smiled. 'Hallo my dear, you *do* look lovely tonight.'

Almost spluttering, Gus interrupted. 'It's not a bloody fashion parade you know. What the *hell's* going on? You can't come to a crime scene dressed like that!' He glared at the kilt as if it was infectious.

Dr McGuire smoothed his kilt with a paddle-sized hand. 'Och, don't worry, Angus ma lad, ah'll be careful. It'll dry clean, you know?'

Gus' mouth fell open, 'I'm not bloody worried about your damn *kilt*! I just don't think it's appropriate for the pathologist to trundle up to a crime scene dressed like Bonnie Prince Bloody Charlie.'

Doc McGuire lowered his voice, leaned towards Gus and jerked his head towards the body. 'Ah hate tae tell ye Angus, but the lassie's already deid. So, ah doubt she'd be bothered if ah wore ma damn birthday suit.'

As Alice turned a giggle into a cough and lowered her mouth into the folds of her scarf, Gus realised he'd hurt his dad's feelings. He felt a momentary pang of guilt which dissipated when he glanced back at his dad and once more saw the offending article of clothing. How long would it have taken him to pull a pair of damn trousers on? Two seconds that's all, just two bloody seconds! But no! He'd got to turn up like some tartan avenger in a Braveheart spoof.

His scowl deepened as Dr McGuire continued, 'I'm not a bloody eejit, Angus. Like always I'll suit up, kilt or no bloody kilt.' And he marched off to examine the body.

'Well done there, Gus,' said Sadia, trying not to laugh, 'If you'd upset him any more that kilt of his would be swinging high enough for us all to see if he's a true Scot.'

Gus let out a puff of air and slouched further into the coat. 'Course he's a bloody true Scotsman. He doesn't do owt by half, does he?'

Alice patted him gently on the arm, 'I'm sure he didn't put it on *just* to annoy you, Gus.'

Gus looked at her, scepticism shining in his eyes. 'You think not, Alice? I'm not so sure. I think my father's main aim in life is to humiliate me in every way imaginable.' He exhaled loudly and rubbed his hand through his hair. 'Bloody silly auld goat!'

Alice laughed. 'Why don't you suit up and join him? At least you'll be able to hold his kilt down for him. After all, it *is* a bit breezy over there.'

Gus raised an eyebrow. 'Yeah, right.' Trying to throw off his annoyance with his dad, Gus, shoulders hunched, turned towards the skinny girl who was now watching his dad don his white suit. Arms wrapped round her frame, she looked so alone and frail; as if a slight breeze would knock her off her feet. He felt sorry for her, knowing from personal experience that the numbness she felt right now would soon give way to something much worse. He sighed and nodded to one of the PCs. 'Get her a cup of coffee or something and a seat. Make sure she's okay.'

Sadia glanced over at the girl and frowned. 'Wait a minute Gus, I think I know her.' She continued to stare at the girl with troubled eyes and then nodded with certainty. 'Yes, it *is* her. I haven't seen her for years, but I was at school with her. She's a year younger than me, but she lived next door to us when we lived in Thornbury.'

Sadia turned to her colleagues. 'She's Arshad Khan's daughter.'

Gus and Alice looked at her. Seeing their blank faces, Sadia tutted and rolled her eyes. 'God, keep up, why don't you? Shahid Khan is Arshad's son. Jessica is Shahid's half-sister. They don't get on. She hates him. Holds him responsible for her mum's death.'

Ah, that's why the name had seemed vaguely familiar to Gus. He remembered hearing about Arshad Khan. It was well before his time but everyone knew he'd been an evil bastard, dealing in drugs, women and weapons. For a while in the late nineties many of Khan's rivals had been 'disappeared' and, although Khan had never been implicated, it was widely believed in the force that he had been responsible. Shahid had a slightly better reputation than his father, but, nonetheless, he still exploited Bradford's vulnerable, and was smart enough to get away with it.

Studying Jessica again, Sadia lowered her voice. 'I was there that night. Saw the whole bloody thing. Jessica's mum set fire to herself.' She sniffed. 'Haven't seen Jess since then. Dad says she went to live with some relatives the other side of Bradford.'

Well, that was a memory that wouldn't go away in a hurry, thought Gus, wishing he could comfort Sadia. He was relieved when Alice put her arm round Sadia's shoulder. All three of them studied Jessica, the fragility of her frame, highlighted by the harsh glare of the crime scene lights.

There was something niggling Gus, though. Something just out of reach. What the hell was it? Shit! That was it. Eyes narrowed, he turned back to Sadia, 'What did you say her surname is?'

Sadia shrugged, 'Khan, I suppose. That was her dad's name.'

Gus lifted his Irn Bru to his lips and swallowed a mouthful. 'Sure it's not Green?'

Sadia began to shake her head and then paused. 'Shit… her mother was called Millie Green. You're not suggesting that…'

Gus nodded. 'Looks like it'

Alice, who'd remained silent, looked at Sadia. 'Someone going to let me in on your little secret then? Telepathy's not my strong point.'

Gus grinned and put the lid back on his bottle before replying. 'Looks like Shahid Khan's estranged half-sister is also Bazza 'The Bampot' Green's niece.'

Alice's eyes narrowed and she flicked through her note book. 'Shit, you're right. Uniform told me her name was Green.'

Running his tongue over his teeth to rid them of the sticky residue, Gus considered Sadia's revelation. Looked like there was personal animosity between Shahid Khan and Bazza Green as well as 'business rivalry'. Had something kicked off to trigger a turf war between these two? After all, for years they'd rubbed along together. Each sticking to their own neck of Bradford. Token rivalry taking the form of low level disruption that, in their infinite wisdom, they'd policed very effectively themselves. Hopefully, Sadia's past relationship with Bazza's niece would elicit some pertinent info. Three working girls dead in Bradford did not augur well. The papers would soon be chuntering on about serial killers and dredging through their archives for some of their favourite stories to regurgitate. Never mind the hysteria their unfounded hypotheses would cause. He sighed. If this was some sort of turf war, Gus wanted to nip it in the bud soon, before anyone else ended up dead.

He looked at Sadia, taking in her pale face and the slight furrow in her brow as she studied Jessica Green. 'Reckon you want to re-establish the link?'

Sadia's lips tightened. She pulled her coat more tightly round her body, and then nodded with a sigh. 'Yeah. Poor sod hasn't had much luck, has she? I'll take care of her for now. Get her preliminary statement.'

Gus and Alice both said, 'Good luck,' as Sadia walked through the fallen leaves towards Jessica.

CHAPTER 6
Killinghall Road

S oon as he'd heard her name he'd known she was his. 'Serafina Nadratowski'! He laughed. What more proof could there be? Serafina; the snake. It was a sign from above that their destinies were linked. It couldn't be clearer. He caressed the snake tattoo that slithered from the collar of his T-shirt. The serpent was his symbol. Their fates were sealed.

He frowned. *She* hadn't been convinced though. Had back chatted him and refused to accept his logic. Maybe he shouldn't have punched her… not then… at least not so soon… and probably not in that club where they had CCTV coming out of their ears. He shrugged. Chances were the Paki bastards would want to hush it all up anyway. They'd not pass it on to the police. Too busy hiding their own secrets and, of course, Serafina would keep schtum. Well, he hoped so anyway. The Old Man had warned him to keep a low profile, had promised him he could have Serafina if he wanted, but not now. Not till after they'd achieved what they'd set out to achieve.

He slammed his fist into the wall, sending sprinkles of plaster fluttering to the floor. He'd have to be more on top of things. He was in the UK now, not in Poland with his network of snitches. He'd have to be a lot more careful. No way did he want to be shunted on to a plane at Leeds Bradford airport bound for Poland and a lifetime in Piotrkow. Especially not with his track record with the Grypsers. If they got their hands on him his 'life' would last no longer than a gnat's.

29

It pissed him off that he was beholden to The Old Man though. Mind you *he* had a lot to lose, too. So, in a way, *he* was dependent on Anastazy. No way did he want to reveal his true identity to the community. He'd managed to cover up for so long in Poland, portraying himself as the perfect family man. Well, until he'd messed up that is. Until he'd pissed off the wrong folk and nearly lost everything. That was when the old man had made a quick exit amid the exodus of Poles to the UK. Luckily for Anastazy, he'd needed his help to do that. Now, although the old man pulled most of the strings, Anastazy had a few of his own to pull. The Old Man may have knowledge of the upper echelons of the Polish underworld, but he, Anastazy had currency too. He knew where the bodies were buried, both literally and figuratively; The Old Man's secrets were like gold and Anastazy knew that, in this game, loyalty was only as deep as the next power struggle.

He exhaled a long breath and turned his thoughts to Serafina again. Frowning he remembered the way she'd thrust her chin out at him so aggressively. She needed taming. He shrugged again. Plenty of time to teach her how to behave later, when he had her hooked. She'd be more pliant then. Much more pliant. He rubbed his jaw. The big beefy bouncer had hit him there and it was tender now. He wouldn't forget. Anastazy Dolinski never forgot and he never forgave. *That* was his strength. The bouncer would get what he was owed.

Anastazy had managed to escape the Polish authorities. He laughed, remembering how easy it had been to evade the bumbling police with their in fighting, corruption and sheer incompetence. A new passport with a new name and Anastazy had, quite literally, resurrected himself. Just like his new name, he *was* the resurrection.

30

It would soon be time to exact revenge on the families of those who'd betrayed him in his motherland. Those vermin responsible for tarnishing his name, his reputation. He would not let them off lightly and now, here in Bradford, he had, with The Old Man, created an infrastructure in which his business could rise from the ashes – a glorious phoenix of destruction. He'd ruin the status quo. The Paki and the English scum would, by the time he was finished with them, beg for his lenience.

As for The Old Man, well maybe Anastazy would turn the tables on him and take over the dynasty *he* was trying to recreate here in Bradford. His anonymity was what made him feared throughout Poland. That's why he would be feared throughout Bradford, and then Yorkshire, and then throughout England as his empire extended and his reputation for 'decisive action' went before him and when the time was ripe, Anastazy would stab him in the back and take everything he held dear. After all the man's family were worthless. His sons were not strong enough to take up the mantle of leadership... no, with the old man gone the way would be clear for Anastazy.

But first, Serafina. It wouldn't be difficult to own her, but in the meantime he'd make do with an inferior product, after all, he had money and knowledge... and the community knew the risks if they refused him. After all, everyone had wives, mothers, daughters, sisters didn't they?

CHAPTER 7
Lilycroft Allotments

S uited up in their abominables, Gus and Alice stood next to Dr McGuire. Having swallowed down his earlier annoyance with his dad, Gus was now focussed on the job in hand and he knew his dad would be too. Gus studied the girl, who was sprawled like an unwanted sack of potatoes at his feet and said, 'Well, what do you have for us?'

Resembling an oversized baby with his kilt bundled up like a nappy under his suit, Dr McGuire replied, 'Well, let me see. She was strangled with her own scarf. A rather pretty pink and mauve one as it happens – cheap, but pleasant.' He moved the scarf slightly away from her neck to reveal an angry ruddy welt.

Irritated by his dad's commentary, Gus grunted. The pathologist turned towards him. 'What's that you say, my boy?'

Knowing better than to engage him in a discussion about keeping to the point, Gus waved his hand in a 'get on with it' gesture. 'Any idea of time of death?'

'Oh, that's easy. The body was still slightly warm. Sometime after eight tonight, I'd say – provisionally though, you understand?'

Gus nodded. The only bonus of having his dad as the on-call pathologist, as opposed to 'the old school' Geoff Chalmers, was that his dad was happy to share his initial impressions with the team, albeit with 'provisionally' tacked on the end. His philosophy, as verbalised to Gus ad infinitum in the past, was that his duty was to the victim and, if his initial thoughts could move the investigation forward, he'd voice them. He was also a stickler for following up if he later found something at the PM to contradict his initial findings.

'As you can see, there's a wine bottle inserted into her vagina.' He continued pointing with a gloved finger, 'Same as the young ladies I examined last week – Camilla and Starlight, I believe they were called.' He bent down to look at the bottle and frowned. 'Doesn't seem to be as much blood as with the other two. Hmm! Maybe he didn't use as much force or maybe it wasn't broken at the neck. Never mind, we'll see when I do the PM tomorrow. Are you coming to that, Angus?'

'Yeah, I'll be there,' said Gus, feeling the colour leave his face at the mere thought of it. After all these years, he still found post-mortems difficult, but, out of pride, he rarely delegated the responsibility.

Fergus patted his arm. 'I'll see you then, son. Well, must get off, lots to do and I fancy a wee dram before I retire for the night.'

Relieved to see his dad finally departing, Gus began to walk carefully over the slabs laid by the crime scene techs to help preserve evidence. Hearing his father's voice calling his name he turned back.

'Oh, one more thing, Angus.'

With an exaggerated sigh Gus, hoping his dad would take the hint and hurry up, looked at his watch. 'Yes?'

'Your mother says you've to come for Sunday lunch and bring your mystery lady with you – she wants to vet her.'

Scowling at Alice's chuckle, Gus' shoulders slumped. He knew everyone was listening and, no doubt, finding it all very amusing. Whilst *they* all loved Dr McGuire's little eccentricities, Gus had, on numerous occasions, wished the ground would open up and swallow him. Was it too much to expect him to behave with a bit of professional decorum at the damn crime scene? Somehow managing to keep a level tone, Gus said, 'How many times do I have to ask you not to mix work and family?' before turning on his heel and moving away.

'Oh, Angus!' his father's sing-song voice rang out, the epitome of innocence.

Gus halted and counted to three under his breath. He really didn't want to lose it with his dad, but he could feel himself coming very close. Shit! Why was he so tightly wound these days? 'What!!!'

'*Are* you coming to lunch on Sunday?'

'*What?*' The word came out sharper than he intended and all of a sudden he was aware of his heart's rapid thud against his chest. His breathing shallowed and became rapid. A wave of dizziness hit him. He swallowed. Not a panic attack. Please, not a panic attack. Not now! Not here! Using all his inner strength, he relaxed his shoulders and forced himself to take slow, deep breaths until the dizziness passed. As if from a distance, he heard his dad still waffling on about lunch and how much it would mean to his mum. With his heart rate slowing, he risked a glance round and was relieved to see that his momentary lapse appeared to have gone unnoticed. Feeling rattled and off-kilter, he looked at his dad who, head tilted to one side, waited for Gus to respond.

Wishing he had something solid he could grip on to for support, Gus tried to focus, 'Sorry?'

His dad threw up his arms and tutted. Then, as if speaking to an imbecile, he said, 'Your mum, she'll want to know.'

With barely concealed irritation, Gus swallowed the words he felt like saying and instead, between half gritted teeth, said, 'I'll be there. On my *own*, okay?'

'Maybe you could bring Alice with you?' His father persisted. Then, lowering his voice to three decibels louder than an explosion, he dropped his final bombshell, 'Gabriella and your sister are coming too.'

Gus froze. Around him everyone went silent. Then, as if orchestrated by an invisible conductor, they broke into loud chatter. Gus glared at them but they all avoided looking at him. Raising his chin, Gus turned to face his dad. Enunciating each word with slow precision, he said, 'I don't need to hide behind anyone. I'm not the guilty party here.'

Clearly uncomfortable, Dr McGuire said, 'You're right, son. Of course, you're right.' And, looking like he carried the weight of the world on his shoulders, he turned and walked away.

Gus felt guilt wash over him. What the hell was he playing at? His dad was just looking out for him. After The Matchmaker fiasco earlier in the year Gus' already fragile mental health had spiralled downwards and it was only the dedicated support of his parents and work colleagues, combined with the persistence of his psychiatrist Dr Mahmood and his medication, that had got him functioning again. He knew he shouldn't take his frustrations out on his dad and he knew he had to get his snappiness under control. It all seemed beyond him at the moment.

His thoughts were interrupted by Alice. 'Em, Gus? I just sort of wondered, *do* you have a mystery lady?'

Gus tutted and then dropped to his knees beside the body, feeling like a grim suitor about to propose, before responding, 'The old man's imagining things, as usual.'

Eyebrows raised, Alice pursed her lips, 'Oh, well, I thought he seemed quite sure of himself. Maybe he's got a point. Maybe you *should* take someone with you for moral

35

support. It'll be the first time you've seen them both together since…' she waved her hand in the air.

Gus ignored her and continued to study the dead prostitute.

Alice cleared her throat. 'Look, I'm free on Sunday if you're stuck. I'll come with you.'

Standing up, Gus looked at her, a slight grin on his face. 'If it was anyone other than my lovely mum cooking, Alice, I'd assume you were after a free slap-up meal. But, seeing as you're familiar with my wee mammy's culinary limitations, I'll just assume you're a masochist.'

Alice shrugged. 'Just a good friend, that's all.'

On the point of telling her he could fight his own battles, he re-considered. Alice was a good friend and she was clearly worried about him. He shouldn't take his bad mood out on her either. He grinned and nudged her arm, 'Okay, Al, you can come… but no using food poisoning as an excuse for bogging off work on Monday, okay? Now, can we get on with some work?'

Alice beamed at him and clapped her gloved hands together, 'I only meant it might be awkward. You know? With Gabriella and Katie there.'

'Alice!' said Gus, his tone brooking no argument. 'Drop it now. Focus. What can you see?'

'Yes, sir,' said Alice, immediately professional and focussed as she studied the crime scene. 'We have a dead female apparently strangled to death by her own scarf. No visible trauma to torso or limbs, but notable drug tracks on legs and arms. Violated, probably post-mortem, with glass wine bottle, inserted neck first. The surrounding scene is heavily covered with debris such as syringes, alcohol bottles, used condoms and spray paint cans, indicating a place regularly used by prostitutes and drug addicts.'

Pleased with Alice's assessment of the scene, he asked, 'What does that mean?'

'Well, we're going to get a lot of trace evidence and it'll be hard to match most of what we get to our killer,' she said.

Gus knew what a nightmare an environment like this could be. Too much trace evidence could be worse than too little and he knew his budget didn't run to analysing everything. They'd just have to hope they got something from the bottle and the area nearest to the body. 'We might get lucky and make a match that will be enough to get the bastard sent to jail.'

Gus, looked round at the crime scene investigators, who were rapidly filling box after box of evidence bags and acknowledged that the chances of that were getting slimmer with every evidence bag logged.

'How do you know the scarf's hers?' he asked, looking back at the Alice.

'Oh.' Alice paused. 'Well, you're right, we don't know that. Your dad said it, but we don't really know that. I just assumed that because the other two girls were killed by their own belongings, Camilla her tights and Starlight her belt.'

Gus rolled his eyes at Alice's use of 'dad' but let it go. 'We can't make assumptions. Until we know for sure that these murders are linked we treat this as we would any other crime scene.'

Alice nodded, 'Yeah, each crime scene stands on its own till we find the link.'

'Now,' said Gus satisfied, 'How about age. You never mentioned age?'

Alice frowned. 'The makeup adds years, but Jessica says she's only eighteen.'

Gus shook his head and sighed. His gaze fell on the girl's skinny, drug-ravaged frame. Eighteen, alone in the world, with only Bazza Green's dubious protection. He wondered if she had a family somewhere or if what she'd run from was worse than the new life she'd carved for herself. One thing Gus *was* certain of was that he'd find out – for her sake, for her family's sake and, perhaps, for his own sake. As he walked away from the body he muttered, 'What a bloody waste. Come on, Alice, let's see what Sadia's got.'

CHAPTER 8

S adia walked towards Jessica carrying two polystyrene cups of coffee. When she reached her, she hesitated before thrusting one under her nose. With a quick glance, Jessica took the cup and turned her gaze back to where the Gus and his dad were talking.

The crime scene lights illuminated the entire area, allowing Sadia to study Jessica as she cupped her drink in two hands, taking the occasional sip. Beneath mascara tear stains, Jess' face was pallid. Her blue eyes looked unnaturally wide, their pupils dilated. In different circumstances Sadia would have assumed she was on something, but, in this case, she knew the shock and adrenalin rush were enough to account for it.

Despite being slim, Sadia felt like a giant next to the girl. Jessica's arms looked fleshless under the harsh lighting and her joints protruded from her body at the shoulders and hips. Her hair was lank and unnourished. Sadia wondered what had happened to the once cheeky, lively girl after her mother had died. Nothing good, she surmised.

'Had a good enough look then, Sadia?' Jessica glanced at her from the corner of her eye. 'Did you think I wouldn't recognise you? Or maybe you don't recognise me?'

Sadia smiled and shrugged. 'Oh, I recognised you, Jess. You always had a filthy face when you were a kid, too.'

Jessica snorted and, despite her best efforts, a crooked half-smile made it to her lips. 'Cheeky cow! And *you* were a bloody know-it-all back then, too.'

Sadia put her arm gently round the other girl's shoulders and squeezed. 'I'm sorry, Jess.' She wasn't sure if her words were related to the present circumstances or to what had happened when they were kids.

Jessica nodded, maintaining her silent vigil over her dead friend. Together, they watched Gus walk over to the body, both engrossed by the way he studied the dead woman. A low cough behind them made them jump. Sadia withdrew her arm as they turned round and saw Dr McGuire, his kindly eyes focussed on Jessica.

'I just wanted to say how sorry I am for your loss, my dear,' he said and patted Jess' arm.

Jessica's eyes welled up and Sadia felt a pang of pity for her when she saw her swallow and, with a sniff, rub her face. The girl asked in a tear-gruff voice, 'Will you cut her up?'

Dr McGuire's lips rose in a half-smile. 'Yes, dear. I'll do the post-mortem on your friend, but I promise I'll take good care of her and, when I'm finished, you'll be able to see her so you won't have to remember her like this.'

Jessica bowed her head and mumbled, 'Thank you.'

The large man raised his hand in a wave. 'Goodbye, my dear.' And then he turned to Sadia. 'Nice to see you again, DC Hussain. Perhaps we'll be seeing a bit more of you in future?' With a wink, he walked off swinging his case by his side.

'Why would you want to see more of him?' Jessica's voice was curious.

Sadia watched the retreating figure with a frown. 'Hmm, Not sure about that.'

Jessica hoisted the blanket more tightly round her shoulders. 'So, you're in the force then, Sad? Like your old man?'

'Yeah, that's right.'

'I suppose you want to interview me, get a statement and all that sort of stuff.'

'We'll need a preliminary statement from you, but then I think you should try to get some rest and we'll finish up tomorrow, okay?'

Jessica wrapped her hands round her body and shivered as Sadia took her notebook and pen from her pocket.

'Come on, we can do this in a car, Jess. There's no need to freeze out here.'

'I don't think I'll ever be warm again. No matter where I am.' Jessica's voice was quiet, her gaze on the crime scene team who were placing bags over her friend's hands and feet.

Sadia's heart skipped a beat at her friend's forlorn tone. It took all her willpower not to allow the tears that stung her eyes to fall. She wiggled her nose and swallowed hard. As they began to put a bag over the dead woman's head, Jessica stepped forward, a strangled cry leaving her lips. Sadia gripped her arm. 'No, Jess. They have to do it. It preserves the evidence.'

Jessica bit her lip and gulped back her tears.

In a quiet voice, Sadia said, 'What was her name?'

Jessica sniffed and looked away from her friend as they lifted her body onto a trolley ready to transport to the morgue.

'Trixie. That was her name. Or that was the one she gave us anyway.'

A snort of laughter came from behind the two women. Sadia frowned and ignored it, moving closer to Jessica. 'Trixie what?'

Jessica shrugged. 'Just Trixie. She didn't give any of us another name.'

As the laughter from behind got louder, Sadia looked over and saw three uniformed officers. One of them had his back to her and was clearly holding forth to his audience, whilst the other two looked uncomfortable and embarrassed. The one who was mouthing off laughed. His head jerking towards the mortuary van. Although she couldn't hear the substance of his conversation, the words 'worthless whore' and 'prossie bitch' reached Sadia's ears. She tensed, debating whether to intervene or just move Jessica to a car and speak to Gus about it later. However, when, the words, 'deserves all they get', splintered the night and hung, loud as thunder in the air, Sadia glanced at Jess and saw her mouth curl.

Crunching autumn leaves beneath her heel as she spun, Sadia said, 'Hold on just a minute, Jess. Something to sort out.' before marching towards the constables.

She'd just reached them, when the one with his back to her spat on the ground and said, 'Bloody whores – bet those two did a double act together – "Trixie and Dixie, twice as risky". Don't know why we waste our time on that sort. You ask me, they get what they ask for.'

Sadia prodded his back. 'Is that so?' Her voice was clipped.

The constable turned round and looked her up and down. His gaze seemed to linger on her breasts. Sadia tensed. *How dare he?*

He stepped closer to her, using his large frame to intimidate her, holding his hands in loose fists by his side.

Cocking her head to one side, Sadia, beyond angry now, mirrored his action and stepped right up to him, her mouth taut. 'Whilst you're on the job, keep your sexist opinions to yourself, okay? Every murder victim gets the same respect, whether or not *you* like it. Each victim leaves behind a heritage of loss and we respect that heritage by making damn sure we find the scum that did it. Got it?'

'Yeees,' he said and saluted her, his elongated agreement and mocking eyes belying respect.

One of the other officers bit his lip. 'For God's sake, Brighton, don't you know who that is? You better watch what you say. She's Detective Chief Superintendent Hussain's daughter.'

Sadia rounded on the other man. 'Doesn't matter who my father is. When we're on the job we represent the force and your *colleague*,' she glanced at Brighton's badge number, 'PC 6312 has demonstrated an appalling breach of our equal opportunities in front of witnesses... you *are* witnesses to that breach aren't you?' Her gaze moved to encompass the other man, who till now had remained silent.

Both officers nodded, the younger one glaring at Brighton, 'You're a pillock, Brighton. You deserve to be reported. That lass heard you, you know? And she's only just found her mate's body. Poor thing.'

Sadia supressed a smile as Brighton glared at his colleagues, his face red with anger as they walked away. Then he turned back to her, his hands splayed before him in a placating manner, 'I was only joking... having a bit of fun. Crime scene humour you know?'

Sadia's eyes narrowed. 'Trouble is, that wasn't funny. Now, who's your superior officer?'

Brighton's eyes narrowed, 'I've just been allocated to DI Gus McGuire for training on the MIT.'

Sadia maintained a neutral expression. Gus had moaned earlier about the 'idiot' her dad had assigned to the major incident team. Looks like Brighton was the 'idiot'. Gus had said the officer had had 'issues' before and that despite strenuous arguments to have him transferred elsewhere, her father had been adamant that he was to join their team.

Presumably his current behaviour was a display of some of his 'issues'.

She smiled. 'Is that so? Well, we'll be seeing a lot more of each other, PC Brighton, because I'm on DI McGuire's team, too. If I were you, I'd practise keeping your bollocks hidden, because if they get in my way, I might just stand on them.'

Sadia, spun on her heel and began to walk back to Jessica when she heard Brighton say in a voice loud enough to reach only her ears, 'Can't abide this positive discrimination. The amount of women in the force is bad enough but when they start giving the Pakistanis detective status it makes you wonder whether it's who they know further up the ladder, who they screw *or* the colour of their skin that got them in.'

Sadia turned back abruptly, 'What did you say?' But Brighton had already walked off whistling under his breath, leaving Sadia clenching and unclenching her fists. Gus was going to have his work cut out with this one.

After several deep breaths and a few quiet curses Sadia felt calm enough to return to Jessica. 'You heard all that?'

Jessica nodded, hands thrust in her pockets. 'Thanks for sticking up for us, but there was no need to. I'm used to pricks like that. In my line of work there's always some like that.'

Sadia shook her head. 'There was every need, Jess. He'd no right. I'll make sure he gets an official reprimand.'

Jessica rested her hand on Sadia's arm. 'Leave it, Sad. It's not worth it and he'll only make trouble for you.'

Sadia shook her head. 'He can't make trouble for me.'

'Well, watch your back, anyway. His sort are nasty'

Sadia guided Jessica over to a waiting police car. 'Tell me what you can about Trixie and how you found her. Then I'll get you home.'

Jessica slipped into the back seat of the car and scooted over to allow Sadia to climb in beside her before speaking. 'We shared a flat. She was one of Bazza's, like me and, at the minute, she was his pet, which meant free rent for us.'

'What do you mean, his "pet"?'

'Well, you know? His pet, his girl, his screw – whatever. She only had to work weekends; the rest of the time she was Bazza's – well, mainly Tuesdays and Thursdays – and, in return, we got free rent.'

'Uggh, Jess, that's horrid.'

Jess grinned. 'Better the devil you know, Sadia. It's much safer doing Bazza than a stranger. At least with Bazza, it's always over quick.'

Sadia shook her head and grinned at the girl. 'You're terrible, Jess.' Then, as the import of Jessica's words sunk in her face fell. 'You mean…? He's your uncle, Jess!'

Jessica shook her head. 'Don't get your knickers in a flap, Sadia. Just winding you up. Not me. He wouldn't fucking dare. Nah, just telling you what the other girls say.'

Sadia frowned, concerned that comparatively, it seemed almost acceptable for Bazza to hold one of his working girls to ransom for free rent rather than screw his niece. What the hell was she thinking? Bazza Green wasn't acceptable in anybody's world. Mind you, she didn't have to survive in Bazza's world – thank God! 'Where did Trixie come from?'

Jessica frowned, 'I'm not sure, you know. She was sort of secretive. But she did talk about Brid a lot.'

'You don't know much about her, yet you say she's your best friend?'

Jessica looked at the ground. 'She *was* my best friend and I'm going to miss her like hell. But you don't know what it's like in this world, Sadia. *Your* parents were always there for you… I lost mine.'

'I know, Jess. I was there. I saw it.'

Jessica lifted her head and met Sadia's eyes. 'You were there that night?'

'Yeah, I saw it from our living room window.'

Jessica sniffed and straightened her back in a gesture Sadia remembered from their childhood. 'Hmm, well that's done now. Fact is Trixie and I trusted each other, but we didn't confide about the past. We both wanted to move on and so we lived for now.'

'How old was she?'

'Younger than me – 'bout eighteen, I suppose.'

'How long had you known her?'

'Two years, give or take.'

'Jessica, I want you to think really hard about this one, okay?'

Jessica nodded.

'Do you have any idea who might have done this to Trixie?'

Jessica thought for a minute and then shook her head.

'No dodgy punters, or a dealer she'd pissed off?'

'Don't know why you're asking that, Sadia. Surely it's the same sicko that did them other two last week?'

Sadia laid a gentle hand on Jess' arm. 'We don't know that for sure. We need to make sure we cover every possibility. We wouldn't be doing our job otherwise.'

Pursing her lips, Jessica hesitated then nodded. 'Yeah, okay, Sad. I see what you mean, but I just can't think of anybody who'd want to hurt her. She was popular, you know? The punters and the other girls liked her.'

Sadia tapped the tip of her pencil on her notebook and frowning said, 'Why was she here tonight though, Jess. You said she was always with Bazza on a Thursday, so she wasn't turning tricks tonight, was she?'

Jessica shrugged, 'No, she should've been with Baz. He phoned, said she wasn't picking up her phone, so I came looking for her. Thought she might've been,' Jess' eyes flitted round the car, 'you know? Like, looking for a hit. She'd been clean for a couple of months, but round here it's easy to slip off the wagon.'

As tears rolled down Jessica's cheeks, she used the corner of the blanket to wipe them away.

Sadia shut her notebook with a sigh. 'Come on, Jess, I'll get someone to drive you home. We'll call round tomorrow. You left your address with someone?'

CHAPTER 9

Gus watched Sadia bundle the girl into the car with a gentleness she didn't often show; at least not in the incident room anyway. 'Anything useful?' he asked, watching as the car carrying Jessica drove off.

'Not a lot.' Sadia tossed their empty coffee cups into the black bin bag that had been hooked on the fence. 'She's about eighteen. Trixie. No surname. Like Alice said she may have come from Bridlington – may not. Been here two years or so. Worked for Bazza Green and,' her mouth screwed up, 'at present she was his "pet" or regular screw. According to Jessica there were no dodgy punters or crazed dealers after payment. No reason for anyone to kill her. What about you?'

Gus hunched into his coat and shoved his hands into his pockets. 'Apart from catching Alice taking a fiver off an unsuspecting plod after winning a bet about what my dad wore under his damn kilt, not a fucking lot. The MO looks almost exactly like the other two girls. We'll have to wait for the PM tomorrow.'

Sadia frowned and stepped closer to him. Her tone sounded accusing when she spoke, 'Do you think your dad knows something?'

Gus turned and studied her face. Judging by the sparks in her eyes, she was in a mood. What had he done now? He cleared his throat. 'About what?'

Before Sadia could reply, Alice bounced towards them balancing three Styrofoam containers in her outstretched hands. 'Does who know something about what?'

Sadia maintained eye contact with Gus, who frowned thinking, *looks like I'll be in for it later on.* With a sigh, he rearranged his face into a smile and turned to Alice.

'Nobody, Al. That's the problem. Nobody seems to know anything.'

'Hmm.' Alice handed a fresh coffee to each of them. Sadia accepted hers with an abrupt 'Thanks' and marched away from them towards her car.

Seeing Alice's lips tighten as her eyes followed Sadia, Gus stifled a groan. What the hell was it with those two? Ever since The Matchmaker case there had been an uneasy truce between them and he always seemed to be the one that got it in the neck from one or other of them. Bracing himself, he waited for the onslaught which wasn't long coming.

Planting her small frame in front of him and pinning him with her dark eyes Alice said, 'What's going on with you and Sadia?'

Gus ran his fingers through his dreads and, feeling like a naughty schoolboy, puffed out a huge waft of air. He hated deceiving Alice. She'd been great earlier in the year and he hated cutting her out of the loop. 'Aw, Al, come on give me a break. I'm not holding anything back. You know we share everything on this team. It's how we work. How *I* work. Now, come on let's see if the door-to-doors have got owt for us, and then we can call it a night. Briefing at 7am prompt, okay?'

Alice shrugged and allowed him to point her in the direction of the waiting officers.

CHAPTER 10
Lilycroft Allotments

A s the heater blasted away the last of her shivers and the wipers cleared away the odd specks of rain and wet leaves, Alice sat in her Mini Cooper thinking about Gus and Sadia. She'd known they were keeping something from her earlier and now she'd seen them huddled together between their cars before they drove off separately.

They'd looked furtive and she couldn't rid herself of the uneasy feeling that their furtiveness was connected to her. She wasn't altogether convinced by Gus' denial earlier. She'd felt excluded for a few weeks now. Nothing too damning, too specific, just the feeling of conversations cut short when she entered the room. Then, there was that one time she'd asked them for a drink after work and they'd both made up an excuse, but later on she'd seen them heading off together in Gus' car. Didn't they trust her? Did they think that because of what happened down in Brent last year she was a detriment to the team? A weak link? Hadn't she proven herself in the child trafficking case? She'd always thought so, and Gus had told her she'd done a good job. After all she'd headed up the investigation at the start before he was fit to come back to work.

Alice heaved a great sigh and banged her hand on the steering wheel. Of course! God, how could she have been such a fool? Sadia's dad, DCS Hussain, was keeping tabs on her via Sadia and Gus. And now DCI Nancy Chalmers wasn't here to watch her back. She should have expected repercussions after everything in Brent, but she'd been lulled into a false sense of security since then. Like the stupid, gullible thing she was, she'd put it behind her and assumed everyone else had too. Well, she'd just have to show them wouldn't she? She'd prove to them she was up to the job – even if it killed her.

CHAPTER 11

Standing in the shadows he flicked the cigarette butt into the air with his index finger, sending a cascade of orange sparks into the petrol-marbled puddle, where they hissed briefly before being extinguished. He pushed himself upright and watched, with a grin, as Alice's brake lights flickered at the end of the road before she turned left. He'd seen her huddled in her car watching the mighty Gus McGuire flirt with that sanctimonious Hussain cow. The light from the passing police cars as they headed back to The Fort had been enough to tell him she was not a happy bunny.

Maybe she fancied a bit of brown cock for herself or maybe she just didn't like her hero showing interest in another bit of skirt. Made no odds to him what her reasons were. He was just pleased to have a bit of inside info. After all, info was currency at The Fort and by the way the Hussain bitch and McGuire were cosying up together it looked like he'd just hit the jackpot. Wonder what DCS Hussain would say to his little Paki bint screwing her boss.

CHAPTER 12
Birmingham

Shahid woke to a dim light breaking through a chink in the floral curtains. An orchestra of snoring assaulted his ears. Uncle Majid's low rumble provided the bass; Imti's sporadic snorts were the flutes; and cousin Aftab's high pitched yelps, the strings section.

Shahid groaned and rolled onto his back, making the precarious bunk bed wobble alarmingly. The attic room was large enough to house two bunk beds and the massive Ikea wardrobes that lined one wall. On the floor were Shahid's and Imti's roller cases. The lids were thrown back and their clothes hung out from when they'd rummaged through them the previous night for something suitable to wear when sharing a room with your uncle.

Shahid's eyes felt gritty and a glance at his phone told him he'd only been asleep for a couple of hours. It'd been late when he and Imti had arrived the previous night. Traffic on the M1 had been appalling and flash flooding compounded it. Then, of course, when they'd arrived, tired and longing for bed, Uncle Majid had wanted to catch up on things in Bradford and Shahid had felt duty-bound to sit with the men, talking about nothing very important, whilst the women served them samosas, bhajia and soft drinks. The atmosphere was festive with wedding garlands strung up inside the house and *Shaadi Mubarak* lights blinking on and off through the darkness in red and gold. His huge extended family were all staying over and for Shahid it was all a bit too much. Imti loved all this stuff, but he hated it. He hated the old aunties teasing him about getting married and threatening to get him a nice girl from Pakistan. His Mirpuri Punjabi was poor and he was well out of practice so he ended up with a headache from trying to concentrate on the various conversations in the crowded room. If Imti hadn't insisted, Shahid knew he would have missed the wedding altogether. It wasn't that he didn't like his cousin. On the contrary, Aftab was a good bloke, but Shahid hated the air of superiority some of his uncles carried. The way they judged him and Imti because of the things his father had done. Imti seemed oblivious, but *he* heard every sneering word and saw every hateful smirk. Shahid could've done with a beer but, even though his uncle was Western in many ways, he still didn't countenance alcohol and Shahid was sensitive enough to respect that.

He'd kept slipping out of the room to check his phone, but there was still nothing from Trixie. From the surreptitious glances Imti kept sending his way, Shahid could sense that he was getting annoyed with him. He probably thought he was checking his phone for some dodgy deal or other. On the journey to Birmingham Imti had done nothing but natter on about cleaning up the business, making it legitimate... on and fucking on. In the end Shahid had turned on the radio and suffered the pounding Bollywood station Imti loved so much in order to get him off his back. As Imti sang along in tuneless Hindi, he'd pretended to doze and instead spent his time worrying about Trixie.

Their cousin Aftab was due to be married later on today. They'd done the civil ceremony last month; today was the Islamic one with the Imam. Shahid was pleased Aftab had broken the mould and married a Gujarati Muslim called Jasmine instead of one of his cousins from the village in Pakistan. Shahid had seen some of his friends marry their cousins only to end up having kids with congenital heart conditions and the like. It was about time things changed. You only had to look at the royal family's history to see how fucked up that had been in the past. He, for one, had no intention of marrying his cousin. Well, he had Trixie now anyway. And he was happy with her. As soon as they could they'd get married and then maybe he would consider what Imti said about cleaning up the business.

Thinking of Trixie, he picked up his phone again and looked at it. Still nothing from the bloody girl. Where the hell was she. Then he smiled. Bet she'd lost her phone again. She was always losing the bloody thing. He scratched his groin and waited for his morning glory to go down, before throwing aside the girly pink duvet and swinging his legs over the edge of the bunk. The faint aroma of Comfort fabric conditioner with faint undertones of male sweat, made him happy. It'd been a long time since he'd shared a room with his cousin, uncle and brother; not since they were kids. Aunt Nusrat had been insistent that they share as the house was full up with wedding guests and though he'd initially balked at the idea, he had to admit it had been fun. They'd reminisced for hours until finally, Aunt Nusrat had banged on their door telling them that Aftab needed his sleep in preparation for his big day

His uncle and cousin, in each of the bottom two bunks, didn't so much as falter in their music-making as Shahid jumped onto the thick carpet. Standing at eye level to Imti who lay with one leg hanging over the side of his bunk, his mouth wide open, made him smile. He leaned over and pushed the stray leg back onto the bunk. Imti mumbled something in his sleep and rolled over.

Rubbing the sleep from his eyes, Shahid pulled on a shirt and left the room. Leaning against the door he quickly punched in Trixie's number, but again it rung out. At this rate he'd have to risk phoning Jessica. Not that he expected any joy from her. If she could make things difficult for him, then she would – and she didn't even know about him and Trixie yet. It'd be damn awkward to try to explain to her why he wanted to know where her flatmate was. He grunted, deciding to hold on till later and was just about to go back into the room when he heard his aunt's voice calling his name.

Popping his head over the bannister he looked down. She was still fully dressed, so Shahid assumed she hadn't been to bed yet. Too busy looking after them last night and then, knowing her, she'd have tidied up after they'd gone to bed. 'What is it, Auntie?'

She looked up at him, her lips tight, a frown furrowing her forehead. When she spoke her voice was clipped. 'I don't want you involving your uncle in all this trouble in Bradford, Shahid. We're out of that sort of life now and I don't want to go back,' she folded her arms under her small breasts, her elbows jutting out as sharply as her cheek bones. 'If you've got trouble with gangs in Manchester or Sheffield, you are on your own. We will not be involved.'

Shahid bit back the angry words that rushed to his mouth and merely nodded before turning back into the room. Clearly she'd been listening to their conversation last night. He knew exactly where she was coming from and, in some ways, he couldn't blame her; but she was a hypocrite. She was happy to take money from him to cover the cost of her precious son's wedding as long as it wasn't her husband or son putting their necks on the line. Where the fuck did she think the money he'd given for the deposit on this house had come from?

Shahid closed the door quietly behind him and climbed back onto his bunk and tried to get comfortable. It was true that he had spoken with his uncle about the possibility of Johnny The Gerbil from Oldham or The Cockroach from Sheffield being responsible for Camilla and Starlight's deaths. Somehow, he didn't really think Bazza had it in him to instigate a turf war and there were no reports of dodgy punters, so it was reasonable to assume that at some point gang bosses from other cities would want to make inroads in Bradford to extend their empires. Hell, he'd thought more than once about extending to Manchester and Sheffield himself, but he'd always considered their fragile truce more beneficial than a turf war.

He punched his pillow and rolled over. Fuck, but he hated family dos. Always full of strife. He wished he was back in Bradford with Trixie. Things were always simple when he was with her.

CHAPTER 13
The Fort

Two huge whiteboards crammed with details, written in a variety of colours, stood against the back wall of The Fort's biggest incident room. Each board had a photo of the previous two victims stuck to the top. Next to them was a third board, which, in vivid contrast to the others, was virgin white. The only addition was a stark crime scene photo of Trixie, taped to the top. In addition to Gus' major incident team a variety of uniformed officers assigned to these murders sat round the huge table in the middle of the room. Others leaned against the back walls and a few had snagged the unoccupied chairs from behind the various computers around the periphery. Replacing the traditional police station odour of stale sweat and cigs was the aroma of bacon sandwiches and fresh coffee – a perk supplied by Gus who couldn't abide instant and didn't see why his team should have to put up with it either.

'Right, settle down folks,' shouted Gus above the chatter. He reeled off a series of instructions to the uniformed officers and sent them on their way before speaking to his team. 'I'll do a quick review of what we've got so far, then open it up for comments, but before that I'd like to introduce our new member. DC Tim Brighton.' He gestured one by one round the table, 'DI Sadia Hussain, DS Alice Cooper and DC John Sampson.'

Gus took a swig from his Wee Bru before continuing. 'For DC Brighton, who's new to the team, I'll just clarify a few things. First of all, you are lucky to be here. We are the first of this type of unit in the country. After our success in nailing The Matchmaker, the powers that be decided our team's diverse skills are "cutting edge".'

He had heard from Sadia about Brighton's behaviour the previous evening and he was determined to be clear, without giving him a rollicking on his first day, that a repeat performance would not be acceptable. He hadn't been allowed the privilege of selecting this new recruit and, though Gus had made his irritation known, DCS Hussain had proved inflexible on this count. Gus knew the DCS, not his biggest fan, was waiting for him to mess up. Gus had decided to give Brighton the benefit of the doubt for now. He'd worked with racists and sexists before and knew that sometimes, despite their obvious personality defects, they had skills that he could use. Hopefully, Brighton was the same – otherwise he'd be out on his arse, DCS Hussain or no DCS Hussain. Gus looked directly at Brighton.

'Our MIT works under the CID umbrella and specifically tackles crimes like this one. This allows the Anti-terrorist and Vice units to continue their specialism, whilst sharing and pooling information that is of relevance to each. In other words, we are a streamlined unit with, so far, a proven track record of speedy, accurate results. To be blunt, we work our balls off, we work as a team and we get the job done. Any questions?'

Brighton cast a glance at Sadia. Gus noted with a smile that she ignored him. He continued. 'I work on the basis that each team member's input, regardless of their rank, is of equal importance. That means that on any investigation you will *all* be proactive. I don't want just paper-pushing sheep. I want you all thinking, putting in your opinion. Yes, some of us have more experience than others, but that doesn't mean we don't all still have something to learn.'

Gus rested one buttock on his desk. 'If you have a thought, no matter how vague or weird or embarrassing, let's hear it, because sometimes the smallest, weirdest things can be what sets an investigation off in the right direction. I want you all thinking. The DCs on my team don't only do the plod work, they input the investigation any way they can, okay?'

Brighton nodded, leaning forward on the table, notebook at the ready as Gus moved on. 'Right, we've had three victims in the space of a week and so far nothing concrete to go on. When we interviewed the working girls last week they said bugger all, as did their pimps. I'm hoping this last murder will have loosened their tongues a bit.'

Gus paused and looked at his team. 'I want this fucker caught before he kills again, okay?'

A low mumble of agreement spread round the table.

'Okay, let's recap.' Gus walked over to the first whiteboard and touched the corner of one of the photos that hung there. 'This is victim number one. Camilla Grant, aged twenty-two years, known prostitute, working for Shahid Khan.'

Gus tapped the photo sharply with his knuckles causing everyone to jump. 'Look at her.'

All eyes were drawn to Camilla, who smiled shyly into the camera. She looked like any other twenty-two-year-old girl, thought Gus.

'Camilla was found last Friday, in Bradford Moor Park by two males taking a shortcut through the park to Killinghall Road after closing time.

Cause of death was strangulation by, what was later identified as, her own belt. However, pre-mortem the bastard savagely and repeatedly rammed a wine bottle, broken at the neck, into her vagina, causing multiple lacerations and severe blood loss. The wine bottle, is unfortunately, available in most supermarkets. There was no semen and no prints.'

'Sick bastard,' said Alice.

'Yeah, this one is a real sicko,' said Gus. 'Now, moving on. This is Starlight.' He glanced round and saw that the team were focussing intently on the photo of the brown skinned beauty with the wide grin and flirtatious eyes.

'The bastard got Starlight on Monday. Again, in Bradford Moor Park. Again, she was one of Shahid Khan's. Nineteen years old, mother of a five-year-old boy.'

He paused to take another swig from his Bru bottle and his cheek muscles contracted as he considered his next words. 'Starlight was discovered by a 7-year-old girl on her way to school with her older brother. She'd chased her ball into the bushes and stumbled on the body. Her mum tells me she has nightmares and has started to wet the bed. She won't talk about it to anyone and has become withdrawn and uncommunicative. Just another one of the unacknowledged victims.'

He allowed his words to sink in before continuing. 'Starlight was strangled with her tights. Again, pre-mortem a broken wine bottle, bearing the same brand name was repeatedly and violently thrust into her vagina.'

Gus shoved his hand in his pocket and moved along to the final board. 'Meet victim three, Trixie (surname unknown) aged around eighteen, probably a runaway according to her flatmate. I've only got the crime scene photo so far,' said Gus. The close-up photo of Trixie with her eyes bulging and her hair splayed behind her like a mane of mucky straw, contrasted sharply with the happy vibe of the other photos.

'Bloody hell!' said DC Sampson drawing everyone's eyes towards him in surprise. He flushed and took a sip of coffee to cover his embarrassment. Alice caught his eye and winked at him, which, unfortunately, rather than reassuring him, made him flush deeper.

'Trixie was found at approximately 9pm last night, in the Lilycroft allotments. She was found by her best friend and flatmate Jessica Green. Trixie was a known prostitute working for Bazza Green. Again, cause of death appears to be strangulation by, possibly, her own scarf. Same or similar MO. For more details, we need to wait for the PM, which I will attend.'

DC Sampson coughed and fidgeted on his chair, 'I was wondering, sir, if maybe we're looking at a sort of prostitute turf war?'

Gus smiled at the young DC but, before he could comment, he heard a snort from the other side of the table. Gus turned and looked at Brighton. 'Yes?'

Brighton stretched his arms out in front of him palm upwards. 'Well, that's a pretty basic question isn't it?' he said, smirking at Sampson.

Gus jumped to his feet and eyes sparking he pierced Brighton with a look. 'I don't care how you managed to wangle your way onto this team, but you need to learn pretty damn quick that I don't tolerate petty point scoring. Everyone is entitled to voice their thoughts without being ridiculed. I don't have time for arses who want to disrupt team dynamics. We've got too serious a job on for that so, let me issue this warning, loud and clear. You do that once more, Brighton and you're out. Nobody, I repeat *nobody*, stays here if they're not a team player. Got it?'

Brighton flushed and sent a glance round the table. Talking a deep breath, he nodded once, 'Look, that probably came out wrong. All I'm trying to say is that it's obviously a sicko prossie serial killer. After all, this one is the third one isn't she? And we all know that three kills equal a serial killer.'

Gus, raised an eyebrow, 'At this point, how can you be sure? It could equally be just what Sampson suggested – a turf war. We rule nothing out until we've investigated it and found it doesn't stand up.'

He turned to Sampson, whose face was as bright as a beetroot. 'That was a valid point, John. Now, what are the pros and cons for either the "serial killer" or the "turf war" theory?'

Alice smiled at Sampson and said, 'Word on the street is that there's a lot of competition for territory at the moment. Apparently, some of the new Eastern European immigrants look like they're trying to stake a claim. With the job market being what it is some of them are desperate and according to Vice more of the women they're picking up are Polish or Romanian and they don't seem to be from either Khan or Green's stables. Interpol reckon some of their more lucrative known criminals have snuck into the UK with the sole intention of cashing in on drugs, weapons and prostitution.'

She rubbed her nose with her hand. 'Then of course there's our own homegrown criminals. Colin "The Cockroach" Roache, from Sheffield's been sighted snooping around and so has Mac Harrison from Glasgow and Johnnie "The Gerbil" Butler from Oldham.' She waved a sheet of paper in the air and continued, 'Vice say they're looking mainly at the drug market so far, but that doesn't mean they won't venture into prostitution and firearms if they can frighten off Bazza or Khan.'

Gus nodded. 'So we may be looking at a turf war after all. Any thoughts on the serial killer angle?'

Again, Alice spoke: 'All the reports from the women indicate that they've not had any dodgy punters. It would be unusual for a serial killer targeting prostitutes to strike three times without leaving some sort of marker... You know, being too rough or asking for kinky stuff outside the girls' comfort zones or the like. Although the MO's and victims match in each of the three incidents, it seems like we've got nothing to go on in that respect. Unless of course he's operating outside Bradford but hunting inside Bradford.'

'That's something we need to follow up on, anyway. I'll get Compo to check out similar crimes outside the district when he gets back from court. Any other thoughts?' When everyone shook their heads, Gus continued, 'Right then, Alice, you and Sampson interview Khan and Green. Get statements from the working girls from both sides.' He grinned. 'That'll be an initiation for Sampson.'

Alice laughed and banged Sampson on the shoulder, 'Oh, you're in for a treat today. I'll be introducing you to aspects of Bradford you've never imagined, not even in your wildest dreams.'

Gus winked at Sampson and then addressed Brighton, 'Contact Missing Persons to see if we can identify Trixie and her family and I want you updating the files. Go through every statement and correlate anything interesting. After we've been to the PM, Sadia and I will interview Jessica Green, see what we can get from her about her uncle and her friend Trixie. Also, to keep everyone up to speed Jessica is Shahid Khan's half-sister and there is no love lost between them. Worth bearing in mind in case it somehow plays into the investigation.'

After Sadia had updated them on the Bazza Green–Jessica–Shahid Khan triangle, Gus wound up the briefing, 'Right any other thoughts?'

Brighton raised a hand, 'Just still thinking about the serial killer thing. It would be difficult to subdue a girl, remove her clothing and force her to stay still while he violated her. I'm thinking maybe there was a second guy to hold her down.'

Gus nodded, but it was Sampson who responded. 'If there were two perps then I think that supports the turf war theory more than the serial killer one.' Taking a deep breath and, ignoring Brighton's frown, Sampson continued, 'Research shows that, although not unknown, it is much less likely for a serial killer to have a partner.'

Sadia glanced at Sampson. 'Actually, you're perfectly right, John.' She turned to Brighton, her expression neutral. 'I can see your point too, Tim, but both girls' tox screens came back with an alcoholic and ketamine level way off the scale. They were so out of it they probably couldn't have put up a lot of resistance. However, if there were two perpetrators it would make it easier. Worth bearing in mind, anyway. I'll add it to the board.'

'What about the door-to-doors?' asked Alice.

'Brighton will liaise with them. A phone line has been set up for information so I want you to be responsible for weeding out anything noteworthy from that, too. Meet back here at 1pm for pizza and feedback.'

CHAPTER 14

Alice glanced over at Gus and Sadia huddled in front of the crime boards and felt a pang. When Gus threw back his head, sending his dreads bouncing as he laughed at something Sadia had said Alice knew her pang had been a combination of jealousy and anger. Since she'd joined the MIT with Gus, she'd been his right-hand person. Now it seemed like Sadia was slowly ousting her and that, combined with her suspicions from the previous night, sat heavy in her chest. She felt side-lined and confused. The cold light of day had made her question her doubts about Gus. Surely, he wouldn't be so duplicitous as to keep tabs on her for DCS Hussain.

What was really bothering her right now, though, was the fact that Gus had elected to take Sadia to interview Jessica. Okay, Sadia knew the girl and had taken her preliminary statement, but Alice had interviewed the other witnesses and she thought she'd done a good job. For continuity's sake she felt *she* should be the one to interview Jessica. Deep down she knew she was being unreasonable and that Gus was perfectly justified in his decision, but somehow, she just couldn't let it go. She hated this feeling and yet, at the same time, she knew she had to do something about it.

Reflected in the large window she saw her multiple ear piercings glistening under the overhead lights as she turned to Sampson. She lifted her hand and touched each one with her fingertip in an attempt to calm herself down saying in a mock cowboy accent, 'Head outside, partner, I'll catch you up in a minute.'

She watched Sampson walk from the room, noting how he avoided looking at Brighton who swaggered behind him, whistling under his breath. Alice waited till they'd left before approaching Gus. 'I interviewed all the key witnesses in the previous two murders so I think I should be the one to interview Jessica, too.'

'Hmm,' said Gus, scratching his head, as he read through the notes on the boards. 'What did you say?'

'I want to interview Jessica Green, Gus.' Her tone came out sharper than she intended and she cursed herself.

Gus glanced up and as he observed her the smile faded from his lips.

Alice knew that she looked pissed off, standing legs apart, hands on hips and her chin stuck out at a pugnacious angle, but it was too late to change her stance.

Gus frowned. 'What's up with you, Al? You and Sampson have enough to do as it is. Surely you're not fighting for extra work?'

Sadia walked over, smiling, making Alice want to slap her superior-looking face. Keeping her eyes on Gus she ignored Sadia when she said, 'I took Jess' preliminary statement last night. I know her *and* her history. I've already got a connection with her.' And she reached out and touched Alice's arm.

Alice pulled away. 'I wasn't asking *you*, Sadia. I was speaking to Gus.'

Gus looked at the two women and then, his tone puzzled said, 'Have I missed something?'

Sadia put her pen down and shrugged as Alice threw a glance in the other girl's direction. '*I* should be the one to take her statement.' Even to her own ears, she sounded churlish. She felt a wave of heat spread up her face as Gus' blue eyes darkened till it was difficult to distinguish the blue of his iris, from the black circle that surrounded it. A sure sign he was pissed off.

'For God's sake, we've got, at worst, a serial killer at large and, at best, a turf war between two rival gangs and you're questioning my decisions. What the fuck's wrong with you?'

Alice swallowed and then straightened her back. 'I feel I'm being side-lined. Maybe my abilities are in question?'

Gus stuck his pen into his dreads. Alice knew from his expression that he was completely flabbergasted. 'What? You think I'm excluding you? Where the hell's that come from?'

Feeling slightly foolish but not wanting to back down, Alice lifted her small chin 'Well are you?'

Gus sighed. 'I don't know what you're on about, Al. I really don't and I don't have time for this.'

Having come this far Alice was determined not to let it go now. 'Is it because of Brent? Because the inquiry's findings will be published soon?'

Gus' face cleared. 'Aw for God's sake, Al. You're in Bradford now. You know you'll be exonerated, so stop dwelling on it.' He walked over to her and placing his hands on her shoulder, he gave them a gentle shake. 'I trust you completely.'

Alice bit her lip. She'd seen the way Sadia rolled her eyes and wanted to slap her but, maybe now wasn't the time. Vowing to keep an eye on the other woman, Alice shrugged, feeling like she'd made a complete tit of herself and said. 'As long as you do.'

Gus glanced from Alice to Sadia and shook his head, 'God, you two are high maintenance.'

CHAPTER 15
Thornbury

S erafina stretched allowing the ebb and flow of the household wakening up to cocoon her. She supposed she was lucky. Her father had lost his job in Poland and they'd been forced to move to Bradford. It had been a real come-down for the entire family and money was tight. Their home in Poland had been palatial in comparison to this little three-bedroomed terraced house but Serafina was beginning to settle now. She'd made friends and she liked her school and being the only girl in a family of three boys meant that she had her own room and she savoured it. Okay, it was only a tiny box room with a single bed and small wardrobe squeezed in and hardly enough room for her to move around when she was standing, but it was all hers and it provided a her with a place to study away from the boisterous teasing of her siblings. Not that she minded their teasing. It was all part of family life and most of the time she enjoyed it.

From downstairs her mum's gentle scolding tones drifted into her room and Serafina smiled, visualising her oldest brother, Jacob, who was always first up, standing shamefaced among the remnants of his breakfast. Her tiny mother, just back from her cleaning job at Barkerend Primary School, would be standing, hands on hips glaring up at her brother. This routine happened every morning. She could hear Jacob's deeper tones now apologising in Polish and she knew he'd be swiftly gathering up his dishes, plonking mum in a chair and switching the kettle on ready to make her a well-deserved cup of tea.

Jacob and her mum had been forced to make the biggest adjustments in their new life. In Poland her mother had enjoyed being a housewife, now here in Bradford she'd been forced to take on a menial job. Serafina knew she hated it. Her mother was an educated woman. She'd been a teacher before Jacob had arrived, but now, speaking little English, and needing to contribute to the household income she'd taken the only job she could find. Serafina knew it caused conflict between her parents. She'd heard her mother crying and her father's harsh tones as he berated her for her selfishness. Once or twice, she thought, he'd even hit her mother. She loved him, of course she did, but at the same time it scared her that he could be so harsh. In Poland, he'd been away on business a lot, but now they were all packed together in this small space and he, too, was forced into a job he hated.

Her alarm clock beeped and, pushing the covers down from under her chin, Serafina grimaced. Ouch! The bruises from that idiot at The Delius last night were making themselves felt. She sighed. She'd enjoyed going to The Delius on a Thursday night. It was something for her to do and was a welcome break from her studies. She was desperate to go to university and her parents and her two elder brothers worked so hard to make it happen for her. Sometimes she felt guilty that they were all contributing to the family income whilst she gave nothing. She knew they all wanted her and Thomas to have the same opportunities as they would have had in Poland if the recession hadn't struck.

It had been a huge decision to move from Gorce, from their extended families, but when her father's business dried up they'd had no choice. Now, he worked nightshift on a zero hours' contract at Farmer's Boy on Cemetery Road, cleaning the huge vats that processed the peas and other vegetables. Her mum's cleaning job didn't bring in much – but it was permanent. Jacob's interest in motorbikes had paid off for him and he'd got a job at Champion Motor Spares on Leeds Road. He'd blagged his way in and shown how much he knew about engines and cars and had just been made permanent. Luka, her middle brother was happy to shelf stack at Pakeezah halal supermarket on Leeds road and was after a bar job at The Delius too. Maybe the cute guy behind the bar, Imti she'd heard the bouncers call him, would give him one if she asked. She sensed he liked her; and she liked him.

Then she grimaced. Best not go back to The Delius for a while, not with that idiot on the loose. She touched her bruised chin and frowned. She'd seen him before. Knew he'd been watching her for a while now and she knew who he was. She really needed to avoid him. She'd heard the rumours from the Polish girls at school. He was bad news and she knew he'd not think twice about using her family to make her do what he wanted. Best if she kept a low profile for a while.

The previous night she'd briefly considered confiding in her brothers but, she knew how headstrong they could be and felt that they'd go all-out to protect her regardless of how powerful Anastazy Dolinski was. They'd all heard the rumours of his real identity and knew that he had contacts within their community both in Bradford and in Poland. They'd heard rumours of the sort of things he did and they made Serafina's blood run cold, but that wouldn't stop her brothers trying to protect her. No, her best bet was to avoid him and hope and pray that he'd gradually forget about her. Maybe develop a new fixation. She lifted the small crucifix she wore round her neck and stroking it with her fingers she sent up a quick prayer.

CHAPTER 16
The Fort

'Do you like it then?' asked Alice, startling Sampson, who was staring at her Mini Cooper. She was used to people staring at it, after all it was a particularly virulent shade of green. Damn near fluorescent really. To crown it all, she'd added a series of aubergine coloured flowers to the intricately painted black ones that intertwined down the doors, up over the roof and down to the bonnet. She loved it. It was like an extension of her personality. She'd always felt like the odd one out as a child but, as an adult, she'd decided to embrace her individuality. She worked very hard at not letting other people's opinions affect her.

Sampson walked slowly round the car, studying the effect from all angles. 'It's different,' he said at last.

Alice pouted, 'You don't like it? Well, I suppose it's an acquired taste. Hop in.'

The gangly officer sighed as he opened the passenger door and bent his frame to squeeze through the opening and into the seat. Stretching his legs, he leaned back. 'Bit roomier than your old one.'

Alice's old Mini had also had a garden on the paintwork but, with that one, she'd restricted herself to black flowers. The purple flowers were a new addition and had taken her ages to apply. She'd looked on it as therapy after the darkness of The Matchmaker case in February and was really chuffed with the outcome. She slid into her seat, inserted her key into the ignition and said, 'New design.'

Sampson grinned. 'And does this new design include the purple pansies?'

Alice stopped mid-way through fastening her seat belt. 'They're not bloody pansies, you idiot.'

Sampson raised an eyebrow. 'No?'

Alice pulled her seatbelt over her coat and clicked it in place, 'They're lilies! You're a peasant, Sampson, you know that?' She started the engine before adding, 'But at least you're not an arse like our new sidekick.'

'You got that right. Brighton's a prize dick. He got himself in trouble last night mouthing off about the victims in front of Sadia. Word is she gave him a right earful.'

'That's not good.'

'Nah, and then he had the nerve to make comments about how Sadia got onto the team.'

Ouch, thought Alice, *that wouldn't have gone down well with Sadia.* She wasn't surprised Sadia had told him off because she was very touchy about her dad at the best of times. 'Yeah well, don't worry about him. Gus has got his mark. He'll deal with him.'

Sampson nodded and as Alice screeched out of the parking lot, he crossed himself, mumbling something about insurance under his breath.

Alice smiled enjoying his discomfort. 'Now, how do you want to handle this? Tell you what, we'll start with Bazza and I'll take the lead, okay? Then you can take the lead with the girls.'

He nodded with a sigh, 'As long as you stay nearby. Those girls are always touching me.'

Alice laughed. She could see why they'd want to wind him up. He looked like a teenager with that endearing blush. Besides which, he was tall, cute and probably one hundred per cent more attractive than most of the johns they put out for. 'Experience with the working girl then, Sampson?'

'Yeah, mainly booking them and trying to get them in the cells overnight without losing any item of clothing.' He put his head to one side and added, 'Mine, not theirs, I hasten to add.'

She laughed and in a mock American accent said, 'Don't worry, babe. I've got your back.'

'Actually, it's more my front I'm bothered about' and he nodded towards his groin.

Alice sucked in a breath. 'Ah, I see what you mean. Never had that problem with them but I have just the thing you need.' She brought the car to a screeching stop outside a kebab shop on Duckworth Lane and reaching behind her, she came up with a large UK road atlas. 'Keep that on your lap during the interviews. That'll save you.'

Sampson laughed and got out of the car to join her on the street. 'Not got satnav, Alice?'

'Always like to have a backup, Sampson. You never know when you'll need a good solid road map.'

Sampson, followed her as she strode along the street.

'Over here,' She nodded towards a small alley between the kebab shop and the Asian clothes shop next door. He lives above the shop.

'Is the kebab shop his, then?'

'Yeah, he rents it out. Same with the clothes shop, I've heard.'

The alley was dank and carried an overpowering stink of urine. As they walked, Alice tried to avoid taking a breath as she dodged the puddles. The stairs leading to Bazza Green's official residence were crumbling. Alice, who'd had occasion in the past to visit both his gym and his 'penthouse' in Manningham was surprised by how neglected his flat looked. Clearly, he ploughed all his money into his business enterprises. The paintwork on the door was peeling and the knocker hung by one screw. There was no doorbell so Alice pulled her glove off and rapped with her knuckles, keeping her hand poised to knock again should Bazza be slow to respond. However, within seconds she heard the sound of an internal door opening and muttered cursing that increased in volume as Bazza neared the door. He opened it a few inches and peered out at them, then with another muttered curse, just loud enough for them to hear, Alice presumed, he yanked it open fully and stood there, proud and arrogant, in all his unkempt glory. Alice met his gaze, not bothering to hide the disgust she felt at the sight of his shrunken, pulled woollen waistcoat and stained trousers.

Angular but stooped, Bazza 'The Bampot' Green was of average height. He was in his fifties and bald and grey in equal measure. When he smiled, Alice noticed that his few remaining teeth were brown and jagged. His fingers were yellow as he beckoned them through and even from this distance she could smell his BO which vied with the smoke and grease that seemed to burst from the flat in a fetid cloud of filth.

With an exaggerated bow, he gestured for them to enter. Alice, wishing she'd thought to wear her old anorak rather than her new winter coat, marched in after him, her face impassive. The heavy, smoke-filled air and the fact that Bazza had already discarded one cigarette and lit up another confirmed Alice's impression of a chain smoker. A wave of pity for Trixie rolled over her. Was it really worth the free rent to bed this disgusting creature?

Once in the small living room, Bazza gestured to a stained sofa and, whilst Sampson took advantage of the offer, Alice shook her head, wary of contaminating her clothing any more than was absolutely necessary. She began to wander idly round the room, taking in her surroundings. The conglomeration of cheap knick-knacks combined with the peeling, yellowing flock wallpaper and faded floral three-piece suite told her that Bazza hadn't done any decorating since his mother died a few years previously. She wandered over and stood in front of the gas fire that was on full bum. 'You heard about Trixie then, Bazza?' she asked.

Bazza sighed. 'Yes, very sad. One of your delightful little PC's came with the news in the early hours of this morning.' He shook his head. 'Very sad indeed. A little cracker she was. Amenable.' He glanced at Sampson and winked, 'in *every* way.'

By the time he'd glanced over to her to gauge her reaction, Alice had banished the disgust from her face, replacing it with a disinterested expression as she walked over to the heavy wood sideboard that ran along the back wall behind Bazza's chair. Objectionable little scrote, she thought taking a deep breath which she immediately regretted when smoke clogged her throat, making her cough. Damned if I'll ask him for a glass of water, I'd rather choke to death than risk consuming anything in here. She waved a hand at Sampson telling him to take over, till she'd recovered.

'I see you're heartbroken,' said Sampson, deadpan.

Bazza leaned back in his chair and flicked ash towards an overfilled ashtray. For a moment, he craned his neck to observe Alice who, having recovered from her coughing fit, was looking at the collection of tat on the sideboard. With a shrug he brought his attention back to Sampson. 'No, not heartbroken. That would be a bit too strong a word. More like… dissatisfied.'

'What do you mean?' asked Alice, standing directly behind him, forcing him to strain to see her.

'She's a business asset or, rather, she was. Now, she's a loss. Causes me a lot of hassle you know? Finding a new girl and all that.'

'You know pimping is illegal, don't you Bazza?' said Alice, lifting a dirty ornament off the sideboard and looking at the 'made in China' label on the underside, 'Nice stuff you've got here.'

'Now, there's no need to be nasty. I'm co-operating because I don't like murder. I'm not a pimp. No. The girls come to me to be looked after and that's what I do. Look at the flat I gave Trixie and Jessica. Rent free it was, though of course I'll have to reconsider that now.'

'Surely not completely rent free, Bazza?' said Sampson 'We heard there were conditions attached. You know, free rent for services rendered?'

Bazza lit another cigarette and threw back his head and laughed. 'Now, you've got that wrong son. Trix and me, well, *we* had a relationship. I treated her right. Took her to my penthouse, bought champagne and such like and we enjoyed ourselves.'

Alice muffled a laugh that had Bazza whirling round in his chair ash flying from his cigarette as he moved. 'That's *not* the word on the street, Bazza. Word is that *you* got the enjoyment and she anaesthetised herself on the free booze to get through it.'

He screwed up his face and turned back to Sampson. 'She's got a nasty tongue in her mouth that one.'

'Yes, well,' said Sampson, straightening up, 'Let's get to business, shall we? We want to catch this guy and we wondered if you'd any thoughts on the matter?'

Bazza shrugged and leaned back, narrowing his eyes against the haze of smoke he exhaled from his nose. 'Well, seems to me that after that business last week it's obvious. Some sicko punter's out there offing the whores and you're wasting time talking to me. I'm bereaved, I am. You should have more respect.'

Behind Bazza's back Alice pretended to stick her fingers down her throat. Little weasel had the cheek to pretend to be grieving over Trixie. She was glad she'd given Sampson carte blanche to take over. Somehow or other he'd managed to establish a rapport of sorts with Bazza… and, with Sampson asking the questions, she was at liberty to explore the room.

Sampson raised his eyebrows, 'Hmm, last week when you were questioned about Camilla Grant's murder, you claimed that Shahid Khan was behind it to incriminate you. Changed your mind now, have you?'

'Well, looks to me like it could well still be him, now I think of it. He might have thought it was me that did Camilla and that other one. He might have done Trixie. You know tit for tat like? Or he might have offed the two whores to send a message.'

'A message to whom?' asked Sampson.

Alice wandered back to her previous position by the fire. Bazza smirked and leaned back in his chair crossing his legs then, chin raised in a challenging manner, he stuck his finger up his nasal cavity and wiggled it around before extracting it and, like a little boy at Christmas, he studied his findings, rolled them between his index finger and his thumb and flicked the bogey ball onto the matted carpet, where it landed close to Alice's feet.

Alice felt her stomach heave, but she refused to give him the satisfaction of reacting as she said, 'You're all class, you are, Bazza.'

Bazza grinned and grabbed his crotch. 'You know you want me, bitch.'

Before Alice could respond, Sampson interrupted, 'Answer the question, Bazza, a message to whom?'

Bazza shrugged. 'To any of his girls that were getting a bit bolshie. That Paki, Khan, wouldn't think twice about offing them. Their sort never does.'

'You got any evidence of that?' asked Alice.

'Nah, just offering an opinion, trying to do my civic duty, that's all.'

Alice snorted. 'It says here that your alibi for Camilla's murder was Trixie. It says here you and Trixie have a regular Tuesday night date. That right, Bazza?

'Yeah, that's right Mondays, Tuesdays and Thursdays were mine.' He prodded his sunken chest with a bony finger. Wednesdays she had a rest and weekends, you know, she worked.'

'So, she was with you this Monday, Tuesday and Thursday?'

'Yeah, that's right.'

'Let me get this clear, the night she was murdered, she was with you?'

'Eh, oh, last night was Thursday. I forgot. No, no I didn't see her last night.'

He stubbed out his cigarette in the ashtray and flicked another one out of the packet, dropping three or four onto the floor. Sampson bent to pick them up and waited whilst Bazza lit up with shaking hands. Alice moved behind Bazza's chair and, against her better judgement, leaned on the head rest so her mouth was close to his ear. Ignoring the staleness that wafted from him, she said, 'So, Trixie wasn't with you last night, even though it was a Thursday and we have it on record that Thursday was one of your "romantic nights" together?'

Bazza inhaled deeply, 'She wasn't well, see? She phoned. Said she was puking and on the rag too. I don't do messy stuff like that.'

'Oh, right,' said Sampson, smiling at Bazza and gaining a nervous smile back. 'So she *wasn't* with you?' Sampson wrote something in his notebook and then said, 'So, who *were* you with Bazza?'

'Me? Well I was on my own, like, at the penthouse.'

Alice, still behind Bazza, grinned. Sampson was doing a grand job of getting Bazza confused. She nodded to Sampson and he continued. 'Who saw you there, Bazza? Come on, we need to eliminate you. *You* need an alibi. Who can vouch for you?'

'Nobody. I was there on my own, maybe Khal saw me going up at around eight but nobody after that.'

Alice whispered in his ear, 'What were you doing, Bazza, up there, all on your own?'

'Drank the champagne and went to bed, that's all.' Bazza began to pull himself up from the chair but Alice gripped his shoulder and pulled him back.

'Come on, Bazz,' she said. 'No porno films on telly last night to keep your right hand exercised, huh?'

Bazza glared up at her, 'You're a cheeky cow, aren't you?'

Alice nodded and, releasing her grip on his shoulder, moved away.

'What DS Cooper means,' said Sampson, 'is that if you could provide us with titles and a description of the contents of your viewing last night, we could verify your statement and that may be enough to convince us of your innocence.'

Bazza stared open eyed at Sampson, 'What?'

'Too many syllables, DC Sampson.' said Alice and walked round to stand in front of Bazza. 'What my colleague means is that you give us the ins and outs (pardon the pun) of your TV viewing last night, along with proof of payment, and that'll go some of the way to establishing your alibi. Understand?'

He nodded, licked his lips and said, 'Well the first film I watched was Gina and her Amazing–'

Alice waved her hand in the air. 'Stop right there. I'm not wasting time listening to replays of your private sexual promiscuities. You'll go down to Lilycroft Police Station before 11am today and give a detailed, recorded statement to this sergeant, okay?' And she scribbled a name on a card and handed it to him.

Bazza took the card and tapped it on his knee. Alice was pleased to note that some of his earlier swagger had vanished. 'What we really need to know is where Trixie came from. Any ideas?

'She appeared a couple of years ago, trying to work on her own. Jessica found her on the street and brought her to me. I've looked after her ever since.'

'Didn't she say where she came from? What her real name was?'

Bazza shook his head. 'Nothing. Just Trixie, that's it, nothing else.'

Minutes later, Alice and Sampson stood outside eagerly inhaling the car fumes, which were a welcome relief after the stench of Bazza's flat. Glad to be away from the disgusting little man, Alice said, 'Wonder what his penthouse is like?'

Sampson grinned. 'Not sure I want to know.'

Thrusting the arm of her coat under Sampson's nose Alice said, 'Smell that! It bloody stinks. I'll need to have it dry cleaned now. Yeauch!' and without waiting for Sampson's response she marched towards her car yelling at two kids who were touching her paintwork, 'I'm a copper, you leave fingerprints and I'll be able to find you.'

The kids grinned at her and ran off. Sighing, Alice slapped Sampson on the arm, with enough force to make him yelp. 'Let's forget about Bazza for a bit, I'm taking you to The Prossie Palace.'

Sampson stopped and stared at her. 'The what?'

Alice grinned and opened the car door. 'You heard right.'

After they'd settled back into the car, Sampson said, 'And what exactly *is* the Prossie Palace?'

'Ah ha, you'll just have to wait and see, won't you?' Alice pulled smoothly into the flow of traffic.

CHAPTER 17
Leeds Old Road

The doorway of the closed laundrette stank of stale sex but, at least it kept the slight drizzle off Anastazy as he watched the bus stop further down the road on the opposite side. He drew deeply on his cigarette before flicking it onto the pavement, narrowly missing a Pakistani woman with a pushchair who was dragging her school-age child behind her. She turned and opened her mouth as if to say something to him but stopped when he stepped towards her, his large body threatening.

Her expression changed from anger to fear as her eyes drifted from his snarling face with its tear drop inks, past his snake tattoo to his muscled upper arms, bulging from the sleeves of his T-shirt. Her fear made his groin twitch. He flexed his muscles and his tattoos coiled and trembled up his arms. 'What, *Bitch*?' he said, enjoying the power. The woman's face blanched, so he stamped his foot into a puddle, sending splashes of rain onto her shalwar and laughed as she scurried off, urging the child forward and steering the pushchair with one hand. Turning to the group of mums who had witnessed the incident and were now giving him a wide berth, he bowed, his gesture slow and flamboyant, before stepping back into the doorway and lighting another fag. He loved commanding respect and he enjoyed seeing other people's fear. Mind you, he needed to keep a bit of a rein on his natural instinct to dominate. No point in drawing too many people's attention to him. Not when The Old Man had told him to keep a low profile. He didn't want to piss him off too much.

Five minutes later his patience was rewarded when he saw Serafina walking down the road towards the bus stop. As usual, she was with her younger brother who towered above her, his limbs all edges and angles as he loped along. To avoid her noticing him, Anastazy took a step backwards into the doorway and continued his secret scrutiny. She seemed more aware of her surroundings than usual. Her eyes darted around her as if she was looking for someone. Anastazy grinned. He knew he'd scared her the previous night and that she was looking for him. Good. Sometimes it was better to keep them on edge. Keep them off kilter.

She wore a hoodie today and he suspected that the hood was up, not only to keep off the rain but as a disguise. She clearly didn't know that he'd been watching her for days and knew exactly where she lived, the places she went and who she hung around with.

He knew that she'd get on the bus down to the Interchange and then get the 626 up Manchester Road to City Academy. He'd followed her before. He drew on his cigarette and frowned. When she was his, she'd be giving that crap up. No way would he let her continue going to school. Not when she could be earning for him. Not as if she'd need A Levels doing what he had in mind for her. A paroxysm of coughing racked him for a second. He hoiked up a glob of phlegm and, using his tongue to direct it, blew it from his mouth in an arc, laughing when it landed on the back of a kid in a poxy blue uniform. The kid didn't notice the green slime dribble down his back, which amused Anastazy even more.

Smiling, he watched as Serafina stood huddled in the bus shelter with her brother and a couple of Polish kids and two Asian lads. They all seemed to be chatting. He frowned as a tall Asian lad put his arm round her shoulder and pulled her into a hug. What the fuck was he playing at? Anastazy was on the point of moving over when he saw Serafina push the boy away with a loud, 'Fuck off, Hasnain!' which caused the other kids to laugh and slag the unfortunate Hasnain off.

That's my girl, thought Anastazy, pleased with Serafina's feistiness. He'd keep an eye on that Paki, Hasnain, though. Damn right he would. Where the fuck did he get off, groping his girl?

The bus pulled up and one by one the waiting schoolkids got on. Anastazy watched Serafina pull her hoodie down and move along the bus. She slid into a window seat, her brother next to her. Stepping from the doorway, Anastazy approached the side of the bus as the rest of the people lined up to get on. Standing on the kerb next to Serafina's seat, he raised a hand and when Serafina's startled eyes met his through the bus window, he grinned and winked. Then, he pointed to Hasnain who sat in the seat behind her. Making a gun shape with his fingers, he pretended to shoot the boy. Anastazy laughed when Serafina's panicked eyes followed his aim and her mouth formed a small O.

CHAPTER 18

She'd been no more than mildly irritated by Hasnain's stupid attentions. For weeks now he'd made no secret of the fact he fancied her but Serafina hadn't been remotely tempted. Not when there was Imti from The Delius. It was a no-brainer. Imti was gorgeous and, although Hasnain was nice enough, he acted like the adolescent boy he was, burping and farting in front of her. As if that would attract her. No Serafina wanted someone a little bit more suave and mature. Yeah, Imti fit the bill for her.

Then, when she got on the bus and settled into her seat next to Thomas she saw *him* standing outside the bus, staring at her. She'd been so careful; keeping her hoodie up, walking a longer way to the bus stop, much to Thomas' annoyance, and *still* he'd found her. She felt her breath quicken in her chest and then he pretended to shoot Hasnain with his pretend gun. Shit! Shit! Shit! What should she do?

As the bus drew away from the bus stop and Anastazy's face faded from her vision, she turned her face to the window and ignored Hasnain, hoping he'd back off. She'd have to find a way to warn him off. Make him realise that, if he didn't back off, his health could be in serious danger. She'd wait till break time, when Thomas wasn't around. The last thing she wanted was for her younger brother to find out about Anastazy and tell her older ones. If Jacob and Luka found out that he was following her all hell would break loose and the new life they'd carved for themselves in Bradford would be at risk. It would all be her fault. She had to try to deal with Anastazy on her own, without the

87

assistance of her hot-headed brothers. But she had a sneaky feeling that would be easier said than done.

CHAPTER 19
BRI Morgue

When Sadia arrived with Gus at the autopsy room, Doc McGuire had already started the post-mortem on Trixie. She smiled as Gus, with his usual stoicism, marched along the corridors with their antiseptic smell, looking as if he was eager to reach his destination. Sadia knew, however, that the tension in his angular face was caused by his teeth being clenched tightly as he fought against nausea. Nearing the morgue, Sadia became aware of a change in the balance between clinical antiseptic and fetid body smells. There was no mistaking the odours that seeped along this corridor in the bowels of the hospital.

With amused sympathy she watched Gus take a deep preparatory breath through his mouth before pulling his hankie from his pocket. He thrust it under his nose and breathed deeply from the depths of its pristine white folds. Sadia could smell the Vicks and grinned. Gus hoped it would disguise the God awful smell, but she knew that the only way to acclimatise was to start off taking shallow breaths, gradually deepening them until you were used to the smells. Never mind, the Vicks would serve as smelling salts when the grinding and sawing noises became too much for his queasy stomach and he landed flat on his back. Sadia grinned: she knew it wouldn't come to that. Gus had too much willpower to faint in public.

She'd never been squeamish around the autopsy room. From a young age she'd been fascinated by the Muslim butcher at the end of her road. She'd watched in fascination as he chopped the chicken or meat into small pieces, frequently asking which parts were which. Sometimes, if she was early enough he would allow her to watch as he slaughtered the chickens by a cut to the neck, from which the bird's blood would drain as he recited the Bismillah, thanking Allah for the food and sanctifying the animal Halal. Sadia smiled remembering how her mother had told her off when she'd caught her, telling her that *her* role was to learn how to cook the chicken not slaughter it. Her father, though, had leapt to her defence, declaring that it was a good thing to understand where food came from and how it should be prepared to make it Halal.

She got changed into her scrubs and by the time Gus had donned his and folded his greasy hankie beneath the mask, Sadia was already in the room, standing as close to the trolley as she could, determined not to miss anything. She glanced back at Gus who stood at the back of the room, leaning against the metal sink. He'd confided to Sadia that he found it reassuring to have the sink within hurling distance, although, to date, he hadn't had to use it.

Dr McGuire, winked at Sadia from above his mask and ignoring Gus he turned his attention back to Trixie's body and continued to remove, examine and weigh her liver. In admiration, Sadia watched his nimble fingers at work and wondered how Gus hadn't managed to develop a thicker lining to his stomach. He'd had told her that Dr McGuire's hopes of him following in his footsteps had taken a nosedive when, at the tender age of twelve, he'd thrown up watching a cow give birth.

She caught the glance that Dr McGuire threw in his son's direction, interpreting it as a combination of concern that Gus would actually faint this time and admiration that, despite the revulsion that gripped him at each PM, he was still strong enough to attend them, time after time.

Dr McGuire directed most of the general data to Sadia as he weighed and dissected organs. 'The cause of death was strangulation, Sadia. From the bruising on her neck, I'd say she was attacked from the front. Look, these are knuckle marks just above her larynx.' He pointed to the front of Trixie's neck. 'Her assailant obviously used his or her knuckles to increase the pressure and strengthen their grip as they pulled the scarf tighter and tighter round her neck'

'Isn't it harder to strangle someone from in front?' asked Sadia

'Well, that depends really on all sorts of things, like the comparative size of victim and assailant, the condition of the victim. Was she drunk like the other two or stone cold sober? Was it erotic asphyxiation?' He shrugged. 'You'll remember, though, the other two victims were definitely strangled from behind'

Sadia glanced at Gus with a raised eyebrow. Maybe Trixie had turned round at the last minute and surprised her assailant at the point of attack. She supposed it was too early to say. 'What else can you tell us, Dr McGuire?'

'Well, Trixie was a drug addict as shown by the state of her organs and the obvious tracks on her legs and arms. This will no doubt be validated when the tox screens come back. I think the age she gave her friend is about right, no older than twenty-one or so, but probably closer to eighteen. In terms of her attack there's another couple of interesting things.'

He moved to the bottom end of the body and pointing to Trixie's genitalia said, 'Firstly, the wine bottle was inserted *post*-mortem, whereas on the other girls they were inserted pre-mortem.'

Sadia frowned. Why would the killer change that part of his MO. Was Trixie not zonked out enough for him to do it pre-mortem or did he decided for some reason to change his MO. Maybe, if Trixie surprised him he had to strangle her quickly and was unable to complete his MO in the correct order. Whatever his reasons though this deviation was very interesting. 'So, this time our killer changed his MO big style?'

'He certainly did,' continued Fergus. 'He also didn't use a *broken* bottle *and* he didn't use nearly as much force as with the other two girls.'

Sadia frowned. 'Do you think he was rushed for time? Disturbed maybe and had to finish off quickly?'

Fergus shrugged. 'Could be either, I suppose, but the other odd thing was that I found traces of semen this time.'

'What?' said Sadia, 'That's weird. Why after being so careful has he suddenly left us a semen trace? Or, wait a minute, it might not be his. It might be a punter she had earlier.'

'Or a boyfriend,' said Gus from his position by the sink. Sadia had been so engrossed in the post-mortem that she'd forgotten Gus was there. A quick glance told her he was fine. She smiled at him. 'Yes, she's less likely to use a condom with a boyfriend than a punter.'

'Unless she was desperate for a fix and the punter offered a good rate,' said Gus

'Well,' said Fergus interrupting their suppositions, 'I've sent it off to the lab, so we'll know soon enough if we have a match. But, I think you might be most interested in this, though.'

He paused, presumably for dramatic effect and leaned against the trolley. 'I removed her womb before you arrived and guess what? She was pregnant. About six weeks along, I'd say. I've also sent the foetus to the lab for analysis. Might support the theory that she had a boyfriend or that she was getting careless to feed her habit. Who knows?' He pushed himself away from the trolley and slipping his gloves off he threw them in the bin. 'I'll leave the whys and wherefores for you super sleuths to find out but, meanwhile, I must say good bye and get on to my next PM. Car crash victims; the male minus his dick after losing control of the vehicle at, I'd hazard a guess, roughly the same time as he orgasmed. The man he was with certainly had strong jaws, is all I can say.'

As the implications of his words sunk in, Sadia released a chirp of laughter and made to follow him from the room. Suddenly, Dr McGuire stopped and swivelled to face them, directing his words at Sadia, 'Ah, Sadia, has Angus invited you to lunch on Sunday?'

Sadia flushed and, caught off-guard, looked at Gus. 'No.'

CHAPTER 20
BRI Morgue

G us grabbed his father's arm and pulled him from the autopsy room. 'What the hell are you playing at? Last night you embarrassed me, and then you ask Al to come to lunch with me and now Sadia. What *is* this?'

Fergus looked at his son and sighed, 'Look Gus, your mother's determined to mend bridges between you, Gabriella and Katie. Sunday is just the start of her shenanigans. You know what she's like. I just thought you'd fare better with a bit of external support around. Besides which, your mother's sure you've got a new girlfriend and she thinks now's the time to parade her in front of those other two.'

Gus looked at his dad's anxious face and his anger evaporated. He pulled his huge father to him in an embrace. 'Thanks, Dad, but I'm a big boy now. Got to face my battles on my own.'

Untying his scrubs and blowing his huge nose, Fergus nodded. 'Aye, Angus laddie, I know. But it's been hard for your mother and me too, you know? Not wanting to take sides. Trying to be fair and seeing you hurting so much. Especially after young Billy's death and then that whole case with The Matchmaker.' He patted Gus on the arm. 'Just come on Sunday, Angus, and bring who you like. It'll be fine. Anyway, you don't need to stay long as we know you're in the middle of a big case, but at least it'll be a step forward... for everyone.'

Still smarting from his previous conversation with his dad, Gus felt like a complete heel. He'd been so busy thinking about himself that he'd failed to realise that this thing with Gabriella and Katie affected his parents too. Fuck, but he was such a selfish bastard at times. After all their support the least he could do was turn up on Sunday and just get on with it. It's not as if he had any feelings left for Gabriella and, as for Katie... well, he was hurt, but she was his sister at the end of the day.

Climbing into the passenger seat, Gus said, 'What the hell do you make of all of that?'

Sadia shook her head. 'Em, you mean your dad or Trixie?'

With a sideways glance at her as he put on his seatbelt Gus said, 'Let's leave my dad for later and think about Trixie first?'

Sadia tapped her fingers on the steering wheel, 'I'm not sure. Maybe Sampson's right and there are two perps and they swapped roles for Trixie. That would explain the change in MO. Or maybe he just got disturbed, or maybe it's a copycat or maybe it's the baby's father trying to make it look like the other two girls.'

'Well, you've about covered every possibility there, Sadia. Let's go and see if Jessica can shed any light on possible boyfriends.'

'Should we mention the pregnancy?'

Gus thought for a minute. 'No, let's keep that quiet for a while, see if she tells us. If she's as close mates as she says she is, then she'll probably know about it anyway. If she doesn't already know, it'll just upset her more *and* she may be less keen to share names with us if she thinks they may get into trouble.'

Sadia nodded and sliding into gear headed towards Jessica's flat on Oak Lane in Manningham whilst Gus mulled over the PM results. When he couldn't come up with anything else concrete, he turned sideways and looked at Sadia. 'Why didn't you come back to mine last night?'

'Don't know. I just got rattled when I thought you'd told your dad about us and, after this morning's little episode, it seems he at least guesses.'

Gus sighed and rubbed at his temples. The after effects of too much Vicks was beginning to make itself known. 'For God's sake, Sad. My dad wouldn't go mouthing off to your dad. Anyway, he doesn't know anything. He's just trying to make me take *someone* to this damn Sunday lunch, that's all.'

Sadia's lips tightened, but she remained silent.

Gus looked out the window, his fingers tapping an erratic rhythm on his knee as he brooded. It was really getting to him that Sadia wouldn't tell her dad about their relationship. He was twenty-nine years old for goodness sake. The last thing he wanted was to be ducking and diving like they were doing something wrong. 'If we told your dad, we could avoid all this subterfuge. He'd have to get used to it eventually.'

Sadia's shoulders slumped and she abruptly swerved into a lay-by, earning annoyed hoots and an obscene hand gesture from the car behind. 'We've been over this before Gus. He wouldn't "get used" to it. That's the problem. He's changed over the years, especially since mum died. He's down the mosque all the time these days and when he comes back he comments on everything. Suddenly my clothes are immodest and suggestive. My make-up too tarty.' She turned and glared at Gus her eyes blazing. 'He even suggested I start covering my hair. My *mother* never covered her hair – he never expected her to, but all of a sudden he's become so judgemental.'

Tears began to pour down Sadia's cheeks. Heedless of her mascara running she dragged her palm across her eyes leaving streaks down her cheeks. Gus sighed and reached over for her, smoothing her hair and holding her till at last she settled. *Looks like I'm on a roll today. First I upset my dad and now Sadia. What is wrong with me?* The truth was he didn't really understand why Sadia couldn't just bite the bullet and he was getting more and more impatient with her. After all, what could her dad do? He knew it was hard for her. Equally, he knew his reactions were part of his illness and that sometimes his anger got the better of him.

Finally, Sadia pulled away from him. Flicking down the mirror, she began repairing the damage to her makeup. 'I know you find it hard to believe, Gus but I *swear*, he's a different man at home. As soon as he comes in, he changes into his shalwar kameez and heads for the mosque. He reads the Qur'an constantly. He's always interrogating me about where I've been and who I've been with… and, I suspect he reads my emails. I have to keep my phone with me at all times because I'm sure he'd check my texts.'

Making a conscious effort to be sympathetic Gus said, 'What's happened to change him?'

Sadia shrugged. 'I just don't know. He's always been a great dad and when mum died he tried his best to make sure I didn't suffer. We don't have any relatives in the UK. Maybe as I got older and more independent he got lonely and the mosque and the friends he's made there have filled the gap. I just know he's not tolerant like he used to be. He wants me to go to Pakistan with him and get married there.'

Gus sat up and turned sideways in his chair to observe. Surely she was joking. Surely in this day and age her father couldn't have those attitudes. His eyes blazed. 'What! When did he say this?'

'He's been saying it off and on for a while, but he's started suggesting we go at Christmas.'

'And what have you said?' asked Gus, looking her straight in the eyes.

Sadia met his gaze. 'I've told him no, of course, Gus. How could I say anything else when I love *you?*'

Gus cocked his head and smiled. 'Well then, Sadia, the sooner we tell him about us the better. I can't have him dragging you off to Pakistan, can I?'

Sadia grabbed his arm. 'Don't be so daft Gus. He'd never agree to me marrying you. When I told him I'd make my own choice of husband he grabbed me by the arms really tightly and said, "*I'll only allow you to choose if he is Muslim.*"' Sadia rubbed her arms, as if she could still feel his hands on her.

Seeing her reaction, Gus felt his own hands clench. What the fuck was Husain thinking? He must know he couldn't force her into marriage against her will. Then the first part of her sentence sunk in. She wanted to marry him? Shit! He ran his fingers through his dreads. Marriage wasn't something he'd considered. His divorce from Gabriella had only just come through and the last thing he wanted to do was to rush into another marriage. But seeing how upset Sadia was he couldn't tell her that right now, could he? Gus was glad when she looked away from him. Maybe she wouldn't see the hesitation in his face.

She continued in almost a whisper, 'That's the first time he's ever threatened me.' Her brown eyes were swimming with tears as she turned to him and gripped his arm, her look earnest, 'If you were to revert, he may be persuaded?'

Gus' heart sank. What the hell was she talking about. Revert? Gus knew that Muslims believed that everyone was born Muslim and that those who came to the faith later in life were considered to 'revert' not 'convert' to Islam. Dreads bouncing, Gus slammed his hand on the dashboard. 'Bloody hell, Sad, you know I'm a Humanist. I can't convert *or* revert or whatever. No bloody way. You know I can't.'

'Well then,' said Sadia, her voice tight, 'There's not much else to say is there?'

Gus turned to stare out the window as Sadia started the car up and headed for Bradford. This had been a complete bolt out of the blue. First the marriage thing and then the conversion thing. Neither of which he was happy with. He loved Sadia, course he did, but it was really early days and he wouldn't be pushed into something he didn't want. No damn way. Sadia would just have to get used to it.

CHAPTER 21
Prossie Palace, Manningham

The Prossie Palace was just off Manningham Lane and it turned out to be a building that Sampson was familiar with. The old Victorian mill owner's semi had eventually become an auction house. Sampson's Uncle Pat had been a regular here, often bringing Sampson along for company when he was a lad as he looked out for bargains to sell in his antique shop. Looking up at the imposing, four-storied building, Sampson could almost smell the musty air and hear the familiar rumble of deep voices speaking in a code that only they could decipher.

They moved towards the solid wooden door and Alice rang the bell. When a tinny voice came from the wall speaker, she looked into the video camera and said, 'Hi, it's Alice Cooper. Can I speak to Carla?'

There was a buzz and Alice pushed the door open and gestured for Sampson to follow her into the airy hallway beyond.

Sampson looked around him at the colourful paintings of old Bradford on lemon painted walls. 'Wow! This has changed a bit since I was last here. Not a musty smell around.'

'Yeah, it's been renovated since Haines, the auctioneer's, had it.' Alice gestured through a doorway. 'It's a charitably-funded health centre and refuge for vulnerable women and their families. Amazing what the lottery funds, isn't it?' She pointed along a bright narrow corridor. 'Along there are the medical rooms. Some local doctors volunteer their services on a rota basis to provide routine testing for STIs, HIV and AIDS. They also give contraceptive advice. Once a week there's a drug service clinic and an AA meeting. The working girls find it easier to come here rather than the infirmary when their pimps or a punter have gotten a bit too heavy handed. The agreement is that, whilst any victim here is treated anonymously, the details of their injuries are officially noted and passed on to us. The doctors and counsellors do a good job trying to get the girls to speak with the designated police officer and offer ongoing support and shelter as necessary.'

Sampson nodded, impressed. To his mind, it was a massive improvement on the auction house and a damn sight more useful. It felt to him like it had the right balance between homely and practical. He pointed to a white gloss-painted door that Alice hadn't mentioned. 'What's through that door?'

'That's the gym and meeting rooms'

He raised an eyebrow, 'A gym? Can't be bad. Very corporate.'

Alice laughed, 'You sound like bloody Brighton, now. Wait till you see it before you sit in judgement.'

Alice pushed the door open and Sampson followed her along another carpeted corridor that smelled of lavender potpourri. At the end she held a door open to let him precede her into the room beyond.

Rotating slowly on the spot, Sampson took in the worn wooden floor, dull despite the smell of floor polish that hung in the air. Bright white walls were punctuated by posters about correct usage of equipment, diet and exercise information and aerobic exercise routines. In one corner lay a pile of floor mats that had seen better days. Against the far wall stood an old fashioned mechanical treadmill next to a mechanical rowing machine. Further along in a blue plastic box Sampson could see a handful of mismatched weights next to two red exercise balls that looked like they needed pumping up.

He caught Alice's eye and grinned. 'This is the gym?'

Samson walked over to the treadmill and stepped on, using his feet to start the machine moving. It creaked and protested before the mechanism kicked in and momentum urged it on. Within seconds he was panting. 'Hope they get a discount in their membership in lieu of the danger factor,' he said, rubbing his back.

Alice laughed. 'Let's just say we could use an influx of new and updated equipment but we get by. We use the gym for other things as well, like self-defence and personal safety classes.'

Hearing the enthusiasm in her voice Sampson said, 'We?'

'Well,' she shrugged. 'I help out sometimes. Do a bit of self-defence with them. Look for grants to get a really good personal safety instructor I know to do a few sessions. They're usually very well attended.'

Feeling miffed that she'd not shared this with her before now, he said, 'I've been working with you for nearly six months, Al, and you've never once mentioned that you do this in your spare time.'

She bit her lip and bent to shuffle the weights about in the box. When she blushed Sampson realised she felt embarrassed and changed the subject. 'What are the other rooms down here used for?'

'Oh, they're just the meeting rooms I told you about before.'

Alice was leading him back to the door when it burst open and a middle-aged woman rushed through, carrying an overflowing box of books in her arms.

'Hey, Al,' she said.

Sampson watched, grinning at Alice's discomfort as the woman slipped an arm round her shoulders and squeezed hard. A handful of books fell to the floor and he bent to retrieve them as Alice kissed the woman on the cheek and extricated herself. 'Hey yourself, Carla. How's it going, girl?'

When Carla hesitated, Sampson sensing that he was the cause of her uncertainty, thrust out a hand introduced himself. Punching him on the arm, Alice added, 'Sampson's okay. He's one of the good ones. Sampson, meet Carla Terrelonge. chief cook, bottle washer and supervisor of the Prossie Palace.'

Sampson grimaced at Alice's use of the name Prossie Palace. Carla, seemingly noticing his expression, grinned, 'Ah, don't worry, John. The girls themselves nicknamed it that. It's a lot easier to say than our official title.'

He waited for her to explain, never imagining what a mouthful it would turn out to be.

'We're officially called *The Outreach Centre for the Health and Wellbeing of Bradford District's Alternatively Employed Women.* Or, if you prefer T.O.C.W.B.A.E.W. I think some politically-correct jackass had a touch of the verbals when he thought that one up, don't you?'

John laughed out loud, enjoying the mischievous twinkle in the woman's eye. The atmosphere in this place was indeed friendly and he reckoned, after some of the things he'd seen on the streets that the working women needed somewhere safe to hang out away from their pimps and the punters.

Alice grabbed the box from Carla and dumped it on Sampson and linking arms with her friend said, 'Can we go upstairs, Carla. We need to talk.'

Carla, all trace of humour gone from her face, nodded. 'About Trixie?'

Alice nodded. Carla told Sampson to put the box in the corner and led the two of them back through the hallway and up a flight of stairs to the first floor.

'These are all offices and storage space' she said, as they walked. 'Up the next flight of stairs are the bedsits for those in need of temporary shelter. Not ideal to be so high up if you've got a child, as we've got no lift, but at least it's further away from the front door if we get any unwelcome visitors.' Carla's grim expression told Sampson she'd seen a few unwelcome visitors in her time.

As he expected Carla's office was an extension of her personality; full of bright coloured throws and just enough ornaments to avoid fussiness. As well as a functional desk and chairs, Carla had created a cosy seating arrangement to one side. It was to this that she led her visitors.

As his unsuspecting bottom hit the loose sofa springs, Sampson released a small yelp. 'Oops, Should've warned you.' said Carla with a grin. 'It's all second-hand and this sofa has had a lot of wear and tear.'

Knowing he'd have a bruise on his backside, Sampson eased himself forward until he found a slightly more padded part to perch on. He could tell by the smug look on Alice's face that she'd known about that particular chair and had chosen not to warn him. He made a mental note to get his own back on her at the first opportunity.

Carla and Alice sat opposite on two old but, judging by the absence of pained yelps, comfy chairs. 'Carla,' began Alice leaning forward, 'What's the word on the street about these killings? Anyone mention a sicko punter or anything odd?'

Carla tutted and shook her head. 'To be honest, the girls from this side of Bradford have been pretty blasé about it all. Well, that is until last night. Now that it's one of their own they might start talking. The officer I spoke to last week seemed to want to put it down to a turf war, but, I wouldn't go down the Bazza–Hussain vendetta route. That's a waste of time.' She flapped her hands to accentuate her point. 'They've co-existed happily till now and I've heard nothing to contradict that.'

Leaning forward elbows on her knees, her expression serious, Carla continued, 'As for a sicko? Well, after Camilla's murder I put the word out and got nothing back so, when Starlight was killed, I went in hard. I personally questioned every girl that came through those doors last Friday and not one of them reported a pervert. I don't think they were lying.'

She inhaled and leaned back against the cushions. 'The only cause for alarm was a report of a couple of new girls, probably underage on the streets. As required, I passed that info on to Vice.'

Sampson digested her information in silence for a few seconds then, 'You said earlier that you cater for the whole of Bradford district. Don't you get any of Hussain's girls in?'

Carla looked at him. 'Yes we do. Not as many, I have to admit, but I suspect that's geography rather than a disinterest in the place. Plenty turn up for the medical checks and suchlike, but only a few hang around, whereas the local girls pop in at all hours of the day and night. We're like a youth club for prossies in that respect.'

She paused and for a moment Sampson saw a flash of sadness dull the vibrancy in her eyes. 'I knew both of the girls that were killed last week; Camilla and Starlight. They were popular and often came in together. They mixed well with all the girls. They were friendly and happy. I was sad to hear what happened to them. Now word has it that Trixie's gone?'

She looked to Alice as if for confirmation. Alice nodded. 'What do you know about her, Carla?'

Carla sighed, 'Sometimes I wonder what I know about any of them. Trixie, hmm?'

She steepled her fingers in front of her mouth and thought for a minute. 'Trixie was troubled. She'd clearly suffered some sort of abuse that had led her to run away from home, but she refused all counselling services and refused to discuss her past at all. In the end we backed off rather than lose her. Jessica brought her in and the two became close. When Bazza chose Trixie as his *pet,*' she said the words with a shudder, 'Jessica and Trixie moved into that little flat together. When she came to us two years ago she was an addict – coke and heroin but, recently, over the past couple of months, she'd been seriously trying to quit. She spent a couple of weeks here at the beginning to get her through the cold turkey and then attended regularly for sessions with the drug advisor. Jessica always stayed with her throughout, even when she stayed in. I doubt Trixie could have done it without Jess.' She threw her hands in the air. 'Lot of damn good that did her in the long run. Poor child. You've got to catch whoever's doing this, Alice… and soon!'

Whilst Alice assured Carla they would do everything in their power to catch the culprit Sampson mulled over what they'd learned about Trixie. 'Any idea what made her want to quit drugs, Carla? It's unusual for an addict to opt to get clean without some sort of enforced treatment. Had she been compelled by the courts to attend rehab?'

Carla smiled. 'No. Trixie had a few minor run-ins with you lot – a bit of shoplifting but nowt serious. No, I suspect that Jessica nagged and nagged until Trixie gave in. Jessica has a persuasive way with her and has often, in the past, helped the girls take the first steps to cleaning up their act. In another life, I think she'd have been a social worker.'

What a waste, thought Sampson, allowing his mind to dwell on the what-ifs of Jessica Green's life. 'So, no weirdoes and no turf war between Bazza and Hussain? What else is there?'

'Weell' said Carla drawing the word out, 'You know those underage girls I told you about?'

Alice and Sampson nodded.

'I think they're Eastern European. New immigrants. You know how it is? They come expecting a Brave New World and end up with dull Yorkshire sandstone, crap weather, no jobs, no benefits and little option but to peddle themselves on street corners. We've had a few Poles and Ukrainians in here, but they've been older and seemed to be working for either themselves, Bazza or Hussain. We've not seen any younger ones but, as I said, a few of the girls did mention it.' She shrugged. 'And Charlotte brought a girl in one night a couple of weeks ago. She was paralytic, covered in blood and bruises; quite clearly sexually assaulted. Charlotte had heard her with a punter in the allotments and didn't like what she was going on so she created a fuss throwing stones and banging things. The bloke legged it.' She hesitated, '…and so did the girl – as soon as she could. We cleaned her up, dressed her wounds, popped her a morning after pill and as soon as she was sober, she checked her phone, started getting agitated and eventually barged her way out, pockets filled with condoms. Charlotte went out looking for her, but she'd disappeared: probably got picked up by whoever is running her.'

'So, you think there's someone else running girls apart from Green and Khan?'

Carla shrugged. 'Might be. Can't be sure. Might be a cousin or brother wanted her to do it for a short time to pay some bills. Who knows?'

Sampson wondered if they could find out more about this. He might ask a few of his contacts, but, he suspected, the girls themselves were the ones with the info. Maybe they'd strike gold with them.

Alice straightened her legs in front of her. 'Look. You know I hate to do this Carla, but can you set us up with a room and see if any of the girls will talk to us. I don't really want to be here with my detective hat on but I reckon it's better me and Sampson than some of the mutts we have on the team at the minute.'

Carla smiled. 'Great minds think alike, Alice. I've already arranged a meeting room for you. Some of the girls are already waiting there. Most of them drifted in this morning when news of Trixie's death reached them. They want to help, but they *are* wary. Don't push too hard and they might spill something juicy.'

CHAPTER 22
City Academy, Manchester Road

Where the hell was he? Serafina desperately needed to speak to Hasnain before school finished for the day and she had the sneaky suspicion his last lesson ended at lunch time. Knowing him he'd head straight home and she might miss him.

Seeing a group of his mates bunched together by the sixth form lockers, Serafina walked up and raised her voice to be heard over their chatter. 'Any idea where Hasnain is?'

Hasnain's best mate Benny turned towards her, a slow grin spreading over his unshaven face when he saw who it was. 'Well, well, well. Maybe Serafina isn't as hard to get as she makes out, hey guys?'

Serafina rolled her eyes, 'Grow up, idiot. Where is he?'

Benny grinned and glanced round as if to make sure he had a willing audience. 'Ooooh, she's getting annoyed boys.' He stepped through the group of boys and eyeing her up and down said, 'Do you want to get all hot and sweaty with Hasnain, is that it?'

Spinning on her heel, Serafina flung a dirty look in Benny's direction and started to walk down the corridor away from them. Why the hell were boys so stupid? Full of testosterone and slathered in Lynx. Didn't that idiot Benny realise how much of a twat he looked with that stupid patchy beard of his? She'd nearly reached the top of the stairs when two lads tumbled off the top stair and, in their haste, barged past her calling Benny's name.

Sensing their panic, she hesitated, holding the bannister and looked back at the group of boys. For some reason her

109

heart began to thump in her chest and a sense of dread overtook her. Please don't let this be something to do with Hasnain she thought. She was glad that she had something to hold on to for, all of a sudden, her knees weakened and she felt as if she would slide to the floor as their words drifted back to her.

'Fucking hell, Benny! Hasnain's in an ambulance. It's fuckin' bad mate. Some Polish geezer grabbed him when he came out of Lidl. He pulled a knife on him. Fuck! It looked bad! Really fucking bad.'

Everything seemed to slow down for Serafina. Her heart seemed to jump up to her throat as she realised what she was hearing. Somehow or other Anastazy had got to Hasnain. She'd been too late. Too damn late. The story of her life. Why hadn't she grabbed him when they got off the bus?

She saw Benny push through the crowd and head for the stairs. The other boy followed still talking. 'There was blood everywhere man. All we could do was phone the pigs. Fuck, Benny, what if he dies?'

Benny turned and lunged at the boy, grabbing him by the throat and thrusting him up against the wall. 'Shut the fuck up, right? Just shut the fuck up. Hasnain'll be alright, okay?'

Tears welled in Serafina's eyes as, when Benny released his friend, she saw him wipe a sleeve across his eyes. Then, taking a deep breath he spoke in a more controlled tone. 'Did they get the bastard?'

The other boy, visibly pale and shaken shook his head as he adjusted his T-shirt. 'Nah. The bastard ran off. He just looked at Hasnain lying on the ground. He fucking spat on him and kicked him in the ribs. Then he said 'That'll teach you to mess with my girl, you Paki bastard' and he kicked him again and ran off.'

Benny took a deep breath and turned towards Serafina. With her heart thumping in her chest, she met his eyes, watching as Benny, all trace of swagger gone, walked towards her. 'This got summat to do with you, bitch?'

CHAPTER 23
Killinghall Road

It had been so fucking easy to deal with the Paki. Anastazy could, of course, have ordered it done but where would be the fun in that? This was a message he wanted to deliver in person. He'd plenty of minions who could do it but it was good to keep his hand in and, despite the risks, he felt it would be well worth it to deliver this particular memo. After all, recently all his 'work' had been completed by a third party. He was wise enough to realise that, for the big issues, he needed to keep a distance between himself and his 'people'.

He was determined to gain a steely hold on the Bradford punks. Punks like Shahid Khan and Bazza Green were slowly but surely being dealt with. Eliminating competition was just phase one of the plan. Phase two; saturating the various markets with their produce and cornering the more specialised markets was already underway. He was pleased. In fact, the only blight on the horizon as far as Anastazy was concerned was Serafina's reluctance to submit gracefully. He grinned, making his teardrop tattoo crinkle. He didn't really mind. He liked them feisty; all the better to break!

He'd gone for a fry-up first. Planning always made him hungry. When he'd finished his breakfast, he'd jumped on his motorbike and headed up Manchester Road. He was smart. He knew they had CCTV all over the Lidl car park, so he'd ridden up to Morrison's and parked up, then jogged back down the hill to the Lidl opposite the school. He was wearing his biker's helmet and leathers so they'd have no way to identify him if they did happen to catch a fleeting glance of him on one of their cameras. He didn't go into the shop but hung about at the bottom end of the car park. He knew it was only a matter of time before the little bastard left school and headed over to the shop. He'd seen him do it before – strutting over the road with his poxy mates, full of swag and shit. Thought he was all that, didn't he? Well, he'd soon discover that meddling with Anastazy's belongings was not a good idea.

When he seen the boy cross the road to the supermarket, Anastazy had thrown his half-smoked cigarette away and dodged behind a car. The boy was so full of himself, laughing and joking with his mates, that the idiot didn't even see him. Anastazy had waited, shuffling his feet as the anticipation built. At last, he'd spotted him as he left the shop carrying what looked like a bag of doughnuts. He'd drawn his knife from the leg of his biker's boot.

He'd considered just blasting the bastard but, in the end, decided that Hasnain's crime warranted a more close-up and personal approach. Looking like any other shopper, he approached the group of lads. God, but they were so stupid. Never paid him any notice at all, too busy being jerks. When he got close enough, he waved the knife in their faces, enjoying the way their smiles died. The tingle in his crotch told him the adrenalin was kicking in. As he took a step towards Hasnain, his hard on pushed against his leathers. He felt great. Invincible. Strong. He flung his head back and laughed, a rough guttural sound that started in his belly and erupted like a volcano of bad breath from his snarling mouth. The boys started to back away, stumbling over their feet in their haste, but he stepped forward and thrust the knife right into the Paki bastard's stomach. Blood, warm and metallic spurted onto his hand. He breathed deep, letting the scent stimulate him even more.

113

As Hasnain fell to the concrete, his fingers cupped his stomach but the blood was already pouring between them. Anastazy studied the startled look on the boy's face and, with his sleeve, wiped away the drops of blood that had landed on the visor of his helmet when he'd pulled the knife out. Turning his head, he noticed, with satisfaction, that the other boys had begun to run, snatching at their phones, trying, no doubt, to phone for help. Anastazy laughed at them and turned back to Hasnain. The other boy's cowardice meant he could devote the little time he had before the pigs showed up making sure the Paki got the message.

CHAPTER 24

Prossie Palace, Manningham

Alice led the way back downstairs to the room Carla had designated for their meeting with the prostitutes. She hadn't expected much more information from Carla, but it was good to get some background on Trixie. The more she heard the more inclined she was to think it was some sort of whacko serial killer. Just what Bradford needs. She dreaded to think what sensationalist headlines would greet them over the next few days. They really needed to get a handle on this. Hopefully the working girls downstairs would come up with something useful. Her thoughts were interrupted when Sampson spoke.

'Do you think she's right about it not being a turf war between Bazza and Hussain?'

Pushing open the fire door at the bottom of the stairs and starting along the corridor, Alice sighed. 'Well, let's put it this way, Carla knows these girls. They trust her and as a result word gets back to her. I'd say she's pretty much on the ball. As for the "sicko" theory – just because there have been no earlier reports of sicko behaviour doesn't mean we don't have one on our hands. These sick bastards have to start somewhere, don't they?'

When they reached the door labelled *Meeting Room Three*, Alice popped her head round. 'Hi all,' she said with a smile and marched into the room, leaving Sampson to follow.

'Woho, Alice, who've you brought for us to play with today?' The girl who sat straddling a chair, arms draped casually along its back, rose to her feet and kicked the chair away. Alice grinned as the girl eyed Sampson with a predatory look in her eye.

Despite Alice's earlier suggestion that he show no weakness Sampson blushed as the tall blond with multiple facial piercings approached him, every part of her slender body undulating suggestively as she moved.

Alice grinned and tutted in mock disapproval. 'For God's sake, Armani, can't you see he's too green for you? You're old enough to be his granny. Now, just sit down and behave.'

The other girls in the room dissolved into raucous laughter. Under cover of their catcalls, Alice gestured for Sampson to move over to the table, where he pulled a chair out and wedged himself behind it, looking to Alice like he was barricading himself in. *Probably a good strategy*, she thought, concealing her smile. She turned her attention to the rest of the girls in the room. There were ten of them and Alice wasn't surprised to recognise only about half of them. Their line of work was transitory and the turnover of clients attending the Palace was high. The women sat around the table. Some were slumped in a mock relaxed pose on chairs, some on adjoining tables, using their elevated position, Alice knew, to show their opposition to any authority she may have thought she had. Truth was, Alice didn't want to hold authority over these women. Too many people already had power over them and she was damned if she was going to be yet another one. So, she sat down next to Sampson and waited.

When they quietened, Alice stood up intending to kick off and frowned when Sampson also stood up. His hand on her arm, indicated he wanted to speak. Alice frowned at him. Her eyes asked him if he was sure. When he nodded, she shrugged and sat down. If he wanted to present himself as a lamb to the slaughter, then that was all part of his learning curve. He needed to toughen up and this was a sure way of doing that.

Sampson cleared his throat and slid his gaze round the room. Alice thought he looked ready to run. She didn't really blame him but, to give him his due, he held his ground. He looked at each woman individually and Alice realised he was implementing his training from the 'crowd control and public speaking' course he'd attended. Hats off to him: he had guts. Realising that she'd inadvertently crossed her fingers Alice uncrossed them and sat up ready to intervene if necessary. Sampson started to speak, his voice calm with just the right amount of self-deprecation to sound authentic. Alice glanced at the woman and saw they were all looking at Sampson, listening, she thought, as he spoke.

'Well, now that you all know I'm the "new kid on the block", I hope you'll be gentle with me.' Some of the women giggled and Sampson winked at them, letting them know he'd set himself up on purpose.

Alice grinned and relaxed. He was fine. He could handle this. Now, she could just sit back and enjoy the floorshow.

'My name's John Sampson and, despite my rather obvious embarrassment earlier, I *am* out of nappies and I am old enough for this job.'

The room erupted in laughter. Alice groaned wondering if she'd relaxed too soon. Was he about to lose them? Armani struck a pose with one hand on her hip, chest stuck out in provocation, 'Well darling. You're one *John* I'd do for free. What do you think girls?'

More laughter and whoops of 'Hell yeah' reverberated through the room. Alice was pleased to see Sampson just ride them out in silence, a benign smile on his lips.

When their catcalls faded away he continued, 'I'm as serious about catching this sick fucker as Alice is. I'm pleased to meet you all and hope we can find him before he strikes again.'

He began to sit down, but seemingly as an afterthought he stopped and said, with a brilliant smile, 'Oh by the way. My granny didn't look like anything like you, Armani.' Amidst hoots of laughter, he continued, 'And for that, I thank God. For, sure as hell, me and my mates would've been down to see Father Lowry every day to confess our filthy thoughts.'

The girls nearest Armani jostled her teasingly.

Alice stared at Sampson and then, under cover of rummaging in her bag she whispered, 'Well done.' He'd broken right through their defences and she reckoned they would trust him now. Sampson smiled and took out his notebook, ready to take notes.

'Right,' said Alice, remaining in her chair. 'Are you all happy to speak to us in a group?'

'Don't usually do groupies,' said one girl, to the accompaniment of a few nervous giggles, 'but for you, Alice, I'll do anything. Just ask away'

Alice raised her eyes heavenward and grinned. 'Alright Cat, enough of the gutter humour. Let's be serious shall we? First, is there anyone who isn't here who you think might have something to contribute?'

Armani spoke up. 'Only Jess. Her and Trixie were mates.'

A babble of catcalls and jokes began, 'And the rest, Armani, and the rest,' said one woman.

'That's a new name for it,' said another.

Armani glared at them, 'Shut the fuck up, you lot, this is serious. Trixie's dead and who knows? It could be one of us tomorrow.'

They settled down and Alice said, 'Yes, we know about Jessica. Someone else is interviewing her.'

'Hey, Alice is it true, she found Trixie?' asked an emaciated woman with greasy black hair.

Alice bit her lip and nodded. 'I'm afraid so.' She waited a moment to give them time to digest this before continuing, 'Any ideas who Trixie was meeting last night at the allotments?'

With a few furtive glances at each other, they remained silent. One woman tapped ragged nailed fingers on the table until Armani stretched over and placed her hand over hers. Alice watched as the woman cast a glance at Armani and then drew her hand away. *Wonder what she knows,* thought Alice, deciding to ask Carla a bit more about her later. Might be worth catching her away from the other women.

'No ideas at all?' asked Alice looking round the group. Again silence. Deciding to mix things up a bit Alice changed tack. 'She was Bazza Green's current pet, wasn't she?' and was pleased when this was met with a few nods of agreement.

'Well, shouldn't she have been at Bazza's last night? It was a Thursday and that's one of Bazza's nights, isn't it?'

Again silence and then another woman spoke up. 'Yeah, she should have been at Bazza's, but she's been making excuses for not going. Saying she was on the rag or summat.'

'Why, Charlotte?' asked Alice, leaning back in her chair and holding her arms by her sides in what was a classic 'I'm being open with you, please confide in me stance'. Hell, if Sampson could employ 'trust' tactics then, so could she.

Charlotte looked at the other girls. Armani shook her head slightly and Charlotte looked back at Alice. 'No idea, but I don't blame her. Do you?'

Thinking back to their earlier interview with Bazza Green, Alice repressed a shudder. 'No I don't blame her. He's a filthy, smelly, little weasel, isn't he?'

A giggle came from behind Armani as the women nodded. Alice thought she heard someone whisper, 'Trix had her hat set on better fish than Bazza.'

Keeping her face expressionless, Alice looked at the speaker. 'What was that?'

But, before she could respond, Alice saw Armani nudge her. The woman blushed and rubbed her arm. 'Nothing,' she said looking at the table.

'Okay,' said Alice with a sigh. 'So, you're telling me you don't know why she'd feed excuses to Bazza and you don't know who she was meeting in the allotments?'

Nods from all round the table.

'Okay then. Were any of you in or near the allotments last night between say eight and nine?'

One by one the women gave their whereabouts the previous evening. Some were off work. Some were working but in other areas and some were at home with their children. Eventually, Armani spoke again. 'Thursday's usually a quiet night, Alice, so we don't all work. All the johns are waiting for payday on Friday, you see?'

'Did Trixie or anyone you know mention a weird punter? Anyone you felt afraid or nervous of? Anyone who was just a bit odd?'

Two or three girls shook their heads. 'Nah. We're old hands at this. You know if there's owt dodgy. We pick up on it straight away and pass the word round. We look out for each other.'

'What about any of the girls who aren't here today, any of them said anything?'

Silence.

Alice sighed and leaned forward. 'Okay, let's do it this way. If you want to tell me something that you think might be related to Trixie's, Camilla's or Starlight's deaths, you tell me.'

She sat back and waited. John kept his head down focussed on his notes.

'Well' said Charlotte, with a shrug. Alice nodded encouragingly.

Charlotte hesitated and then said. 'Well, it's about that foreign bird.'

'The one you helped?'

'Yeah, that's her.'

Charlotte lit up a cigarette and took a deep puff. Alice had long since accepted that to implement the smoking laws in the Prossie Palace would alienate the girls so she ignored it. Thankfully, Sampson had the sense to ignore it, too. 'Tell us what happened?'

'Well, I'd just finished with my john, you know? I was feeling a bit flush so I bought myself a bottle of Asti Spumante. I wandered into the allotments to drink it in peace when I heard a fuss at the other end near the big conker tree. I ignored it for a while. Just wanted to mind my own business, like. Then, I heard a bit of banging against the fence and I knew it was one of the girls with a punter.' She looked at Alice. 'Shagging, you know?'

Alice nodded and Charlotte took another draw on her fag before continuing. 'Suddenly I heard a really big crack and then someone crying, like. It sounded like a cat. I moved a bit closer until I could see them. There was this huge bloke in a baseball cap holding onto this skinny little girl and banging her head on the fence. She was crying and with the moon and that I could see summat shining on her face. It were blood.' Charlotte looked round at the other women, nodding all the time as if she thought they would disagree. 'Then he slapped her across the face and said something. Something foreign like, in another language, not one o' them Paki languages though, a different kind. Then, he shouted summat and this other bloke appeared from the shadows. He turned her round and pushed her face against the fence. Next thing he was pulling her skirt up and jerking her legs apart. He were going to give it to her up the arse. By this time she looked like she'd fainted, so I ran back down the other end and round the back of the allotment near the houses and I started throwing stones and shouting in a right deep voice. Then, I smashed my Asti bottle on the fence and kept banging it and banging it till I heard them run away.'

'Good for you, Charlotte.' said Alice quietly, as the other woman ran her sleeve over her eyes. Charlotte swallowed and sat up straighter. 'Phew, wouldn't have minded so much but I'd hardly drunk any of my Asti. Bloody waste.'

Everyone laughed and Cat put an arm round Charlotte's shoulders. 'Way to go, girl,' she said.

Alice gave them a moment, then said, 'How did you get her back to The Prossie Palace?'

'Well, I dragged her along till she were near the other entrance. Then I ran and got Armani'

Armani nodded, 'Yeah, we carried her back here.' She shook her head. 'Poor kid was in some mess. Covered in shit and blood and spunk. That bastard Charlotte stopped obviously wasn't the only one she'd had to do, that night. The only saving grace was that she was so drunk, she maybe didn't feel all of it.'

Charlotte shook her head. 'But she'd have felt it the next day, poor cow. Those injuries would take ages to get over.'

'Was she treated by one of the rota doctors?' asked Alice

Charlotte sniffed. 'Yeah, that nice Pakistani one, Dr Kauser. She were nearly in tears herself when she saw what they'd done to the girl. Then, after we got her sobered up, she got a text. Next minute she looked petrified and were fighting her way past us like we were the enemy. I ran after her, but she'd gone.'

'Have you seen her since?'

Armani and Charlotte shook their heads.

'What about the two men you saw? Have you seen them since?'

Again Charlotte and Armani said, 'No', but another girl said, 'I'm not sure, but I saw a big bloke skirting round the allotments last week. He had a baseball hat on and looked as big as Charlotte said, but it could've been someone else.'

'Anything else? Anything at all?' Sensing that she'd got all she was going to get from them for now Alice smiled and stood up. 'Well, you know you can talk to me in confidence any time. Just get Carla to phone me, yeah? Okay then, thanks.'

Alice began gathering her stuff together and began walking towards the door. Without notice she swung round, her gaze narrowed in on Armani

'Oh, by the way, Armani, what's the big secret about Jessica and Trixie you're all trying to hide?'

Armani glared at Alice, then lowered her gaze. 'Don't know what you mean. You must be imagining it. There's no big secret?'

'No?' Alice inclined her head. 'Next you'll be telling me you haven't a clue who her boyfriend was?'

Armani paled and then stared straight into Alice's eyes. 'We don't know owt else, Alice.'

Alice, shrugged and pulled the door open. 'Oh, one last thing, have any of you seen Trixie wearing a mauve or crimson coloured scarf.'

Charlotte laughed. 'That's Jessica's. She'll go daft if she finds out Trixie borrowed it. She hates it when Trixie does that.' She stopped and stared at Alice. 'You don't mean he used her scarf? *That* scarf? Oh fuck!' and Charlotte fell back onto a chair. When Alice and Sampson left Armani and the other women where shoving Charlotte's head between her knees.

CHAPTER 25
Oak Lane

For the rest of the journey from the mortuary in Halifax they remained silent. To Gus it felt like the air had been sucked out of the car and he hated it. Stony silences weren't his bag, but he knew better than to attempt a reconciliation with Sadia right now. Better to let her work off some of her anger in her own way. Anyway, she'd floored him too with the 'M' word and he needed time as well.

As they drove past the bottom end of Lister Park, Gus recognised the group of women; one in a shalwar kameez, two in Burkhas and two in lycra jogging pants, power-walking at a rate of knots round the boating lake. One was Mo's wife, Naila, and the others worked for Mo in his samosa shop on Oak Lane. They were going nearly as fast as the men in prayer hats with heavy beards who were all out jogging round. When he'd jogged through the park before work this morning, the bowling green had been covered by a slight mist of dew and the park had been all but deserted. Only a few weeks earlier, during the summer, it had been alive with mixed cultural groups enjoying the fresh air. The play park had been filled with children and parents whilst youngsters idled on bikes or bounced balls around the basketball courts. It was still one of the best used parks in Bradford, though, even in this drab weather.

Sadia turned off onto Oak Lane, drove up as far as Mo's Sa'MO'sa's and pulled into a vacant spot on the main street outside a small vegetable shop with trays of chillies, garlic, ginger and onions lined up in front. Pointing through the windscreen to the mucky windows above the shop she said,

'That's where Jessica lives. Apparently, we have to go round the back to get in.'

Gus pulled his lanky frame from the car, rolling his tense shoulders, well aware of the iciness coming off Sadia in waves. He stopped on the pavement and glanced at her, wishing she'd lighten up a bit. The job was hard enough without her being in a bloody mood. She really needed to compartmentalise or they wouldn't be able to work together effectively. Sadia reached into the back seat to retrieve the MacDonald's bag with the Big Mac she'd insisted they bring for Jessica and then brushed past him on the pavement. He reached out and grabbed her arm, spinning her towards him, 'Come on, Sadia. It'll all work out, I promise, we can make this work.'

Sadia nodded, but the tightness round her mouth told Gus she was unconvinced. Stretching out his hand, he made to touch her face, but she jerked her head away, glancing round and looking nervous. 'Don't, Gus. Not here, not outside, someone might see us.'

Gus sighed and glanced round too. This was Manningham, heart of the Muslim area and very close to The Fort. Knowing Sadia was worried about one of her dad's friends reporting back to him, Gus took a deep breath to calm himself. This was so bloody stupid and he was getting more and more fed up of the subterfuge. From the corner of his eye, he saw a movement from Jessica's window. The raggedy curtain swayed as if someone had just moved away from it and as he glanced at Sadia, she raised one precisely plucked eye brow as if to say 'see'.

Gus turned with a grimace and made his way between the bags of onions and potatoes that were piled high under a makeshift shelter. Sadia followed, pushing her way through the haze of fruit flies that, attracted by the pulp of vegetation scattered along the alley, whizzed around their heads. Once clear of the odour, they climbed worn concrete stairs that led to a faded door with peeling blue paint on it. Before Gus could raise his hand to knock, the door swung open and Jessica stood there. The bags under her eyes and her pallor told Gus she'd hardly slept. She stood aside without speaking and indicated that they should follow her through.

The flat smelt fresh and looked tidy except for a handful of woman's magazines and two cups scattered on the small well-used coffee table. Realising that he was surprised by this fact, Gus smiled ruefully, making a mental note not to be so judgemental in future. Just because Jessica was Bazza Green's niece didn't mean *she* lived by his less than salubrious hygiene standards.

'Sit,' said Jessica, and looking as though her skinny legs couldn't hold her upright a moment longer she sank into an enormous armchair. Sitting childlike between the oversize padded cushions, she scrunched her legs up beneath her and proceeded, with agitated movements, to fold and unfold the tissue she held in her hands. At some point since the previous night she had showered and changed into skin tight jeans and a bobbled old woolly jumper. Replacing the dark mascara smudges, on her face were angry red blotches and flaky skin. Further evidence of her tears lay in the bundles of screwed up tissues that filled the waste paper basket and overflowed onto the threadbare carpet.

Despite feeling sorry for the girl, Gus knew that the best way they could help her would be to get down to business. He'd dealt with too many victims in the past to allow their sorrow to submerge him. He could pity her later, but for now he needed to extract whatever information she had.

'Jessica,' said Gus, positioning himself on a chair opposite her, his arms loosely draped over his knees as he leaned towards her, deliberately maintaining a non-threatening stance. 'I'm Gus McGuire and I'm in charge of finding out who did this to Trixie.'

Jessica's lips trembled as she nodded, her eyes flicking over to Sadia as if for reassurance. It was clear that Jessica and Sadia had a rapport so, Gus with a brief nod to his colleague, indicated that she should take over.

'Look, before we start I'll make us a cup of tea.' said Gus, 'and I bet you haven't eaten?'

Jessica shook her head, looking slightly confused, presumably by Gus' solicitousness. Like a magician Sadia drew a bag from behind her. 'Dada – MacDonald's Big Mac with cheese. Dig in, Jess, or I'll be offended.'

A ghost of a smile flitted over Jessica's face as she pushed her sleeves up her arm and accepted the bag. Withdrawing the boxes, as eagerly as puppy would unearth a bone, she said, 'Oh, Sadia, you got me, girl!' Then took a huge slurp of milk shake. 'Chocolate's my favourite.'

As Jess stuffed her face, Gus sidled into the small kitchen that had been created by placing a grubby plaster board partition in the corner of the room. Busying himself making the drinks, Gus took the opportunity to glance round the cramped space.

A variety of brightly coloured magnets on the fridge held a selection of photos of Trixie and Jessica, arms round each other, cheeks together. Gus placed a finger on Trixie's face. She was slightly shorter than Jessica, and he thought she had an air of sadness about her – as if her smile didn't quite reach her eyes. His eyes moved to a jumbled pile of letters that lay next to a plate with a smear of jam on its rim and covered in crumbs. Humming to cover the noise, Gus sifted through them. They were mainly bills addressed to both girls, but amongst them was a single sheet of scruffy paper without an envelope. Gus glanced through to the other room where Jessica was still stuffing fries into her mouth. He flipped the single page over and read: *Lost your phone again? Thursday 8pm. If you can't make it text me. Luv Sx*

Interesting, thought Gus. Wonder which of the girls it was for and wonder who 'S' is. No date so nothing to say the meeting was arranged for last night but, this 'S' is a definite person of interest. As the kettle pinged off he put the letters back tossed a couple of Bettabuy tea bags into the teapot and sloshed in the boiling water. A final glance round showed him another picture of Jessica and Trixie together. This time Trixie looked vibrant and smiled widely straight into the camera, whilst Jessica looked intently up at the other girl, with a faint smile on her face. Gus frowned and leaned over to get a better look. He shook his head and moved away. There was something about the picture but he couldn't think what right now. It would come to him later if he didn't push it.

When Sadia came to help carry the tea cups through, he brought her up to date on the scribbled note.

'Good snooping, Hercule,' she whispered following him through with a cup of tea in each hand.

Jessica, looking slightly better for having eaten, leaned back balancing the tea on the arm of the chair. Sadia took out a small recorder and placed it on the table between them. 'You don't mind do you, Jessica? It saves me having to worry about missing anything out when I'm taking notes.'

Jessica shook her head and Gus leaned forward. 'First of all, Jessica, have remembered anything that might help us with finding Trixie's family?'

Jessica sipped her tea and shook her head.

'Nothing at all?'

'Nothing. She said I was all the family she needed.'

Gus smiled and in a gentle tone said, 'I'm just wondering if her family could have something to do with this. It would be good to eliminate them from our enquiries.'

'She hasn't been in touch with them since she left. They don't even know where she is. I mean was.' Her voice caught slightly and she grabbed a tissue and rubbed her eyes.

'Okay, Jessica. You're doing really well. Any idea what she was doing at the allotments last night?'

Jess shrugged, 'Seeing a john, I suppose'

'Didn't you tell each other when you had appointments? You know for safety and that.'

'Well yes, if we knew in advance but, if we were picked up off the street we'd just go.'

Sadia leaned forward. 'Jessica, last night was Thursday.'

Jessica looked puzzled. 'Yeah I know.'

'Didn't you say that Trixie was Bazza's pet and didn't have to work during the week? Wasn't Thursdays one of his nights?'

Jessica glanced quickly from Gus to Sadia and frowned. 'So what? She shouldn't have been working, but she'd done it before. I told her Bazza would kill her if he ever found out.' She paused, hand to her mouth, 'Oh Fuck! I didn't mean that. Bazza wouldn't kill her.'

'Would Bazza arrange to meet her there, Jess... at the allotments?'

'What? Down the allotments?' Jessica, laughed. 'No way! Bazza took his pet to his flat and used his king-size bed. Fed them champagne and strawberries like in that *Pretty Woman* film. It's the only way he could get off. He even had a picture of Julia "Blow Job Lips" Roberts, above his bed. He wouldn't shag down the allotments. He thought he was a cut above that sort of thing...' She paused head to one side, '... not that nylon sheets, carpet sticky with spunk and Millions scent with an underlying tone of Eau de BO Bazza, was upmarket by anyone else's standards.'

How the other half live, thought Gus? Jessica's words were conjuring up images he'd rather not see. Poor Trixie... it was a toss-up whether she was better off on the streets or holed up with the delectable Bazza Green. 'Okay then, not Bazza. But, would she meet someone else down there in secret, maybe?'

Jessica looked down at her hands, her chin trembling, 'No, she wouldn't. We didn't have secrets, me and Trix'

'Do you think Shahid could have something to do with this?' asked Sadia.

Jessica reached for her tea and carried it to her mouth too quickly, spilling it on her jeans. She shoved her mug on the table and jumped to her feet, grabbing tissues to soak up the tea. Gus raised an eyebrow and Sadia grimaced.

'Don't know who you mean?' said Jessica finally sitting back down

Sadia leaned towards her and clasped Jessica's hands in hers. 'Come on Jess, don't be a pain, we need your help. For Trixie's sake.'

Jessica threw a tissue in the general direction of the bin and said nothing.

'Come on, Jessica, we're asking about your brother, Shahid Khan.'

'I've not got a brother.' And tears began to roll down her cheeks.

'Oh, Jess,' said Sadia, 'Shahid Khan is your half-brother and he pimps the girls in Bradford 3. Last week two of his

131

girls, Camilla and Starlight, were killed just like Trixie. We *need* to find out if we've got some sick fucker out there doing this or if it's a turf war between Bazza and Shahid.'

Jessica sniffed and rubbed her eyes vigorously. 'Look, Shahid is *not* my family. Trixie was. If he did this, get him and string him up by the balls. If he *didn't* do this, still get him and still string him up because he killed my mother on his dad's orders, so he should die anyway.'

'Jessica! Come on, this is about Trixie, not your mum. Help us!'

'Look, there's no turf war going on. Bazza has a few girls that work this area but Shahid's got the biggest business.'

She stared Gus in the eye and continued, 'Bazza's happy with what he's got. He doesn't flaunt us in the Muslim community, so they ignore us.' She grimaced. 'Well, them that don't visit us ignore us, anyway. We're discreet. But, more than that Bazza's just not the sort to kill the girls. *Or* order anyone else to do it either,' she added quickly, as if sensing that would be their next question. 'Shahid, on the other hand has the morals of his father. He deals in drugs, guns, knives, organises robberies and everything.'

'Don't you and Shahid share a father?' he asked.

Jessica snorted. 'Arshad Khan was no father to me... I'm glad he's dead.'

Gus decided to change tack. 'How do you know so much about Shahid's business?'

'He hassles me sometimes. Doesn't like that I work for Bazza. Doesn't like the work I do. Says I can have an office job with him if I leave Bazza. I'd rather die than earn anything from *him*.'

'Has he told you what he does?'

Jessica shrugged. 'Look, he's capable of killing Trix. My mother damn near brought him up. He was always at our house. He hated his mum, hated his dad too but still, despite everything she did for him, the bastard poured petrol over her, threw a match on her and watched her burn. So, no, I don't think he'd struggle too much with strangling a whore, do you?'

Gus studied her silently and then said very quietly, 'Jessica, why are you so sure he was responsible for your mother's death?'

Jessica looked straight at him. 'He was there that night just after it happened and when I ran to help my mum, he grabbed me and stopped me. He stank of petrol. He did it.'

'Did you tell anyone at the time, Jessica?'

Jessica gulped. 'Phew, do you think I'm stupid? No, I ran straight to Bazza as soon as I could and he's looked out for me since.'

Sadia shook her head. 'Your mum wouldn't have wanted that for you.'

Jessica shrugged. 'No, but I'm sure burning to death wasn't in her plans either. You do what you have to, Sad.'

Gus pushed his hand through his hair, and considered his next move. Could Jessica's relationship with Shahid and Bazza be at the crux of this whole business? It didn't really seem credible to him. Not after so long. If they'd wanted some sort of retaliation surely it would have happened when Shahid's dad was still alive. Unless something drastic had happened that he didn't know about, he didn't think their animosity was enough to have them popping off each other's girls. It just didn't make sound business sense and these men were nothing if not business men.

'So,' he said finally, 'Could you be a source of animosity between the two men?'

Jessica jumped to her feet, agitated, 'For God's sake, I thought you were here to find out who killed Trixie not to make up stuff about Bazza and Hussain. They didn't like each other. Khan may have wanted Bazza's business but, he wouldn't do owt to him… for *my* sake. For some reason he feels responsible for me.'

'Okay, okay settle down,' said Sadia. 'I *know* this is hard but we really do have to ask these questions.'

Jessica flung herself back into the chair and glared at them.

'What about dodgy punters?' asked Gus. 'Any talk of a weirdo amongst the girls?'

Jess thought for a moment and then shook her head, 'They're all bloody weird if you ask me, but nobody new on the scene. Nobody that we couldn't handle. You know, just the usual.'

'What about boyfriends? Did Trixie have a boyfriend?'

Jessica picked up a tissue, blew her nose and looked down at her knees before answering. 'Nah, no boyfriends. Not easy in this line of work.'

Bullshit antennae on the alert, he persevered. 'Are you sure? No boyfriends? Nobody new in the last couple of months? Somebody she might not tell you about, maybe?'

'Fuck sake, what do you want me to do? Lie?' shouted Jessica, glaring at him 'I said *no* boyfriend and I meant it, okay? We had no secrets, none at all. I'd have known if she had a boyfriend, and she didn't – right?'

Gus raised an eyebrow. Well, that line of questioning had certainly provoked a response. 'No need to get agitated. What about condoms? She always use them or what?'

Jessica stared at him and then at Sadia. 'Is he for real? Condoms? Of course we bloody use condoms.'

134

Leaning closer, he said, 'We know Trixie was an addict, and we know that addicts get desperate, and we know that, when addicts get desperate, they get careless. You get my meaning?'

Face sulky, Jessica nodded.

'So, think again. Did she always use condoms or were there times when she was so desperate for a fix that she'd let a punter do it nude for a few extra pounds?'

'She was clean.' Her voice was barely audible as she continued, 'She'd been clean for weeks. Nearly two months in fact. She was going to do it this time. She really was.' She looked pleadingly at Sadia.

'Ssh, Jessica, ssh, I'm sure she was,' Sadia put her arm around the distraught girl's shoulder.

'She used to sometimes do it without a condom. Just when she was desperate like. But not any more. Not now she was clean.'

'Did she owe anybody any money?'

'Nah, I don't think so. I helped her pay off her debts two months ago, so I'm sure she was clear.'

'Who was her dealer? Was it Bazza?'

She shook her head, 'Not Bazza. He only deals in ecstasy and tranqs for raves. I think she sometimes went to one of Shahid's fences and,' she frowned, 'yes, now I think about it there was one bloke with an accent I caught her dealing with a few months ago. But I think it was a one-off. I've not seen him again.'

'What was he like? White? Asian? Tall? Short?'

'White, medium– I don't know, didn't pay attention. Ask one of the other girls who do drugs, they'd know.'

Gus paused. 'You know, when she was with Bazza, did he use a condom?'

Looking pale and defeated, she nodded. 'Yes, Bazza *always* looked after his health. He'd never do it without a condom'

Gus stood up. 'We're nearly finished here and you look like you could do with a good rest. We'll get your statement typed up and someone will bring it round for you to sign tomorrow. But, before we leave I'd like to have a look through Trixie's things, okay?'

She pointed him towards a door leading off the living room. 'That's Trixie's room.'

Entering the room, he closed the door behind him, pulled on a pair of latex gloves and took out a small hand-held tape recorder. Standing, by the door, he glanced around and, in a low voice, recorded what he saw.

'Very small box room with a single bed against the wall under the window, dressing table against opposite wall, with a single wardrobe beside it. Barely enough room to walk between the bed and the other furniture. The room is neat but feels empty. There is no clutter and no personal bits and pieces on the dressing table... Has Jessica cleared it out?'

He moved over to the dressing table and drew his finger through a layer of dust and then opened the drawers. *'Thick layer of dust covering dressing table. Top drawer contains two pairs of old panties and an open pack of Tampax. Second drawer contains an assortment of pens and paper – no diary or address book. Third drawer contains two shrunk T-shirts and a jumper.'*

Since when did any woman own only two pairs of knickers, and scruffy ones at that? Moving over to the bed, he pulled back the duvet, *'no sheet on bed... Query... washed or hidden or what? Mattress has an assortment of old stains.*

He spun on his heel and glanced round. Never had he been in a room so lacking in personality. Seemed like Trixie was a minimalist but, even to Gus' male eyes her lack of belongings seemed extreme. Maybe she'd packed up ready to move. Without telling Jessica? That could explain it and it would certainly put a different complexion on things. He didn't get the impression from Jessica that Trixie was planning on moving out.

Opening the wardrobe door, he moved a few empty hangers around and studied the two pairs of old jeans and the parka jacket that hung there. Then, he stepped to the foot of the bed and stopped, slowly turning in a circle, taking in all that he saw. '*Query: where are all the posters and pictures on the walls, the cuddly toys, make-up, shoes?*'

On a whim he fell to his knees and looked under the bed. Nothing. He stood up and went towards the door then, nodding to himself, he went back and lifted the mattress up. There flattened against the wooden slats was a Morrison's bag. He picked it up and opened it. Inside were two cards. One was a Valentine's card with '*To T luv S xx*' on it. The other was a birthday card addressed '*To Trix*' and signed '*Love forever Shahid xx*'.

Gus sprang to his feet flipped his hand in the air and said, 'Gotcha!'

CHAPTER 26
Oak Lane

Glancing at Jessica for the fifth time, Sadia wondered what the hell was keeping Gus. Jessica looked ready to drop off and she felt guilty for keeping her up when she was so clearly exhausted. 'Come on, Jess,' she said, pulling the girl to her feet, 'Let's get you to bed, huh?'

Jessica made to protest, but Sadia said, 'Look you're knackered. A sleep will do you good, okay?'

With a quick nod, Jessica got to her feet. As she turned to head to her bedroom she turned and gripped Sadia's arm, her fingers pressing so hard Sadia was sure they'd leave a bruise. 'Sad, will you do me a favour? For old time's sake?'

Sadia felt her heart sink. She had a sneaking suspicion about what Jessica was going to ask and she just didn't know how she'd be able to refuse this girl; the girl whose mother she'd seen burn to death outside her childhood home.

Before she had a chance to respond, Jessica continued, her voice earnest. 'I need you to look into it for me, Sad. I *need* to know for sure. No-one else will take me seriously but you were there. You saw it.' Tears welled up in her eyes. 'I need you to prove once and for all that Shahid did it.' She let go of Sadia's arm and began kneading her hands together. 'Especially now, Sad. Especially now I've lost Trixie too. I *need* to know.'

Sadia took a deep breath. What could she say to this girl who'd already been through so much? She glanced at the closed door of Trixie's room cursing Gus for taking so long. If he'd been quicker she could've avoided having to answer. But, one look at the girl's anguished face and she knew what her answer would be. Jessica needed closure. She handed the other girl a tissue and said, 'Dry your eyes.' When Jessica had wiped her face and blown her nose, Sadia continued, 'Okay, Jess, this is what I'll do. I'll look into it. I can't promise anything but, I'll have a look at the old files and see what I can find out.'

Jessica began to thank her but Sadia interrupted, 'Look, I'm not promising I'll find proof that Shahid did it. Personally, I don't think he did but, I promise you, I'll look into it and *if* I find something – and I'm telling you now, Jess, it's a very big if – I'll try to pressurise the powers that be to reopen the case. This is a real long-shot. Do you understand that?'

Jessica nodded but Sadia knew that she didn't really believe it. She knew Jess had pinned her hopes on Shahid being discovered culpable for her mother's death. The thing was, she knew how unlikely that was. Shahid had been pretty much a kid himself when it happened and Sadia knew he'd loved Millie to bits. No, she didn't think he was responsible but, if she could find something to prove his innocence then at least Jessica would have closure and perhaps she, Shahid and Imti could be reunited.

'Now bed for you.' Sadia pushed open the door leading to the second bedroom and guiding the girl into the room, she gently pushed her onto the huge double bed that stood against the central wall. Eyelids already drooping, she scooted over to the far side of the bed and, pulling the duvet up to her chin, fell asleep.

Feeling sorry for her, Sadia studied the sleeping girl for a second before turning to look round Jess' room. Two bedside cabinets with matching alarm clocks stood on either side of the bed. The room was filled with pictures, cuddly toys and junk ornaments, the sort you could win at fun fairs. Two slim wardrobes stood side by side with a dressing table beside it covered with make-up and bits and pieces of jewellery. Sadia was glad that Jessica's flat was at least homely. She thought momentarily about setting one of the alarm clocks, decided against it and left the room to find Gus waiting for her by the door.

'What?' She whispered when she saw his smile

'Love letters from Shahid.'

Sadia grinned back and then with a finger to her lips, she gestured to the door and setting the lock they left the flat.

CHAPTER 27
Off Ingleby Road

The courier had delivered, not just the guns as scheduled, but also some unexpected news. News that upset The Old Man very much. When he'd enlisted Anastazy's help, he'd known he was taking a risk. The man was unpredictable with no boundaries and, despite being made aware of the benefits of keeping a low profile, he'd gone and done something stupid. The Old Man knew it was because of Serafina. From the minute Anastazy had set eyes on the girl he'd been besotted and that had been alright… until now. He had no quibble with Anastazy pursuing her: the girl meant nothing to him and, if it kept him happy, then that was a bonus. But now he'd gone and drawn attention to himself by stabbing the boy. Serafina would not keep quiet about Anastazy… it wasn't in her nature. They'd have to come up with a solution quickly. Things were still too fragile for him to dispose of Anastazy and, unfortunately, Anastazy knew too much about his operations for The Old Man to allow him to be caught.

Packing the guns away in the storeroom at the back of the warehouse, The Old Man was content. The smell of gun oil and metal had always soothed him and, as he checked each gun to ensure the serial numbers had been properly removed, he felt relaxed. Putting Anastazy's stupidity to the back of his mind, he reflected on his life. His moniker, The Old Man, was misleading in itself, something the stupid Polish police hadn't realised. For thirty years they'd been searching for an old man, never stopping to consider that the nickname was designed to mislead. He wasn't old now and he certainly hadn't been old when he first started out. It had taken them thirty years to even get close and in that time he'd amassed a wealth that should have taken him gracefully into his retirement. That was until that Detective Jankowski had begun to peel away the layers and close in on him. He spat on the concrete floor. Now, most of his wealth was tied up in Poland and he had been forced to escape to the UK. He'd started from nothing before, so this time it would be easier. He had contacts, he had some money, maybe not the huge wealth that was unavailable to him at the moment but enough to make a dent. Most importantly though, he had knowledge… information that afforded him certain benefits that he fully intended to exploit. He'd chosen Bradford because he wanted to hide among his own community. Only a few people knew who he really was and, of course, he had leverage… they all had people they cared for and that was their weakness, one he had no compunction about exploiting.

He himself had no time for women and family. He considered them a distraction. Yet getting married and fathering children had provided the smokescreen he had needed in Poland and again when he'd had to uproot. He had always maintained the illusion of a perfect family with almost religious fervour. The fruits of his many enterprises had, until recently, provided his wife and children with a near decadent lifestyle. The only proviso he made of his wife was that she keep their sham of a marriage secret from the children and uphold their pretence. He didn't love her, or the children… was that strange? He didn't dwell on that much, preferring to concentrate on how useful they were. When the Polish authorities had gotten a little too close he'd been able to utilise the privilege of family to keep them off the scent long enough for him to flee.

Of course, Anastazy, with his ability to transfer his assets, had been an essential requirement. Sometimes he wondered if, perhaps, he'd overestimated the influence he held over the younger man. He knew that as soon as Anastazy had outlived his usefulness, he would have to be disposed of, before *he* tried to dispose of The Old Man... but, for now, he needed him. He needed Anastazy to implement every stage of the takeover, whilst he himself fine-tuned the planning. From a safe distance

Guns counted, The Old Man entered his office space. When they'd taken over the old supermarket warehouse, he'd spent a lot of money having it soundproofed and secured. He felt completely safe here. When he needed to, he could bring reluctant contributors here to convince them of the error of their ways, secure in the knowledge that they would not be interrupted. It was distant enough from the squalid little terraced house that was his temporary home, yet close enough to get to quickly. He was satisfied with his headquarters. Now, as he waited for the drug delivery that was due shortly, he considered how to minimise the damage caused by Anastazy's rash actions. He trusted Anastazy not to have revealed himself to the boy so, that only left Serafina to consider. He needed to make sure she would keep quiet and there was only one way to do that.

CHAPTER 28
Birmingham

Imti had spent a futile half-hour looking for Shahid. His uncle had been asking where Shahid was and Imti was getting fed up lying and making excuses for him. Why the hell couldn't he just be there for their uncle? After all, it was their cousin's wedding. He could at least make an effort, even if family stuff wasn't his top priority. For God's sake it was only for a few more hours. Wasn't too much to ask was it?

Imti walked round the back of the mosque to the small meditative garden that the community tended. Plants and shrubs were beginning to die back with the onset of the colder autumnal weather and the slight drizzle meant that the guests were mainly indoors; the women in their gold embroidered Lengha with ornate Mehndi decorating their hands and feet were in the main hall with the bride, and the men in less ornate, but none the less exotic-looking *kurta pajama* chatted in the smaller hall. Imti knew this sort of segregation irritated Shahid. He often told Imti it was backward, but as far as Imti was concerned that was just the way it was. It was their culture and although he himself wasn't fully supportive of it, it didn't rile him in the same way it did Shahid. Imti saw it as just part and parcel of being a community, a community that, at the moment, seemed to be constantly under attack in the media and, sometimes, even in the streets. It wasn't as if he had such a huge family anyway: he'd no intention of alienating the relatives he did have by being arsy about things he knew he'd never change.

He walked down the crazy-paved path to the Moghul-style gazebo. Shahid was sitting inside it, huddled over his phone. He and Imti wore matching suits. Shahid had railed against wearing traditional dress but Imti had ignored him. He'd gone along to Bombay Stores in Bradford and spent ages choosing the matching *kurta* in cream with traditional hand-sewn gold threading and midnight blue skinny *pajama* cuffs, collar and scarf. Shahid had moaned at the expense but Imti knew deep down he liked them… besides they looked smart, as smart as any of the Birmingham lot, anyway.

Another wave of annoyance hit him as he strode towards his brother. He knew fine and well he was chasing around after that girl of Bazza Green's. Idiot! Didn't he get that this was all going to end in tears? He'd heard on the rumour mill that not only was she Bazza's pet but she was also Jess' friend. This was not going to end well for anyone. He suspected. Bazza would be pissed off that Shahid was diddling his girl and Jess would be absolutely furious. It's not as if she and Shahid were even on speaking terms. Jess hated him and this would do nothing to pour oil on troubled waters.

As Imti climbed the two shallow stairs that led into the gazebo, he saw the look on Shahid's face and his earlier anger died away. Shahid looked bereft as he stared at his phone. So lost in his own thoughts was he that he didn't even hear Imti's approach.

'You okay, bro?' asked Imti, wiping a hand over the marble seating before sitting beside Shahid.

Shahid looked startled and then, seeing it was Imti he smiled. 'I'm fine Imti. You should be up at the wedding, not looking for me.'

Imti nudged his brother on the arm. 'Missed your scintillating convo. Everyone was asking where "the light of the party" was.' He made bunny ears with his fingers and laughed at Shahid's incredulous expression. 'Okay, okay, I'm exaggerating. The only person that missed you was Uncle Majid. Auntie Nusrat was quite glad that you weren't around, I suspect. She doesn't really like you much, does she?'

Shahid grinned. 'No, miserable old cow. Had a go at me this morning. Just want to get this fucking wedding over so I can get back to Bradford.'

Shahid jumped to his feet and started to walk towards the steps. 'Come on, Imti, let's get this charade over with.'

Imti stood and put out arm to make his brother stop. 'What's wrong Shahid? Your face looks like a slapped arse.'

Shahid raised an eyebrow, his lips twitched into a near smile and then settled into a sigh. 'It's nowt. Just can't get a hold of Trixie, that's all. She was supposed to phone me last night but, she didn't and I've been texting and phoning her all morning. Nothing.'

'She'd probably just busy or lost her phone or summat, Shahid. Don't get why you're so worried. She's bad news, you know?'

'Fuck's sake, Imti!' said Shahid pulling his arm away, 'This is serious, right? Not just a silly fling – she's pregnant, okay?'

Imti watched open-mouthed as Shahid strode up the path back towards the mosque, then he ran down the steps and ran towards his brother. This was bad news, but he'd have his brother's back, same as Shahid had his. Guilt for upsetting Shahid when he was already so distraught flooded through him. Catching up with him, he grabbed his shoulder and pulled him into an embrace. 'Shit, I'm sorry, Shahid. Really sorry, okay? If she's your girl, then that's fine. We'll deal with Bazza together, you and me.'

Shahid allowed Imti to hold him, then pulled himself away, 'And Jess?'

Imti exhaled and then grinned 'Hell yeah, and Jess. She'll just have to get used to it, won't she? Maybe this baby will make her forget all her silly accusations.'

Shahid looked uncertain. 'Not sure it'll be as easy as that. It's not like she thinks I stole her sweets, for fuck's sake. She thinks I killed her mum.'

'Yeah, yeah I know, but she'll come round. Now, come on, let's get this wedding over with and we'll head back to Bradford in a bit and look for your Trixie.'

Arms linked, the two brothers walked into the mosque.

CHAPTER 29
Oak Lane, Bradford

After leaving Jessica sleeping in her flat, Gus and Sadia emerged onto Oak Lane. Something niggled in Sadia's mind but she couldn't quite put her finger on it. Maybe she was just still pissed off with Gus. For God's sake, did he have to be such a bloody *man* about things. All she wanted was a bit of commitment. Maybe some compromise. It's not like she could just cut herself off from her own father. His faith was important to him. More important even than the damn job and she knew just how important *that* was to him.

All those weeks, when her mother was so ill and he'd still worked all the hours he could. Maybe he just wanted to escape the claustrophobic atmosphere at home. Sadia's lips tightened… maybe he should have considered that she might have wanted a break from it all too. Funny how, now she's gone, he seems to have eased back a bit at work. All of a sudden he's got more time for the mosque. She could've done with him being there with her when her mother was upstairs dying, instead of leaving her with a series of 'aunties' who swanned in, cooked, gossiped, cleaned and tended her mum but, through no fault of their own, couldn't provide what a teenage Sadia needed. How could they give the things her mother had? Not that her mum had ever been overly demonstrative but at least she was always there and Sadia knew deep down that, although distant, she loved her.

What she'd missed most during that time was her father's hugs and kisses. He'd always been more loving, more affectionate than her mother. He'd always been the one to provide relief from her mother's more serious nature. He'd

148

been the light and laughter in the house. Not any more, though. Gradually, she'd become aware, since her mother's death, of a tightening of his emotions. A more controlled way with him, a stricter, more judgemental attitude. She'd first noticed it when she'd told him, expecting him to be over the moon, that she wanted to follow in his footsteps, that she wanted to join the police force. He'd almost exploded before her eyes. You'd think she'd told him she wanted to pose nude for *Playboy* the way he went on, quoting the Quran and saying it was no job for a young Muslim girl.

She shrugged off her thoughts and brought her mind back to the present. She wasn't quite ready to forgive Gus. For fuck's sake, being a Muslim wasn't so bloody bad after all and, if he loved her, surely he could revert, just to placate her father. She jumped when Gus spoke, interrupting her thoughts.

'We're going to have to re-interview her later, Sad'

Pulling her coat up against the persistent drizzle, Sadia took a step back to allow a group of girls in Grammar School uniforms to walk past, before replying, 'Yeah I know. Clearly there's a link between Shahid Khan and Trixie which could've complicated Jess' relationship with her friend. You'd think she'd have mentioned it if she knew though, wouldn't you?'

Gus looked thoughtful. 'Maybe Trixie kept it secret, knowing how much Jess hated Shahid.' He pursed his lips. 'What's the betting he's the father of the baby?'

'Hmm, he seems the most likely candidate so far, doesn't he? Wonder if *he* knows about it.'

Gus' phone rang in his pocket. Retrieving it from his pocket he nodded, 'Yeah, well, it's time to bring him in again, I reckon.' Then, looking at his phone, he cursed. 'It's my mum. You take the car back. I'm going to nip home to let Bingo out. I need to clear my head a bit and my leg's stiffening up. See you at the briefing.' He smiled in what Sadia took to be a half-hearted apology and answered his phone.

Sadia watched him, standing with his habitual hunch, his short mucky brown dreads speckled with droplets of rain, his coat unfastened and his blue eyes sparking with affection as he spoke to the woman he loved more than any other; his mum. She had noticed the way the Grammar School girls had eyed him up as they passed earlier. Not surprising really. He *was* one handsome bugger. From his side of the conversation, she deduced that his mum had dropped off some of her inedible cookies to the station and that Compo, who'd been testifying at court for the past week in a fraud case, looked very handsome in his suit. A fact Sadia found difficult to imagine, as Compo was, in her experience, not only incapable of looking smart but actively opposed to it. Some reference to hell dog Bingo told Sadia that Gus' mum, Corrine, planned to take the mutt for a long walk at some point. *Hopefully she'll lose the bloody thing,* thought Sadia and then, immediately, felt guilty, for she knew Gus would be devastated if the dog was cut from his life. He'd had more than enough losses to contend with recently.

She took her keys from her pocket and unlocked her car. Slipping behind the wheel, she watched Gus stride down Oak Lane to the ornate gates that marked the entrance to Lister Park, phone still held to his ear. An unexpected wave of emotion flooded her and turning the key in the ignition she came to a decision and, instead of heading up Oak Lane to The Fort, she headed towards the traffic lights at the bottom and took a left, heading along Keighley Road.

CHAPTER 30
Marriners Drive

W hen he arrived home, Gus was surprised to see Sadia's car sitting in the drive and assumed there'd been a breakthrough on the case. He sped up and burst through the front door to find Sadia standing at the bottom of the stairs waiting for him. He knew at once, from the look on her face, that she had something other than work on her mind and, after the debacle on the way back from Halifax in the morning, he was only too willing to comply. Without uttering a word, she held out her hand to him and when he clasped it, she led him upstairs, her arse swaying as she moved, making him feel like one of Pavlov's dogs as he all but salivated in anticipation.

'This is so naughty,' murmured Sadia heading over to the bedroom window. As she stretched to pull the curtains closed, Gus came up behind her and, nuzzling her neck, he slipped her jacket off her shoulders and propelled her over to the bed. As soon as the back of her knees hit the side of his king size bed, he pushed her so she landed at an angle on top smiling up at him. Their earlier disagreement thrust aside, Gus returned her smile. He didn't want the hassle with her father to get in the way of their relationship. He knew it was going to be a very fine balancing act, but she was worth it. He knew they'd find a way forward that kept everyone happy, but for now he was going to live for the moment. He slid on top of her and began placing small kisses along her jawline. 'You started this, Sadia, besides, we've worked all morning *and* we've been at that damn PM. We deserve a half-hour's break before we head back.'

151

He continued to kiss her until the sound of paws half scampering, half skidding on the laminate flooring had him groaning in frustration. He pushed himself up, ignoring her grin and loped over to kick the bedroom door shut, narrowly avoiding Bingo's snout. Bingo scraped loudly at the woodwork and, from the depths of his belly, emitted a woebegone whimper. Gus cast a disgruntled look at the door and ambled back to the bed kicking off his shoes as he went.

Sadia lay, eyes smouldering behind dark lashes. God, she was beautiful, thought Gus as he pulled her to him again. But Sadia pulled away and looked him straight in the eye, her eyes pleading. 'Gus, I'm sorry about earlier. I don't expect you to revert. How could I? I'm hardly an advert for a good Muslim myself, am I? I just hate all this deceit. It wears me down and I suppose I was looking for an easy option.'

'Look, Sad, it doesn't matter. Let's just take this one step at a time, yeah? Let's just enjoy being with each other. We'll deal with the shit when it hits the fan, okay?'

He rolled on top of her, moulding her body to his and with an exaggerated wink said, 'I know you're not keen on this but, I'm the boss and, well, the boss gets what the boss wants, right?' and as she giggled, he kissed her gently on each eyelid and pulling her hair from its band, he smoothed it over the pillow.

Sadia, already unbuckling his belt, laughed. 'That, *sir,* smacks just a little bit of sexual harassment. I might just have to do something about it.'

'It's your own fault Sadia, all morning that perfume of yours has been egging me on. It's been driving me crazy.'

'Has it now?' she asked, pulling up her skirt to reveal that she'd already removed her underwear.

'Oh, I'm in heaven,' he whispered, as he slipped inside her. 'I think you're doing something about it right now.'

'Yes, but be quick, darling' she arched backwards, wound her legs round his waist and thrust upwards, 'I don't want to miss the samosas.'

Gus threw his head back and laughed. Then, very slowly he pulled himself out from her. 'Oh, you know, I *never* rush a good thing.'

With a growl, she tensed her legs and pulled him back into her before suddenly flipping him over onto his back so that she was straddling him.

Gus closed his eyes and giving himself over to the sensations flooding his body, thought I've died and gone to heaven. Without warning, he sensed her body tense and she stilled. His eyes flew open and he too became aware of the thud of footsteps ascending the stairs accompanied by his mother shouting, 'Bingo, Bingo walkies!'

He looked at Sadia, 'Shit!'

Sadia scrambled off him cursing under her breath and Gus, still half-dressed, shot up and to the door, zipping up his trousers as he went. He stepped onto the upstairs landing, closing the bedroom door behind him. 'Oh, hi, Mum. What're you doing here?'

'What do you think I'm doing here, Gus? I'm collecting Bingo for a walk. More to the point what are *you* doing here? And who does that car in the drive belong to?'

Gus hated lying to his mum but he was damned if he was going to tell her the truth. Knowing her she'd be delighted to know he had a woman in his life but he wasn't sure Sadia was ready for his mother's inimitable presence. Feeling as if his face gave him away he tried to avoid eye contact with her as he replied. 'I do live here, you know?' Then as his mum put her hands on her hips he shrugged, 'I just nipped back to let Bingo out. I borrowed DS Hussain's car.'

Corrine nodded and clicked her fingers for Bingo, who was gazing up at Gus his tail wagging nineteen-to-the-dozen, to follow. She turned to retrace her steps downstairs and then, foot poised to step off the bottom step, she looked up at Gus. 'You do realise particular Issey Miyake is a woman's fragrance, don't you Angus?'

Momentarily flustered, Gus raked his fingers through his dreads, 'Eh?'

His mum sniffed in an exaggerated manner. 'I smelled it as soon as I came in. It just happens to be one of my favourite scents, too.' She stepped onto hallway carpet, before adding, 'And, of course, you are, and always have been, a dreadful liar. Say hi to DS Hussain for me, won't you?' and with a wink, she headed along the hallway to the door, Bingo, tail wagging in anticipation of a walk, following, leaving Gus staring after them, feeling like he'd been exposed as a fraud of mammoth proportions. He mentally kicked himself. He should have known better than to try to get one over on his mum. Hearing the front door bang closed, he re-entered the bedroom to find Sadia still lying on the bed, grinning, 'Your mum's bloody awesome, isn't she?'

Gus sunk to the bed and pulled Sadia to him, feeling that 'awesome' was the last word he'd use to describe his mum at that precise moment. 'Katie and I could never get away with owt when we were kids, but you'd think I could pull off a minor deceit as an adult. Seems I was mistaken.'

Sadia laughed and ruffled his hair. 'Now, where were we before we were so rudely interrupted?' she said, nibbling his lip before he could reply.

Later, sweaty and satisfied Gus lay panting on the bed, 'Bloody hell Sadia! Where in heavens name did you learn to do that?'

Sadia grinned at him and wiggled her eyebrows. 'That's for me to know and you to worry about.'

She jumped from the bed winding her hair into a bun so it wouldn't get wet it in the shower. Gus laughed and threw a pillow at her naked bottom as she wandered at a leisurely pace to his en suite. As the shower ran, Gus contemplated joining, her but knowing they were cutting things tight for the briefing, he got dressed instead.

When she'd done Sadia brushed her hair back into its ponytail, whilst Gus opened the curtains and looked out the window. 'Wonder if that's the neighbour's new car,' he said, watching a red Vectra idling part way down the hill. Sadia circled her arms round his waist and looked over his shoulder at the car.

'Mmm, nice model isn't it? She pulled him round towards her and pirouetted on the spot. 'Do I look sexed up or will I do for work?'

Gus turned to look at her. 'You look sexy, but you'll do for work.'

CHAPTER 31
Marriners Drive

W hat a stroke of luck that he'd recognised her car as she turned left onto Emm Lane. He'd been at the Subway next to The Turf pub for his lunch and was heading back to work when he'd noticed her turning off Keighley Road. So, he'd quickly slipped into the right hand lane and followed her in time to see her turning into McGuire's street.

He couldn't have planned it better if he'd tried. He'd seen her pull into McGuire's drive and managed to get a few photos of her taking the key out of her pocket and using it to gain access to Gus' home. The fact that she had her own key was a loaded gun as far as he was concerned.

He'd driven past the car and gone down to the bottom of the road that was blocked off by bollards to stop people using it as a shortcut to avoid the lights. He'd done a U-turn and ended up parking halfway up the incline in prime position to see Gus heading along the road on foot. Things just got better and better. He picked up the camera from the passenger seat where he'd put it moments earlier and thanked God for digital dates and times. More incriminating evidence. He fired off a few more shots as Gus glanced at Sadia's car and then ran up the few steps, slipped his own key into the lock and entered the house.

Wonder what those two will be getting up to… in the middle of the day too. Naughty, naughty!

Barely five minutes later he was aware of movement at the upstairs front window; the master bedroom, he presumed. He raised his camera on zoom and laughed to himself as he took a series of pictures of Sadia arms raised to close the curtains and Gus' distinctive dreads bouncing in the frame as he nuzzled her neck and slipped her jacket off. You beauty! Conclusive, indisputable evidence. He giggled, knowing exactly what was going on behind those closed curtains, and knowing he'd captured enough to prove it. Putting the camera down, prepared for a long wait, he picked up his Subway roll and unwrapped it. He'd taken only a single bite when another car pulled up at the bottom of Gus' drive. Shoving the roll onto the dashboard and hastily wiping his fingers, he grabbed his camera and took a few photos of the diminutive woman who alighted from the Range Rover. Catching a glimpse of the woman's features as she walked round her vehicle he realised that she must be McGuire's mother.

Again, he watched as she went up the steps and used a key to enter the house. Maybe McGuire should be a bit more discerning about who he gives a key to. He smirked, wishing he could be a fly on the wall right now. Wonder what Mumsie will make of her son bedding a Paki. Mind you half those bloody blacks'll shag owt that moves by all accounts.

Minutes later he saw Gus' mum leave the house with a yapping dog which jumped into her car before she drove off. He grinned. Wonder how McGuire reacted to coitus interruptus. Wonder if Mumsie's presence put the kybosh on him getting his leg over. Fifteen minutes later the curtains opened and he saw Gus silhouetted against the window. Seconds later Sadia joined him resting her chin on his window, as they looked out. Brighton flicked his cigarette out the partly open window and again took a few photos. Happy with the day's work he put the camera down and headed off before Gus and Sadia came out and saw him waiting there.

Liz Mistry

CHAPTER 32
The Fort

'Right, dig in,' said Gus dropping three huge boxes of Mo's samosas on the table. He was a firm believer in rewarding hard work and he knew his team deserved a treat so, he and Sadia had stopped off at Mo's to grab the food and cans of Rubicon Mango for everyone.

Compo, nose in the air sniffing like a bloodhound, jumped to his feet and dived on the box marked 'meat'. 'Bloody starving' he said, 'Takes it out of you giving evidence in court you know?'

Gus laughed, 'Thought you'd already had cookies from my mum.'

Mouth half filled with samosa, pastry flakes floating down to land on his white shirt, Compo nodded. 'Yeah, great. Had some earlier. I've left a few in the tub by the Tassimo machine.'

Alice nudged Compo out of the way and homed in on the veggie samosas. 'You've left crumbs, Compo. Just crumbs and, to be frank, I'm surprised you didn't hoover *them* up too.'

Compo stopped chewing and looked up at Gus, contrite. Alice nudged him again 'Idiot! I'm only teasing. You should know by now you're the only one that ever eats Mrs McGuire's cookies – they're perfectly vile.'

Shaking his head, Compo gulped down the last of his samosa and hand outstretched to grab another said, 'I think they're great. Dunk them in some hot chocolate and you'd never even know they're slightly charred.'

Gus patted him on the back, 'Just glad you're here to eat them, Compo. She'd be right offended if no-one ate them.'

After the others had gathered round and helped themselves to samosas, Gus called the briefing to order. 'Updates? Who's going first.' He perched himself on the corner of his desk and looked round his team. Alice and Sampson looked like they were buzzing. Sampson was grinning and Alice was flushed. Brighton sat at his desk, his expression guarded. He was the only one who hadn't availed himself of Gus' hospitality stating that he'd eaten his lunch already. Gus didn't like the vibe the other man was giving off. He felt there was an arrogance in the way he swung on the back two legs of his chair like an arrogant adolescent cheeking the teacher. He hoped Brighton had come up with the goods in his absence. That would go a long way to dispelling some of the doubts Gus had about the man.

'Sampson and I'll start, if you like?' said Alice, bouncing in her chair like an eager schoolgirl.

God thought Gus *what is it with the school analogies today. Anybody'd think I was a damn head teacher or something.* He nodded at Alice and, picking up the marker pen, stood to update the crime board as she spoke.

When she'd finished he said, 'So, none of Bazza's girls added anything other than possible underage girls from Eastern Europe and a big foreign guy in a baseball hat. Better check that out with Khan's girls. See if they've seen him. You and Sampson'll do that this after?'

Alice nodded, 'Sure. Mind you, Gus, I think there was something they were holding back. Something to do with a boyfriend, I'm sure, but they wouldn't spill. What did you think, Sampson?'

Sampson's habitual flush stole across his cheeks. 'Yeah, they looked edgy. And Armani shut them up before they slipped up.'

A loud snort interrupted Sampson and everyone turned to look at Brighton. 'Yes?' said Gus, his expression stern.

Brighton shrugged and dropped his chair back onto four legs with a bang. He grinned, 'It's just some of the names they come up with. Makes me laugh.'

Gus stared the other man out, then, 'You have a strange sense of humour, Brighton, and it's not one I appreciate, so just can it, eh?'

Brighton held Gus' gaze and swung his chair back onto two legs. Whilst his voice sounded contrite when he apologised, his look said otherwise. Gus was unconvinced of his sincerity, but let it pass.

Alice sending a dirty look in Brighton's direction said. 'I'll try with them again tomorrow, if we don't get anything else to go on. I'll take Sampson with me. He earned his stripes this afternoon at The Prossie Palace, didn't you, Sampson?'

Sampson nodded with a slight smile. 'Think I did alright.'

'Alright?' Alice looked at Gus. 'This guy had them eating out of his hand and you know how hard that can be.'

Gus grinned, remembering his first encounter with the working girls at The Prossie Palace three years previously, when it had first opened up. He'd barely made it out alive, especially after Scarlet, the ringleader had taken a fancy to him. Hats off to Sampson if he coped so well on his first visit. 'Well done, I'm in awe. I embarrassed myself totally on my first visit and couldn't get out of there quickly enough.'

Gus turned to Brighton. 'Well how did you get on this morning? Anything from the door-to-doors or the phone line?'

Brighton frowned, 'Not a bloody thing. Selective hearing and vision if you ask me. Half of them don't want to get involved, according to the troops on the ground.'

'You're probably right, but keep on top of it, will you? Something might pop. Any luck with tracing Trixie or possible similar crimes elsewhere?'

'Well, I did have a go looking for crimes with a similar MO, but nothing so far. I'll keep at it though, there's still a lot to get through. I've sent a photo of Trixie to the Bridlington area Missing Persons in the hope that something'll pop. If it's okay with you I'd like to enlist the media to circulate her photo so we reach a wider audience. Maybe that'll help.'

Gus nodded, wondering if his blow up earlier had done Brighton some good: he seemed to be pulling his weight, even if his attitude left a lot to be desired. 'Yeah, good idea. Get onto that.'

Sadia took over updating the crime boards whilst Gus updated his team on the preliminary PM report and what they'd discovered in Trixie's room. 'So, I sent two PCs to The Delius to pick Shahid Khan up, but seems he's attending a family wedding in Birmingham and isn't due back till Sunday. Naturally, the bouncer in charge doesn't know where the wedding is. I've got my contact on the Birmingham force checking out Arshad and Shahid's relatives in Birmingham. Hopefully they'll get back to us with an address soon'

Compo raised his hand, looking like a naughty schoolboy with his white shirt, now splodged with the ketchup he'd dipped his fourth samosa in. His tie hung loose with one bit flipped over his left shoulder.

'Is the baby Shahid's then, Gus?'

'Well until we get proper confirmation we can't be certain.'

'Well, in that case, do you want me just to bypass the Birmingham lot and get Shahid's relatives' addresses in Birmingham. It'll only take five minutes or so.'

Gus nearly got up and kissed Compo. 'You're a whizz kid, Compo. Do it.'

CHAPTER 33

As everyone got back to work Brighton sidled over to Sadia who was inputting her report form the morning's work on her computer. In a quiet voice, he said, 'You feeling okay, DS Khan?'

Sadia glanced at him, looking puzzled. Brighton smiled, satisfied that he'd put her on the back foot, as she said, clearly forcing a neutral tone, 'Perfectly, DC Brighton. Why?'

He shrugged. 'Just thought you looked a bit flushed like. And your hair looks a bit damp. Wondered if you're running a temperature. You know, coming down with something? Maybe you've been overdoing it?'

Sadia frowned, but continued writing, 'I'm fine, Brighton, but when I'm poorly you'll be the first to know, okay?'

Brighton nodded. 'That's good, wouldn't like to think the boss has been taking advantage of you.'

Sadia darted a glance at him, but Brighton stood hands in pocket, an innocent expression on his face. He knew she was wondering what he was up to and he enjoyed the feeling of power that gave her. He disliked her supercilious expression, her arrogant assumption that everyone would jump when she asked. Her dad was nearly as bad, but, as far as Brighton was concerned at least he was a male, albeit a Paki, so he had the right to act a bit superior. Enjoying toying with her he continued, 'Maybe you should get a bit of exercise. They say getting a bit of a sweat going is good for the endorphins you know?'

This time when Sadia looked at him, he replaced his innocent expression with a blatant smirk. Let the cow wonder what he was on about. Make her squirm. She deserved it after the way she'd treated him the previous night and judging by McGuire's reaction today she'd indulged in a bit of pillow talk. Well she'd soon see. The last laugh would be on him.

She narrowed her eyes and glared at him. 'Something on your mind Brighton?'

With pointed arrogance, he increased his smirk, raising one eyebrow to accentuate his amusement and said, 'No, nothing at all.'

He walked over to the table and helped himself to a samosa. He took a bite and then raising his voice said, 'DNA on the sperm's come through.'

'*What*?' said everyone at once, all turning to look at him.

'Came in earlier. They put it on your desk, Gus, but I picked it up in case it got misplaced.'

Gus stood up, swallowed a too large mouthful of samosa, coughed and spluttered crumbs all over his desk before moving over to Brighton and in a quiet voice said, 'What the fuck were you doing, removing things from my desk? What you should have done is contacted me straight away. What the hell were you thinking?'

Brighton glanced at Sadia, 'I thought you might be busy.'

Gus slammed his hand on the table, but kept his voice low. 'Busy? Course I'm busy. We've got three unsolved murders here. *That* evidence is crucial to the investigation. Why didn't you include it in your report a minute ago?'

Brighton blanched and his shoulders tensed. *Who the hell does McGuire think he is, talking to me like that? He wouldn't even have noticed the fucking report on his desk if not for me. Worst case scenario that idiot Compo would have spilled something on it or, at least, it would have got covered with the rest of the files everyone kept piling up there. He should be grateful to me.* He handed the report to Gus, annoyed when he noticed his hand was shaking.

Gus glanced through the report and then punched the air with his fist. *Ugly bastard,* thought Brighton as Gus' dreadlocks bounced around in his enthusiasm. *Looks downright manic with those dark rims round his pupils. Like the fucking devil. How the hell does a darkie end up with blue eyes anyway?*

With effort, Brighton managed to maintain a bland expression as Gus told the team, 'Right the sperm matches DNA on file from Shahid Khan. That places him with Trixie sometime before she was killed.' He snapped his fingers at Compo, 'Got that address in Birmingham?'

Compo nodded and pointed to the printer which had just whirred into action. Gus grabbed the printout and thrust it at Alice. 'Get Shahid Khan picked up, ASAP.'

Whilst Alice scurried off to activate the request, Brighton cleared his throat again. He knew he was pushing his luck but, if he played his cards right, he'd wouldn't have to worry about DI Gus McGuire for much bloody longer. He'd have someone with a bit more clout in his pocket. He lowered his head and feigned and apologetic look, 'Em, the fingerprint results from the bottle came through too.'

'Give me bloody strength' said Gus, grabbing his head with both hands 'Don't tell me the fingerprints are Hussain's too?'

Covering his smirk, Brighton continued, his tone placatory, 'No, No they're not. They belong to one Patrick O'Donnell, previously arrested on public disorder.'

Gus ran his fingers across his forehead, 'Please someone tell me why Patrick O'Donnell sounds familiar?'

Sampson stood up. 'Well, sir, when I was in bookings, I remember one Patrick O'Donnell got picked up most weekends. Special needs like, you know? Alcoholic but simple as well. Tended to sit outside the church singing hymns all night so the locals couldn't get to sleep on a Saturday night. That church near the allotments, now I come to think of it, St Augustine's, I think it is.'

'Right, Sampson, see if you can locate him and bring him in. If he's drunk, try to sober him up with black coffee and sandwiches.'

Gus turned back to Brighton and said, 'I suppose Doc McGuire's written report's back too?'

Brighton sifted through a pile of papers on the desk. 'Yes, it's here too. Looks exactly like you said; cause of death, strangulation. Evidence of unprotected sexual activity. No evidence of rough sex, unlike with whore one. Tox report's not in yet, though.'

For seconds everyone in the room stood still, waiting for Gus' response. Brighton knew he'd blown the placatory attempt. Fuck's sake why'd they have to be so PC about everything? The girl was a whore and no using fancy terms, like sex worker, changed the fact that they opened their orifices, in exchange for cash, from any punter that happened to take a fancy to them.

Gus' response blasted across the room like a firebrand. 'Are you a fucking arsehole on purpose or can you just not help it, Brighton? If you've got Tourette's, get it diagnosed and I'll ignore your disgusting unfeelingness for the deceased, otherwise get yourself a dictionary and look up some respectful ways to refer to murder victims. You are seriously trying my patience and its only day one.'

Gus turned away, but swiftly swivelled back his sharp features pinched in anger 'and while we're at it my "dad" as you call him, has a title. He's a renowned and well respected

167

pathologist and it is in *that* capacity, *not* in the capacity of being my parent, that he makes his post-mortem reports.' And prodding Brighton fiercely in the chest he ended, 'Use his bloody title.'

CHAPTER 34
M1 North

Shahid was content to let Imti drive. He was by far the better driver and he didn't get stressed by the motorway queues in the same way Shahid did. Besides which, Shahid had enough to worry about. They'd finally dragged themselves away from their cousin's wedding. He'd noticed that despite his uncle's obvious sincerity in begging them to stay longer, his aunt had looked distinctly relieved to see the back of them. There was no love lost between Shahid and her, although to give her her due she did always treat Imti as if he was one of her own kids and that redeemed her in Shahid's book. She could be a prize bitch to him as long as she kept her toxic attitude away from Imti.

What had started as mild annoyance with Trixie for not picking up the previous night had escalated to outright anger after a couple of hours. However, now, nearly twenty-four hours later, Shahid's anger had given way to a deep and persistent sense of foreboding. This was so not like Trix. Yeah, she could be a bit erratic but they had something to celebrate now. She was happy and he was getting ready to move her away from Bazza. He bit his fingernail, grimacing when he drew blood and wondered if Jessica had something to do with Trixie's radio silence. He'd promised Trixie he'd let her break the news to Jess, but who knew how she would've reacted.

His phone rang, breaking him out of his thoughts. He flicked the screen, saw Jai's name on the screen and answered. 'What's up, Jai?'

169

Frowning, he listened as Jai explained that the police had been round looking for him. What the hell did they want? He'd not got anything dodgy on the go at the minute. Nothing that warranted a piggy visit anyway. When he hung up, he glanced at Imti who had turned the music down in order to listen into the conversation. He was tempted to ask Imti to contact Sadia Hussain to see if she knew what was going on, but decided against it. It was probably about Camilla and Starlight and, as he knew nothing about their deaths, he reckoned he needn't worry about the police for now. Not when he had Trixie to worry about.

Halfway through explaining to Imti what Jai had said his phone rang again, this time it was his Uncle Majid. Assuming that Imti, as usual, had forgotten something, Shahid grinned at his brother and answered, 'What's he forgotten this time, Uncle?'

However, when he heard the police had gone to the trouble of tracking him down at his uncle's house, Shahid felt the first stirrings of unease form in the pit of his stomach.

This didn't seem like just routine enquiries. This had the feel of something altogether more serious. Why else would they track him down in Birmingham when he was due back in Bradford soon?

Hanging up, he looked at Imti. 'Put your foot down, Imti, something's not right.'

He just hoped it wasn't anything to do with Trixie.

CHAPTER 35
The Fort

Gus walked over to a chair carrying his umpteenth mug of coffee of the day in one hand and a sheaf of papers in the other. He sat down and rolled his shoulder. A stab wound to that shoulder had been followed, a few months later, by a bullet wound earlier in the year and it was prone to seize up if he didn't move it regularly – and for the past couple of hours he'd been hunched over his desk doing paper work. The office radiators, which, for some obscure reason, were regulated centrally, blasted out heat making him feel lethargic. Raising his arm up to stretch his stiff shoulder, he exhaled before pulling his jumper off. He tucked his shirt back into his jeans, grimacing when he noticed the numerous creases he'd hoped would stay hidden under his jumper when he'd put it on this morning. He really did need to get on top of his laundry. Either that or invest in some crease-free shirts for work.

Glancing up, he saw Alice grinning at him. God, couldn't a man forget to do his ironing without getting found out? He jutted his chin out, 'Yeah, got something to say, Cooper?'

Her grin widened, 'Not a word boss. Your sartorial elegance is, as usual, unsurpassed by us mere mortals who utilise irons.'

Trying to hide his embarrassment he opted for an indignant response. 'Hmph! Waste of bloody time ironing clothes. All it does is add to global warming.'

'Yeah, yeah if you say so.' Alice took a bite of a Mars bar and chewed. 'You know you could just pay someone to do your ironing if it's an issue.'

Gus looked at her, assuming she was taking the piss but she looked quite serious. Did people really pay to have their ironing done? Hmm, maybe he could ask Mo's wife if she knew someone who'd do it... then again, maybe not. He could imagine the slagging he'd get from Mo. Pushing the pile of paperwork away from him, Gus stood, stretching his leg. 'Apparently, Shahid Khan's on his way back from Birmingham. What do you reckon to the DNA results, Al? Think he's the father?'

'I think those letters you found in her room combined with the fact that it's his sperm is pretty conclusive evidence of some sort of relationship with Trixie.' Alice perched on the edge of Gus' desk and, popping the last of her Mars, into her mouth, she chewed furiously before continuing, 'Maybe a relationship gone bad? I mean the unprotected sex makes me think "relationship" as opposed to a quick shag. I mean, why would Khan, with all those girls of his, fraternise with one of Bazza's if there wasn't something more to it?' She licked her fingers and popped the wrapper into an empty Irn Bru can, that stood on Gus' desk. 'Most of the women are pretty health-conscious, you know? The Prossie Palace drums it into them. Mind you Trixie was a recovering addict, maybe she lapsed and took a risk in exchange for a quick fix... but it doesn't seem Shahid's style, does it?'

Gus had been thinking that himself. Khan wasn't the sort to fraternise with the enemy's girls, nor was he the sort to take unnecessary health risks. Besides which Trixie's tox screen results had come back. 'There were no drugs in her blood. Jess said she was clean and it looks like she was right. Hopefully, we'll find out more from Khan when we pull him in. What I'm having difficulty with is working out if the three murders are linked or not. Trixie's makes me feel uneasy'

'Okay, we have a relationship between Trixie and Khan, but what about the other girls? Are all three murders linked or not?' asked Alice

'Why were Patrick's fingerprints on Trixie's bottle when the others were wiped completely clean?' said Gus standing up and stretching his leg using the rubber physio band that looped around one leg of his desk.

'Well,' said Alice, jumping down and moving back to her own desk, 'My money's on two perps, the second being a copycat. I reckon Khan did Trixie in a fit of passion and then tried to cover up by using the bottle. After all, he knows exactly how Camilla and Starlight died.'

'It's one theory, but let's keep our options open. I'm still intrigued by the report from The Prossie Palace of the Eastern European girl being beaten by an unidentified punter. We need to look into a possible takeover bid from an external company. I'm waiting on reports from Vice about that.'

'I suppose Sadia will be interviewing Khan with you, Gus?'

Gus shook his head. He knew Alice still thought he was favouring Sadia but he couldn't be arsed getting into that at the minute. 'No, Alice, it'll be you and me. Sadia's close to his brother Imti and she knows Shahid. She'll not be involved in this aspect of the investigation.'

CHAPTER 36

Sampson heard Patrick O'Donnell before he saw him and, following his dulcet tones along the corridor, he also smelled him first. Alcohol fumes floated after him, strong but unfortunately, not strong enough to cover the fetid stench of his unwashed body or the waft of dried urine that seemed determined to clog Sampson's throat. Raising an eyebrow at the duty officer who had escorted O'Donnell up to the interview room Sampson said, 'Give him a trough full of black coffee will you, Bob. Maybe he'll sober up enough to be interviewed in a bit.'

Bob humphed, shaking his head, 'It'll take more than coffee to sober *him* up.'

Sampson suspected he was right but he knew he had to try anyway. Neither he nor Gus held high hopes of the interview with Patrick O'Donnell proving fruitful but they had to try. It seemed likely that O'Donnell had just chucked the empty bottle in the allotments and the killer had just grabbed it to use on Trixie. Mind you, that didn't explain why he hadn't wiped the prints off this time like he had with the other two women. Maybe he had been disturbed.

Sampson looked through the peep hole and saw Patrick O'Donnell sprawled on a chair, legs spread out, revealing a spreading wet patch blossoming out from his groin area. From the bottom of his trouser leg urine dripped in an expanding puddle. His head was flung back and quite clearly his lungs were in excellent working order as he belted out an upbeat rendition of *Onward Christian Soldiers*. Lovely! No wonder the locals complained. O'Donnell's singing was bloody tortuous.

By the time he'd managed to interview O'Donnell, Sampson had been regaled with *The Lord's My Shepherd*, *All Things Bright and Beautiful* and a rather ponderous rendition of *Once In Royal David's City*. It appeared that O'Donnell's choices were not entirely seasonal. It was also very clear that the only murder committed by the warbler, was of the songs he sang with unmelodious gusto.

CHAPTER 37

Gus' nerves felt frazzled and he knew it was because he'd drunk too much coffee today. He usually limited himself knowing that an excess of caffeine often preceded a panic attack, but, in the middle of a big case he often found it difficult to find the time to make a pot of decaffeinated. He was just considering making himself some when Sadia walked over to his desk. He raised an eyebrow and waited. He knew from her expression and the way she looked round at her colleagues, who were engrossed in their work, that she was about to ask him something he might not be happy with. She bit her lower lip. Yes, she was after a favour of some sort. Hope it was nothing to do with cutting Shahid Khan some slack. No, he corrected himself. She wouldn't ever ask him to compromise an investigation, especially not for the likes of Shahid Khan. He leaned back, linking his hands behind his head and waited.

'I want to look out the files of Jessica's mum's death. Maybe we'll find something there that'll give us an in with Shahid. It's quite interesting that Khan was there that night *and* smelling of petrol and we've got a witness who will say that.'

Gus studied her for a moment. He knew from the way she avoided meeting his eyes that there was more to this than she'd revealed. He considered his response then said, 'That was a long time ago, Sadia. It's a cold case and it's not directly relevant to this. I'm not sure I can justify one of my officers spending time looking into something with such a tenuous link to our current case.'

Sadia's shoulders slumped and he saw a tell-tale flush spread across her cheeks as she glanced at Alice and then

176

lowered her tone. 'It's Jess. She begged me to look into it and…' biting her lip, she wrung her hands together, her face anguished, 'I sort of promised. I know it's not related really and I know it happened years ago, but Jessica is convinced Shahid killed her mother. Stands to reason that if he did that, he might just as easily be responsible for these murders.'

'There's a vast difference between the isolated killing of a woman twenty years ago and the current three murders linked by a similar MO, Sadia.'

'Yeah, I know, but maybe there's something to it. Stranger things have happened.'

On the one hand, Gus was sceptical but, on the other, he had to admit to some curiosity about the Millie Green case. It seemed strange that no-one had ever been held accountable for it. Especially, with Millie's links to Arshad Khan. He'd have thought the police would've been all over it, hoping to get something on him. Aware that Alice was earwigging Gus said, 'And what do you think? Don't you think you're a bit too emotionally involved in all of this?'

Gus hated interrogating her like this, but he'd no intention of treating her any differently from the rest of the team. If she wanted to follow a lead away from the main investigation then she'd have to justify it, just like any of the others would.

She sighed, 'I'm not sure. Maybe I am. It's just I *saw* it, Gus. I saw Millie Green burn to death that night. I was just a kid myself but I *know* Shahid loved Millie. She was like a mother to him. I can't see that he'd do it. Not really. His dad maybe, but not Shahid… but someone did, didn't they? And, whoever it was, they've got off scot free.' She brushed away a tear and sniffed, 'I just want Jess to have some closure. If I can prove that Shahid didn't do it, maybe Shahid and Imti and her could be a family together.'

'And if he did?'

'Well then he deserves to rot in hell then, doesn't he?'

As Alice walked over to join them, Gus saw Sadia tense and he wanted to bang their heads together. Why the hell couldn't they just get on? He had enough to think about without their damn nonsense. He hoped Alice wasn't going to stir things up.

'Look, Sad,' said Alice, 'what if you do prove Shahid didn't kill Jess' mum, but then we find out he killed her best friend. What then?'

Sadia's eyes narrowed and, still looking at Gus, she said, her tone abrupt, 'At least Jessica would know Shahid hadn't killed her mother *and* she'd see him put away for Trixie's murder.'

Lowering her tone as if to exclude Alice she continued, 'I don't want to cover owt up, Gus. I just want to help Jess out. She's had a shit life to date and this is hanging over her. Just let me have a look at the files. I'll do it in my own time.'

Gus looked from Sadia to Alice. Alice grinned at him and nodded moving slightly closer to Sadia. 'Can't do any harm can it, Gus? She says she'll do it in her own time, so where's the harm?'

Never in a million years would he understand women. First they're at loggerheads now they're acting like co-conspirators. He threw his arms up in the air. 'Fine. In your own time only though, okay?'

Shaking his head, he watched, incredulous as Sadia turned and hugged Alice. He saw Alice's blush as she extricated herself from Sadia's hold and judged she was happy. He was just about to say something about a group hug when the door clattered open and DCS Hussain walked in. He looked briefly round the room, acknowledging the officers and then looked at Gus, his face stern. 'Update please, McGuire'

Hiding his annoyance at being spoken to so abruptly in front of his team, Gus moved round to the boards and began to explain where they were with the case and that they were waiting on Shahid Khan's imminent return to Bradford to interview him. He noticed that, on her father's entrance, Sadia had moved to sit next to Alice at her desk, where she now sat, hands clasped in front of her and her head bowed. From the corner of his eye he saw Alice flash her a supportive smile and was pleased that the tension between his two detective sergeants appeared to be easing, at least for the time being.

Whilst Gus summarised, DCS Hussain, pulled out a chair and sat next to Sampson. Gus inwardly groaned when he saw Sampson's face flush. Sampson and the DCS had had a run-in on their previous case and he knew Sampson was nervous in his vicinity. He wished the lad wouldn't exhibit any weakness because, in his experience, the likes of Hussain fed on their victim's insecurities

DCS Hussain frowned at Sampson and said 'Don't slouch boy, you're a police officer, for goodness sake. Look like one!' After ascertaining that the long cold pizza was halal, he helped himself to a slice. Gus hoped he choked on it, supercilious bastard that he was, and catching Sampson's tightened lips he realised he too shared the sentiment.

With the DCS nodding periodically, Gus, hoping that the creases in his shirt had fallen out or that Hussain wouldn't notice them and see fit to humiliate him any more in front of everyone, mentioned Jessica's assertion that Shahid Khan had murdered her mother and was surprised when DCS Hussain got abruptly to his feet, and interrupted him.

179

'Solving these current murders seems to be stretching your limited capabilities quite enough without you bothering about a case that's well and truly in the past. I'm very disappointed in your performance thus far, McGuire. I'd have expected results by now, not a hotchpotch of loose ends. For Goodness' sake, you haven't even interviewed your main suspect in this case and yet, you're thinking about a red herring from twenty years ago. Not satisfactory, McGuire, not satisfactory at all.'

Gus, heart accelerated in response to the other man's antagonistic tone. There was no need for him to adopt that tone and especially not in front of his team. Never in his police career had Gus come across anyone as abrasive as DCS Hussain. His previous boss, DCI Chalmers, had an emotional intelligence in dealing with the team that brought the best from them. Hussain, on the other hand, seemed to believe that humiliating, criticising and badgering was the way to get results. He felt a compulsion to slam his fist into his boss's face, yet, when he spoke, he somehow managed to kept his tone neutral. 'A crime's a crime, sir. If I can rattle Hussain by using Millie Green's murder, then I will.'

DCS Husain's expression darkened, 'I don't want you wasting time and resources on the word of a prostitute, McGuire… and *that's* an order!'

Gus heard Sadia's sharp intake of breath, but he kept his gaze on her father who was too busy smirking at Gus to notice that she'd stood up, until she spoke.

'Excuse me, sir,' she said.

Gus winced, hearing the insincerity dripping from each word and hoping that her father would be so far up his own arse that he'd be oblivious to her tone. What exactly was she playing at? This was not the time for her to put herself in the firing line. He was perfectly capable of withstanding whatever acerbic slights Hussain could throw at him.

DCS Hussain turned towards his daughter, frowning as if surprised to see here there. With an abrupt hand movement, he gestured for her to sit down. 'Yes, Sadia, what is it? You don't need to stand on ceremony, I'm your father after all.'

Sadia, hands clenched into fists by her side, did not move. 'I'll stand if you don't mind, sir.'

Hussain sighed and waved his hand in a dismissive manner that again made Gus want to clock him one. 'Have it your own way, child.'

Gus thrust his hands into his pockets, his face like thunder, wondering if the other man chose his words deliberately to patronise or, if he was just an arse. He suspected a combination of the two.

Sadia, her cheeks flushed, thrust her chin out and continued, 'Jessica Green *is* a prostitute but, she *wasn't* one when her mother burned to death before her eyes. She was a child, younger than me. No one ever listened to her or helped her. She believed Shahid Khan killed her mother on his father's instructions and I think she's got a point. Surely we can at least investigate it, sir?'

Noting the pointed hesitation before she said 'sir', Gus sighed, willing her to take the challenging look off her face, as she glared at her father. Why did she always have to be so bloody confrontational? Didn't she realise that this was a battle she wasn't going to win and that drawing attention to it would just make it more difficult for her to look into the Millie Green case without her father finding out. Whilst finding her honest bravery commendable, Gus thought she had a lot to earn about diplomacy.

DCS Hussain shook his head, in a way that reminded Gus of his nursery teacher when he'd done something silly. 'You were always too impetuous, Sadia. Too quick to believe what you're told. That's not a good trait in a DS. Insh'Allah, you will outgrow it one day and then, maybe, you'll be worthy of your position.'

Gus opened his mouth to respond but before he could object to his superior officer's assertions, Hussain continued. 'No, I won't sanction reopening that investigation. It was investigated robustly at the time. Clear up here and I'll be happy. Is that understood?' he glared, first at his daughter and then at Gus, adding, 'You need to keep better control of your team, McGuire.' He glanced at Sampson. 'We've had trouble with them before.'

Taking another slice of pizza, he looked at Gus, 'As the investigation isn't progressing as quickly as I'd like, I've taken the liberty of making an appointment for you to consult with a forensic psychologist. A Professor Carlton. Tomorrow at 2pm, Leeds Trinity University. There is a serial killer at large and *you* could do with some expert help on this one.'

A sudden flash of anger, burst through Gus. Not because he'd been told to consult with a forensic psychologist – he admired their skills and welcomed their contributions to profiling offenders. No, Gus was pissed off that Hussain had made the appointment without consulting him first. When he replied, his tone was clipped but polite. 'With all due respect DCS Hussain, much as I welcome the input, I'd rather make my own appointments. If you give me the number, I'll reschedule the appointment to a more convenient time.'

Hussain stood, his thin lips in a semblance of a smile, 'No, McGuire. I'm issuing a direct order to you. You *will* consult with Professor Carlton at the time given. I thought you'd be champing at the bit to get some input from a renowned psychologist who has worked for a number of years at Quantico. Or… perhaps you think *you're* better qualified.'

The last statement, Gus knew, was a dig at his own degree in forensic psychology that had got him on the fast track scheme in the first place. He knew Hussain devalued the work of fast-tracked graduates at every opportunity. Gus was fine with that when it was merited. He was all too aware that some of his fellow fast-trackers had fallen short of the expectations their superiors had placed on them. However, he was equally aware that he was one of the success stories, with a proven track record behind him.

Feeling ready to explode at the man's arsiness, Gus took a deep breath as Hussain walked out, closing the door behind him. For seconds the air held a palpable chill before, as one, everyone released a huge breath. Then, just as they relaxed, the air was sucked from the room, when Hussain popped his head back round the door and spoke to his daughter.

'Shamila phoned for you last night, Sadia. Strange really, as I was sure you said you were with her.' He shrugged and smiled in, what Gus knew, reeked of insincerity. 'Never mind, beti, we can clear that little mystery up tonight after prayers, can't we?' and he pulled the door closed with a sharp click.

Sadia's face paled and she glanced at Gus, who shook his head with a worried smile. *Shit, it looked like Sadia would be in for it tonight.* Although she'd told him repeatedly how domineering and controlling her father was, Gus had, until now thought she must be exaggerating. However, the behaviour he'd just witnessed left him in no doubt that every word Sadia had told him was true.

The next thing he knew was that Alice had grabbed Sadia's hand and was dragging her from the room announcing, 'Toilet break, now. Come on.'

CHAPTER 38

Brighton had watched the interaction from behind his computer screen feeling smug. Earlier he'd seen what appeared to be a thaw in relations between Alice and Sadia when they'd been blabbing on to McGuire about something or other. They'd lowered their voices, so he'd been unable to work out what had caused this. However, from the bitch's reaction to her father's orders regarding the Millie Green murder, followed by Alice's almost immediate evacuation, Sadia in tow, he surmised it had been concerning this.

He intimated to Gus that he was taking a smoking break and, humming under his breath, left the incident room in time to see the two women disappear into the ladies' loos. He'd give anything to be a fly on the wall during their conversation in there.

Finding himself alone in the smoker's shelter to the side of The Fort entrance, he used the time to consider his next actions. How soon should he give DCS Hussain the evidence he'd compiled about McGuire and the DCS's spoilt daughter? He'd do it anonymously if could. He knew only too well how often it was the messenger who was shot and he'd no intention of succumbing to that fate. However, Hussain had entrusted him to keep an eye on his precious daughter and the rest of McGuire's team, and he'd agreed. With the prospect of a promotion looming on the horizon, Brighton couldn't risk DCS Hussain finding out about Sadia and McGuire himself. No, he'd just need to bite the bullet and hope things would work out.

He inhaled deeply, savouring the hit of smoke in his lungs. He'd print the photos off tonight and take them personally to the DCS in the morning. He grinned. Then he could sit back and watch the fireworks fly. DI McGuire's days would be numbered and that bitch would be put on a tight leash. She'd probably be shipped off to Pakistan to marry her cousin or something… that's what Pakis did after all. Yeah, that would be even better, and whilst McGuire was busy sorting out his career, Brighton could get his feet under the table by playing Hussain and McGuire off against each other. He frowned. He'd have to play it carefully though. He'd maybe been a bit too obviously disruptive earlier with the DNA and PM reports. Better ingratiate myself a bit more with McGuire and not rock the boat.

Brighton flicked his cigarette towards the large metal ashtray and made his way back indoors as two bits of skirt from the offices walked into the shelter. As the women lit up Brighton eyed them up. One was a bit fat for his liking but the other? Well, he wouldn't kick her out of the bed for farting, that's for sure.

CHAPTER 39

S adia followed Alice down the corridor and into the ladies' toilet where, she watched with barely concealed amusement as Alice checked each cubicle and, after ascertaining that they were empty, locked the external door and turned to face Sadia. Hands on her hips, she looked like an indignant elf. 'Bloody hell, Sadia, what are you up to?'

Sadia raised one eyebrow, feigning puzzlement, 'What, Al?'

Alice snorted, inelegant as ever. Again, Sadia refrained from smiling, sensing the other girl was in no mood to be teased.

'Don't you "what?" me, Sadia. Spit it out, right now!'

In an attempt to delay responding, Sadia turned and began to fill the sink with cold water. A single glance in the mirror that ran behind the row of sinks confirmed that her face looked clammy and pale after the run-in with her father. Reaching round Alice, she grabbed a handful of paper towels and dampened them in the basin before mopping her face. Studying Alice's reflection, she wondered what exactly it was that Alice wanted her to 'spit out'. Not wanting to give anything away, she hedged her bets. 'Not sure what you're on about, Alice. It's not news to anyone that me and my dad don't get on very well.'

'Look, I'm not a bloody idiot, you know?' Alice huffed and, folding her arms over her chest, she leaned her bottom against the adjacent sink and glared as Sadia began to dry her face.

Turning to face her, Sadia knew that Alice wasn't going to let her get away with this so easily and she was proved right when Alice straightened and, chin jutting out, said, 'How long's it been going on?'

Sadia tossed her used towels into the bin, 'Don't know what you're talking about.'

'You and Gus aren't keeping an eye on me because of what happened in Brent are you?'

Sadia frowned. God, had Alice really thought she was spying on her? No wonder things had been chilly between them for the past few weeks. 'Hell no, Alice. I wouldn't do that. Neither would Gus. If someone wanted you monitored, Gus would have told you up front. He doesn't do stuff behind the team's back.'

Alice grinned. 'Yeah, that's what he said too. So, you and Gus have nothing going on that you're keeping from the rest of the team.?'

Sadia felt her cheeks colour as she tried to maintain eye contact with Alice without flinching. Finally, when it was clear Alice wasn't going to budge she flung her hands in the air, 'Okay, what do you *think* you know?'

Alice's grin deepened, 'Well, judging by the way Gus looked ready to clout your dad when he spoke to you like that, I'd say Gus has more than just a professional interest in you. It's me you're talking to, Sad, and in case you wondered, I'm not bloody stupid.'

Deciding that one more bluff was worth a try, Sadia looked straight at Alice and, tone firm, said, 'Rubbish! You've got an over-active imagination, Alice, that's all.'

Alice laughed. 'Yeah right and the way you looked when your dad was being arsy with Gus wasn't more personal than professional, was it? I knew it. I should have guessed last night, but I got myself all aeriated about Brent'

'Oh Alice,' said Sadia, her voice angry, 'Let London go. It's finished. Over. You've been exonerated. Graham Willis was the bad officer not you. We all know that.'

Alice shook her head, 'Stop deflecting, Sadia.'

Sadia closed her eyes and shook her head slowly from side to side for effect.

Alice nudged her, 'Again, at the risk of repeating myself, you and Gus are getting it on.' And, in what Sadia considered to be a childish tone, but one that nevertheless had her creasing up with laughter, Alice began to sing, 'Gus and Sadia up a tree K.I.S.S.I.N.G…'

Sadia, realising that she was beaten, nudged Alice, 'Okay, okay shut up! Yes, we're in a relationship. We didn't want everyone to know. Mainly because of what my dad would do, but also because it's new and with him being my boss it's a bit iffy. Not that he makes any exceptions for me.' As soon as the words left her mouth Sadia felt a huge weight lift from her shoulders. The past few months had been a strain. Keeping secrets wasn't in her nature and she was relieved to finally share it with someone other than Gus.

Alice sniffed, 'Well, I'm relieved to be honest. I was going round the twist thinking you two didn't trust me,' she cocked her head to one side, 'Professionally that is, because of course you didn't actually trust me on a *personal* level.' She paused and face serious she looked at Sadia, 'What are you going to do, Sad?'

Sadia shook her head. After her dad's performance she felt even more confused. She loved him, course she did, but right at this minute she wanted to disown him. Did he have to be such a pompous git with the team. And the way he'd treated Sampson? That was just unforgiveable… it was nothing short of bullying. 'Gus thinks I should tell him but I can't. He'd destroy Gus. His career, his life and maybe even Doc McGuire's, too. He's got weight you know he could make sure Doc McGuire doesn't work for us again.'

'I don't get it. Gus is great. A good guy. Doesn't womanise, holds a good job.'

Sadia smiled. She was well used to this sort of reaction. At school she'd constantly had to explain aspects of her culture to her non-Muslim friends. But this was something she didn't really have an explanation for... it just was. 'Gus isn't Muslim, Alice, and if he's not Muslim, my dad won't even consider him.'

'It's serious then?'

'Oh, yeah,' said Sadia, tears rolling down her cheeks, 'But I know how it will end.'

Alice frowned, 'How?'

'Gus hurt again and me married to some bloke I hardly know.' She hated the tone of self-pity in her voice.

Alice snorted, 'Oh, get real, Sadia. You're twenty-five. You're a woman not a little girl. He can't decide for you.'

Sadia realised how limp she was being, but she just didn't know what she could do about it. How could she keep everyone happy when they all wanted and expected very different things?

'No, you're right. My dad can't decide for me. He'll just make the options very clear and then leave it for me to decide.'

'Well, that's okay then.'

'You don't understand Alice. I'll have to let Gus go. Since my mum died I'm all my dad's got left. He brought me up almost single-handedly. My mum was never in very good health and I can't repay him in this way.'

'Have you spoken to Gus about all this? Surely there's a solution.'

Sadia smiled. 'I did mention the possibility of him reverting to Islam, but as you can imagine that didn't go down too well.'

Alice snorted. 'God, I can imagine. Gus has got no time for religion, I can't see him becoming Muslim, but, at the end of the day, Sadia, your dad's not God. He can't touch Gus or the Doc, for that matter.'

'Hmm, you don't know my dad.'

CHAPTER 40
Thornbury

Serafina had stayed late at school hoping to find out how Hasnain was doing, but the last she'd heard was that he was still critical in Bradford Royal Infirmary. Of course she felt responsible. Hasnain's friend, Benny's words kept reverberating in her mind. She was certain in her own mind that Anastazy was behind the attack and it was her fault that he'd done this. Now, her mood matching the drizzle that speckled the streets and the darkness that the warm glow of streetlights did little to dispel, she trudged home. Anxiety had made her restless so she'd trudged down the side streets to the interchange before catching her bus up Leeds Road to Thornbury. The hustle of crowded bodies, in damp steaming clothes had done nothing to restore her spirits as she waited for her stop, near the Pakeezah supermarket.

Memories of Anastazy's taunting face at the bus window before he 'shot' Hasnain merged with the hatred on Benny's face when he'd heard about Hasnain until both became contorted in the pool of blood she'd seen in the Lidl car park. She felt like throwing up and even her crucifix offered her no comfort as she jumped from the bus, and headed home.

Pushing open the front door and stepping into the warm hallway, Serafina felt a frisson of fear. Something was different, the atmosphere felt heavy, the air malevolent and stagnant. She hesitated, head cocked to one side and then it clicked. The Polish radio station her mum normally listened to was silent. Her mum's gentle humming, as she pottered about the kitchen was absent and there was no sign of her father upstairs getting ready for his night shift. Heart hammering, she threw her school bag in the corner near her brothers' discarded trainers and, coat half-fastened, she burst through the kitchen door and ground to a sudden halt.

Seeing her mother standing by the sink, her father beside her with his arms round her shoulders she felt immediate relief followed by the realisation that something must be very wrong for her father to hold her mother so. The most affection they ever shared was her mother's clipped civility in response to her father's silent expectations. Her eldest brother, Jacob leaned against the back wall and, as Serafina's glance drifted over him to the figure seated at the table, she noted his fists were clenched by his side. A jolt of fear had her raising her hand in silent warning, her eyes wide and pleading as she willed him to be quiet. Thankfully, neither Luka nor Thomas were present.

She turned, eyes flashing, to Anastazy, who straddled a chair, his arms balanced along its back grinning and swallowed. Her instincts told her to march over and pummel him till he admitted what he'd done to Hasnain, but, fortunately, her survival instincts kicked in before she could move. Anastazy had hurt Hasnain because of her and now, his presence in her home was a clear threat against her family. This was his way of telling her that, not only *could* he hurt anyone she cared about but that he most definitely *would*.

Unable to contain herself, Serafina glared at him, her chest heaving. Finally, speaking in Polish she said, 'You are an animal. Why did you do that to Hasnain? He's just a boy. You had no need to hurt him.'

Anastazy's grin deepened. He glanced at her parents, 'Your daughter has spirit, but maybe she needs to be taught respect.' He scraped his chair back and jumped to his feet in one fluid motion. Before either Serafina or Jacob could protest, he grabbed her mother by the hair and dragged her to the centre of the room.

Serafina looked at her dad but he stood motionless his expression unreadable. Why didn't he react? Why hadn't he done something? Cursing in Polish under her breath, Serafina ran over, tears flooding her face, and managed to grab Anastazy's arm as he pulled it back, his hand formed into a fist ready to punch her mother. 'Okay, okay. I am sorry. I'm sorry. I spoke out of turn. Please don't hurt my mother.'

Anastazy jerked away from her grasping hands and followed the punch through, hitting her mother on the jaw. He let her arm go and she slid to the ground. Serafina hands covering her mouth, looked with appalled eyes from Anastazy to her father, who remained glued to his position by the sink. With her eyes she beseeched him to do something, but he looked straight through her a strange half-smile on his lips. Realising he wasn't going to move to help his wife, Serafina stepped forward and helped her sobbing mother to her feet.

Behind her Jacob roared and she felt a waft of air as he lunged towards Anastazy. Releasing her mother, Serafina spun on her heel and placed herself between the two men. 'No Jacob, no! Let me deal with this. It's me he wants. I'll handle this.' She forced her brother to look her in the eyes and begging him to back down. Breathing heavily, Jacob took a step back and lowered his arm.

Anastazy laughed and spat in Jacob's face. Head on one side, eyes narrowed he waited for a reaction. Jacob, a muscle in his cheek the only outwards sign of his anger looked at Serafina, who shook her head. He backed off to the sink and running cold water on a cloth, he began to dab it on his mother's bleeding lips. Serafina kept her eyes lowered in what she hoped looked like supplication to Anastazy but, beneath her lowered lashes they sparked in anger. 'What do you want?'

Anastazy leaned close to her, put his index finger under her chin and jerked her head upwards. Serafina made her expression neutral. He leaned in closer until she could smell a nauseous combination of nicotine and garlic. Trying not to flinch, she held her breath and waited. As if in slow motion, he lowered his mouth to hers and captured her lips, thrusting his tongue between them, as if he owned her. Then his hands reached up and grabbed her breasts, squeezing tightly, causing a small squeal to leave her mouth. Serafina heard her brother's sharp intake of breath, as if from a distance and a single tear, escaping her closed eye, rolled down her cheek. Reaching up, she surreptitiously touched her crucifix, praying that, Jacob would find the strength to ignore Anastazy's provocation.

After what seemed like an eternity, he lifted his mouth from hers and leered into her face before tugging her hair hard. 'You are mine, Serafina, don't you forget it!' He pushed her away and marched over to the door. Hesitating, he turned and allowed his malignant gaze to drift over each of them in turn before speaking. 'You know what will happen if you speak out of turn about that boy don't you?' When Serafina nodded, he smiled and said, 'I'll be back!'

After the bang of the front door had signified his departure Serafina stood motionless, her eyes closed. Had that really just happened? Her heart began to slow and her thoughts became more ordered. Anastazy had just issued a warning and she knew it was one she would have to pay heed to. The way he'd punched her mother made his intentions perfectly clear. She glanced at her mum who

Jacob had seated at the kitchen table. She held a damp rag to her mouth and her eyes shimmered with tears. Jacob spoke reassuring words into the silent room. Her father hadn't moved since Anastazy's departure.

Serafina pushed out her tongue to lick her dry lips and the sharp taste of nicotine made her stomach heave. She rushed over to the sink and vomited.

CHAPTER 41
The Fort

It was one of those nights when all Gus wanted to do was get out of The Fort. He'd already taken an hour out for a swim up at the university but it didn't seem to have hit the mark… He still felt lethargic and although some of his anger with DCS Hussain had receded, the lingering tension in his shoulders persisted. He knew he needed to let it go before it consumed him. He was also pretty fed up that Shahid Khan had still not been found. The police had gone to his uncle's house in Birmingham, interrupting the wedding and, no doubt, doing sod all for community relations in the process, but Shahid had already left for Bradford. To date there'd been no sight of him.

Looking out the window, the heat from the radiators blasting onto his face, he wished he was anywhere but here. Heaton woods would be a great place to be. Well, maybe not at this time of night in the dark and probably not in the torrential rain that had just begun to splatter against the window, distorting his reflection in the glass. He turned away, considering packing up for the night when his desk phone rang. It appeared that Shahid Khan had presented himself voluntarily for interview and was now in an interview room. According to the duty officer, Shahid had said he'd learned of Trixie's murder from his bouncer, on his return from a family wedding in Birmingham and had come to 'help you lot catch the bastard who did this.'

Gus walked down the corridor to the interview room with Alice in tow. The duty officer had, as per Gus' instructions, put Shahid in one of the less hospitable rooms and Gus had

197

waited half an hour before entering the room. No reason to make it easy for Khan: after all, at the moment, he was one of their main suspects. Gus was intrigued that Khan had opted to come into the station. There was no love lost between him and the police, so what had prompted his compliance?

Khan, Gus presumed, was still wearing his wedding clothes. The Asian suit was far too ornate to be normal daily wear, besides which Gus reckoned Khan wasn't the sort to wear traditional clothes if it wasn't for a special occasion. Gus nodded at Shahid and sat down, Alice beside him, whilst Shahid continued to pace the floor, the fabric of his suit rustling as he moved. Gus' eyes narrowed as he tried to gauge the younger man's mood. Shahid looked upset, his eyes were red rimmed and Gus wondered if this was because of Trixie's death. Clearing his throat, he began, 'Well, Mr Khan, it's really good of you to come for this little chat. Could you confirm that you are Shahid Khan?'

Khan, pulled a chair out and sat straight backed in the chair. In an exaggerated gesture he raised his arm, elbow bent and flipping his cuff back with a finger, he looked at the state-of-the-art Rolex watch on his wrist. He looked at Gus and inclined his head. Gus could almost feel the frustration oozing from the other man's pores. He didn't feel bad for keeping him waiting. Gus had had too much experience of being messed around by Khan to spare him even a moment's sympathy. He'd waited for hours for this interview and he was bloody sure it would be on his terms.

'Could you confirm verbally, Mr Khan?' said Gus, his voice pleasant. As ever the contrast between the two pimps struck Gus. Where Bazza Green was seedy and made your skin crawl, Khan was smooth, clean shaven and, when not decked out for a Muslim wedding, could easily pass for any young professional working in a bank or office. His usual clothes were designer smart and, if the thick gold chain that hung round his neck had anything to do with it, top of the range. No Asda sale items on his shoulders, thought Gus making a mental note to reassess his own wardrobe. Khan was a living advertisement that crime actually did pay… and big bucks by the looks of it.

Gus was pleased that for the time being, Khan had opted not to contact his lawyer. He seemed perfectly relaxed. *Obviously got a good alibi,* thought Gus. Leaning forward to rest his elbows on the table, Gus noted with interest, the way his right leg jogged on the spot, as if he were channelling all the nervous energy contained in the well- muscled body into that one limb.

'Good wedding?' asked Gus sifting through a pile of papers he'd brought into the room with him.

'What?'

Whatever Khan had been expecting, it wasn't that. He frowned and then leaned forward. 'Yeah, great wedding. Loads of hot totty and booze. Bridesmaid was a bit of a goer.' Then scraping his chair back from the table he jumped to his feet and shouted, 'What the fuck's the wedding got to do with owt?'

DS Cooper tutted and tapped her foot on the floor whilst Gus raised an eyebrow but remained silent.

'Okay, okay,' said Shahid, running his fingers through well gelled hair. He hooked the chair with his foot and dragging it towards him he sat back down. 'Typical Muslim wedding, you know? Never got near any girls, stayed with the blokes and compared cars and watches. Satisfied?'

Gus nodded, 'Glad you enjoyed yourself. Tell me where you were on Thursday night?'

'What?'

'Thursday night?' repeated Gus 'You got a hearing problem? I can speak louder if you like.'

Shahid shook his head. 'You can't think *I* did this. Fuck! Trixie was my girl, you know? Bet it were the same fucker that offed Camilla and Starlight. You should be out looking for that sicko. I came in to try to help you lot, cos I care about her… cared about her.' He took a deep breath and looking beyond Gus's right shoulder he added, 'We were going to get married.'

Gus considered this for a moment. Shahid did look distraught. His usual arrogance was toned down a notch and Gus' experience told him that Khan was covering up just how cut up he was about Trixie's death. The fact that he'd turned up without coercion was a first for Khan. In Gus' previous dealings with the man it had been like pulling teeth.

'You care about Trixie, right?' he waited for Shahid's nod, then, 'Well answer the question.'

Khan shrugged. 'Here and there, you know? Round and about.'

Gus released an exaggerated sigh and leaned back crossing one leg over the other as if he was settling in for the long haul, 'Look we're all here for the same thing. Be more specific and we'll be able to rule you out of our enquiries. Where's here, there, round and about?'

Shahid raised an eyebrow, that told Gus in no uncertain terms that he was sceptical of Gus' good intentions. 'Forgive me if I don't fully believe that you're not trying to fit me up for this. You know fine and well you had me in here and raked me over the coals about Camilla, poor cow, then again after Starlight. Stands to reason you're trying to put Trixie on me but, you see, this is different. She was my girlfriend. I *wouldn't* hurt her.'

Gus leaned forward, 'You still haven't answered my question, Shahid. Thursday night. Think back. I want all the gory details'

'Oh, for crying out loud, why are you wasting time with me? It's obviously a sicko punter on the loose. You should be out there looking for him, not hassling me. That's what I pay me taxes for. To fund the likes of you.'

'Well, I'm not so sure about your taxes, Shahid but, if you like we can go into that another time?' Gus looked Shahid straight in the eyes until the younger man looked away, seeming a little less sure of himself. 'Right, Shahid. Last time. Thursday night, where were you? And I promise I won't bring up your tax situation again.'

'Fuck's sake. If it'll get you off my case, I was with Trixie till about eight or so, then I was at The Delius. Imti does this underage disco thing on a Thursday night, so I worked upstairs in the office. Trixie were supposed to phone me at tenish, but she didn't. I kept ringing and ringing her but she didn't pick up.' His voice caught and he rubbed his sleeve over his eyes and bit his lip. He stared straight ahead for nearly a minute then, with a belligerent expression on his face he looked at Gus. 'I was in the office all night till closing. Then me and Imti drove to Birmingham for the wedding.'

Shahid looked down at the table and sniffed, 'I was cursing her, you know? Thought she was with Bazza. She'd *promised* me she wouldn't go with him, no more. Not now. Bastard made Trixie his pet. She hated it, his sweaty paws all over her. Made my skin crawl. But I were taking her away from all that.'

When he saw another tear roll down Shahid's cheek, Gus signalled to Alice. 'DS Cooper will get you a drink. What do you want?'

Shahid shook his head. When he spoke his voice was full of despair, 'The only thing I want is Trixie. Find who did this to her.'

'That's the plan.' said Gus, 'Where did you go with Trixie on Thursday? Somewhere nice and quiet?'

Shahid nodded.

'Aah, yes, I know the sort of place you mean. Quiet and secluded where you can be a bit intimate, yeah?'

Shahid nodded, 'Yeah, that's right'

Gus continued, 'Dim romantic lighting? Maybe moonlight and a few stars?'

Again, Shahid nodded, his shoulders hunched. He looked defeated but Gus wasn't finished yet. He needed to be sure. Glancing at Alice, he continued, 'What have I missed out, DS Cooper'

Alice folded her arms and shook her head, 'Beats me, sir'

Gus snapped his fingers. 'Oh that's it. I've got it. It's the scent I forgot?'

Shahid looked puzzled, 'What scent?'

'That distinctive aroma of rotten vegetation, stale sex and sweat from the druggies that can only be found at Lilycroft allotments.'

Shahid's mouth gaped open and his face paled. Without waiting for him to recover, Gus said 'That's where we found Trixie's strangled body.'

Shahid shot to his feet, his chest heaving. He put his hands over his ears like a small child. 'Shut up, shut up, shut up.' He chanted backing into the far corner of the room.

Gus glanced at Alice who shrugged, her eyes telling Gus she was as unsure of Shahid's guilt as he was. Gus leaned over the table and in a quiet voice said, 'Sit down, Shahid, sit down.'

But Shahid was too far gone to respond. Leaning against the wall for support he allowed his body to sink to the floor and with his elbows resting on his knees he cradled his head and wept. Gus stood and walked over to stand beside him. He gently pulled the other man by the arms until he was upright and, arm round his shoulders he walked him over to sit back down at the table. Meanwhile Alice had gone to the door and ordered a mug of tea for Shahid. When it arrived she poured in two sachets of sugar and pushed the mug over to Shahid saying, 'Drink.'

She handed him a tissue and then sat down beside Gus. After a few sips of tea, some colour returned to his cheeks. He pushed the mug away and wrapped his arms round his body, rocking to and fro, in the same way he'd learned as a boy in mosque school, when he was learning the Quran.

Gus broke the silence. 'Look at me, Shahid. We know you were with her cause we've got a DNA match to your sperm. Do you deny it?'

Shahid shook his head 'No, she was my girl so I met her Thursday cause I was going to be away for a few days and yes, we had sex. Why shouldn't we? We're getting married?'

'Not any more, you're not.' said Gus, his voice gentle.

Shahid nodded in acknowledgement and fresh tears flowed down his face. 'Where is she? I need to see her.'

Gus laid a gentle hand on his arm, 'Later, son, later, okay? I need to get your statement.'

Shahid nodded and straightened up. Taking a deep breath, he said, 'Okay, I'm ready. Trix and I met up around twoish. She told me that she'd told Bazza she was on. Having a period, like?' He glanced at Alice as if for confirmation and when she nodded he continued.

'We walked about in town for ages but we were always on the lookout in case somebody saw us so we ended up at the allotments and, well, you know we were having a laugh and we made love.'

'I don't get it Shahid. You've got plenty of dosh. Why didn't you take her to a hotel? I mean, if you were getting married, I'd have thought you'd have wanted to treat her... not shag her down Lilycroft allotments like any old whore?'

Shahid rubbed the heels of his hands against his eyes. 'I know, I know! We normally did go to a hotel. Don't know why we ended up there. We were just mucking around like and one thing led to another and then I needed to get back and she needed to avoid Bazza. I wish to fuck I'd never gone near that fucking place with her.'

Gus waited to give Shahid a chance to compose himself, then when he seemed to have calmed down he said, 'So, when did you leave, Shahid?'

'Well at around eight or half past. We thought we heard someone and she were worried that it might have been Je–' He hesitated and then said, 'One of the other girls who'd tell Bazza she was with me. Then she'd lose her free rent and all.'

Gus nodded, stood up and paced the room for a few seconds.

'Look Shahid, don't get me wrong, I sympathise with your loss but I'm just not getting it. Why was she still working for Bazza if you two were getting married? What did it matter if she lost her free rent – you're loaded? Why was it all kept such a secret? Do you see where I'm coming from, Shahid? It doesn't add up.'

Shahid's face flushed and some of his earlier arrogance returned. 'It's true. I loved her and I wanted to get married, look after her.' He lowered his eyes and wringing his hands together on the table top, he added in a voice so quiet, they barely heard his words, 'She were pregnant. We were going to have my baby.'

'Then why not just whisk her away from Bazza? You're not scared of him, are you? Unless of course that's why Camilla and Starlight were killed. Was that Bazza's way of warning you off his pet?'

Shahid shook his head, 'Nah, he's not got the guts to do owt like that, not Bazza!'

'No, then who killed the girls? We've got three dead working girls, one of whom is your girlfriend and who works for Bazza. It stinks of turf war to me, Shahid. Especially when you tell me Trixie was scared to leave Bazza. That doesn't tally with you saying he didn't have the guts to kill your girls. Makes me wonder if you and Bazza were sorting things out between yourselves. If Bazza's so gutless why was Trixie so scared of leaving him?'

Shahid glared at Gus, 'It weren't fucking Bazza that was the problem. It were Jessica, okay?'

Gus frowned and pretended to be confused, 'Why would Trixie's best friend not want her to get out of this life?'

Shahid snorted. 'You having a laugh? You know damn well Jessica's my half-sister and you also know, because that fucking Hussain bitch will have delighted in telling you, that Jess and I don't get on. That's why it was so awkward for Trixie. She didn't want to tell Jessica she were seeing me. Jess would've gone ballistic if she found out.'

'You telling me Jessica didn't know about you and Trixie?'

'Nobody did. It were a secret.'

Gus felt that Shahid's words rang true. Going by what Sadia had gleaned from Jessica, she wouldn't have been happy at all about Trixie and Shahid, but was that enough of a reason to keep it all a big secret. He decided to push a bit more, 'Still don't get it Shahid. You sure it's not all about Jessica blaming you for her mother's death? After all Jessica thinks you killed her, doesn't she? Maybe you did. *Maybe* if you were capable of killing Millie Green all those years ago, you'd be capable of killing two of your "girls" and your girlfriend now.'

Shahid groaned, 'Aw for fuck's sake, maybe I should just lawyer up now. I didn't before because I just wanted to help you find who killed Trix, but now you're just taking the piss. Dragging up Millie. Fuck! I loved her. She were like my mum. I've spent the last twenty years trying to convince Jess I'd nothing to do with it and now you lot are dragging it all up. If I knew who'd killed Millie, I'd have given them up and, sure as fuck, if I knew who killed Trix, I'd make sure they were sorted, okay?'

Gus nodded at Alice to take over and watched as she rested her arms on the table and with a sympathetic look on her face said, 'See Shahid, what DI McGuire is wondering is, that maybe Trixie wasn't so keen to settle down and play happy families with you. Maybe she heard how you Muslim lads make your white wives cover their bodies and hair and stay at home looking after the kids?'

'Get a life,' said Shahid. 'It's not like that now. I wanted her to have the chances she'd missed as a kid. I wanted her to train as a nurse, like she wanted. All I wanted was Trixie.'

Gus decided to push one last time. 'Yeah, but you see where we're going? If she kept rejecting you, saying no, refusing to get married... Well, it's understandable that a hot-blooded lad like yourself might lose it and hurt her. Course you didn't mean it, did you Shahid? Didn't mean to strangle her.'

Shahid shook his head. 'That's *not* what happened. I've told you we made love and then I went when we heard a noise. She was fine when I left. She was supposed to phone me later, after she'd told Jessica about us.'

Gus gathered up his papers and walked to the door with Alice following.

Shahid stood up. 'Where are you going?'

'Giving you a chance to reconsider what you've told us. Oh, and here.' Gus handed Shahid a piece of paper and a pencil. 'Write down anything Trixie told you about herself. Where she came from, birthday, all that sort of thing, so we can locate any family she may have.'

Shahid took the paper and crumpled it and threw it on the floor. 'No way would I give you that information. Those people aren't fit to see her again or go to her funeral.' And he flung himself back into his chair.

Gus looked at him and then said quietly, 'I'd get yourself a lawyer now, Shahid, I think you're going to need one.'

Shahid looked up with tear-filled eyes and nodded.

Back in the incident room Alice brewed some coffee whilst Gus discussed what had happened with the rest of the team. 'I really don't think he murdered Trixie. I've interviewed him plenty of times before and he's always cool as the proverbial cucumber. Today he was distraught. I'm not saying he didn't have something to do with the Camilla and Starlight's deaths but, I'm not convinced about that either. We need to re-interview Jessica, see if she knew about the relationship between Shahid and Trixie; and Bazza too. We need to find out more about the Eastern European girl and what happened to her. Who knows? That could be related.'

CHAPTER 42
Killinghall Road

Anastazy sprawled on a large sofa in front of a 48-inch state-of-the-art TV that dominated his living room. The volume was at least two notches louder than necessary but Anastazy liked the feeling of being surrounded by constant movement. It made him feel secure. Solitude, on the other hand freaked him out. He wasn't one for enjoying his own company – but some things were best done in private.

His large detached house stood at the corner of the crossroads separating Leeds Old Road from Killinghall Road. He loved that his address was Killinghall, thought it was apt, bearing in mind his chosen profession. He lived rent free, having secured the house from a Polish landlord in exchange for allowing the man's mother back in Poland to live out the rest of her years in safety. Of course, *that* deal was open to negotiation. As far as Anastazy was concerned nothing was written in stone and any 'deal' was subject to reassessment whenever he fancied. For now, though, it served his purpose to keep his side of the bargain.

He glanced round the spacious living room and compared it to the cramped space that was Serafina's home. As befitted his tastes the décor was sparse but clean. The landlord's daughter came in and 'did' for him. He grinned: she also did the housework. Anastazy had no respect for any man who'd prostitute his daughter but, then again, he'd made it only too clear what would happen to the rest of the man's family if he didn't comply and, if he got fed up with little Mathilde, well, that was okay; for Mathilde had three younger sisters, each as ripe for the picking as she.

On the glass coffee table in front of him was a bag of throwaway mobile phones. He selected one that was already charged and pumped in a number. After a rapid exchange in Polish with one of his contacts, he sat back and started flicking through the TV channels. He felt happy. He'd considered ramping up the pressure on Shahid Khan, especially since his sources told him the pigs had been practically camped out at both his home *and* The Delius, but his 'unfinished business' with Khan's brother Imti had felt more pressing... well, that was until Serafina's brother, Jacob, had dared to challenge him. He'd consulted with The Old Man and, with his usual callousness, the boss had agreed that Jacob should be the final message to keep Serafina on-side.

Much as taking Imti Khan down a peg or two was tempting, Anastazy was a business man at heart and he agreed with The Old Man that taking care of business should be his first priority. His anger with Anastazy for stabbing the boy on Manchester Road had been scorching. Clearly, The Old Man didn't like his people going off-piste and, in hindsight Anastazy couldn't really blame him. It had been risky and if they hadn't worked out a plan to get Serafina on-side, it could have been disastrous. If she'd gone to the police with her suspicions, it could have jeopardised everything. Anastazy was glad The Old Man had had his back on that one, although he was still smarting from the scathing words he'd used.

Anastazy's instructions to his contact had, therefore, been twofold. First, deliver another blow to Bazza Green's infrastructure then, as a reward, the man could employ his carving skills on a big Polish turkey. For this one, Anastazy was keeping *his* hands well and truly clean. No point in alienating Serafina any more than the blow to her mother had already done. He was convinced that after his man was done with Jacob, Serafina would be only too willing to acquiesce to his every demand. After all, she had the health of her other two   brothers   to   consider.

CHAPTER 43
The Fort

Gus sprawled in his chair with his legs stretched out in front of him a glass of whisky in his hand, glad, for once, to be on his own with his thoughts. The interview with Shahid Khan had lent a different complexion to the investigation and, to his mind anyway, Khan could be taken off the list of suspects. His earlier lethargy was replaced by a slow burning desire to think things through so he'd sent everyone home and lowered the lights, creating a less sterile, more productive atmosphere. He knew his shoulder would suffer for his bad posture later but, right now he was too knackered to move, besides which, from where he sat he had a prime view of the crime boards, illuminated as they were by a single spotlight above. He still couldn't decide whether the three murders were connected. The MO was the same and popular opinion in the press appeared to be that there was a serial killer, targeting prostitutes, on the loose.

Gus felt the other option of a turf war had its own merits too. But a niggle at the back of his mind made him doubt that it was a turf war between Khan and Green. They'd lived reasonably amicably in their own stables for nearly twenty years and ears on the ground reported no stressor that that would have escalated their passive hostility to this type of activity. He shook his head. Bazza Green wasn't above a bit of firebombing and Shahid Khan wouldn't have to lower himself far to rough up some of Bazza's girls, but this felt way too extreme for either of them.

He took another sip of whisky, rolled it round his mouth allowing the chocolatey warmth to spread down his oesophagus as he swallowed and considered the other information that had just come in from one of the special constables. Apparently, a young lad, stabbed on Manchester Road, had come round and identified his attacker as being Eastern European. His description of his attacker was circulated to the specials and one of them had got back to the officer in charge saying that she'd had a similar description from a Polish man on Leeds Old Road. This man claimed that he was being forced to 'allow' his daughters to work for this man. He'd been too scared to name the man, but had demanded police protection. Although the specials increased their patrols in the area, the man was found stabbed to death the following week and his family had disappeared.

What had piqued the special constable's curiosity was the similar description of the attackers alongside the fact that both were stabbings and that both victims lived in Bradford Three. She'd also wondered why the Eastern European community in that postcode had closed rank when she questioned them about the incidents. She'd thought that they seemed frightened. This, for Gus, resonated with Alice's report from The Prossie Palace about the young Eastern European girl being attacked and then fleeing in fear from The Palace. The question was whether this was related to his murders or not.

He heard the door open behind him and, for a moment, imagined that it was his boss DCI Nancy Chalmers. Of course it wasn't. After the Matchmaker case, Nancy had taken a sabbatical and, as far as Gus knew, was sunning herself in the South of France. He wished she was here right now. He'd gotten used to running his ideas by her over a whisky.

He shrugged and spun his chair round as Sadia approached.

'You okay, Gus.'

As she plonked herself down in the chair opposite his desk he held up his whisky glass to offer her a dram too.

Shuddering, she shook her head, 'Hell no. Drain cleaner, that is.'

Gus laughed and pushed himself upright, feeling the tension in his shoulder as he did so. 'The trouble with you is, you've got no bloody taste.'

Pouting she inclined her head to one side. 'Well I admit my taste in men's a bit dodgy, but I'll have you know I'm connoisseur of vodka.'

'Sacrilege,' said Gus, swirling the last of the amber nectar in his glass, before swallowing it and depositing his empty glass on the desk. 'Thought I told you to go home.'

'Yeah, well I decided to do a bit of digging about Millie Green before you gave me the direct order not to.'

Gus smiled. 'I've no intention of telling you to leave that alone. Far as I'm concerned it's part of our ongoing investigation.' He paused, 'just try to keep it on the QT though. No sense in inflaming an already volatile situation with the "high heid yin".' The last three words were a reasonable imitation of his dad's accent. 'Maybe best you keep me out of the loop unless you find anything. That way, I can claim no knowledge of it if your dad happens to ask.'

Sadia grinned. 'Thank God for that, thought you might shut it down before I'd even started.'

Gus stood and grabbed his coat from where he'd flung it over the back of his chair. 'Nah, too scared of you,' he said, dodging as she jumped to her feet and aimed a playful punch in his direction.

'Drink?' he said, heading towards the door.

Sadia, grabbed her coat from the coat rack and followed him. She'd just flicked the switch to plunge the room into darkness when Gus' mobile rang.

Fumbling in his pocket, he pulled it out. Head to one side, he listened to what the desk sergeant said and then, with a glance at Sadia, said, 'Get DS Cooper and DC Sampson to meet us there. DS Hussain and I are on our way.'

He shoved his phone back in his pocket and said, 'Northcliffe Park, Sadia. There's been another attack and I'm presuming she's one of Bazza Green's.'

CHAPTER 44
Bradford Royal Infirmary

Serafina huddled in the corner of the waiting room holding her mother in her arms. Her father sat in silence opposite them, spinning his cigarette lighter between his fingers. Her brothers Luka and Thomas sat, heads bowed, on two of the blue plastic chairs that were lined against three of the waiting room's four walls. Thomas stared at the blood that coated his hands. Serafina would have given anything to be able to go to Thomas, but her mother had fallen apart when she'd heard how critical Jacob's condition was and her father was useless. He'd not said a word since they'd contacted him earlier. Initially they'd been unable to contact him. Bloody Farmer's Boy switchboard kept saying they had no Mathias Nadratowski working night shift. Fortunately, he'd eventually picked up his mobile and arrived at almost the same time as she, Luka and Thomas.

Stretching one of her legs, she kicked Luka and nodded towards Thomas. 'Luka, help him. Get him cleaned up. Then, she reached into her mother's handbag and took out her purse, 'Get hot drinks for everybody. Put in plenty of sugar.'

Her father stopped his pacing and turned to his daughter, his face expressionless, despite the venom in his words. 'This is *your* fault. You've brought this down on our family.'

Serafina felt the colour fade from her face and a chill settle in her belly. She lowered her head. 'I'm sorry, Dad. I'm so sorry.' She knew from experience that her father's wrath was to be avoided at all costs, but for once he was right. It *was* her fault so she was happy to absorb his anger. She began to sob.

Her father made a tsch! sound and standing up, began pacing the room. Serafina's mother, face tear-stained and pale, pulled away from her daughter and stood up. Walking towards her husband on unsteady legs, she gripped his arms, forcing him to stop moving and spoke in quiet Polish. 'This is not Serafina's fault. The only person to blame for this is that monster Anastazy Dolinski. As a community, we stood by and let him kill David the other week. I will not stand by now and let him get away with what he's done to Jacob.' She shook her husband, seemingly oblivious of his darkening expression, and continued in a louder voice. 'Nor will I let him split our family up. He is to blame, not Serafina, and I will make sure he pays. Are you with me?'

Serafina watched as her father's face hardened. He shrugged away from her mother nearly knocking her to the floor and swore. 'Serafina is no angel, you understand?' He glared at Serafina, making her blood freeze in her veins. 'And as for Jacob? He would have done better to stay quiet. We all know what Dolinski's like. He should have kept his mouth shut.'

Her mother, eyes wide shook her head, 'No, Mathias. You can stop this. You need to speak to Dolinksi. He'll speak to you.'

Mathias Nadratowski spun round, his eyes flashing with an anger that had Serafina's mum backing away from him. 'Mind your tongue, woman. You need to be quiet right now. Do you understand?'

As her mother crumpled into her chair, wringing her hands together, Serafina again put her arms round her.' What the hell was going on? How could her father speak to her mum like that when she was so upset? The way he was behaving was vile. She almost wished things were like they'd been in Poland when they hardly ever saw him. At least there wasn't this atmosphere all the time.

As if he knew what Serafina was thinking, he looked at her, his dark eyes seemingly boring into her soul. 'We will not retaliate, is that understood?' His gaze moved from Serafina to each of her brothers in turn.

Serafina opened her mouth to respond, but her mum shook her head her eyes pleading. Nodding Serafina bit her lip. Her mother was right: now was not the time to contradict him – but she was at a loss to understand why he was, behaving like this. Maybe he wasn't thinking straight. After all, his eldest child was battling for his life right now. That was enough to make any parent erratic.

Serafina had no doubt that her brother was now in surgery because Anastazy Dolinski did not like the way he'd defended his sister. That in turn made her remember how little her own father had done to defend her. She sighed. Why was her family, and her dad in particular, so difficult? She turned and gently pushed Thomas and Luka to the door. 'Get cleaned up.'

Sitting apart from her parents, who now sat stony faced and opposite each other, their faces pale, Serafina took deep breaths trying to calm the pounding in her chest. First Hasnain and now Jacob. From the moment she'd seen Anastazy leering at her she'd known he was trouble, but she'd underestimated just how dangerous he was. The man was pure evil. If he hadn't actually stabbed her brother, she knew he had arranged it. She shuddered. If Thomas hadn't come home early and found Jacob lying in a pool of blood in the front garden, she dreaded to think what would have happened. Thomas saved Jacob's life. For someone so young, he'd acted responsibly, applying pressure to the wound in Jacob's abdomen and yelling as loudly as he could for help. The paramedics had arrived in record time and, as her mum stumbled into the ambulance beside her deathly pale brother, Serafina had arranged a taxi to take them BRI.

Now, an hour and a half after they'd arrived, all they knew was that Jacob was in surgery and was critically ill. It was likely that he'd lose his spleen, if not his life. Serafina tried to quell the last thought from surfacing but she knew that they were all thinking it. She summoned a half-smile as Thomas, wearing a borrowed hospital gown to replace his bloodied clothes, thrust a mug of tea into her hand. He settled himself beside her and blew on his drink. 'The nurse let me make it in the staff room. Nice of them.'

Serafina nodded, grimacing as the too-sweet liquid made her teeth throb. She felt Thomas's gaze on her face and looked up.

'He stabbed Hasnain too, didn't he?' said Thomas, his voice quiet for her ears only.

Serafina glanced away with a single nod. Thomas moved closer, 'Hasnain's okay. I bumped into Benny earlier this evening and he told me. Missed all his vital organs. Lot of blood but a few stitches and a few week's rest and he'll be okay.'

Serafina heaved a relieved sigh, 'Thank God. I've been so worried about him.'

Thomas nodded, 'Yeah, I know. I saw that Anastazy watching us at the bus stop when Hasnain was pratting about. Didn't think he'd do that, though.'

She snorted, 'No, neither did I.' Tears flowed unimpeded down her face. 'After what happened to Hasnain, I should have known he'd do something to Jacob. Jacob cheeked him earlier. I should've known he'd do this.'

Thomas grabbed her hand in his, 'No, you shouldn't have known. Why would you think he'd do that? You're normal and normal people don't do this sort of thing. Anastazy's a psycho. We need to sort him out.'

Serafina glanced at her dad to see if he'd heard Thomas' words and shook her head. 'No, *we* don't need to sort him out, Thomas. We need to let the police do that. We need to get the community to unite on this. We can't do it on our own. He's got too many friends.'

Thomas looked doubtful, but Serafina grabbed his arm, 'I mean it, Thomas. We do this properly, okay? Promise me? No matter what dad says we get the police involved and we direct them to Anastazy?'

Thomas nodded and, satisfied, Serafina rested her head on the wall, closed her eyes and waited to find out the fate of her brother. She may have told Thomas they should go to the police, but in her own mind she wasn't at all sure what they could do. After all, she'd no real proof of any of it; Anastazy was too clever to make mistakes like that.

Uncoiled Lies

CHAPTER 45
Northcliffe Park, Shipley

Gus nodded at the officer who was securing crime scene tape across the outer cordon and, with Sadia following, marched over to the paramedics who were positioning a trolley at the back of the ambulance prior to raising it into the back. He could see a young woman lying prone on the stretcher, an oxygen mask obscuring her features.

'What's the prognosis?' he asked, as the female paramedic jumped into the ambulance beside her patient and the other medic ran round to jump into the cab. With a brief smile at Gus, she said, 'Stable, unconscious and we'll know more later. We're taking her to BRI.'

Gus backed off as the doors slammed shut. The engine started and the blue ambulance lights flashed as they turned right and sped off along Keighley road towards the hospital. Turning, he saw that Hissing Sid was approaching from the entrance of the park. He gestured to Gus and, as he and Sadia approached, he thrust two bunny suits at them. 'Suit up and follow me. I'll show you the scene. At least this girl's alive. One of her mates found her. Apparently, they're doubling up where they can these days.'

Struggling into his suit, Gus peered into the depths of the park where he could see the crime scene lights shining. 'What you got for us, Sid?' Then, hearing Sadia groan, he turned towards her and saw her wriggling her nose moments before Hissing Sid's offering hit his own nostrils, 'Fuck's sake, Sid. That's bloody toxic.' It never ceased to amaze Gus that so intelligent a man in his late forties could still reap such childlike enjoyment from producing noxious gasses.

'Well, you asked what I'd got… and I showed you. You should be careful what you wish for.'

Gus could see Sid's eyes sparkle behind his mask and, despite himself, a grin spread over his face as he chided, 'No need to be so bloody proud of yourself. Come on, let's go before we need to fumigate the area.'

Chortling, Sid, after waiting for them to sign in, led them towards the scene. 'As you can see the bastard violated her with a broken bottle – that's where all the blood has come from.' He shook his head. 'That poor girl will never be the same again, you know?'

Seeing the glitter of tears in the other man's eyes before he blinked them away, Gus sympathised. He knew that at scenes like this, Sid normally worked around the dead bodies and his focus was on reading the scene. This was one of this rare cases where Sid was faced with a living victim and that was hard. To see the pain and trauma in a living person was always different. Not that Sid wasn't sympathetic to the dead. Gus knew he was and that's why he did his job so well – but there was always one case or situation that hit you in the solar plexus and kept you awake at night. Gus suspected that this was one of those cases for Sid.

Sid turned to his right and pointed to a girl who, bundled in a blanket, sat sideways on in the passenger seat of a paramedic first responder van. 'That girl over there saved her life. Her name's–'

'Armani' said Alice, who'd approached, without them hearing her.

Gus turned, 'Hi Al, you know her then?'

Alice nodded. 'She's a regular at The Prossie Palace. She was in the group Sampson and I spoke with earlier on today.' She frowned, 'We both got the idea that she was the leader and that she was stopping the other girl's from telling us something. Maybe this'll change her mind. Who's the girl who was attacked?'

'Charlotte something or other,' said Sid walking off to direct his team.

Alice exhaled. 'She was there today too. She was the one who brought the Eastern European girl to the Prossie Palace. She seemed to be a friend of Armani's, poor thing. I'll get her statement if you like, Gus?'

Knowing how heavily invested Alice was in The Prossie Palace, Gus nodded. 'Great. Sadia and I will head to BRI see if we can talk to Charlotte.'

He turned back to Sid, 'Don't suppose you've got anything else?'

Sid walked over to a marker and crouched down, indicating that Gus should follow suit. 'Because of all the damn rain we've been lucky.' And he pointed to the floor.

Gus grinned, 'Footprints in the mud. Brilliant!'

'They're clearly from the struggle as he tried to subdue Charlotte. You can see some are overlapped with Charlottes shoes but there are a few prints that are notably clear and, luckily for us, we've been able to cast them before the rain started causing more deterioration.'

The prints indicated quite a ferocious struggle. Charlotte clearly fought hard yet, he'd still managed to subdue her enough, presumably through asphyxiation, to violate her with the bottle. She must have been absolutely petrified and, because of the previous murders she'd have known what was to come. He hoped she'd recover well, but he knew her injuries would be as much psychological as physical.

'Yep.' continued Sid, clearly pleased with himself, 'You find me the footwear and we'll match these prints to the bastard. It's practically indisputable in a court of law because everyone's gait is different. It would be almost unheard of for two different people to produce the same footprints from the same brand of shoe, or in this case trainer. My folk will get back to you with make and size et cetera later. All you need to do is bring me the suspect and the trainers.'

Gus could've kissed Sid. This was the first concrete piece of evidence they'd found so far and when they found the bastard who was doing this it'd go a long way towards ensuring a conviction.

CHAPTER 46
Wyke

With a sizeable glass of Bombay Sapphire and tonic on the table beside him, Brighton flicked through the photographs he'd taken earlier. He'd printed them off minutes before on his home printer, after selecting the clearest, most incriminating ones from the bunch. Living on his own, he enjoyed the freedom that came from being divorced. He had everything he needed: his gin, the adult channels on his TV, and a pile of takeaway menus from every continent, from the Chinky's down the road to the Iti's and the Paki's in Wyke village itself. Then of course there was the odd visit from Sam from across the road. She knew he was always willing when she fancied being serviced by a real man rather than a poncy banker with a limp wrist.

Taking a sip of his gin, he picked up the photos one by one, twisting them this way and that. He was particularly pleased with the close ups. They clearly showed Gus nuzzling Sadia's neck as she closed the curtains. *No room for misinterpretation there*, he thought. *Clear view, steady hand; I've excelled myself. Almost up to a professional standard*, he thought. Then he frowned. It was all fine and well that he'd done what he was asked to do, but he suspected that this wasn't evidence DCS Hussain had expected and he didn't want to be shot as the messenger. He'd seen that happen too many times before and he'd no desire to incur the wrath of Hannibal Hussain. On the other hand, needs must. He'd been entrusted, by the man himself, to 'keep an eye on his daughter' and he took his responsibilities very seriously.

He might not actually like DCS Hussain, but he accepted that Hussain was his ticket forward. He'd blotted his copy book too many times in the past and he knew that this unlikely alliance with Hussain was his last chance to progress in the force. The fact that he'd managed to ingratiate himself with Hussain by covering for his three stooges after that unsuccessful drug raid two months ago, had put him in prime position to exploit his advantage. Hussain was blinded by his fears for his daughter's moral well-being and he hated her being on Gus' team so it had been easy for Brighton to get him to agree to reward his loyalty by placing him on the team with her: in DCI Nancy Chalmers' absence, Hussain was in charge. The move out of uniform was something Brighton had wanted for ages and Hussain had been more than happy to oblige. His displeasure with Gus was well know at the Fort and Brighton was happy to exploit that.

He spread the photos across the table and sipped his gin. The thing he had to consider was the risk factor in giving Hussain the incriminating photos at this point. Who knew how the man would react to his Muslim daughter screwing a half-caste wog. God, these Pakis could be really defensive when it came to their daughters. Last thing he needed was for Hussain to flip and do one of those honour killings. He laughed out loud at the very thought of the staid Hussain doing something so crass. As Pakis went, he supposed Hussain wasn't too bad. At least he didn't waltz around in one of those bloody nightdresses like some of them did.

He drained his glass and poured himself another. He'd gone above and beyond the call of duty in staking out McGuire's house and following Sadia, but it had paid off. He just wasn't too sure if the results would weigh in his favour, or if Hussain might think he'd gone too far. He *was* quite unpredictable. He'd a bit of a reputation of being a stickler for the rules, but he'd been happy to bend them to save his minions earlier.

Sighing, Brighton swept the photos into a pile in the centre of the table and decided to make up his mind in the morning. Standing up, he checked the living room curtains were drawn fully, grabbed the bottle of baby oil he hid in his kitchen cupboard, settled himself in his comfy sofa, undid his flies and put on one of the adult channels he liked so much... nothing like a good wank to round off a productive day.

CHAPTER 47
Bradford Royal Infirmary

It had taken two minutes for Anastazy to sweet talk his way into the Critical Care Unit. He'd lied and said he was Jacob's brother and, whether it was because she liked a 'bad boy' or because she was nervous of him, the little nurse with the red hair had smiled and directed him to the relatives waiting room.

He stood outside the door, staring through the small window into the room. They'd dimmed the lights, but he could clearly see four distinct bundles slumped in chairs pulled together to make makeshift beds where they could rest their feet. Serafina had scrunched up her coat and was using it as a pillow, whilst her brothers had pulled their hoodies up over their heads and down past their foreheads to cover their eyes. Her parents sat at opposite ends of the room – very telling, Anastazy thought, smiling. He glanced towards the entrance as a trolley burst through the doors. It was carrying a young woman attached to various monitors and with an oxygen mask covering her face. The wheels squeaked obscenely, jarring with the silence of the unit as it was guided by the same red haired nurse into a room further along. A registrar in green scrubs followed looking frazzled. *Looks like Jacob's not the only one having a rough night tonight.* Anastazy turned his attention back to the occupants of the waiting room.

Pushing the door open, he slithered in without making a noise; a silent snake prowling for sustenance. Taking a single step towards Serafina, he felt someone's eyes on him. He spun round and saw that her mother was awake and watching him, her face pale and her skinny frame dwarfed by the padded chair she sprawled in. He nodded once and refocussed his attention on Serafina who, eyes shut, rubbed her thumb over her crucifix. No doubt praying for Jacob, a stupid gesture that irked Anastazy beyond reason. He couldn't understand the faith people put in God even after being dealt so many harsh blows. His lips tightened. When she was his she could forget about that stupid crucifix and her stupid God. The only person he'd allow her to worship would be him. He stepped towards her, intent on ripping the necklace from her hands but, before he reached her he felt small fists pummel his back.

Annoyed by the interruption, he reached behind him and, with one hand, effortlessly circled both of Serafina's mum's wrists. He yanked her round to stand in front of him like a ragdoll and, aware, but uncaring, that the scuffle had drawn the attention of her dad and brothers, he raised his free hand, bunched his fingers into a fist and, before the petite woman could react, he hit her, putting all his weight behind the punch. A dark bubble rose in his chest as his fist connected with flesh. What was wrong with this woman? Twice in the one day he'd had to reprimand her. He felt his breathing quicken and white lights flashed in his eyes as he lifted his hand ready to punch her again. From somewhere in the depths of his consciousness he heard a voice telling him to 'stop'. It may have been Serafina's but, he didn't know for sure. The flashing lights faded and were replaced by the dazed expression of Serafina's mum. Her eyes were dilated and already he could see a bruise forming on her jaw. He'd expected her to have raised her hands to protect herself but instead they hung limp by her side. Her complete recapitulation left him drained. He was better than this. More powerful, stronger. He didn't need to dominate Serafina's mother to make her do his bidding… not when she had two brothers who were much more interesting adversaries.

He turned to the two boys who, still half asleep, were attempting to process the scene. With a sneer, he raised two fingers in a horizontal V to his eyes and then flicked them to each boy in turn, in the universal 'I've got my eye on you' sign. Their bodies tensed, but as they each too a step back, Anastazy laughed, flicking a glance at their dad who'd remained in his chair, his eyes hooded, betraying no emotion.

With a derisive snort he directed his attention to Serafina. As he released her mum, allowing her to slip to the floor like a discarded marionette, he heard a gasp catch in the girl's throat. Stepped over her mum's prone figure, he approached Serafina as she scrambled to her feet. Seeing the anger flashing from her eyes and the way her entire body seemed to shudder in reaction, he felt himself harden. God, but she was beautiful, exquisite even. He looked forward to savouring her. When she launched herself at him, he laughed, enjoying her spirit and, more importantly, the prospect of taming it, as he blocked her ferocious, but ineffectual, punches. Behind him he was aware that her brothers were helping her mother to her feet, but he didn't care. The older woman had been an obstacle and he'd dealt with her with his usual efficiency. Perhaps a step too far… But, he just didn't care.

Using his superior strength, he pulled the struggling girl into his embrace, sniffing her hair, breathing her in. Then, with a suddenness that took Anastazy by surprise, Mathias prised his daughter away from the younger man and inserted himself between them. When he spoke his voice was chilling. 'You forget yourself, Anastazy. My son is in intensive care and my family are distraught, yet you come here and assault my wife and my daughter?'

For long seconds the two men stared each other out, then Anastazy smiled, splaying his hands before him in apology. 'You're right, Mathias, I'm sorry.' He turned to Serafina's mother. 'I'm sorry, you took me by surprise and I was momentarily disorientated. Thought I was under attack. I hope you are okay?'

Drawing the back of her hand over her mouth, Sofia leaving a smear of blood on her chin, looked from Anastazy, to her husband and back. Her puzzlement was clear, yet she nodded before resuming her seat and pulling her coat under her chin as if it were a suit of armour that could protect her from everything that was going on in the room. Her fear fed Anastazy, who savoured the euphoria that surged through his veins. Now he knew he had the Nadratowski family exactly where he wanted them and it felt good… damn good.

Ignoring the rest of the family, he directed his words to Mathias. 'I heard what happened to Jacob and rushed straight here to offer my support to you all.'

Serafina snorted, chin raised, eyes narrowed she glared at him, 'You did this. I know you did. Just as you stabbed Hasnain this afternoon, you stabbed Jacob.'

Feigning anguish Anastazy frowned. 'Serafina, my sweetheart, how can you think I am responsible for this. I wouldn't hurt someone you hold dear.'

'You just punched my mother, didn't you, and you hit her earlier too. You are an animal, Anastazy.'

Anastazy's lips tightened. 'I've explained that, Serafina. She took me by surprise and I regret my reaction. But, you know as well as I do that in the area of Poland I'm from, quick reflexes are essential. Now I'm safe here, in Bradford,

I need to learn to control my instincts a little bit. Please forgive me.'

Mathias glared at his daughter and said in a warning tone 'Serafina!'

After a second, Serafina, avoiding eye contact with either of them, nodded once.

Satisfied, Anastazy lifted his gaze to encompass Luka and Thomas. For a moment, he studied the boys' sullen expressions. Recognising that they would not be easy to appease, he smiled and held out a hand to Luka. The boy looked at it but made no move to reciprocate until his father, with a growl, ordered him to. After repeating the gesture with Thomas, Anastazy nodded to Mathias and said, 'A word please. Outside?'

CHAPTER 48
Bradford Royal Infirmary

G us pressed the bell for entry to the Critical Care Unit at BRI. Charlotte had been admitted to the CCU after being stabilised in A&E. Gus had been told the bleeding had been extensive but had been stopped. Charlotte was now in an induced coma for the shock. She'd been strangled repeatedly and they were unsure how long she'd been starved of oxygen. He'd been told that bruising covered most of her body and he knew there was no way they'd get a statement from her any time soon. Nonetheless, he wanted to introduce himself to the ward staff and see her for himself. He always felt this way about the victims he represented, whether they were alive or dead... fortunately for Charlotte, she'd been found in time... or so he hoped.

A smiley red haired nurse who inspired confidence walked them along the corridor. As they reached the door to Charlotte's room, she turned to greet two men who were leaving the ward, 'Everything okay, Mr Nadratowski?' she asked.

Gus saw the older man, his face set in a grim expression nod. The younger man didn't even acknowledge the nurse's greeting.

Entering the room, Sadia said to Gus in a quiet voice, 'Did you see those tear tattoos on the younger man? They give me the creeps.'

The nurse hesitated at the door then said, 'I noticed them. They're scary. His brother was stabbed earlier on tonight. The family's distraught.'

Gus shrugged, preoccupied with studying the fragility of the girl lying in the bed. Gus hated hospitals at the best of times but he was full of admiration for the work the doctors and nurses did. If it hadn't been for the dedicated staff at BRI he'd have died, so he knew Charlotte was in the best possible place. He reached out and touched the girl's hand, his fingers gentle. 'You're safe here, Charlotte,' he whispered, 'We'll catch the bastard who did this to you. Just you get well. That's all you need to think about right now.'

He glanced round the spartan room with its pale blue paint and yellow blinds. His gaze drifted over the various monitors that beeped and flashed rhythmically, and came to rest once more on Charlottes face. A series of bruises were beginning to bloom over her cheeks and eyes making her barely recognisable. The raw welts around her neck were swollen and a tube ran into her mouth, presumably to help with her breathing. Gus and Sadia spent a few more minutes with Charlotte, then left, after issuing instructions that they were to be contacted as soon as there was any change in her condition.

As they were leaving the hospital via the main entrance Sadia nudged Gus and pointed to the smoking shelter that was illuminated by the light from the wards to the rear. 'There's those two men again. The ones from the CCU. Can you see the tattoos now?'

Gus rolled his eyes, 'For God's sake, Sadia, I'm not going to stare at the relatives of some poor kid who's been stabbed just because you find some tatts creepy.'

Sadia pulled her coat tighter round her body and grunted, 'Okay, point taken. Come on, its bloody freezing, the wind's picking up and I'm knackered. Take me back to my car so I can get home.'

Gus opened the car and slid into the driver's seat. 'Not coming to mine then?'

Sadia grimaced. 'Not tonight, no. Don't want to push my luck with my dad. He's already on my case and now I have to convince him that he misheard me say I was with Shamila last night when in reality I was with Jamilla. Not sure he'll fall for it.'

Gus laughed. 'With your powers of persuasion I think you'll convince him.'

Saturday

CHAPTER 49
The Delius

The wind hadn't blown itself out overnight and as Sadia pulled into The Delius car park, she shuddered. After last night's events and having heard Gus' account of the interview with Shahid Khan, Sadia felt compelled to check up on Imti. Whatever affected Shahid would have an effect on Imti, too, and she wanted to make sure he was okay. A driving rain hammered against her windscreen and the short drive from her house had barely allowed the car heating to kick in. Bracing herself, she struggled out of the car and pulling her hood over her head, she ran to the entrance. Hopping from foot to foot, wishing they'd hurry up and answer, she brayed on the door, glaring up at the not-so-discreet camera that was angled downwards. When, after a few seconds, the door still hadn't opened, she raised her hand to hammer again and, her vision obscured by her furry hood, nearly hit Jai on the chest as he yanked it open. He raised one eyebrow without saying a word, which made Sadia giggle. Jai always treated her with a degree of reluctant indulgence making her want to tease him to provoke a response.

'Sorry, Jai. Mistook your taut pecs for the door. Imti around?'

With a snort, Jai, mouth pursed in what Sadia took to be disapproval, shook his head and stepped back to allow her to enter. Once inside Sadia shrugged out of her coat and shook it sending droplets of rain all over Jai's very shiny black shoes. Glancing up, she saw his resigned expression and bit her lip to cover her smile. Knowing it would irritate the hell

237

out of him she stood on her tiptoes, raised her hand and, with more pressure than was strictly necessary, she pinched his cheek in mock affection. 'Lighten up Jai. It's only a bit of rain,' she said, before flouncing past and making her way into the main bar, where she assumed Imti was.

Two steps in she registered the presence of another man wearing a prayer hat and sporting a full Muslim beard. She stopped and glanced at Imti who was behind the bar setting the coffee machine up for the day's trade not, thought Sadia, that The Delius made a roaring trade in coffee. Never mind, she'd welcome one right now to heat her up. As the other man turned round Sadia's heart sank. It was Councillor Majid who attended the Leeds Road Mosque – the one her father frequented. Clearly recognising her, Councillor Majid, took a step towards her. 'Assalamu Alaikum, Sadia. How lovely to see you?' He frowned, 'Mind you, I'm not sure your father would appreciate you frequenting such premises.'

Sadia tensed but, with great effort, she maintained a neutral expression. 'Wa Alaikum salaam. I'm here on official business.' She frowned and continued, her tone deadpan, 'Bit early in the day for you to be in for a drink, isn't it?'

The flicker of anger that crossed the councillor's face was so fleeting that had Sadia not been waiting for it she'd have missed it. She risked a glance at Imti who, shaking his head, was trying not to laugh at her cheek.

The councillor clasped his hands in front of him, disapproval written all over his expression. 'Now, now Sadia, there's no need for rudeness, is there?'

Sadia, instantly bounced back to when she was a little girl at Mosque school, bowed her head. She knew she was being deliberately provocative, and also that there was no need for it. Councillor Majid had never been anything but kind to her and he deserved better from her. It wasn't his fault she was having a crisis with her father at the minute and her doubts about the faith were hers to sort out. She had no need to take it out on him. 'I'm sorry, you're right, that was uncalled for.'

Seemingly not completely mollified he continued, 'Maybe your father is right, Sadia. Maybe you need to spend a bit more time at the mosque. You should join the unmarried girls' group. I'm sure you'd find it very useful to receive guidance in your marriage preparations from your Muslim sisters.'

Sadia opened her mouth to reply that she, most certainly, was *not* making any wedding preparations, but he directed his gaze over her shoulder and took a step forward arm outstretched as he said 'Assalamu alaikum, Shahid. Imti said you were indisposed, so I'm very glad to have bumped into you. I really need to speak with you.'

Sadia turned round and saw Shahid standing just inside the bar running his fingers through his hair. He looked dreadful. Sadia could see he still wore the previous day's clothes. His shirt was half untucked and unfastened at the neck, but it was his eyes that affected Sadia the most. They were red and glazed and, despite her reservations about Shahid as a person, she felt sorry for him. He looked desolate. Without acknowledging the councillor, Shahid walked round and joined Imti behind the bar. He picked up a glass, went over to the optics and took two measures of whisky, which he downed in one.

Sadia heard Councillor Majid's disapproving intake of breath and bit her lip wondering how this scenario was going to play out. She knew from experience that both men could be stubborn irascible characters and this seemed like an

239

explosive situation in the making. Imti took a step forward, placing himself between the two men, 'Shahid's had some bad news. He's not himself. Perhaps we can leave this for a few days, till he's feeling better?'

Sadia could tell from his focussed expression that Councillor Majid wouldn't be deterred and she felt for Imti. As always the two brothers did their best to protect each other, but she knew Imti hated confrontation. Councillor Majid stepped to the side and, as if Imti hadn't spoken, addressed Shahid. 'We've had complaints in the community about rowdy, drunken behaviour from some of the patrons of The Delius.'

Shahid, in the process of refilling his glass, grunted, 'So what?'

Councillor Majid's shoulders went back, in a gesture Sadia recognised as being the precursor to a major challenge. He ran one hand down the length of his beard as if attempting to smooth out its unruly curls and leaned on the bar, 'It's your responsibility, as a Muslim, to ensure the community is not disrupted. *You* assured us that when you opened this den of infidels that you would ensure the community was not adversely affected.'

Sadia caught Imti's eye and grimaced. This was not going to end well. Shahid had clearly had more to drink than the two doubles he'd just downed and the Iman was not about to be deflected from his self-righteous indignation.

Shahid turned round, his eyes flashing, 'Aw shut up, you sanctimonious prick. You and your fucking mosque get more than enough money from me to compensate for the *inconvenience* of a few kids enjoying themselves of a weekend.'

Imti's gasp was audible and, for a second, the tableau before them seemed frozen. Then, Jai appeared as if from nowhere and, at Imti's nod, he wrapped his arm round Shahid's shoulders and guided him out of the bar, leaving Imti to build bridges with the angry Imam. Minutes later, anger only partially abated, he flounced from the bar leaving the words 'You haven't heard the last of this' hanging in the air behind him.

'Shit!' said Sadia, 'I only came in to see how you were and have a quick coffee before briefing, but I could do with some of what Shahid had and it's barely nine o'clock.'

Imti pushed a coffee across the bar to her as she climbed onto a bar stool and watched him prepare the tills for the afternoon's trade. 'You're getting sorted early today, Imti.'

He shrugged. 'Been away. Need to check the tills and stuff.'

Sadia nodded and studied the boy. She had a soft spot for him. She'd known him since he was a baby. Shahid used to bring him next door to Jessica's house and she and Jess had enjoyed having a real live doll of their own to play with. He'd been an angel and, even after Millie's death when Jess had disappeared, she'd still bump into Imti when Shahid took him to Bradford Moor Park. She only realised later that Shahid had been the younger boy's main carer since he was born. She'd discovered that Shahid's dad was always too busy with his crime empire to bother with the boys and Imti's mum was twenty years younger than her husband and ill-quipped to look after herself, never mind an unruly teenager and a baby.

Millie Green had been the only mother either boy had ever known. Sadia couldn't believe that Shahid would have killed Millie, even under instruction from his father. Or... maybe she just didn't want to believe that the earnest teenager that she'd had a secret crush on all those years ago could do something so awful.

'How's Shahid?'

Imti snorted, 'You saw how he was, Sad. He's broken.' He slammed the till shut and took a deep breath. 'He didn't kill Trixie. I know Jessica thinks he's a cold-blooded killer but I know him, Sad. He's not capable of that. He loved her.'

Sadia's lips tightened, 'Don't try to romanticise your brother to me, Imti. We all know he's a drug dealer, pimp and God knows what else.'

Imti flushed and looked at her, his eyes full of suppressed anger, '…but he's not a killer.'

Sadia exhaled. They'd been through this so many times but his loyalty to his brother was unshakeable. He loved him and, though he didn't condone Shahid's career choices, he would never hear a word against him.

Sadia bit her lip and then with a shrug said, 'Look, Imti, I'm not on duty right now but, between you and me, we're desperate. Rack your brains for anything you can tell me that'll give us a clue. Anything about Camilla or Starlight? Anything you or your bouncers have heard in the club? Anything at all?'

Imti busied himself polishing glasses for a minute. And Sadia, savouring her coffee, allowed him the time. Finally, he said, 'Camilla and Starlight were really nice, you know? When they were working they got tarted up and put on a front but, the rest of the time they were just normal. They'd have a laugh with us, tease Jai and they wouldn't let Shahid undercut them. They stood up for themselves.' He smiled. 'If I knew owt I'd tell you, Sad. Promise I would, but there's nowt. Not a bloody thing.'

Sadia leaned over and squeezed his arm, 'Thanks for trying, Imti. If you do remember something will you let me know?' She jumped from the stool and pulling her coat back on, headed for the door with a final wave in Imti's direction. Nearly through the door, she heard Imti called her. 'There is one thing, though.'

Sadia turned round and stepped towards him one eyebrow raised in question.

Imti shrugged, 'It's probably nowt, but the other night, Thursday it were, some bloody thug caused a bit of a scene her in the bar... punched a girl in the face. Took three of the bouncers to chuck him out.'

'Really?'

Imti nodded and pointed to the CCTV screen behind the bar, 'Come round here and I'll show you. We recorded it.'

Sadia moved round the bar as Imti set up the recording. As she watched her face broke into a big smile, 'I recognise him, Imti. Saw him yesterday at BRI.'

'Hope he was in plaster' said Imti, his voice gruff, 'That girl will have a shiner, I reckon. She said her brothers would deal with him.'

'Nah, he was visiting his brother who was stabbed not far from here last night.

Imti frowned. 'Jacob?'

Sadia shrugged 'Is that the name of the lad who was stabbed?'

'Yeah, but Jacob has two brothers, Luka and a younger one, Thomas, I think, and none of them are him,' he jerked his thumb at the now still footage on the TV that showed the tattooed man making a crude gesture towards the screen. 'Friend of mine told me that guys with those tattoos are ex-cons from Poland. Violent ex-cons from Poland. The worst kind.'

Sadia looked at the man on the screen. His snake tattoo and his tear drops weren't the only scary thing about him... even from here she could see that his eyes were vacant... lacking in emotion. She shuddered.

CHAPTER 50
The Fort

When he arrived at The Fort, Gus was surprised to find Brighton already huddled behind his computer, fingers flying over the keys, a steaming mug of coffee on the desk beside him. In light of the fact it was a Saturday and the absence of any further developments since Charlotte's attack the previous night, he'd scheduled the briefing for ten o'clock and had expected to have the room to himself. He glanced over and saw that Brighton had also filled the coffee machine. *Maybe he's turned over a new leaf,* thought Gus. He was happy to give Brighton the benefit of the doubt when fresh caffeine first thing on a Saturday morning was on offer.

He nodded at the other man and, shaking the rain from his battered fisherman's jacket, he hung it on the coat stand before grabbing a steaming coffee for himself and settling behind his desk. He hadn't slept well the previous night. Worries about Sadia and her dad had jostled for prime position with his thoughts about the ongoing investigation. Alice had reported that Armani had been too hysterical to say much other than that the man who attacked Charlotte had been 'a big fucker'. *Not really enough to go on,* thought Gus, smiling as he imagined the reactions of the press if they released a description like that. Didn't bear thinking about. Mind you, if they didn't give the press something to work with soon, there'd be an even bigger backlash against the police.

Scrutinising a report that told him there was no evidence of any moves by other gang leaders onto Bradford's turf,

Gus felt frustrated. He sighed and pushed the paperwork to the side and leaned back in his chair, feet resting on top of his desk, mug in hand, and thought.

Three working girls dead, one critically ill. Two were Shahid Khan's, two were Bazza Green's. Judging by the various forensic reports, all but one of the girls were penetrated by a broken bottle pre-mortem. Which begged the question, why the hell was Trixie different? Why was she violated post-mortem? The rest of the MO was consistent with the other victims. Even Charlotte, the survivor, had been injured this way. Had Trixie died quicker than her attacker intended? Is that why she'd been violated post-mortem? It seemed that he'd throttled them to unconsciousness and revived them a few times before the fatal strangulation.

And where the hell did Shahid Khan fit into all of this? His relationship with Trixie complicated things. It added another dimension to the attacks. Khan had lawyered up and been released late the previous night but, in truth, Gus wasn't that bothered by that fact. He'd felt Shahid's grief was genuine and, although he knew that didn't necessarily signify innocence, he felt inclined to believe him. He couldn't see any reason for Shahid to kill either his own girls or his girlfriend. His past experience with Shahid made him doubt his culpability.

A constable came in with the day's newspapers, and as Gus spread them out side by side on his desk he felt his stomach clench in anger at the way they dehumanised the victim's, emphasising their 'professions' and 'vulnerable lifestyles' rather than the fact that their life had been snuffed out violently by a monster and that they left behind family and friends who cared for them. The police, as usual, came in for a huge amount of stick with words like 'incompetence' being a common thread throughout the tabloids. He knew to expect a visit from DCS Hussain before the day was over. No way would he be able to resist twisting the knife. He'd clearly missed the emotional intelligence training that was, supposedly, compulsory for all police managers, regardless of rank. Not for the first time, Gus wished DCI Nancy Chalmers was back from her sabbatical. Not only was she fully supportive of Gus but, her clear thinking made her a valuable asset to any investigation. And she also provided a useful buffer between him and the DCS.

As the room filled up, Gus began the briefing. In light of a lack of additional information, he focussed on directing Compo and Brighton to continue trying to track down Trixie's relatives. He decided to change tack with Jessica Green, who he was sure was hiding something, and directed Alice to accompany him in a follow-up interview after which they'd re-interview Armani and, he hoped, Charlotte, if she regained consciousness. Then, of course, he had to waste precious time driving to Horsforth to consult with Dr bloody Carlton. As if he hadn't got enough to do today. Never mind, he'd take Al with him and they could use the drive to bounce some ideas about.

After the briefing, he pulled Sadia and Sampson to the side. He'd been thinking about Millie Green and Jessica and the more he thought about them, the more he felt compelled to help Jessica. 'Today we've got a bit of a lull going on. The groundwork's being done by uniform and we're waiting on all sorts of results to come through, so, before all hell breaks loose again, I want you to use the time to review the Millie Green case.' He looked at Sadia, saying, 'You mayn't get another chance for a while, so make the most of it. Fill Sampson in and, until further notice or until something else breaks on this case, he's at your disposal.' He glanced at Sampson and grinned. 'Look on this as a little training project for you, but keep schtum about it. I know nowt about this, okay?'

Sampson, face flushed, clearly pleased to be chosen, nodded.

Smiling, Sadia looked at Gus. 'Before I go I just wanted to run something by you about that bloke with the tear tattoos we saw at BRI yesterday.'

When Gus nodded, she recounted what Imti had told her earlier. Gus raised an eyebrow, 'Hmm, interesting, I'll make a point of finding out a bit more about him when I head up to BRI later. Maybe that nurse will be able to tell us something about the family. Worth keeping an eye on him if he's inclined to violence. Get Compo to see if he can get an ID on him. Chances are he'll turn up again. The type that're prepared to hit a woman in public aren't usually the sort to suppress their violent tendencies for long.'

Sadia grinned, 'If he can get an ID on the girl he hit, that'd be useful too. Our Imti's got a soft spot for her, I think.'

Gus shook his head. 'Playing matchmaker now, Sad?'

CHAPTER 51

Brighton had waited till after the briefing to make his move. Seeing that sanctimonious cow sucking up to McGuire and acting all coy had made him determined to bring the bitch down. She deserved every piece of shit that was about to descend on her. He chuckled. And he'd have the added satisfaction of seeing her snooty dad wrong-footed. No matter how much he was prepared to bend over backwards for Hussain it still irked that the bastard felt superior to him. Never mind, not for much longer. His decision to pass on the good news himself had the added bonus of allowing him to witness Hussain's reaction. Well worth braving the 'shoot the messenger' scenario.

After making sure McGuire was otherwise engaged chatting up Sadia, he slipped out of the room. Not that McGuire could really say much to him: he'd been in early this morning and besides, chances were he'd assume he was on a cig break. Walking along the corridor to Hussain's office, he tried to ignore the flutters of unease in his stomach. Hussain's PA was absent from her desk so, after a tentative knock and the resultant instruction to enter, he opened the door and walked into Hussain's inner sanctum.

The room was pristine; white and devoid of the usual sweaty, greasy smell that permeated the rest of the building. Despite The Fort's very efficient central heating, in that room the starkness lent a chill to the air. Brighton moved over to take the chair offered by the DCS. His desk was bare, except for a computer, a nearly empty in-tray and a framed photo. There were no coffee mug stains on it and all his pens were neatly organised in a pen holder. The scent of furniture polish teased Brighton's nostrils as he sat down.

'Well?' Hussain's tone was clipped, as if Brighton was some sort of time waster.

The unjustness of this combined with the other man's superior air annoyed Brighton, who barely managing to suppress his grimace managed a weak smile. 'I've got something to report, sir, but I don't think you'll like it. Are you sure you want to go down this route?'

Hussain glared at him, making him want to flinch. Instead he raised one eyebrow, feigning indifference and pushed the A4 padded envelope across the oak desk. This was exactly the tone he'd aimed for. He knew that the air of mystery would make it near impossible for Hussain to back out now. As Hussain made to pick up the envelope, Brighton slapped his hand on top. 'Again, this will not make you happy. You *will* be upset and I want you to know how deeply sorry I am to be the bearer of this news.'

Seeing a frown spread across Hussain's forehead, Brighton felt a wave of pleasure engulf him. He'd made Hussain nervous and that made him feel good. About time Hussain felt at a disadvantage. He was altogether too used to having the upper hand and Brighton was pleased to be the one to bring him down a peg or two.

He lifted his hand from the envelope allowing the other man to lift it. Picking up a wooden letter opener – pretentious twat, thought Brighton – Hussain slit the envelope open. He held Brighton's gaze as he opened the envelope and pulled the contents out. When he looked down at the topmost photograph, Brighton saw the colour drain from DCS Hussain's face and only just managed not to smile.

Hussain quickly scanned the other photos then, without looking at Brighton, he said in a quiet voice, 'Get out.'

Milking the situation, Brighton pushed his chair back and, taking his time, got to his feet and walked to the door. Once there he looked back, hesitating, and in his most sombre voice said, 'I'm very sorry, Sir.'

Exiting the office, Brighton closed the door behind him with a quiet click and leaned on the door for a moment as a grin spread across his face. Hussain's expression had been even more than he had wished for. The man was clearly devastated and Brighton, feeling ecstatic at being the bearer of such bad tidings, was jubilant.

CHAPTER 52

Hussain sat unmoving staring at the photo of Gus, his dreads clearly silhouetted in the window as he nuzzled Sadia's neck. Her arms were raised, each hand gripping the curtain on either side of the window. Her smile was evident. Their intentions were clear.

Thrusting the photos back into the envelope, Hussain threw it on his desk and whirled his chair round till he could look out the window. A cold sweat covered his entire body making him shiver in his shirt sleeves. He felt his right eye twitch and the beginnings of a headache niggled behind it. He hadn't expected this. No, the most he'd expected was a minor infarction by Sadia. Maybe a bit of clubbing or being too friendly with that Alice girl or those two buffoons, Sampson and Compo but, not this. Never this.

What the hell was she thinking? McGuire of all people, for heaven's sake, she could do better than *that*. There were so many eligible Muslim men around and she needn't be confined to Bradford… she could have her pick.

His face grim, he smiled without humour. He should have stuck to that old policing mantra, 'Only ask the question if you know the answer'. It had served him well for the past thirty years… until now. He'd asked the question and the answer he'd received was wholly unpalatable. The question now was, what could he do about it?

With a blank gaze, he looked up as his PA knocked and entered his office, carrying a mug of coffee in one hand and a sheaf of paperwork in the other. He saw her expression falter as she approached his desk and asked, 'Are you okay, sir?'

Pulling himself together, he waved a hand, indicating she should put his coffee on the table and then his tone abrupt, he said, 'Come back later. I'm not ready for you.'

He saw her look of disbelief but he didn't care. For once in his life he'd abandon his routine. He needed to think. So what if it disorientated his staff? She got paid enough to do what she was told. When she clicked the door shut, he looked at the steaming mug. Sadia had decorated it years ago at one of those pottery events. In gaudy colours and with an unsteady hand she'd written '*To the best daddy in the world. I love you, love Sadia xxx*'

He reached out a finger and traced the words then, he grabbed the full mug and with an anguished roar he hurled it at the wall next to the door. Almost immediately, his PA burst through the door, her expression startled. Her gaze moved from her boss to the wall next to the door. Hussain saw her eyes widen as she took in the splatter of sludgy coffee dripping down the wall to pool in droplets on the carpet among the broken pieces of coloured china from the mug.

He grinned, feeling a strange satisfaction that he'd discombobulated the woman. Without uttering a word, she, once more backed from the room. Hussain knew his uncharacteristic behaviour would be the topic of conversation among the other PAs for the rest of the afternoon but, with atypical bravado, he realised that, for once, he didn't actually care what anyone else thought about him.

He exhaled and stood up to pace the room. When his pacing slowed he went over to the window and looked out onto Oak Lane. From his position he could see the steps leading from The Fort's entrance and the queue of traffic lining up outside. As he watched he saw Sadia jog down the steps followed by that idiot Sampson, seconds later McGuire and Cooper also walked down the steps. McGuire, he noticed, was still limping slightly. Pity that bastard last year hadn't had a better aim. If he'd had none of this would be happening. As he watched McGuire's dreads bounce around his head with ebullient energy, he felt an almost uncontrollable anger engulf him.

He didn't register the fact that his hands had clenched into fists until he felt the force of his well-manicured fingernails break the surface of his palms. Taking a deep breath, he unclenched them and eyes narrowed observed Sadia's surreptitious glance towards Gus as she crossed the road and Gus smiling back, equally surreptitiously. He wanted to thrash the man to within an inch of his life. How dare he lay hands on his daughter? It had been a struggle to bring Sadia up alone after his wife died twelve years ago; a young teenage girl and a busy police officer were a difficult combination but, somehow, they managed. She was the apple of his eye and, until fairly recently, he'd been her hero. He frowned. That had all changed when she insisted on joining the force. He'd wanted more for her. She was clever, pretty and would make a wonderful wife and mother. Was it really too much to expect her to do the right thing? Why couldn't she just do get married to a nice Muslim boy like his friends' daughters. But no, Sadia had always had an independent mind and somewhere, it seemed, he'd allowed her to drift away from what was right. It was time to change this, redirect her and end this damn, foolhardy 'relationship' she'd forged with the devil. He didn't care how he'd achieve it but, he knew that he would ensure that Gus McGuire suffered greatly for what he'd done... and Sadia? Well, Sadia would be forced to toe the line.

Uncoiled Lies

CHAPTER 53
The Chaat Café, Oak Lane

Sadia decided that, rather than risk her dad finding her poring over the Millie Green files in The Fort, she and Sampson would work in The Chaat Café. Relieved that the perpetual rain had faltered to a drizzle, she left the police station with Sampson and made her way across the road, ignoring the huddle of paparazzi that jostled her for a quote. Fortunately, they lost interest in her and Sampson when Gus and Alice alighted onto the steps behind them. With a sneaky glance at Gus, she waited at the kerb.

As Sampson took advantage of a gap in the traffic, Sadia glanced to her right and saw a car she recognised. Distracted she faltered, craning her neck to confirm that it was indeed, Gus' wife, Gabriella with his sister, Katie in the passenger seat. The car had come out of the Lister Mills complex and was heading up Lilycroft Road. Looking behind her she saw that Gus and Alice had already rounded the corner to The Fort's car park. Thank God! The last thing she needed was Gus getting riled up again by his sister and ex-wife's betrayal. That wound was still very raw and a chance sighting of the two lovebirds would only add a liberal dose of salt – not something she wanted for Gus. Not when the prospect of the dreaded Sunday lunch loomed like a dark cloud on the horizon.

Sampson, who'd already bounded across the road, waved as she took her chance and jogged across to join him after Gabriella's car had passed her. She hated to admit it to herself but seeing Gabriella made her feel a little bit jealous. Gabriella was gorgeous and, although Gus assured her that their marriage had been over before Gabriella left, Sadia still felt a bit like one of the ugly sisters compared to his ex-wife.

'What held you up?' asked Sampson.

'Aw, just got distracted. Come on, coffee's on me.' And she marched past him through the revolving glass doors and into the entrance to the building.

The Chaat Café, as its name suggested, did a mean spicy chick pea and yogurt salad but, it also catered for a wider palate with a range of home-baked cakes as well as fry-ups of every variety from halal to veggie to red-blooded meat. It was a regular haunt of most of the officers working in The Fort as well as the locals. It was a community project with funding from charitable organisations and Bradford Council. One of its main remits was to provide culinary catering training for adults with learning disabilities. Its various rooms were available for groups from armchair aerobics to Zumba classes to mindfulness training and were well attended.

Sadia walked past the security guard stationed at a desk covered in leaflets and continued past the various community rooms, following the corridor to the café. If her nose was to be believed, a fresh batch of scones were either ready or soon to be ready. God, but she loved those scones. Approaching the counter, her eyes flicked across the array of cakes until they alighted on the still steaming scones piled up at the end of the line. Eyes sparkling, she smiled at the head chef, Tony, 'Great timing Tony. Two cappuccinos, please, and two scones with butter and jam.' She looked beyond Tony to a figure wearing an apron and pink Marigolds, who was drying a pile of plates by the sink. 'Hey, Rizwan. You make the scones?'

Rizwan turned and his face creased into a huge smile. He stripped off his gloves, rushed over and threw his arms round Sadia. 'Yeah, Sadia, I did and they're delicious.'

Sadia caught the chef's eye and winked, 'I hope you made them specially for me.'

When Rizwan replied, 'Yes, just for you', she smiled, envying him his ability to lie so blatantly to please her. She knew she could do with taking some lessons from Rizwan in that area as her customary bluntness had gotten her into trouble in the past.

Leaving Tony and Rizwan preparing her order, she joined Sampson at the table he'd chosen in the corner of the room. She was pleased that, without being told, he'd chosen the most discreet table right at the back behind a pillar. She sank into the faux leather chair next to him and cast her eye round the walls of the café. They'd recently changed the artwork on display and, as ever, Sadia was fascinated by the skill of the local artists. The current artwork was textile collages inspired by the work of International artist Imran Qureshi that provided welcome splashes of colour on the magnolia walls and combined with the baking smells and muted background music made the café one of her favourite coffee stops.

Coffee served and scones demolished, Sadia pushed the thin file across the table to Sampson. 'This is the file on Millie Green's death.'

Sampson used a napkin to wipe his jammy fingers and weighed the folder in one hand. 'Not very substantial, is it?'

Sadia grimaced. 'Tell me about it. I've not had a chance to look through it properly myself yet, but it is a bit too thin for my liking.'

Head to one side, Sampson flicked the cover open and Sadia continued, 'I was there that night. Saw it from my living room window. It was bad. No way would Millie have chosen to commit suicide that way – who the hell would?'

'So, you think Jessica may have a point? You think Shahid Khan may have done it?'

'Not sure. I'm keeping an open mind. Jess thinks he did. But, me? I just don't know.' She gestured to the file in Sampson's hand, 'Maybe the answer's in there.'

Sampson pursed his lips, then shuffled the papers in his hands and handed Sadia a small pile. 'Half for you, half for me. Won't take long to shuffle through these, will it?'

Sadia could have kissed him for his understated acceptance, and taking her share of the paper work she settled down to reading the details of the police investigation into Millie Green's tragic death.

First, she glanced at the post-mortem report, but quickly put it to one side – after all, she knew what had caused Millie's death. Gritting her teeth, she flicked through the post-mortem and crime scene photos, which made up part of her bundle, feeling like a masochistic voyeur but, nonetheless feeling the need to see each and every one. When she'd done that she picked up the witness statements and scowled. Why were there so few witness statements? A quick glance told her that Sampson was nearly finished scrutinising his paltry share of the file, so where was all the rest of the paperwork? Most murder books were much heftier than this. Interview statements took up a lot of space. Could things have been misfiled? Unlikely. She remembered that night, vividly. The whole street had been out and the police had surely interviewed everyone at the scene. She knew her dad wouldn't have missed a trick like that, even as a young officer.

Frowning, she jotted down the names on the few interview statements and then took a plain piece of paper and concentrated on drawing a plan of the street as she remembered it. If she had the time tomorrow, she'd drive through to make sure her street plan was correct. Satisfied that she'd got it as accurate as she could for now, she marked the name of the families she remembered who had lived in each of the houses at the time of Millie's death. When she was done she was pleased to see only three houses where she couldn't identify the inhabitants.

So engrossed in her work was she that she didn't notice that Sampson had left the table for more coffee and now, depositing a fresh cup before her, was curiously studying her plan.

'We could google them,' he said pointing to the names Sadia had listed

Startled Sadia looked up and flicked her hair from her face. 'What?'

'It'll only take me a minute to find out who lives in those houses you've not named. Then, I can cross-reference it with the list from 1998 and see if any of them are still there. I'll probably be able to get current addresses for those that've moved too.'

Sadia studied him. His enthusiasm was commendable but, she needed to reinforce the fact that they were working under the wire on this one. 'Did you hear what DCS Hussain said yesterday regarding this case?' She tapped the file with her manicured fingernail.

He shrugged. 'Yeah, but Gus also asked me to help you and that's what I'm doing. Let's cross-match the statements we have with the names you've remembered and see if any are missing. We could take it from there.'

Sadia smiled at him. 'Two minutes on the job and you're already taking risks. Good show.' She lowered her head, matching the few statements she had to the house numbers, before handing him the sheet. 'Take it from there, Sampson.'

With Sampson busy beside her, she buried herself into the file again until with a frown she threw her pencil across the table. 'Half this bloody file's missing. I know damn well they interviewed my dad *and* my mum, so where the hell are their interview statements? So bloody frustrating.'

Sampson mumbled an agreement, but was clearly concentrating on his task.

Sadia, sighed, leaned back closing her eyes and racked her brain to remember. Yes, that was right, she'd just jumped off the sofa, trying to escape from that God awful image of Millie Green burning on the pavement outside when her dad rushed in and grabbed her. Even in that short space of time his clothes seemed impregnated with the foul stench of burning flesh and petrol.

The police constable who'd taken her parents statement was on the drugs squad in Manningham now. Sadia remembered how he'd stuttered and stammered through his questions, embarrassed at interviewing a superior officer's daughter. She remembered her dad patting him on the arm and saying, 'Pretend you don't know me, lad, and it'll be easier.'

Her mother, she remembered, had looked shocked. She'd stared straight ahead, her eyes glazed, as she answered each question in a robotic tone. Throughout the interview, her dad had kept his arms round her shoulders and held her shaking hand. Sadia doubted she'd even been aware of his presence, so affected had she been by the tragic death of her neighbour and friend.

Her parents' statement was missing, as was Mr Malik's from number 38 and Mr Amjad from 49 as well as Mr and Mrs Dhosangs' from next door. Annoyed by the incompetent filing, Sadia scanned the rest of the statements.

It was quite clear from two eye-witness statements that Millie Green had been standing just inside her gate when something made her turn round. As she had turned the witnesses saw her raise her hands to her face and then back away, towards the gate. According to them, Millie then opened the gate and seemed to be trying to run away when a flash of light sailed through the air and landed on her. It was later discovered that someone had managed to cover Millie in petrol, before throwing a lit petrol filled milk bottle at her to ignite the petrol. An empty bowl, containing traces of petrol was also found later under the hedge. It was clear of prints.

Millie had run from her gate to the street engulfed in flames and screaming and, soon after, the fire brigade and paramedics had arrived bringing the police with them. By then it was too late. Jackie Oliver stated that he saw a young Asian lad run round the side of Millie's hedge. Sadia stopped and considered. Yes, that tallied with Jessica saying Shahid appeared behind her stinking of petrol and holding her back whilst she listened to her mother's screams. He could have thrown the petrol and the milk bottle and ran round the side to arrive through the back garden.

As Sadia made a note to check out Jackie Oliver, someone she couldn't remember from that time, Sampson cleared his throat. 'Got those names, for you. It looks like quite a few people still live there. Want me to ask around tomorrow? See if I can find anyone who puts Shahid Khan at the scene.

'You don't have to do that. You heard what Gus said: we've got to play this under the radar. You could end up on the wrong side of my dad and, believe me, that's the last thing you want this early in your career.' She stood up and drew her coat on.

'Yes, I got that impression today but the thing is, I'm like a dog with a bone. I can't let it alone once I've started. Anyway, *you* can't interview them. They'll still remember you as the wee lass that lived in the street.'

She laughed, 'Okay, you've got a point. But be careful and don't get caught! Anyway, I'm off home now. Good work, Sampson.'

Sampson began to shuffle the paperwork together into a neat pile. 'Night Sadia. Oh, and Good luck.'

She frowned, surprised, 'What do you mean?'

Sampson blushed, 'Sorry, didn't mean to get personal. It's just, well, after yesterday I sensed a bit of family conflict between you and your dad. Believe me, I get on the wrong side of my sisters often enough to know how hellish a "family situation" can be.'

Sadia grinned, 'Yeah, you're right about that.' Then realising she knew practically nothing about Sampson she asked, 'How many sisters have you got?'

'Only the six still at home.'

Unable to hide her surprise she said, 'What?'

He grinned, 'Two married sisters and six still at home… and me and my mum and dad, of course.'

*'Hells bells! I thought us Muslims had big families.'

Sampson laughed, 'No, the Catholics will beat you every time. Anyway, you're an only child so obviously not *all* Muslims go down the big family route.'

'Yes, but, in my parents' case, it wasn't through choice. They'd have liked more after me but after many miscarriages they decided it wasn't to be.' She scrunched up her face as, thinking that, perhaps, her dad wouldn't be such a control freak if she had siblings. Then she shuddered. No, knowing her luck she'd have been lumbered with a herd of over-protective brothers who would be as bad as her dad. After all, she had friends who complained that their brothers put the kybosh on half the things they wanted to do. On the other hand, she also had girlfriends whose parents were much more reasonable than her dad had become in recent years. Suppose it's the luck of the draw really.

Sampson settled back in his chair and began to flick through the PM report. "What the hell?" Scanning the document his eager eyes had picked out the words pregnant. How could Sadia have missed this. He shrugged. He'd known how upset she'd been just thinking about Millie's death. No wonder she hadn't wanted to read the gory ins and outs of it too. But bloody hell this was hot. He glanced up to see if he could see her, but she'd gone. He considered phoning her but then decided not to bother. Exciting though it was, it could wait till tomorrow.

How had it not come to light before now that Millie Green had been eleven weeks pregnant when she died? Looks like we've got the beginnings of a motive. Maybe Shahid didn't want another little half-brother or sister. Or maybe his dad didn't want to support another kid from his mistress. Well, it stood to reason. All the neighbours said he paid her rent and gave her money. It seems logical he got something in return… and, of course, he was Jess' dad. This was certainly interesting.

Uncoiled Lies

CHAPTER 54
Killinghall Road

Anastazy lay back on the fluffed up pillows of his king-sized bed ignoring the muffled sobs coming from the girl who lay shivering by his side. Mathilde was becoming a bit of a pain, sniffling and whimpering like a bloody kitten. The bruises on her skinny body were a real turn off, too. Maybe he'd lay off her a bit… at least for a while. He kicked off the duvet, uncovering one hairy leg and kicked the girl so hard in the kidneys that she fell out of the bed, her head ricocheting off the bedside cabinet before she landed in a heap on the floor.

'Piss off, you little whore!'

Not waiting to be told again, the girl grabbed her clothes and stumbled out of the room as Anastazy, scratching his groin area laughed at her scared retreat. He was physically sated, yet, still, he felt unsettled. He knew it was because of Serafina, but there was nothing he could do about that right now. He was pissed off that she hadn't appreciated the fact that he'd come to BRI to see her after Jacob was stabbed. Ungrateful bitch! He grinned. Slapping her mother had been a real bonus. She was a cow and she deserved it, interfering. What had she been thinking, attacking him like that? He'd only been defending himself when he retaliated… self-defence, that's what it was. Shame Serafina didn't feel the same way, really.

He'd enjoyed his little talk with her dad though. He'd set out his intentions regarding Serafina and, although Mathias was less than happy about it, in the end, he'd agreed. What choice did he have when Anastazy had so many shots?

Now, he had to decide on his course of action. The old man wanted to increase the pressure on Shahid Khan – and he was more than happy to do that. The only thing was that The Old Man wanted him to target another girl but Anastazy had a different plan. He had a better way to increase the pressure on Shahid... one that would have a harder impact, a more personal one, than offing one of his whores. Been there done that. Time now to change the boundaries... get them on the hop, keep them on edge.

CHAPTER 55
Leeds Trinity University, Horsforth

T he drive from Bradford through Rawdon was pleasant. The rain had stopped and autumnal foliage dressed the roadsides in a range of deep golds, yellows and maroons. Gus liked autumn. He liked the changing of seasons. His friend Mo was always going on about how he'd like to avoid the winter months in Bradford by spending them in the warmth of the Pakistani climate. Gus, on the other hand, liked the variety. Yes, he moaned about the snow and rain and wind but, in general, the changing seasons grounded him, made him more attuned to his environment, more appreciative of the beauty each season provided.

He'd gotten over his earlier annoyance at having to make the trip to Horsforth. He and Alice had already had a relatively unproductive day, so he was optimistic that this Professor Carlton would be able to give him some pointers. He'd got Compo to email over the files, such as they were, yesterday so hopefully the psychologist would have had time to give them the once over.

Despite Alice's best efforts, Armani had remained stubbornly silent and Gus had been unsure whether to attribute her reticence to shock or fear. Her description of Charlotte's attacker was sketchy but it had been dark, with limited lighting. She refused to comment on Alice's suggestion that she'd held something back about Trixie during her previous interview. Gus had felt sorry for the girl who chain-smoked her way through their questions, her hand shaking, her fingers barely able to keep hold of the cigarette she seemed to rely on for sustenance. At the same time he admired her bravery; the pugnacious way she stuck out her chin and the fire that shone in her eyes.

Their trip to the hospital hadn't garnered much more information. Charlotte was still sedated. Her internal injuries meant the chances of her being able to carry a baby to full term in the future were slim and that, apparently, was if she could even conceive. It made Gus' blood boil that men used their superior strength to inflict such atrocities on women and it saddened him that it was the most vulnerable in society that suffered the greatest harm. However, what made him despair the most was when women themselves were instrumental in facilitating this sort of abuse. Charlotte's mother had recently been released from a five-year stretch in New Hall prison in Wakefield for prostituting Charlotte and her sister from their home in the Canterbury Estate.

Now, sensing something in it for herself, the woman had come crawling out of the woodwork. That morning, Gus had read in one of the Nationals the story – largely fabricated, he suspected – of the miscarriage of justice that led to Charlotte and her mother being separated. He was well used to the mercenary actions of addicts and the disenfranchised, yet it still stuck in his throat when it was a mother selling her daughter out for a poxy fifty quid from an unscrupulous journalist.

They'd also been unsuccessful in re-interviewing Jessica who, according to the shop owner downstairs, was at home, but refused to answer. He understood that. Sometimes it was easier to grieve on your own. Both Jess and Armani had refused the services of a family liaison officer and Gus was damned if he'd waste any resources on Charlotte's mother. He'd stationed a uniformed officer at the door of Charlotte's room and issued strict instructions that under no circumstances was Charlotte's mother to be allowed access to her daughter.

As Alice and he had been leaving the ward, the red-haired nurse from the previous day had turned up to start her shift. Gus, remembering Sadia's comments about the man with the tear-shaped tattoos, had taken a moment to ask her about that family. She clearly remembered the man and suggested that he didn't seem to 'fit in' with the rest of the family. The young man who'd been stabbed was Jacob Nadratowski and, according to the nurse, was the second of two young men to be stabbed in Bradford yesterday. She said there seemed to be a spate of stabbings recently, with a Polish man being killed in the Thornbury area only the previous week. Despite Alice's teasing afterwards about working his charm on the nurse, Gus made no apologies for asking her to keep her eyes and ears open for any more information on the tattooed man.

He'd got Compo scrolling through reams of CCTV footage of Bradford Road as well as accessing ANPR records for that area in the hope that he could cross-match a vehicle with one picked up in the Bradford Moor area around the time of either Camilla or Starlight's murders. He knew a lot of the information Compo came up with would only be useful when they had a viable suspect but it all had to be done. He'd also asked Sadia to call in to BRI to get an update on Charlotte. He knew she and Sampson were working under the radar on the Millie Green case but they needed to pull their weight on this case, too.

As Alice, who was driving, turned into the main entrance of the university, Gus' phone rang. Seeing it was his mum he answered, 'Hi, Mum, you okay?'

As Alice pulled into a vacant spot next to the university doctor's reserved parking space Gus listened. Rolling his eyes at Alice, who, he was sure, could hear his mum's voice from where she sat he wondered if he'd ever be able to get a word in. His mum, like his dad, seemed to think that you had to raise your voice to a near shout when on the phone. Gus suspected that both parents could forgo using the phone altogether and just shout their conversations the length and breadth of Bradford.

After five minutes of Gus being unable to interject, his mum got to the point of her call. 'I'm just making sure you've not forgotten about Sunday lunch tomorrow, Angus. I'll expect you at 2pm with both Alice and that lovely girl, Sadia.'

Gus rolled his eyes at a smirking Alice. 'Well, the thing is, Mum, another woman was attacked last night and, what with the investigation into the three murders still ongoing, I doubt I'll be able to afford the time.'

He held the phone away from his ear as his mum's 'Tut' followed by a tirade threatened to do permanent damage to his ear drums. 'Mum, Mum, listen. I'll see what I can do, okay? Yes, I know we all have to eat. Yes, I know you love cooking.' At his mum's last assertion about her love of cooking, Gus risked another glance at Alice who now sported an even bigger grin on her face and was rubbing her tummy in an exaggerated way whilst mouthing the words, 'Yummy, Sunday lunch.'

Gus, grinning turned away before he started to laugh and focussed on trying to wind up the conversation. 'Okay, okay Mum, I give up. I'll be there. Yes, yes I'll bring the whole bloody team with me if you want.' His tone held a note of warning. 'But, if something crops up on this case, it may be a flying lunch date, okay?'

He could visualise his tiny mum's satisfied smile as she ended in a sweet voice, 'Oh that's great, Angus. We'll see you then.' And he was left with the dialling tone buzzing in his ear. He turned to Alice and shrugged, 'I've just been played, haven't I?'

Alice opened her door and got out. 'Yup, by the master. Now, let's get a move on. Don't want Professor Carlton reporting back to Hannibal Hussain that we were late for our appointment now, do we?'

Gus scowled and shoulders slumping, followed her.

CHAPTER 56
Rushton Crescent, Thornbury

T he McDonald's on the Thornbury roundabout was heaving because it was October half-term. Kids in clown masks carrying plastic machetes ran amok, making Sampson wonder at the sanity of their parents, bearing in mind the reported epidemic of clowns terrorising people. The children's Happy Meal toy was one of a choice of wind-up Halloween characters. Sampson's preference was the orange pumpkin that the little girl on the next table was playing with, but he also had a grudging admiration for the red devil with its trident and the ultra-white spook that appeared to issue a ghostly wail when wound up.

Trying to ignore the background noise he took out his notebook and began to make a list of possible questions he could ask the Dhosangs, should they prove willing to be questioned. He'd decided to get a better picture of what happened that night by speaking with some of the neighbours whose statements had apparently gone missing, regardless of the possible risk of word getting back to DCS Hussain. Despite the scone he'd eaten earlier he was hungry and the McDonalds was handy. As he was stuffing the last of his fries into his mouth, his appetite wholly unsatisfied, Sampson looked through the window and caught sight of the huge elephant that stood outside the renowned Aagrah Restaurant on the opposite side of the roundabout. To Sampson it was the equivalent of a 'Welcome to Bradford' sign. He wished he'd opted for their buffet instead of the Maccie D's meal he'd just consumed.

273

Pocketing his notebook, he exited onto Leeds Road and, dodging two young lads on bikes, headed towards Rushton Road. Once there he walked part way along before turning off, realising that if he hadn't been looking for it, he might have missed the entrance to Rushton Crescent. As he walked into the cul de sac, he tried to imagine a dark night filled by a woman's screams of agony and the stench of burning petrol vying with burning flesh. It was difficult in the autumn sunshine to imagine the horror of that night but, Sampson hoped that the few residents who had remained living here since 1998 would still remember. It was hard to imagine they would be able to forget.

He paused near a broken fence about six houses in and gazed at the semi-detached house. In the front yard a child's swing and sandpit sat atop concrete slabs each one edged by a liberal growth of weeds. This was where Sadia had lived. For a second, he looked at the front window and imagined a small Sadia, gazing out through the darkness expecting to see a colourful firework display. The rattly wooden windows Sadia had described had been replaced by double glazing and, despite the neglected garden, Sampson could tell that the house had been upgraded during the intervening eighteen years.

The house was separated from its neighbour by a privet hedge, badly in need of a trim. As he studied the house that had once belonged to Millie Green, the front door opened and a young woman began struggling to bump a pushchair carrying a squawking toddler down the front steps to the path. Pushchair safely deposited on the flat ground, she turned to lock the door, before mumbling something that Sampson couldn't hear to the child and started to push the pram through the gate. Sampson nodded with a smile as she passed. It was good that the house was occupied – a young family starting out, children's laughter to chase away the despair that must have hung over the house after Millie's death.

Walking on, Sampson laid his hand on the gate of the house adjoining Millie Green's, and pushed the gate open. He knew that it was still occupied by the Dhosangs. According to the electoral roll only Mr and Mrs Dhosang remained in residence. Presumably, their kids had grown up and moved away. He wondered what their memories of that fateful night were. He hoped they'd be able to add something to the information contained in the meagre file he and Sadia had read earlier.

Before he'd even knocked on the door, it swung open and a small woman, grey hair pulled back and falling in a long plait over one shoulder, stood there. She wore a shalwar kameez and Sampson thought the brown eyes that looked up at him held a sparkiness that belied her advanced years.

He smiled down at her. 'Hallo, Mrs Dhosang?'

The old lady frowned. Her skinny hand was firmly on the door jamb and looked ready to push it shut in his face if she felt at all threatened. Her tone held a challenge that made Sampson smile. 'Yes, and you are?'

Her English, though accented, was perfect. Sampson took out his ID and introduced himself explaining why he was there.

'Hi hoi!' said the old lady, using the same sing-song words Sampson remembered his old school friend Ranjit using. It was an expression of surprise universally used in the Indian sub-continent. Opening the door wider and gesturing him in, Mrs Dhosang continued, 'It was a tragedy. A terrible, dreadful tragedy. That poor girl left without a mother. Hmm, and all for nothing.' She shook her head woefully from side to side. 'All for nothing.'

'You remember that night, then?'

Mrs Dhosang snorted, 'Course I remember that night. How could I ever forget? I'm not in my dotage yet, young man.' She gestured for him to follow her into a room heavily scented with incense, where a large man wearing a turban sat in an armchair. Sampson noted that the turban was an exact match to the blue of his tie. Mrs Dhosang addressed the man who laid the newspaper, folded in quarters, onto his lap. 'We both do. Don't we?'

The man barely glanced at Sampson, as if he were used to his wife bringing unfamiliar people through his house. With a frown he removed his glasses and waited as Sampson held out his hand and introduced himself.

'Sit,' said Mr Dhosang, leaning back, his fingers stroking his silver striated beard. 'You're only about twenty years late.'

Sampson grimaced his acknowledgment of the older man's words and perched on the edge of a matching settee that had antimacassars draped over the back and arms, putting him in mind of his granny's house in County Cork. 'What do you mean?'

'Well,' said Mr Dhosang, his eyes twinkling, 'I know the police are busy, but eighteen years before being interviewed is ridiculous.'

Sampson glanced at Mrs Dhosang who stood by the door, arms folded across her chest. As if satisfied that the point had been made she nodded before exiting the living room leaving Sampson alone with her husband. 'Are you telling me that no one interviewed you at the time, Mr Dhosang?'

'That's right. No-one interviewed us then. Not that we could have said any different than anyone else, but perhaps we might have felt that the poor girl's death was important to *someone* if we'd seen the police looking for reasons.'

Mr Dhosang certainly has a point, thought Sampson. What he couldn't decide was whether it was just police incompetence or something more sinister that had led to a half-baked investigation. He sincerely hoped that he wouldn't discover that the police had been in the pocket of Arshad Khan or that they just didn't care enough to investigate an ex-prostitute's death. The world, so his dad always said, was very different in the 90s.

On her husband's instructions, Sampson waited until Mrs Dhosang came back, carrying a tray with a plate of biscuits and three china tea cups containing steaming, aromatic, spicy tea. Fearing that her fragile hands weren't strong enough to carry the weight, Sampson jumped up, took the tray from her and deposited it on the large glass coffee table that separated the settee from the fireplace. 'You shouldn't have, Mrs Dhosang,' he said smiling at her.

She shooed his protests away and busied herself with the cups 'I was making it when you knocked, anyway.'

She handed Sampson his cup on a saucer and offered him a KitKat, then repeated the process with her husband before settling back with her own tea saying, 'We felt he'd covered it all up, didn't we, Perminder?'

Despite the fact that her feet dangled three inches above the floor, Sampson sensed that this woman was a force to be reckoned with and that her husband willingly submitted to her personality. He was sure that nothing slipped past her eagle eyes.

He took a sip of the milky tea, savouring its sweet spiciness. He loved masala chai and he'd not had any for

277

years. Not since Ranjit got married and left Bradford, in fact. 'Who'd you think covered it up, then?'

Mrs Dhosang glanced at her husband, 'Him next door to her on t'other side.'

'You mean DCS Hussain?'

'Oh, that's what he is now is it?' she said and pursed her lips up as if she wasn't impressed. 'Well, he wasn't so high up then but, he still had enough clout to keep things quiet.'

'Stop talking in riddles, Harpreet,' chided her husband. 'Just tell the young man. He obviously needs to know *now*, even if it *is* a bit late.'

Mrs Dhosang again pursed her lips, 'He visited her, you know? All times of the day and night. Thought he was being careful sneaking through the hedge halfway up the back garden, but I could see him letting himself in her back door.'

Sampson frowned in confusion. 'Who did?'

Her lips tight, Mrs Dhosang jerked her thumb towards Sadia's old house, 'Him! Hussain, that's who.'

Sampson bit his lip, considering the implications of Mrs Dhosang's words. 'Are you telling me that DCS Hussain was having an affair with Millie Green?'

Mrs Dhosang slapped her thigh, 'That's right! He was having what they call "illicit relations" with Millie.'

Shaking his head, her husband said, 'Too many soaps… she watches far too many soaps.'

Sampson, torn between smiling at Mr Dhosang's deadpan delivery and being horrified by his wife's revelation, said, 'Are you sure about this?'

Although he'd directed the question to Mrs Dhosang it was her husband who replied, 'Yes, she's sure. The whole cul de sac knew about it. It was one of those sort of open secrets. Everyone felt sorry for Mrs Hussain. *She* was the only one who didn't know.'

'Ach, Perminder. That's not true. She must have known. A woman always knows when her man is unfaithful. She must have known. She wasn't blind after all.'

Mr Dhosang shrugged, clearly intimating his disagreement with his wife's assessment of the situation. Mrs Dhosang glared at him and then, jumping to her feet, she grabbed the saucer from his hand. From startled look on the other man's face, Sampson surmised he hadn't finished with his drink. However, it didn't seem like he was going to complain, as his wife continued, her tone brooking no argument. 'Well, I know it wasn't Shahid. No matter what Jessica thought, that boy loved Millie. He was heartbroken when it happened. It must have been Hussain. That's what we've always thought, isn't it?' She looked to her husband who nodded.

'What about Shahid's dad?' asked Sampson 'Arshad Khan?'

Mr Dhosang flicked his hand as if swatting a fly. 'No, Arshad wasn't interested enough. He'd moved on and anyway, wasn't he abroad when it happened, Harpreet?'

'Yes he was, but he could have hired a hitman if he'd wanted to,' said Harpreet, her eyes sparkling as if she were relishing the thought.

Mr Dhosang sighed and said in a side tone to Sampson, 'Too much CSI too, I'm afraid. In fact, altogether too much TV, full stop.' He turned back to his wife. 'You know he didn't do that. You know that he, although not a nice man, just couldn't get enough of Millie. That's why he paid her rent. But she knew what he was like and wanted nowt to do with him.'

Nodding, Mrs Dhosang agreed, 'Yes that's true. He wasn't interested in changing his ways. Not interested in his

279

daughter. Only in her mum.' She threw her hands up in the air, 'He paid for the house and absolved himself of responsibility. And that's how Millie liked it. She owed him nothing.'

Sampson thought for a moment, then, 'But she kept in touch with Shahid and the baby and they weren't even her blood relatives.'

'Well, Shahid didn't like his father's new wife but he doted on Jessica and that little lad, what was his name? Imtiaz, I think. Shahid used to bring him over all the time and Millie didn't mind.'

A few more questions ascertained that the Dhosangs hadn't been alerted to what had happened until after the fire brigade arrived; nor had they heard anyone pointing fingers at anyone. So, sensing that he'd learned all he was going to from the Dhosangs, Sampson put his empty cup on the tray and stood up. He headed into the hallway, Mrs Dhosang following behind. As she removed the chain and unlocked the door for him she said, 'One thing I never understood though, was how did he manage to cover up about the baby?'

'What?' Sampson looked down into the old woman's eyes.

She nodded, 'She was pregnant, you know? Early days no more than three months gone. She told me in confidence one morning when I went over with a letter that had come to us instead of her. Just as she opened the door, she had to rush to be sick. Well, there was no point lying to me. I knew morning sickness when I saw it, so she admitted it and swore me to secrecy.'

She paused and looked up at me with steady eyes. 'I've always wondered why the Hussains moved house so suddenly after the fire.'

Sampson nodded and then turned away, wondering what to make of everything. It seemed that the neighbourhood knew about Millie's pregnancy and now he had another contender for the paternity of her child. Why did things have to be so complicated?

CHAPTER 57
Leeds Trinity University, Horsforth

By the time Gus and Alice had ascertained the whereabouts of Professor Carlton's office and weaved their way past the hordes of students milling about for the university's open day, they were running late. Gus hated being late. It made him feel at a disadvantage and he knew that some of these academic types could be real sticklers for punctuality, regardless of the fact he was running a major investigation.

Ignoring the twinge in his upper thigh, he took the stairs two at a time leaving Alice puffing and moaning behind him. Following the directions, he'd been given at the reception he walked along a corridor, reading each of the names on the office doors as he went. At the second to last door, he paused. It bore the name Professor Carlton, and was half open. Gus could see two people inside. An elegant woman sat at the desk wearing a flowing skirt, her hair bundled on top of her head in one of those messy buns Sadia sometimes sported when she wasn't working. Pacing the small office was a short dumpy man in an ill-fitting suit, wearing a pair of luminous green Nike trainers. A pair of thick lensed glasses, one leg held together with parcel tape, were perched at an angle across his nose. Gus hoped the professor would be able to get rid of the man quickly as he didn't want to waste any more time than he had to.

With Alice standing behind him, Gus rapped lightly on the door with his knuckles. Professor Carlton looked up, so he took a step into the room, hand extended and introduced himself. However, before she had a chance to shake his proffered hand, the other man snorted, 'You see, Andrea, that's just the sort of reverse fucking stereotyping I've been talking about.'

Professor Carlton looked apologetic as she shook Gus' hand, 'I'm pleased to meet you, DI McGuire but, I'm not actually Professor Carlton. This,' she turned to her male colleague, who with his chest thrust out, looked like a triumphant penguin, '…is Professor Sebastian Carlton.'

Gus blinked, trying to reconcile the fact that he'd probably offended Professor Carlton with the information that the man in front of him bore the comparatively exotic name of Sebastian. He'd never met anyone less like a Sebastian. Looking sheepish, Gus grinned, realising that the other man's 'reverse stereotyping' comment was all too accurate. He hoped that Carlton didn't bear grudges.

Professor Carlton gripped Gus's hand in a very firm hold and continued as if he'd not been interrupted, 'Just been talking to Andrea here about how, in this day and age of being "PC",' he enclosed the letters PC by bending two chubby nicotine stained fingers in the air, 'we're at risk of introducing reverse stereotypes. Take what happened just then. 'He pushed his glasses up the bridge of his nose, making them wobble even more. 'You knew one of us had to be Professor Carlton and, rather than opt for the male "Prof",' again air quotes with his chubby fingers, 'which, statistically, would have been correct seventy-eight per cent of the time, *you* opted for the PC option which, had only a twenty-two per cent chance of accuracy, as reported by the Higher Education Statistics Agency 2013 to 2014.'

He peered at Gus and grinned. 'As I said, reverse stereotyping.'

Gus couldn't prevent the smile that spread across his face. There was something incredibly likeable about this man.

'Actually, Professor Carlton, not that I want to burst your bubble, but my deduction wasn't based on reverse stereotyping by sex, but rather, I'm ashamed to admit it, through stereotyping by appearance.'

Carlton studied Gus for a minute and then, flinging his head back, he chortled, reminding Gus of a smaller, non-Scottish version of his dad, 'Ah, the fucking scruffy man with his glasses taped up is statistically less likely to be a professor than the à la Primark elegant Andrea? Well, that's another variable I'll pose to my third-year imbeciles. They need something to get their brains geared up.' He waved his fingers at Andrea, 'Toddle off then, I've got to talk to the police now. You can bail me out later if they arrest me.'

Andrea shook her head in way that told Gus she was well used to her colleague's idiosyncrasies, 'Yeah you'll be lucky. If you're banged up, I'd have peace and quiet. What makes you think I'd jeopardise that by bailing you out?'

Carlton sashayed over to the chair she'd vacated and plonked himself down, clasping his fingers together over his chest, 'Ah, but you'd miss my suave wit and incisive humour.'

Andrea snorted and turned to Gus and Alice, 'Well, good luck with him… you'll need it.'

Sebastian Carlton, waved them into the two visitors chairs opposite his desk and placed his elbows on the table, steepling his fingers under his chin. After Gus had moved a pile of paperwork onto the edge of the already overflowing desk and sat down, Carlton said, 'So, what do you expect me to tell you?'

Gus shrugged, 'To be honest, we'd be grateful for anything that would point us in the right direction.'

Carlton nodded and moved his computer mouse. After a few moments studying the screen he said, 'Well, let's see.

First up, because of the limited amount of time I've had to study this, my offerings are purely provisional, okay?'

Gus nodded.

Seemingly satisfied, Carlton continued, 'Your DCS is a bit of an arse, isn't he?' he winked at Alice. 'Don't answer that. I'll make my own judgements. His agenda wasn't for me to help you. He just wanted to piss on your parade. I could have emailed you my findings, saved you some time but, he was insistent you trail out here to get them. Fucking wasting my time too. Hmph! Never mind, I'll tell you what I've got but it's not much... nor, I suspect, is it anything you've not considered yourselves.'

Gus risked a glance at Alice. It was good to have his own opinions of Hussain's motives reinforced by a renowned forensic profiler and judging by Alice's smug expression, she was pleased, too.

Carlton pushed his specs back up into position. 'The first two women and the fourth one were attacked, I reckon, by the same person. The third one was a "copycat". I'm only giving you the highlights now. I'll send you the reasoning later.'

That tallied with Gus' thoughts on the killings too, which of course meant they were dealing with not one but two murderers. He hoped that Trixie's killer wouldn't opt to increase his body count to match the other one.

With a sniff, Professor Carlton pursed his lips, as if gathering his thoughts before beginning, 'It's not a crazed serial killer as the press are speculating. The MO and forensic reports indicate that Camilla, Starlight and Charlotte were attacked by the same perp, excuse the Americanism, but I've just got back from Quantico.' His expression indicated he wasn't wholly enamoured with his most recent foray to the FBI headquarters,

'However, none of these girls have been displayed with any precision. No ritual, no specific placing of the body or manoeuvring of the limbs… and more importantly, no apparent trophy taking.' He looked over the top of his glasses. 'That's not to say the "perp" isn't a sociopath; he probably is. He certainly gets off on pain: why else violate them when they're conscious? But, each of these three is dissimilar in looks and stature. There's no sign that he's unravelling, yet the attacks have no clear time frame. He doesn't appear to be evolving either. He's not "fine-tuned" his approach, he's left no calling card, other than the bottle which, your forensic report states, contain trace evidence indicating they've been left discarded in the vicinity. Thus, he's not brought the bottle with him, but relied on finding one nearby. If he was an organised killer, he'd wouldn't rely on that chance. So, what would he do if he couldn't find a bottle? Would his MO vary? I suspect he'd use anything that came to hand to make his point.'

So, thought Gus, *although we're looking for a sociopath of some description, we are looking for a sadist.* It would be worth finding out more about the Eastern European girl Charlotte had found being beaten and brought to the Prossie Palace. Maybe when Charlotte came round she'd be able to say if it had been the same man who attacked her.

Carlton continued, 'He enjoys dominating his victims, there's no doubt of that. He's clearly a misogynist and yes, he has committed a series of killings, but he seems to employ a quite arbitrary victim selection procedure… unless his motive reaches beyond just killing and maiming prostitutes.'

He turned his computer screen showing photographs of the bodies of Camilla and Starlight in situ. 'The way Camilla

286

is lying face down whilst Starlight is rolled partly onto her side, seems like the attacker finished his "job" and just left them however they landed. Why go to the bother of doing his thing with the bottle if he wasn't going to display his work? That makes me think it's more of an execution type of kill. He strangles them repeatedly because he enjoys watching them suffer. He waits till they're unable to struggle any more before using the bottle and then he strangles them one last time and just leaves their bodies as they are. This smacks to me of murder to order... gang related? Turf war? And, if it is territorial, there *will* be other similar crimes, stabbings, strangulations going on locally too. They *will* be linked but, they probably haven't crossed your radar yet. Follow the patterns of low-level crime and it'll lead you to the organisers... this perpetrator will, more than likely, be a sadist employed by bigger fish.'

Without warning, he jumped to his feet and headed for the door leaving them still sitting, 'Got to go, got a lecture to prospective students to deliver... lucky little fuckers! You need owt else, email me.' And he was off, leaving Gus and Alice looking at each other, speechless.

On the drive back to Bradford, Alice said, 'Well, if what he says is right, and I think it sounds reasonable, that doesn't rule out Shahid Khan for Trixie's murder does it?'

Gus had been thinking along those very lines himself, but he still couldn't work out why Shahid would kill Trixie. He seemed serious about wanting to settle down with her and raise the baby. His grief seemed real and, although he'd seen murderers display seemingly real grief for their victims in the past, Gus felt disinclined to think that Shahid's masked culpability. He'd been wrong before though, so he wouldn't rule it out. 'No, it doesn't, and it makes me think we need to look a bit more closely at those stabbings that nurse told us about. See if we can find a link. I'll get Compo on it when we get back.'

'Maybe Charlotte will come round soon and give us a positive ID on her attacker.'

'That would be great but, she's been through a lot and we don't know what her prognosis is yet. We'll keep digging and we will eventually come up with something, Al.'

CHAPTER 58
The Delius

Shahid sat slumped over his desk, his eyes fixed on the bank of TVs that looked over The Delius. He felt numb. He knew he was stewing in his own sweat but he'd no energy or inclination to do anything about it. What was the point? He'd lost Trixie, he'd lost his baby. He had nothing left. Nothing to look forward to, no future. He opened his desk drawer and rummaged about until he found what he was looking for… three packets of an antidepressant that had been prescribed to his step-mum years earlier. Probably out of date by now but, they'd do the job. He peered into the depths and, lurking in the corner, found two packets of Paracetamol. That should do the trick. He slammed the drawer shut and opening the lower one, he took out the bottle of whisky he kept there for emergencies.

He rubbed his hand over his stubbly chin and then rubbed his sore eyes, savouring the gritty sensation beneath his lids. Sniffing, he began to pop each pill from its blister pack until they lay in a sizeable pile on his desktop. Strangely calm now, he poured whisky into a pint glass and lifting it to his lips he took a preparatory sip. Ready now, he raised his eyes to the TV monitors to take a last look round the most important part of his empire. As he watched, Imti opened the back door and, swinging a black bin bag in one hand, he walked across the concrete paving to the huge industrial bins that stood against the back wall. Without warning, a figure emerged from between two of the bins. Shahid saw the figure look straight at the camera and then, smirking, he raised his hand and pulled it back. Before Shahid had time to

289

register what was in the man's hand, he heard a crash through the speakers and then the monitor covering that area flickered and died. *Fuck!* thought Shahid, his heart thudding as he jumped to his feet. 'Imti!'

In his haste he scattered the pills and upturned his glass over the desk, where it soaked into a pile of paperwork before dripping onto the wooden floor splashing whisky onto his jeans. Storming out of his office, he took the stairs two at a time, yelling for Jai to 'Get to the fucking back door. Pronto.' What the fuck had he just seen? He'd recognised that bloke but, for the moment, couldn't think where from. All he knew was that his brother was in danger and he had to get to him quickly.

Reaching the door, seconds before, Jai appeared from the lounge area, he barrelled into the metal fire escape bar and when it bounced open, he fell out into the back yard. All of his earlier lethargy dissipated now, Shahid regained his balance and whirling round he ran towards the bins. He was praying frantically to a God he'd never depended on before and his breath came in short gasps. *Please let Imti be alright. I couldn't bear to lose him too.*

Aware of Jai pounding at his heels, he reached the spot where he'd last seen Imti. He stopped momentarily when he saw the dark oozing liquid seep across the concrete from the side of the bin and with a primal yell, he rounded the corner and there, sprawled in an unmoving heap like a discarded pile of rubbish was Imti, the contents of the black bin bag he'd carried scattered all around him.

Shahid fell to his knees, heedless of the blood soaking into his jeans and seeing Imti's eyes flutter, he pulled his T-shirt up to check out the wound. Sensing Jai beside him, he yelled, 'Get an ambulance here, *now*.' And, as Jai got out his phone, Shahid pressed his hands onto the oozing wound in

Imti's stomach, barely aware of Jai's urgent mutterings on the phone.

When Jai knelt beside him, Shahid, ignoring the tears that streamed down his face and diluted the blood on his hands, said, 'It was that bastard from the other night. Saw him on the monitors. See if you can find him. He can't have got far. Get him.'

CHAPTER 59
The Hare and Hounds, Toller Lane

Sampson had left the Dhosang's house with his head reeling and had gravitated to The Hare and Hounds on Toller Lane, craving the homely comforts of wood fires, friendly faces and a good pint. He also knew that the chances of bumping into someone from work were miniscule. Most of his colleagues frequented The Kings Arms right next door to The Fort and, until he got his head round all he'd discovered earlier, he needed some space. His mind was full of too many questions and no bloody answers.

What was he supposed to tell Sadia? How could he tell her that her dad was having an affair with Millie Green? Was it even relevant? He'd fleetingly thought that, maybe, he could avoid sharing that information with Sadia, but he knew deep down that that would be impossible. He'd have to bite the bullet and tell her.

Fuck, this was a car crash. He wished he hadn't been so keen to work with Sadia on this when Gus had suggested it. Not only that but, Gus had made it plain that he wanted nothing to do with it. Deniability or some such thing. Now, *he* was in the firing line and he'd no idea what to do. Nodding to Adam, the bartender, for a refill, Sampson settled in for a long night of worry.

CHAPTER 60
Bradford Royal Infirmary

Having reprimanded three teenagers in clown masks who been running around the grounds frightening hospital visitors when she'd parked up, Sadia wasn't in the mood for visiting. She'd spent the afternoon avoiding her dad when she'd have liked nothing better than to go home, run a warm bath and have a long soak. She guessed that by now, Councillor Majid would have reported her earlier visit to The Delius and was certain that this would prompt yet another lecture from her dad about who she mixed with, the unsuitability of her job and, of course, the old chestnut about going to Pakistan to get married. She just didn't have the energy for it.

She felt physically and mentally exhausted. It had been a long day following on from a longer night and all this emotional stuff combined with the pressures of the current investigation just added to her anxiety. Gus was at the end of his tether and she wasn't sure how much longer he'd be able to keep a lid on their relationship without confronting her dad. A confrontation between Gus and her dad was the last thing she wanted. It could only end badly.

It infuriated her that her father, who'd had the freedom to choose his own wife, albeit it within the Islamic community, could employ such double standards where she was concerned. Apart from the fact that things were getting serious between her and Gus, did her dad really think that she'd find a better life partner by trolling for a spouse in Pakistan than in scouring the streets of Bradford? It's not like there was a dearth of Muslims to choose from in the district. But the problem for Sadia was that she didn't want that. No, she wasn't prepared to forsake her independence and that was one of the reasons that Gus was so appealing. He put no constraints on her independence. In fact, he expected her to be her own woman, make her own decisions. It was sexy as hell to know her opinions were valued… and of course he'd a great body too. She smiled. Thinking of Gus always made her smile.

Realising that she'd attracted the attention of the security guard at the main entrance by grinning like an idiot, she waved at him, before heading up to the intensive care wards to check out Charlotte. If there had been any significant change in her condition, they would have been informed but Gus wanted to make sure that whichever officer on duty was aware that Charlotte's mother was definitely not allowed near her.

Buzzing through the entrance she was pleased to see that the nursing staff had provided the uniformed officer, with a chair, a cup of tea and some toast. Sadia grinned and threw the officer the bag of crisps and chocolate bar she'd brought. 'Any change?'

Ripping the wrapper from the chocolate, the officer shook her head. 'Not really. The consultant's been in and they've reduced her meds but, she's still not stirring. They're not worried though. Say it's a matter of time.'

Remembering from her own experience, how mind-numbingly boring guard duty could be, Sadia sent the officer off for a fifteen-minute break. Taking her coat off, she flung it over the chair and prepared to watch the ward activity. It was busy, but quiet. The nurses moved around the ward with a purposefulness that Sadia envied. She wished she felt as purposeful. Instead, she felt that the Millie Green investigation was a dead end. They seemed to be treading water on the murders and her home life was tense. The only thing giving her any satisfaction, at the minute, was Gus.

Standing up, she looked through the square window into Charlotte's room. She was hooked up to a range of monitors that stood around the top of her bed. Flashing numbers, zig zag lines accompanied by the occasional beep accentuated the desperation of her condition. Her already fragile frame seemed dwarfed under the tightly secured sheets that covered her body. From the back of her skinny hand sprouted a cannula which led to a drip that hung like a towering triffid beside the bed. From where she stood, Sadia could see that Charlotte looked ashen, the healthy coffee complexion she remembered replaced by a deathly pallor. Beneath her bruised eyelids, her eyes flickered but, as far as Sadia could see she was otherwise motionless. Sadia bit her lip as angry tears sprung in her eyes. What sort of bastard did that to a young girl? As the intensive care nurse took Charlotte's pulse, Sadia turned away with a sigh. It looked like it could be a long wait before they could speak to Charlotte.

Down the corridor a young girl walked out the relatives' room and approached one of the side rooms. Sadia frowned. The girl looked vaguely familiar. She shook her head... no, probably mistaken. As she watched the girl hesitated and then waved to a figure who was walking up the corridor from the ward entrance. It was a boy, maybe a couple of years younger than the girl. As he approached the girl, Sadia heard them speaking in Polish and the girl turned and walked back up the ward with the boy. *Clearly siblings,* she thought. Then, as they got nearer the girl flicked a glance in Sadia's direction and Sadia froze. She *did* recognise this girl. She'd seen her on the CCTV Imti had shown her from The Delius. According to Imti the tear tattooed man was not her brother, so what had he been doing at the hospital the previous night? From the footage she'd seen, there was no love lost between the two of them.

The girl had her hand ready to push open the door of a side when Sadia spoke. 'Excuse me, I just wanted to have a quick word with you.'

The boy turned, angling himself slightly in front of his sister as if to protect her. Sadia smiled and held out her warrant card. 'I'm DS Sadia Hussain. I wanted to speak with you about an incident at The Delius club in Thornbury on Thursday night.'

The boy raised an eyebrow and looked at his sister as she took a step forward. Darting what Sadia took to be nervous glances back down the corridor towards the ward entrance, she spoke in a quiet but rushed tone. 'I can't speak to you here. Please wait. I'll come when I can.'

Not wanting to cause the girl any discomfort, Sadia nodded and backed away, allowing the girl to push open the door and, with a grateful smile, disappear inside. Moments later the main ward door buzzed open admitting the man Sadia assumed was the girl's father. Looks like the girl wasn't too keen on letting her dad know she was willing to talk to the police. Wonder why?

Trusting the girl to make an appearance and knowing she couldn't leave without passing her, Sadia chatted with the uniformed officer, who'd returned from her break. Sadia had recognised the flicker of fear in the Polish girl's eyes when she'd flashed her warrant card, but, if she was right, that fear had quickly been replaced by a look of determination. She felt sure this girl had something important to share.

CHAPTER 61
Duckworth Lane

Since dropping the bombshell on DCS Hussain earlier, Brighton had busied himself trying to trace Trixie's relatives. If they were anything like that Charlotte's mum, the whore would probably have been better off without them anyway. He grimaced. No matter how bad her parents had been though, it didn't mean she'd got to go whoring herself for the likes of Bazza Green. Plenty of help out there for young girls without them slutting around like that. Half of them probably deserved what they got anyway, flaunting themselves on the streets, playing hard to get and then backing out last minute. Yes, he'd had a few girlfriends like that. Gagging for it to begin with and then all of a sudden crying 'no'. He'd soon set them straight, though. He shrugged. Since his last divorce he was happy on his own. A bit of porn and a gin and tonic of an evening were a lot less hassle than a woman any day.

He'd not managed to get a line on Trixie by the time Sadia got back from whatever little rendezvous she'd had with Sampson. Stupid bitch thought he hadn't noticed her sodding off with the lad. Probably letting him get his leg over as well. So when she got up to leave a while since, he'd decided to follow. Hussain hadn't told him to keep following her, but, then again, he hadn't instructed him to stop either. Besides which, the way the bitch, McGuire and Sampson had cosied up earlier, made Brighton sure he was being kept out of the loop on something important… and that would never do.

So far she'd not done anything very exciting. He'd heard Gus tell her to check on the whore that was in intensive care and that seemed to be what she was doing. Brighton was too smart to park in the BRI car park so he'd parked near Bradford Girls' Grammar School and walked up to Duckworth Lane. He could see her car from where he stood on the opposite side of the road, but he doubted she'd notice him from the car park. When she came back he'd have time to run back to his car and be ready to follow her.

Standing under a tree, which protected him from the light drizzle that had started, he wondered what Sadia's dad would do. He'd seen the man's Paki face lose colour when he'd looked at the photos and recognised his daughter. The way his hands had bunched into fists on top of the desk had made Brighton wonder for a second if he was going to punch him. But then he'd relaxed and his expression had loosened. Brighton had breathed a silent sigh of relief. He didn't want to take a punch from the DCS but he knew that he'd be quids in if Hussain had lost control and lashed out. He'd mentally prepared himself not to retaliate should that happen, but the other man had managed to keep control. He wondered what Hussain was thinking about him. The last thing he wanted was to be in his bad books. He suspected he'd got off lightly so far.

Mind you, it was early days. Hussain could still turn round and take it out on him if he wanted to. He could make his life miserable but, then again, maybe he'd decide to keep him sweet. Maybe he'd realise that, if he wanted to keep his precious daughter's reputation intact, his best option would be to keep Brighton on-side. After all, he'd kept copies of the photos and he knew that the press were all too keen to soak up any stories to discredit the police. Yes, Hussain would do well to remember that Brighton held a royal flush.

Lighting up another cig, he grinned. Oh, how he'd love to be a fly on the wall of the Hussain house when Sadia finally got home.

CHAPTER 62
Bradford Royal Infirmary

The heat of the hospital made Sadia feel sleepy and, when the girl from The Delius came out of the side ward, she was stifling a yawn. The girl approached Sadia, her eyes scanning the length of the ward, reinforcing Sadia's feeling that she didn't want to be seen talking to her. Sadia was glad she'd thought to ask the ward sister earlier for permission to use the nurse's staffroom.

Smiling, she led the girl to the room and once inside she closed the door behind them. 'I reckoned the relatives room may not be private enough for our chat,' she held out her hand, 'I'm Sadia, I don't know your name, though.'

Tentatively, the girl shook Sadia's hand, 'Serafina. My name's Serafina Nadratowski.'

Sadia sat down and waited for Serafina to join her. Despite the fact they were in a private space, away from the main ward, Serafina kept darting glances towards the door as if she expected someone to burst through at any moment. Sadia could see the faint remnants of a bruise at the girl's chin and knew it was from when she'd been hit at The Delius on Thursday. Serafina's lips looked dry and cracked and, as Sadia watched, she chewed on her bottom lip and fiddled with her hair, twisting strands of her long ponytail round and round her index finger. Sadia stretched out a hand to stop her, 'Serafina, you look petrified. Can you tell me who you're so afraid of and why? Is it the man with the teardrop tattoos?'

Serafina snorted in what was half hiccup, half tearful gasp, then shook her head from side to side. The words 'like a rabbit caught in the headlights' sprung to Sadia's mind and she wished there was an easier way to do this. 'Look, sweetheart, why don't you give me the name of the man from The Delius for starters and we'll go from there.'

Looking down at her hands, Serafina said, 'Anastazy. Anastazy Dolinski. That's his name and he's a *monster*.' She spat the last word out as if it were a poisoned sweet she'd been forced to taste.

Seeing how distraught Serafina became at the mere mention of the man's name, Sadia changed the subject. She'd revisit the subject of Anastazy later but, for now, she wanted the girl to relax. 'Who are you visiting in the CCU, Serafina?'

The tightness round Serafina's lips eased and her mouth twitched in a tired smile, 'My brother, Jacob. He was stabbed. Anastazy stabbed him. He lost his spleen, but they say he'll be okay.'

Sadia allowed the words to sink in before speaking again. 'So, Serafina, why, if Anastazy was the one to stab your brother, was he visiting your family last night?'

Serafina's eyes again darted to the door. She shifting on her seat, she shrugged but said nothing.

'Look, sweetie, you've come this far; said this much. I think you want to tell me. I think you *need* to tell me. If this Anastazy stabbed your brother, then we need to know, don't we?'

Pulling the sleeves of her jumper down over her palms, Serafina gripped the cuffs with her finger tips, swiped one arm over her eyes and swallowed hard. 'He stabbed Hasnain yesterday too… but my dad made me promise not to speak to the police about it.' And she broke down, sobs wracking her body. Sadia moved closer to her and put her arms round the crying girl. Holding her tightly, she smoothed Serafina's hair and muttered reassurances. All the while, Sadia was remembering the conversation she'd had with Gus earlier. The forensic psychologist had intimated that he believed the MO to be more akin to a turf war scenario than the work of a serial killer. He reckoned that, alongside the attacks on the prostitutes, this villain would likely indulge in lower level violence to enforce his will over others. Was this what the psychologist meant? Could this Anastazy be linked to or even responsible for the murders and the attack on Charlotte, which had been intended to create confusion and antipathy between Bazza Green and Shahid Khan?

When Serafina was calmer, Sadia teased out the details of the attacks on her friend Hasnain and her brother Jacob. 'What I don't understand though, is why your dad has prevented you from reporting this. Is he scared too?'

Serafina scowled, 'No. I don't think he's scared of Anastazy. Not like I am.' She thought for a moment before continuing, 'It's more like he wants to keep him sweet, no matter what he does to the rest of us. Like Anastazy has something on him maybe.' She waved her arms. 'Oh, I don't know. I just don't know. After my dad spoke to him, he told us that Anastazy hadn't stabbed Jacob and that we better not say otherwise to anyone.'

'Is that typical of your dad?'

Serafina laughed, 'Don't know. We didn't see him much before we moved to the UK. In Poland we were well off, not like we are here, but then, something happened and he lost his job or something and we moved to Bradford.'

'Any idea where Anastazy lives?'

Serafina shook her head, 'Bradford Three, maybe Killinghall Road area?'

Sadia texted Anastazy's name to Compo, asking him to see what he could find out about him. Then, she texted Imti asking him to email the footage of Anastazy to Compo and Gus to let him know what she'd discovered. Feeling pleased with her evening's work she stood and, after checking no one was on the corridor, they left the staff room.

Sadia decided to take one last look at Charlotte before she left and, making sure she walked behind Serafina, she headed along the corridor. When she drew level with her brother's door, Serafina paused and mouthed, 'Thank you,' to Sadia, but before she could enter the room the main ward door burst open, ricocheting off the wall. Both women spun round and Sadia spotted the other girl's sheer panic as she instinctively grabbed her crucifix, her eyes wide, pupils dilated. In an instant, all thoughts of Serafina were driven from Sadia's mind when she saw who had entered the ward.

Heart hammering, Sadia ran towards the figure that stood unsteadily in the entrance. A nurse approached but Sadia waved her away, 'It's okay, I've got this.' She said and concerned she put her hand on the man's arm, 'Shahid, what's happened?'

It was then that Jai approached like a towering brick wall behind Shahid, breathing heavily as if he'd exerted himself. When Shahid, stared blankly at Sadia without responding, Jai interjected, 'It's Imti.' His usual patronising arrogance was absent from his tone for once and Sadia felt her heart skip a beat. It must be bad for both Shahid and Jai to be so strongly affected. Her gaze fell to Shahid's hands. In a surreal Lady Macbeth type action, he kneaded them together sending little flakes of dried blood floating to the floor. The front of his T-shirt and the knees of his jeans were splodged a deep red colour and waves of alcohol wafted from him as Sadia tried to make sense of the tableau before her.

Jai, his voice catching in his throat put his arm round Shahid as he spoke. 'Shahid saw someone on the CCTV attack Imti when he was putting out the rubbish. He ran down and tried to staunch the blood.'

Sadia, wide-eyed, stepped forward and began to guide Shahid towards the relatives' room. Her hands shook, but she wouldn't allow the tears that clogged her throat to fall. Not till she knew everything. '...and Imti? Where is he now?' She felt like her heart was about to implode. How could this have happened? She'd only just seen him this morning. Who the hell would do this to Imti? Everyone loved him. But, as this last thought flitted through her mind, Serafina, who had followed her to Shahid, spoke, her voice trembling, 'Anastazy. It was Anastazy.'

Jai, eyes narrowed looked at Serafina, then nodded once before turning back to Sadia, 'Imti's in surgery. They wouldn't let us come in the ambulance, so I drove Shahid over. It was bad, Sadia, really bad.'

Settling Shahid on a chair in the relatives' room, she sent Serafina for coffee before saying, 'You stink, Shahid. You been drinking?'

Jai shook his head. 'I think he spilled whisky down himself. He's not as drunk as you think.' He glanced at Shahid and then moved closer to Sadia and said for her ears alone, 'I think he was going to top himself, Sad. I found a whole bunch of pills scattered over the table in his office.'

Sadia ran a trembling hand through her hair. 'Because of Trixie. God, I could kill him. Didn't he stop to think about what that would do to Imti?'

Jai laid a warning hand on her arm, 'That's not important now, though, is it?' and he inclined his head to where Shahid sat staring into space, seemingly oblivious to the tears pouring down his cheeks.

Sadia took a deep breath. 'Get a nurse, Jai. He's in shock.' She slipped her coat off and wrapped it round an unprotesting Shahid's shoulders. In another time the image of Shahid Khan, her pink coat with its fur collar draped round his shoulders, would have made her laugh… right now she wondered if things could get any worse.

CHAPTER 63
Duckworth Lane

Brighton kicked at the small pile of cigarette ends he'd thrown at his feet whilst he'd been waiting for Sadia's return. Where the fuck was the stupid bint? How long did it take her to check on a comatose whore? If it wasn't for the fact he could still see her car sitting where she'd parked it earlier, he would have thought he'd missed her. It was bloody freezing and he was getting fed up growling at kids in stupid clown masks to piss off and leave him alone.

Talking of piss, his bladder was protesting strongly now. If she didn't turn up soon he'd have to go. He glanced around. It was too busy here though, what with the never-ending flow of car headlights spotlighting him and the regular pedestrian activity. No, he'd have to risk heading up to the hospital and if he missed her... He shrugged. Well so fucking what. Not as if he was being paid hard cash for this. Besides if he went up there he'd be able to get a warm drink too. He blew on his hands. God, but he'd murder for a scalding hot coffee right now – even one of those poncy ones McGuire drank.

He pushed himself away from the tree, stamped the cig butts into the ground, crossed the road when the lights turned red and scurried up the steps into the hospital grounds. If the bitch saw him, he'd just tell her he was worried about the whore and was checking up on her. He grinned, not that he'd call her a whore though. No, he'd be as polite as he could and wrong-foot the cow. Make her think he'd turned over a new leaf.

Near the entrance to accident and emergency, he saw an ambulance screech up, sirens blaring and, even when the paramedic jumped out of the driver's seat and rushed to the back, the lights continued to rotate in a blaze of blue. Hands thrust deep in his pockets, he began to cross the asphalt, thinking 'probably some drunk started early on a Saturday night and over done it'. Typical fucking Bradistan. If it weren't the damn Pakis rioting and dealing drugs, it was the scumbags from Holme Wood and the like, dragging the city to the ground.

Heading for the illuminated 'Main Entrance' sign, he was distracted when a car braked hard near him, skidding to a stop. A man all but fell out of the passenger seat, slamming the door shut behind him and nearly rolling over the bonnet of the car in his haste to get to the entrance. Brighton glanced at the driver and recognised him as the bouncer from The Delius. He swung his gaze to the other man who had reached the disabled access slope and was grabbing the handrail to propel himself over like an Olympian hurdler before slamming through the double doors. As the light from the reception fell through the door, Brighton saw that it was Shahid Khan. *Wonder what the fuck's got into him now,* he thought, following at a more sedate pace.

CHAPTER 64
Marriners Drive

L eaving the cloying heat of the hospital, Sadia welcomed the blast of cold fresh air that hit her as she exited the double doors. Her head felt fuggy and she could feel the beginnings of a tension headache behind her eyes. Feeling as if she was moving through sludge, she walked towards her car and as she approached she saw that she'd been ticketed. She'd only put in enough money for an hour earlier and, after everything that had happened, she hadn't given parking a moment's thought. She lifted a leaden arm and pulled the plastic bag from beneath her wiper. Scrunching it up, she shoved it in the pocket of her coat, unable to even summon the energy to curse.

Climbing into her car, she savoured the stillness after the frenetic activity of the hospital and leaning forward, she rested her head on the steering wheel and closed her eyes, feeling the tension leave her body. She suspected that she'd suffer in the morning after holding her body so taut all day, however now she could relax a little. Imti was out of surgery and in the CCU. He'd lost a lot of blood but they'd managed to stop the bleeding in time and the knife had missed all his major organs. Thank God! For the first time in years, Sadia had prayed, as she'd waited for news with Shahid and Jai.

Gus had arrived with Alice, but then quickly left to deal with the crime scene and to see what headway they could make locating Anastazy Dolinski. He'd reported earlier that they were no further forward, but that Compo had made contact with Detective Jankowski, the Polish detective they'd worked with on The Matchmaker case, and would report back as soon as he had anything.

Serafina had alternated between visiting her brother and keeping Sadia company in the relatives' room. Her father had left shortly after Imti had been admitted and Serafina said she had no idea where he'd gone. Sadia texted his name to Compo too, on the off-chance it flagged something up.

Now, thankful that Imti was stable, Sadia turned the key in the ignition. She needed to get some rest, but she knew Gus would worry if she didn't see him so she made her way there, oblivious to the red car that followed her along Duckworth Lane, through Heaton and down Emm Lane, before turning into Marriners Drive.

When she pulled into the drive the security light came on and, even before she'd climbed out of the car, Gus opened the front door, holding a barking Bingo in his arms. A wave of longing engulfed her as she watched Gus, with his mucky blond mussed up dreads, trying to control the dog. She walked up the path, smiling when she detected the change in tone of Bingo's bark when he realised it was her. The welcoming tail wagging and barking became a pitiful whine accompanied by drooping ears and enlarged eyes. Sadia ran the last few steps and threw herself at Gus, grabbing his head with both hands and pulling his mouth to hers as she kissed him thoroughly, ignoring Bingo's squirms as he struggled to escape from between their embrace.

'Wow! Someone's pleased to see me,' said Gus.

Sadia laughed and ruffled Bingo's head. 'And someone's pissed off to see *me.*'

Gus laughed and led the way indoors and, as Sadia refused to take her coat off, saying she needed to get some rest, he said, 'Tomorrow's going to be a hellish busy day, but,' he shrugged, 'I've sort of promised my mum we'll go to hers for lunch. I'm planning on taking anyone who's on duty, but I thought I'd better give you a heads-up. No doubt she'll give you the third degree.'

Sadia sighed. There was nothing she felt less like doing than dodging questions from Gus' over-enthusiastic parents. 'Aw, Gus, can't you just take Al and the rest of the team for moral support? I feel like crap and I'll need to visit Imti.'

Gus shrugged and put Bingo down on the couch, 'Gabriella and Katie will be there.'

Sadia turned to him and wrapped her arms round him, squeezing tightly. She knew how difficult this would be for Gus. He hadn't seen his sister and his ex-wife together in the same room since he'd found out about their relationship. She kissed the side of his mouth and summoning an enthusiasm she didn't feel said, 'Then I'll definitely be there, but first I need to go home and grab some beauty sleep.'

CHAPTER 65
Astor Avenue, Idle

Sadia parked in front of her home. The warm glow of the porch light warned her that her father was expecting her and, after the events of the day, the last thing she needed was a confrontation. She sat for a moment looking at the home she'd shared with her parents for most of her life. They'd moved here soon after Millie Green's death. It had been difficult for a young Sadia. The trauma of what she'd witnessed that night stayed with her in the form of nightmares for many months afterwards and she could see why her parents had thought a move to a different area would be best for her. However, she'd felt isolated.

She was used to Thornbury, where the colour of her skin had never seemed to be an issue. At school she'd happily played with children from all faiths and cultures but the Idle of the 1990s was a completely different ethnic and class mix. In school she had found herself ridiculed for her skin colour and her faith and had quickly learned to stick up for herself. Slowly, she'd made friends and, as her school became more ethnically mixed, things improved. It angered her that, in Bradford in 2016, it appeared that the concept of not ghettoising children into mono-cultural schools was being largely ignored by the local authority, despite the rigorous report by Lord Ousely that had emphasised a cohesive community policy. Through her work, she knew that schools were becoming less and less mixed and this made her worry about how Bradford's children would rub along together in the real world if their cultural experiences in childhood were so narrow.

She switched off the ignition and geared herself up for the lecture that she knew was due to happen. Her father, not convinced she'd been with Shamila the other night, was clearly ready to have another go at her. No doubt he'd bring up the option of travelling to Pakistan for a husband. Ever since her mother had died her father had become more devout, spending more time with the Quran, both at home and at the mosque. Sadia knew loneliness made him seek the company of his own people but, over the years he'd become less cosmopolitan in outlook and held less open-minded views. She knew he loved her and that he worried she was putting her career before marriage and settling down. She knew he wanted to feel secure in the knowledge that she was taken care of should anything happen to him. Unusual among Muslim families, Sadia was an only child, and her only relatives lived in Lahore in Pakistan. She could not remember the last time she'd seen them.

Her father wanted her to visit his home country with him again, but Sadia's memories of heat, mosquitoes and basic toilets put her off and she'd refused. Maybe she should go with him, she thought now. What's a couple of weeks of hardship if it makes him happy? Of course, she'd have to be clear that looking for a groom was *not* on the agenda. Maybe it'd deflect him from questioning her too much if she were to suggest a visit after this case closes.

With a heavy heart, she got out of the car and trudged up the path. Opening the porch door, she bent down to take her shoes off and as soon as she opened the inner door her father called out, 'I'm in here, Sadia, come in, please.'

She grimaced. He was in his office and that meant that he wasn't going to give up easily. She knew to expect the third degree. Walking through the hallway with its lush green carpet, she pushed open the office door. Her father sat with his hands clasped together on the desk in front of him. He wore his prayer hat and a plain white shalwar kameez. His beard was freshly trimmed and his eyes looked stern as he gestured her to sit down in the opposite chair.

'I've been praying tonight that Allah will give me the strength to know the right path to take with you, Sadia beti'

Sadia frowned. 'What do you mean, Apo?'

'Ah, Sadia, I wonder if perhaps I have been too lenient with you. If I've allowed some of the rules of Islam to go unheeded. If I've neglected to teach you the ways of our religion. Perhaps, that is why you lie and are deceitful to me?' He rose to his feet and shouted the last sentence at her. His tone hit her like a slap and she flinched. This was so much worse than she'd expected. What had gotten into him?

'I don't understand. What have I done?'

He paced around her, making her feel like prey to a trapped tiger in a zoo. She swallowed, scared because she'd never seen him in this mood before.

'When is the last time you prayed, Sadia?' he asked, his voice quiet.

Sadia hung her head, completely forgetting her ardent prayers for Imti earlier. 'I'm not sure, Father. You know I'm not as devout as you.' To her own ears her voice sounded weak and pleading and she resented feeling like a naughty child when she was a grown woman.

'Well, you must change your ways, Sadia. From now on, I expect you to follow *all* of Allah's rules. Maybe that will teach you right from wrong and prevent further sinning.'

'Sinning?' asked Sadia, standing up to face her father now. 'I haven't sinned.'

Her father slammed both hands on the desk and glared at her. His voice when he spoke was razor sharp and accusing.

'So, you haven't been sleeping with a man out of wedlock, then?'

Sadia took a step back and shook her head, less in denial of the situation than of his accusation. What was going on? Did he know something about Gus? But how could he? Other than herself and Gus, Alice was the only other person who knew and Alice wouldn't betray her, would she? She rested a hand on the desk and stared at him. All tiredness had left her body, replaced by the adrenalin surge brought on by the charged atmosphere. He closed his eyes and, when he spoke, it was in a whisper. Sadia had to strain to hear his words. 'I see from your expression that your accuser is not wrong.'

He sat down in his chair and threw a brown envelope towards her. A bundle of photos fell out landing in a heap on the polished surface. Sadia glanced down at them. The envelope had no address on it which puzzled Sadia, but what drew her attention was the topmost photograph. She could clearly see that it was of her and Gus at his bedroom window. Sadia picked it up and looked at the next photo before sifting through the remaining photos. The realisation that someone had been stalking and spying on made her heart skip a beat. Then, a bubble of anger started in her chest. Who the hell would do this? What would anyone have to gain by giving these photos to her father?

Sadia grabbed a handful of photos and ripped them in half, her face flushed, her chest heaving as she looked at her father. As he ran one hand through his hair she became aware of how much he seemed to have aged. Guilt that she'd caused this flooded through her. He looked old and frail and her heart went out to him. With tears in her eyes, Sadia went over to where he sat and kneeled beside him. Gently, she took his hand in hers. It was frozen cold. She lifted it to her cheek and whispered, 'I'm so sorry, Bapa. I'm so sorry that I can't be what you want me to be. I'm sorry that I've hurt you but, I still love you and I am your daughter, always.'

Her father let out a keening sound and then, with unexpected force he whipped his hand from Sadia's and smashed it backhanded across her face, causing her to fall backwards and bang her head on the wall. He jumped to his feet, towering over her. 'Enough! You. Are. A. Muslim. And. You. Will. Behave. Like. One.'

Sadia hand held at her cheek, eyes wide looked at him in disbelief. He had *never* hit her as a child! How dare he do it now? Without stopping to think of the consequences, Sadia scrambled to her feet and pushed past him.

He let her go assuming she was headed upstairs. It wasn't until he heard the front door rattle on its hinges as she slammed it shut behind her that he realised she'd left the house. He leapt after her, rushed through the house and pulled open the porch door, noting that she hadn't even waited to collect her coat or put her shoes on. As he ran into the drive, all he saw were her brake lights as she turned the corner at the end of the street.

He threw his hands in the air and yowled like a werewolf at the moon. Then, falling to his knees, heedless of the dirt on his white clothes, he wrapped his arms round his body. Tears stormed down his face, landing among the puddles already gathering on the crazy paving. Where had he gone wrong? He looked up to the sky and asked Allah where he had failed.

CHAPTER 66
Marriner's Drive

The hammering on the door jolted Gus awake. After Sadia had left, he'd fallen asleep on the sofa with Bingo sprawled over his chest. Disorientated he pushed a reluctant Bingo onto the floor and rubbing his eyes walked through the hallway. He could hear thrashing rain against the window and, as he approached the door, he saw Sadia's silhouette through the glass. Wondering what the emergency was, he pushed Bingo out of the way and stepped closer, hoping that Imti's condition hadn't worsened.

As he pulled the door open, Sadia stumbled in, giving Gus barely enough time to see that she had no coat on, was barefoot and drenched. Her hair hung in dripping lengths to her shoulders and mascara blackened her cheeks. Even Bingo, appearing to pick up on her distress, whimpered and nudged her legs with his nose, his eyes looking up at her till, with a half-hearted motion, she patted his head.

Gus' heart contracted as he closed the door behind her and guided her through to the living room. Her vacant expression told him she was in shock so, after settling her onto the sofa and bunging a couple of extra logs on the fire, he headed into the kitchen, flicked on the kettle and rushed upstairs reappearing moments later with his skimpy robe. As he sat beside her gently chaffing her frozen between his hands he saw the bruise blossoming on her cheek and the trail of blood where her lip had cracked. Had she been in a car accident? He glanced down at her feet, wondering where her shoes were. Bingo jumped up beside her, resting his chin on her leg. A faint smile appeared on Sadia's lips and Gus released a grateful sigh. He hadn't realised until that point that he'd been holding his breath.

Leaving her with Bingo, Gus disappeared into the kitchen, reappearing minutes later with buttered toast and a steaming mug of hot chocolate. Sadia smiled when she accepted the mug and nursing it in her hands she allowed Gus to minister her injuries.

First, he applied a cold compress to her swollen cheeks before gently wiping away her blotched mascara and the trail of blood from her lip. Then he soaked and washed her scraped feet and administered a few arnica pills to help with the swelling. As he worked, his brain was in overdrive, wondering what had happened to her in such a short space of time. He felt sick and was struggling to control his own panic. It was only the knowledge that she needed him to be calm right now that prevented him from losing it. It was clear that, although she was distressed, her injuries were superficial and he understood that any questions could wait until she was calmer.

When he'd finished, he was relieved to see that some colour had returned to her face and she'd stopped shivering. Time to find out what was wrong. He pulled her into his lap and as he smoothed her hair back off her forehead, she told him what had happened. When she got to the part where her dad hit her, Gus felt an almost overpowering urge to rush over to Idle and deal with him there and then. How dare he lay a hand on Sadia? It was only her beseeching look and the way she gripped his hand so tightly that kept him there. Sadia needed him right now but, as soon as he was able he would have it out with her father. No way was he going to get away with this.

317

Between them, they'd tried to work out who'd taken the photos. Gus remembered the red car he'd seen hanging around and made a mental note to check that out. They'd thought they were being discreet, but obviously they hadn't been careful enough. Someone, though, had decided to stalk them and that someone had done so with malicious intent. Were they both targets, or was it just one of them?

'Nobody knew about us, Sadia. We didn't flaunt it, so maybe it was just by chance,' Gus snorted, 'Nah, strike that. There's no way somebody could, just by chance, have been outside my house at the exact same time we were having an afternoon quickie. No, it seems like premeditated stalking to me. Which brings us back to the question of who knew about us?''

'Alice did,' said Sadia. 'She confronted me in the loo yesterday.'

'Yeah, she got at me too.' Gus grinned, remembering Alice's serious face as she'd chided him for not confiding in her. 'She warned me to be careful… but it wasn't a threat Sad. She was just concerned because of your dad.'

Sadia nodded. 'I agree. Alice hasn't got a bitter, nasty bone in her body. It wasn't her. Besides which, I don't think she rates my dad much. Doubt she'd give him any ammunition.'

Cuddled up next to him, with the heat from the fire making her drowsy, Sadia continued, 'Do you reckon Brighton or Sampson would do something like that?'

Gus didn't even have to think about it. He shook his head, 'Not Sampson, but Brighton… well, who knows? He's a nasty piece of work.'

'I gave him a rollicking that first night and yesterday I came down on him like a tonne of bricks,' said Sadia. 'He doesn't like me and I'm afraid the feeling is very definitely mutual. My money's on him.'

Gus grimaced. 'I know what you mean. He's an "eejit", as my dad would say, and a nasty one at that. Worth keeping an eye on him.'

'Yeah and he made those weird comments at the briefing, about me being flushed and my hair being damp. I thought he was just being an arse at the time but, what if he'd followed us?' She pulled away from Gus and opened her mouth to expand on her thoughts but that was as far as she got before Gus had swooped her into his arms and stood up. 'We'll think about all this in the morning. Right now, I think we both need our bed.' And with a lascivious grin that had Sadia laughing he took her upstairs.

Sadia lay on the bed, her eyes huge, her lashes skimming her cheek bones when she looked down. Gus lay beside her and undid the tie on the oversized terry bath robe. He opened it and looked down at her. Slender, soft and inviting, her skin, the colour of a good whisky. 'You're beautiful,' he whispered.

Her eyes filled with tears as she reached for him. He kissed her eyes, her nose, her swollen cheek and her lips. Then, breathing in the scent of her, he moved down to kiss every part of her. His tongue explored every contour of her perfect body as he enjoyed her whimpers. No rush this time... Sadia was staying the night.

CHAPTER 67
The Delius

The air was heavy with smoke and, even from halfway up Leeds Road, near the Hindu Temple, Gus could hear the screeching of fire engines against the backdrop of flames that lit up the distant dark sky. When the call had come in, Sadia hadn't even stirred beyond burrowing her head further into the pillow and when Gus had crept from the bed and got dressed in the dark she hadn't moved a muscle. He'd made the decision not to wake her, reckoning that the events of the previous day warranted her having a lie in. He knew though, that when she found out, she'd be furious... but hell, he'd deal with that later.

Now, he parked on Leeds Road just beyond the cordon and, flicking the tape up and over his head, he marched through uniformed officers and fire fighters looking for Alice or Sampson, both of whom he'd called earlier. When he found them, Alice was standing beside Jai. For the first time since Gus had met him, the bouncer looked dishevelled. His normal taciturn expression was replaced by an angry curling lip and frown lines on his forehead. Alice had her notebook out and was scribbling furiously by the light from the blaze.

Gus let her get on with it and, instead of approaching them, he studied the fire. It seemed like it was concentrated at the back of the building and, although it looked and smelled bad, Gus thought that the Khan brothers had been lucky this time. It looked like the administrative part of the club had suffered most of the damage but that the main area had escaped lightly. Gus knew that, bearing in mind everything that had gone on recently, the likelihood of this

320

fire being an accident was miniscule. He suspected the fire officer's official report would define the cause of the fire as arson. Taking out his phone Gus shot an email to Compo who had headed into The Fort, asking him to access CCTV footage along Leeds Road and Lower Rushton Road, which backed onto The Delius.

As Alice shut her notebook, clearly having completed her interview with Jai, Gus saw a man in a prayer hat, wearing a duffle coat over, what looked like, a pair of striped pyjamas, approach Jai. With interest, he noted how Jai bristled when the man touched him on the shoulder. When he turned to reply to whatever the man had said Gus saw the anger on his face. Jai gesticulated with his hands and then, strode off towards one of the firefighters.

'Wonder what that was about.' said Gus, as Alice joined him.

'Well, my money's on that man being Councillor Majid from the local mosque. Jai said he had a run-in with Shahid yesterday. Moaning about the rowdiness of some of The Delius' patrons.' She grinned, 'Jai was pretty pissed off, said, and, I quote, "the old bastard's an ungrateful git. Shahid paid the mosque thousands, so he should put up and shut up".'

'Not sure how strong that motive is if he was getting money from Shahid. Stands to reason that if The Delius stopped bringing money in, the mosque would lose out.'

'Jai also went on about that Anastazy bloke. He's convinced he's behind it.'

Gus couldn't really fault his logic, but so far they'd been unable to find anything concrete on the bloke or even establish an address. It was like he was a ghost.

'Who discovered the fire, Al?

'That would be our trusty bodyguard bouncer, Jai. Shahid's still up at BRI with Imti so Jai was kipping on the couch in Shahid's office. Said it was so uncomfortable he couldn't sleep, lucky for him, because he smelt the smoke and phoned 999 straightaway. If he hadn't acted so quickly the damage would have been much more extensive.' She glanced over Gus' shoulder, 'Oh and here's Sampson. He's been chatting with the fire officer.'

Watching Sampson yawn widely as he approached made Gus smile. 'We keeping you up, Sampson?'

With bleary eyes Sampson peered at Gus, 'Well, I'd no better offers, sir, so I might as well be here.' He began to rub one eye with his knuckle, leaving a sooty mark on his face.

Gus thought it made him look as if he'd got lost on the way to a Halloween party. 'What did you get from the fire officer?'

'Not much really. He reckons from the flash points it was set by pouring petrol through the letterbox at the back. Clearly an arson attempt, but he'll know more later when he can sift through the rubble.'

A flurry of activity near one of the fire engines had Gus turning his head in that direction. A firefighting team was running to the engine nearest the cordon and almost before they'd all jumped in, it began to back out with its siren on. Another fire officer, recognising Gus shouted 'There's another fire over in Bradford Nine. Looks like we've got a spree on our hands.'

Bradford Nine? Shit, thought Gus, *I bet I know where that fire is.* Just then his phone began to vibrate, followed almost immediately by Alice's and Sampson's. Gus took off back towards his car, with Alice and Sampson following.

CHAPTER 68
The Fort

The incident room in The Fort was steeped in a strange combination of petrol fumes, smoke and coffee. The petrol and smoke were from Gus, Alice and Sampson's clothes. Having attended two fires in the space of as many hours, they had lost any residue of fabric conditioner, perfume or deodorant that might have otherwise lingered. The coffee was down to Compo, who'd got the machine up and running in readiness for an all-nighter as soon as he'd arrived in the early hours of the morning.

Gus could've kissed him when he'd walked through the door and been greeted by a piping hot mug of coffee and the promise of a bacon butty, which was being delivered by Tony from the Chaat café. Nothing like two arson attacks to build up an appetite, thought Gus, relieved that there'd been no injuries from either fire except for Bazza Green who'd fallen flat on his face in his haste to jump off the young girl he was screwing and get out the door first. Stupid bastard had broken his nose and bruised his knee. Served him right, thought Gus, who'd felt like punching him when the seventeen-year-old had told him what had happened.

Gus had had an uncomfortable phone call with Sadia, who, as expected, was angry that he'd let her sleep through all the activity. However, the fact that she had a huge bruise on her cheek that she couldn't disguise meant that she was reluctant to face everybody, especially as she'd left home with no make-up to cover it. Besides which, she didn't feel ready to risk bumping into her father yet. He'd been phoning and texting her off and on all night but Sadia wasn't in the frame of mind to respond. Gus didn't blame her. He knew she was in shock. Not just about her dad's aggressive behaviour but also about Imti. Gus had told her to get her friend Shamila to bring her some clothes and makeup and told her to work from home. There were plenty of reports she could be filling in. He grinned. It wasn't her favourite job but, at least it'd keep her out of harm's way for now.

When he'd entered The Fort this morning he'd hoped he wouldn't bump into DCS Hussain. He wasn't sure he'd be able to contain himself if he saw the man. The memory of Sadia's swollen cheek and the anguish in her eyes was just too fresh for Gus to take a dispassionate stance just yet. He knew he'd have a 'conversation' with the other man, but he was determined that, when that time came, it would be on his own terms and away from The Fort. This was personal, not professional and he'd be damned if he would allow Hussain to pull rank on him.

From the incident room he could see that Hussain's parking space was empty. Maybe he was too ashamed to show his face here. *He bloody well should be too*, thought Gus, anger resurfacing in his chest as he thought about what he'd done to Sadia. *What sort of parent does that to his daughter?* He ignored the sneaky little voice at the back of his head that whispered, *one who's desperate and scared he's losing his daughter*. As far as Gus was concerned that was no excuse.

Butties eaten, Gus opened the briefing, recounting the events of the previous day. Brighton, who Gus had decided not to call to the fires, looked clean and relaxed. The way he swung back on the back two legs of his chair annoyed the hell out of Gus. He looked like a bloody overgrown schoolboy and Gus had an almost uncontrollable urge to knock the legs from under the chair. Besides which, Gus had a sneaky suspicion that he was the secret photographer. Although he'd like to challenge the man about it, Gus decided he'd get clarification from Sadia's dad before doing anything rash. For the time being though, visions of Brighton landing on his fat arse would have to do. Brighton raised a hand. 'What is it, Brighton?'

'Just wondered where DS Hussain is? We could do with her input on this couldn't we? Especially as she took the statements from Shahid Khan and the Polish bint, whassername?'

Gus, with difficulty, refrained from snapping at the other man… but only just. 'DS Hussain is pursuing other enquiries and, for your information the female witness who, presumably, at considerable personal risk, is helping us in our enquiries, is called Serafina. Please call her that from now on.'

Brighton nodded, 'Yes sir, will do. Just not familiar with a lot of those foreign names, you know?'

Alice tutted. 'Hardly a bloody tongue twister, is it Brighton. You pronounce it phonetically – that means you say it as it's spelled. Too difficult for you?'

Gus sighed, 'Right you two, stop it, okay. We've too much to do to be argy-bargying amongst ourselves. Brighton, you need watch your attitude. It's distasteful and unproductive. Wise up, huh?'

Head down, Brighton mumbled what Gus suspected was a half-hearted apology. He knew he'd have to deal with the other man at some point, but now wasn't the time. He'd have to put up with him till after this case was over. He shot him a warning look and then explained the forensic psychologist Professor Carlton's assessment before turning to Compo. For once the computer whizz kid looked marginally better groomed than any of them. Amazing how the absence of soot grime and smoke could elevate you to the best dressed person in the room. 'What have you got for us, Comps?'

Shoving the last of his butty in his mouth, leaving a residue of greasy ketchup round his lips, Compo took a swig of coffee, gargled it round his mouth a bit and took a deep swallow before speaking. 'Well, I spoke with Detective Jankowski earlier. Thought I'd have more success going to him directly. The name Anastazy Dolonski meant nothing to him, but he put it thorough the system and still came up blank. Then I sent him the CCTV footage from The Delius and …' he looked round the room grinning as if he'd just invented the wheel, 'He recognised him. He's one bad son of a–,' he blushed, 'you know what I mean.'

He pressed a button and the interactive whiteboard sprung to life revealing a much clearer photo of Anastazy Dolinski. This is our man. His rap sheet is extensive,' another document appeared next to the photo, revealing a list that went from petty crimes like carjacking and shoplifting as a teen, through to gang activity involving murder, rape and prostitution offences. 'According to Jankowski, Dolinski was part of the notorious Grypsers gang – note the teardrop tattoos on the face – until he got on the wrong side of them. The trouble is, the only way to leave the Grypsers is in a coffin. Dolinski apparently thought he'd find another way and tried to set up a rival gang with funding from a renowned Polish gangster. However, that all fell through and after raping and murdering the gangster's wife and daughter, Dolinski went in the wind. That's probably when he escaped Poland to come to the UK.'

Another series of mug shots came on the screen. 'These are his known associates. The ones at the top are known to have fled Poland, so may well be in Bradford as we speak.

Jankowski's got someone to locate and interview the others to see if they can shed any light on Dolinski's plans.'

'Good work, Compo,' said Gus, studying the profiles on the screen.

Compo held up a finger, 'One more thing, Gus. Detective Jankowski said that another Polish kingpin, much more influential than Dolinski, made a dodgy drug deal that screwed with a rival gang with international connections. This guy ended up being hounded out of Poland. The only thing is, he'd always played it clever until that point. He had someone fronting for him to conceal his identity. The authorities had their suspicions but could never confirm his identity and he always seemed to fly under the radar. However, they have no proof.'

Gus frowned. 'What's the relevance of this?'

Compo slapped his hand down on his desk making Alice jump. 'That's just it, Jankowski says this bloke, codenamed 'The Old Man' is desperate. His sources tell him he's left Poland and is seeking to make new liaisons in order to re-establish an empire somewhere in Europe. Jankowski's sources reckon he's in the UK *and* they reckon he's just about desperate enough to make a deal with the devil, in the form of Dolinski.'

'Well, it all seems a bit tenuous to me,' said Brighton, 'There must be loads of criminals hot-footing it to the UK from Poland. Seems a bit much to link these two together.'

Gus noted how Compo's cheeks flushed at Brighton's condescending tone and was just about to intervene when Compo, turned and faced Brighton. When he spoke his tone was firm, 'If Detective Jankowski is suggesting there may be a link between these two men then it is because he believes it to be a very real possibility. He says "The Old Man is losing his grip in Poland. Allies he previously relied on are coming under the scrutiny of the Polish police and some are beginning to realise that their knowledge of The Old Man is the best bargaining tool they have." Detective Jankowski would like him returned to Poland to face the Polish courts for his crimes. He reckons that hiding his identity is crucial to The Old Man and that might be enough for him to strike up a deal with Dolinski. If Dolinski knows who he is then he has a very strong hold over The Old Man... maybe strong enough to warrant a partnership.'

Gus grinned at Compo, 'From our previous dealings with Jankowski, I trust him implicitly. Keep working with him. Get Dolinski's photo circulated and see about getting a photo of the other man too. Any word in placing Anastazy Dolinski at either of the arson sites? Or better still any word on the ground regarding where he lives.'

Compo shook his head. 'Nah, still working on it.'

'Right then. This morning we'll focus our energies on re-interviewing everyone, armed with these mug shots. Alice and I will take Jessica Green and Shahid Khan. Sampson, you work with the fire officer and co-ordinate the arson investigations. The focus of these attacks on Bazza Green and Shahid Khan are too co-incidental not to be part of Dolinski's apparent takeover bid. Brighton, you're co-ordinating the paper trail from here, okay?'

As everyone gathered up their paperwork, he added, 'Oh and by the way, Sunday lunch at my parents', 2pm sharp. You're all invited.'

Compo, jumped to his feet and punched the air, 'Yippee!'

Gus exchanged a glance with Alice who shook her head saying, 'Constitution of a bloody ox, that boy.'

CHAPTER 69
Marriners Drive

Huddled in Gus's oversized towelling robe, Sadia sat on the couch, legs curled up beneath her, nibbling toast liberally slathered in butter and jam. Despite everything that had happened, she felt happy. She'd phoned the hospital and found out that Imti was out of danger, stable and comfortable. The relief that flooded through her made her have a little weep but now, tears wiped up, she was doing her best to forget about her dad. She knew she'd never forgive him for hitting her but, in truth, his actions had made it easier to admit the extent of her feelings for Gus. The weight of secrecy she'd carried for months was gone now and, in spite of her father's reaction, she felt optimistic for the future. Hell, even Bingo had declared a truce for now and was curled up beside her on the couch. She leaned over and ruffled his head, smiling when his small tail wagged.

In a daydream bubble Sadia was only half aware of the door rattling and, forgetting it was a Sunday, she assumed it was the post. Seconds later, Bingo's little feet jumped over her, his bottom wiggling from side to side in excitement as he dived for the living room door, barking an energetic greeting. Sadia smiled assuming it was Gus then when a voice Sadia recognised only too well drifted through the door, her smile faltered

'Halloooo! Anyone home?'

Frozen to the spot, Sadia was debating what to do when the door was flung open and Corrine McGuire stood there. The two women stared at each other; Corrine with a grin

329

illuminating her face, Sadia with her mouth open like a stranded goldfish.

Corrine reacted first moving into the room, hand extended, 'I'm Gus' mum, Corrine, and you, I take it, are Sadia?'

Conscious of the shortness of her robe and the fact that she was naked underneath it, Sadia tried to pull it down with one hand, whilst shaking Corrine's with the other.

'Gus not in?' said Corrine, settling herself into the armchair opposite Sadia.

Sadia shook her head, 'No, no, there were a couple of arson attacks last night that we think are linked to our current case so he went into The Fort. Not sure when he'll be back.'

She felt like she should explain what she was doing here, in Gus' house in his absence but, she really didn't know where to begin. As a first introduction to her partner's mum, this left a hell of a lot to be desired. She uncurled her legs, trying to retain what modesty she could, preparatory to heading upstairs to get dressed, but as if anticipating her actions, Corrine waved her hand, to stop her an amused look on her face. Sadia wanted to curl up and die, but Gus' mum seemed intent on prolonging her agony by having a conversation.

'I only popped in on my way back from Sainsbury's. Don't really need him for owt. I was going to take Bingo back with me, but you could always bring him with you when you come for lunch.'

Shit, she'd forgotten about lunch at Gus's parents'. She wasn't sure she was looking forward to it any more than Gus was, especially not with a huge bruise on the side of her face. Without thinking she raised her fingers to touch the swollen skin then, seeing Corrine's gaze follow her actions she lowered them, hoping Corrine wouldn't notice it. Chance would be a fine thing. By the look of concern that flitted across the other woman's face she knew those laser eyes that were so like Gus' had homed in on the mark. Thankfully though, Corrine diverted her gaze to Sadia's bare legs. God, this situation was getting worse and worse. The last thing she needed was for his mum to let slip to the rest of the team that she'd caught her nearly naked in Gus' living room... and that was before you considered the atmosphere that would surely erupt between Gus, his sister and his ex-wife. Not a lunch made in heaven, she suspected.

'Em, I'm not sure I'll be able...'

But before she could finish her sentence, Corrine again waved her tiny hand in the air, effectively brushing off Sadia's excuses, 'Rubbish! Course you'll be there... Everyone will.'

Corrine settled more comfortably into the chair, letting Bingo rain her with kisses as she fondled his ears. *Was she ever going to leave!* Sadia would have jumped up and offered her a drink... anything to escape for a moment, but her inability to extricate her legs from beneath her bum without flashing her arse, followed by the prospect of a walk to the kitchen with her buttocks barely covered squashed that idea. No, far less embarrassing to risk being considered rude than to *expose* herself further to her boyfriend's mum.

With Bingo calmed down a fraction, Corrine studied Sadia, then she touched her own cheek and in a tone that dripped with concern said, 'What have you done? That looks really sore.'

Feeling like a complete fool, Sadia found that her eyes were full of tears and that despite her trying to blink them away, they began to roll down her cheeks. She sniffed and wiped them away with her sleeve.

Corrine tutted, 'Oh dear, now I've upset you. Gus will be so cross.'

Sadia, in the face of Corrine's distress found herself smiling. Deciding that honesty would be the best policy with this woman, she shook her head. 'No, no, it doesn't matter. What happened was that my father discovered I was seeing Gus and he hit me. That's why I'm here, trying to work out what to do next.'

Corrine gasped and a look of horror crossed her face, 'That's awful, Sadia. It angers me when men use their strength to physically punish women because of their own inadequacies but it saddens me when a father uses violence against his daughter.' She leaned over and squeezed Sadia's arm. 'There is *never* an excuse for violence in the home… *never*… and I should know. I suffered it enough as a child.' She paused, a slight frown marring the smoothness of her forehead. Her unusual eyes narrowed, as if, perhaps, she was remembering a very bad memory. Then, her face broke into a smile that left Sadia wondering if she'd imagined the desperation of Corrine's earlier expression.

Standing up, she looked at Sadia. 'Thank you for being honest with me. I much prefer straight-talking sensible women and I sense that you're one of those.' She raised an eyebrow and winked, 'Maybe if Gabriella had been a bit more straight-talking in the first place, Gus wouldn't have been hurt. I'm sorry your dad found it necessary to resort to hitting you. Some men have an unfortunate habit of trying to offload their guilt for their actions on their victims. Don't allow him to, Sadia. You're worth so much more than that.'

She leaned over and hugged her, 'I'll leave you to your thoughts and look forward to seeing you at lunch.' She placed two fingers under Sadia's chin and raised it slightly so Sadia was looking into her eyes. 'You'll be fine. I know you will. Now, I've got a lunch to prepare and you, my dear, will feel much more comfortable when you meet me later on with your clothes on.'

And with another wink, she headed for the door, leaving Sadia feeling as if she'd just endured a tsunami.

CHAPTER 70
Oak Lane

Alice and Gus chose to walk the short distance from The Fort to Jessica's flat. Oak Lane, despite it being Sunday morning, had a steady flow of traffic heading down towards Manningham Lane. Gus' thoughts were partly on the interview ahead and partly with Sadia. She'd texted earlier to say his mum had dropped in. Gus hoped his mum hadn't embarrassed him too much. Why did he have to be lumbered with two lovely but extremely eccentric parents? Mind you, according to Alice, he didn't have the monopoly on weird parents.

As they waited to cross the road at the Oak Lane traffic lights, he was aware of Alice studying him. She'd been throwing covert glances at him since they left the briefing and he'd known it was only a matter of time before she said whatever was on her mind. He suspected it was something to do with Sadia and he was proved right when she spoke moments later.

'Come on, Gussy boy, spill the beans.'

Gus seeing a gap in the traffic stepped onto the road, grinning when he heard Alice's 'bloody hell' as she ran to keep up with his long strides. 'That's no way to talk to a superior officer, Al.' he said when they reached the other side.

'Well, the thing is,' said Alice, popping a chewing gum in her mouth before offering the packet to him, 'I've got one of those new breeds of DIs who believe that respect is earned and isn't always denoted with a yes sir, no sir, Let me lick your arse, sir!'

'Touché, young Alice, you do me proud.' said Gus. You could always rely on Alice to make you laugh.

'How is she?' asked Alice, her tone serious now. 'You, for some strange reason look happy as Larry, humming that stupid Robbie Williams song to yourself, but Sadia's off work, which isn't like her *and* I haven't seen the DCS today either.'

Gus realised that, despite worrying about Sadia, he had in fact been relieved at the turn of events. He was pretty sure he hadn't been humming Robbie Williams but, he wasn't entirely certain. 'In case you hadn't noticed it *is* a Sunday and the powers that be don't often deign to grace us with their presence on a weekend... well not unless it's to give us a rollicking.'

Alice gave an expressive humph that told Gus she wasn't going to be put off so easily, so he continued, 'She's at mine.' Anticipating Alice's next question, he added '...and she's fine.'

'And?' said Alice, her impatient tone telling him to get a move on.

Shaking his head at her persistence, he said, 'Okay then Al. You win but this is strictly confidential.'

'God yes, I wouldn't gossip about you two.' Alice looked shocked at the mere suggestion of her betraying him, making Gus feel like an arse for spelling it out to her.

'The thing is, Al, the bastard hit her... well, slapped her really. Her cheek's bruised. It happened last night after she got home after all the Imti trauma. She ran out and came to me.'

Alice stopped dead in the street, one hand raised to her mouth. 'Oh, my God! Poor Sadia, she must be gutted. Why

335

would he hit her? He dotes on her. Don't tell me he's done it before?'

Gus sighed, 'No, no he's never hit her in the past. Some bastard's been stalking us and he took incriminating photos of me and her together. As expected, Hannibal Hussain wasn't happy about it. He snapped and hit her.'

'Fucking hell!'

'She wants it kept quiet. She's not going to do anything about it. Not going to report it. But me? Well, that's a different matter. I'll be paying him a visit later on today.' He started walking again, 'If we ever bloody get there, that is.'

Alice grabbed his arm and pulled him to a standstill again. 'Gus, you can't do that. You can't hit a senior officer. Not even a bastard that hits his daughter.'

Gus smiled. 'Who said anything about hitting him. I don't need to use my fists on an old man. I'll just verbally pulverise him… and I'll make damn sure he never touches her again.'

'Oh, well,' said Alice with a shrug, 'That's okay then.'

Gus frowned. 'It is?'

'Yes, because you'll take me with you as your witness that you did nothing but talk,' she said and folded her arms across her chest as if that settled the matter. Then, she added, 'but, if I were you, Gus I'd be more worried about who's been following you two and why.'

'You've got a point there, Al. I've been wracking my brains to think of someone who'd be malicious enough to do that, but short of Brighton, I can't think of anyone.'

'Brighton? Don't think he'd have the brains to do that… unless of course Hussain asked him to. He's Hussain's lapdog isn't he? Maybe he put him on the team to keep an eye on Sadia.'

Gus, hands in his pocket, shoulders slumped, frowned. 'Nah, surely not?'

Now that Alice had planted the thought in his mind, Gus began to wonder if she was right. Brighton was an unwelcome addition to the team and was there purely on Hussain's insistence. There was no doubt it was all a bit co-incidental.

Nearing the greengrocer's underneath Jessica's flat Gus became aware that a crowd had gathered. At first he thought they were looking at the boxes of tomatoes, chillies and fresh coriander that were displayed on upturned crates on the pavement, but then he heard the raised voices. He turned to Alice, 'What the hell's going on?'

From the alleyway leading to Jessica's flat he could hear banging and a man's voice shouting, 'Come on, Jessica. Let me in. We've got to talk. Please.'

'Fuck off! I've nowt to say to you.'

'Jessica, we both loved her. You've got to let me in. Come on, Trixie wouldn't want me to leave you here with Bazza. I need to speak to you about Imti, too. He's been hurt.'

Gus heard a door opening and, as Alice made to go down the alley, he grabbed her arm shaking his head. This wasn't the time to rush in guns blazing. He turned to the crowd and told them to disperse, before edging forward to get a view of what was happening at the end of the ally.

Jessica stood at the top of the steps, her face pale and grimy, her hair tangled and dank. She was wearing the same clothes she'd worn at their first interview on Thursday and, Gus suspected, she hadn't left the flat since then. She appeared oblivious to Gus and Alice standing behind Shahid. Her furious gaze was focussed only on Shahid Khan who, hands stretched out before him, pleaded for her to hear him out. Jessica was having none of it though. 'You've got a fuckin' cheek. You've no right to say her name, you're not good enough to say it. She'd never have gone with you, Shahid, never. She loved me!' and, before Gus could react, Jessica darted down the stairs and began pummelling Shahid with her fists.

Shahid lowered his hands to his side and took it, until, without warning, Jessica fell at his feet crying as if she'd never stop. Shahid bent down and put his arms round Jessica. With tears pouring down his cheeks too, he pulled her to him, smoothing her wild hair and patting her back as she cried, holding onto him as if for dear life.

'Sssh, sis. It's okay. I've got you now. Sssh.' He rocked her back and forth like a baby until eventually her tears subsided to the occasional hiccup.

Gus watched in silence as Shahid pulled her to her feet and, still holding her, led her to the stairs. Turning, Shahid looked at the small group that still loitered at the end of the alley and said, 'Show's over folks.' Turning to Gus, he said, 'I'll leave the door open, but give us five minutes, huh?'

Gus nodded and walked back round the front to wait, with Alice following him.

Alice rubbed her hands together, 'Great! I've got time to grab one of Mo's samosas.' And she darted across the road, leaving Gus to wonder where the hell she put it all.

Ten minutes later, samosa taste still in their mouths, they climbed the stairs to Jessica's flat. Shahid, true to his word, had left the door open and, with a cursory knock, Gus and Alice walked in.

Jessica sat, legs curled under her in her usual seat. Shahid, looking dishevelled but cleaner than he'd looked at the hospital the previous night, popped his head out from the kitchen. 'Tea?'

His tone was grudging and Gus nearly laughed out loud when Alice smiled and said in a too-sweet tone, 'How lovely. Yes, please, Shahid.'

She got a grunt for her efforts, which amused Gus even more. There would never be any love lost between the police and the likes of Shahid Khan, but Alice's sassiness at least took the sting out of it. Sitting down, Gus watched as Alice wandered around the room. It was her first visit here and he knew she wanted to get a feel for the place. It was a technique he also employed. He'd done his snooping last time but he'd be interested to hear what her thoughts were. He grinned as she threw a glance at Jessica, making sure she wasn't watching, before poking her head through the open bedroom door. Leaving her to her exploration, Gus turned his attention to Jessica. Staring at the carpet in front of her, cigarette between her fingers, the faint whiff of stale sweat hanging heavy in the air, Gus thought she looked worse than she had on Friday. Poor thing was taking Trixie's death very hard. Maybe she'd have thought of something for them. It still worried Gus that Trixie's death varied, even if only slightly from Camilla and Starlight's. He'd put his money on Professor Carlton being right about it being a copycat. He just hoped Jess would give them something to work on… a punter who'd taken too much of a liking to Trixie or a dealer she owed money to.

Shahid walked through carrying a plate of toast for Jessica and mugs of tea for everyone else. Gus was surprised that Jessica had capitulated so much in the space of ten minutes that she was allowing Shahid to look after her. Maybe the news of Imti's stabbing had been too much for her so soon after Trixie's murder. He found it hard to believe that all the animosity she'd felt towards Shahid had vanished so completely.

'Surprised to see you here, Shahid,' said Gus, smiling.

'Why? Jess is my sister in't she? She needed to know about Imti … *and* Trixie was her best mate.'

'Half-sister,' said Alice, taking a sip of tea

Shahid snorted, 'What's the difference? Sister, half-sister? What's it matter?'

Gus shrugged, 'Last time Jessica took great pains to make sure we knew you were only her *half*-brother. She really didn't want to acknowledge you as her brother, did you, Jessica? So, what's changed?'

The look of hatred Jessica threw at Shahid was unmistakeable, but so was the leaden way she moved and the dullness in her eyes. Jessica was very near to breaking point. Speaking quietly with no inflection in her tone, she said, 'Nothing's changed. I still hate him. Just make him go.' she raised her hand, fingernails bitten to the quick, and clumped her hair in it, her palm resting on her forehead as she spoke. 'I'm just so tired. Please make him go.' Letting go of her hair she wrapped her arms diagonally round her shoulders and began to rock back and forth. Gus felt his heart contract at the pitiful picture she made. He wondered if she'd eaten anything since the MacDonald's that Sadia had brought her. Lowering his voice, deliberately making his tone gentle, Gus pushed the toast towards her and said, 'Eat this, Jess. You need to eat.'

He turned to Shahid, who looked as if she'd slapped him. 'Jessica wants you to go, Shahid. Why don't you just go and stop upsetting her. I thought you'd have had enough to worry about, what with Imti and the arson attack on The Delius this morning,'

To Gus, it seemed that Shahid's body caved in on itself. Instead of the confident young man, full of swagger, he looked like a bereft little boy. Despite himself Gus felt a momentary pang of pity for Shahid as he ran a trembling hand through his short black hair and stood up. Then he remembered all the things Shahid did and his face hardened.

Shahid looked at Gus and shrugged. 'Only bricks and mortar, innit? Imti's safe and that's all that matters right now.' Hesitating, he looked at Jessica, 'Jess?'

She refused to lift her head. Shahid stepped nearer and knelt in front of her, 'Come on, Jess. Now Trixie's gone it's just you, me and Imti. Imti needs us now. Please.'

Feeling like a jerk, Gus deliberately made is voice dismissive, 'Oh, that'll be why she's accusing *you* of setting fire to her mum then, Shahid? Because she needs you? Because you're family? It didn't stop you frying her mum, did it?'

Shahid jumped to his feet, 'What? That's fuckin crazy. I've told you before. I was with Jess that night. How could I have done it?'

'She smelt the petrol on you?' said Gus, watching for a reaction. 'Says you weren't with her all the time.'

Shahid shook his head, 'We all smelt of fuckin petrol that night mate.' Gus appreciated what Shahid was saying. After all The Fort smelt like a bonfire right now because he, Sampson and Alice had spent a couple of hours near a fire.

Shahid, his Adam's apple visibly moving as he swallowed, glared, wide-eyed at Gus. 'It was fucking awful.' He wiped a tear from his eye and looked down at Jessica. 'I didn't do that to your mum. I'd *never* have done that to her. She was good to me. More of a parent than my dad was. I didn't ever know my real mum, so *yours* was the next best thing. My dad didn't like me visiting your house, but I still did. I didn't kill her, Jess. I swear, I didn't. I've told you again and again, it weren't me.'

Jessica's head whipped up. Her eyes flashed and her mouth curled, 'Then who did Shahid? Who the fuck did?'

Shahid took a deep breath. 'It weren't my dad either, Jess. He was in Pakistan. God! I'd tell you if it were him, but it weren't. Maybe you should ask them from next door. Maybe they'll know.'

Jessica frowned. 'Who from next door?'

Shahid jerked a thumb in Gus' direction, 'Their mate and her fucking dad,' he said and marched to the door. 'Maybe their lot did a big fucking cover-up for all I know. But I swear it weren't fucking me, okay?'

Well that was interesting thought Gus when Shahid had gone, banging the door behind him. He'd felt Shahid was telling the truth about Millie Green's death when he'd interviewed him, and he felt the same today. He really did believe Shahid about this… he wasn't so sure about Trixie's murder, but he *was* convinced that he was innocent of Millie Green's. Which posed the question, who did murder Millie Green?

Jessica's eyes narrowed. 'He means, Sadia doesn't he? He thinks Sadia knows something about my mum's death. But how could she? She were only a kid herself. How could she know owt about it?'

'I don't think she does, Jess. Sadia got the file out to look into it again. She's as much in the dark as the rest of us.'

Jessica, picked up a piece of toast and took a bite, 'Look, I'm done in. Ask whatever you need to ask and then just let me get some sleep, okay?'

Pleased that she was at least eating some toast, Gus smiled. 'That's fine Jess. We just wanted to see if you'd thought of anyone who might have had it in for Trixie.'

Jessica sighed and shook her head, 'Just that tosser, Shahid. Trix was going to dump him. She told me so.'

Gus leaned forward, 'Jess, last time we spoke you told me Trixie didn't even have a boyfriend. Now you're telling me you knew she was seeing Shahid Khan. Why wouldn't you have told us that last time.'

Jessica's eyes darted from him to Alice, she shrugged, 'Must've forgot.'

'Really, you forgot that your very best friend was in a relationship with your enemy Shahid Khan. That seems a bit odd to me? What do you think, Al?'

Alice tilted her head to one side before responding, 'Yep, seems odd to me too.'

Jessica flung the half-eaten slice of toast onto the plate, 'Fuck off! I was upset, got confused, that's all. It's no big fucking deal, okay?'

Gus leaned back and crossed his legs, 'So, it's no big deal that Trixie was pregnant with Khan's baby, either?'

Jessica jumped to her feet, 'What? What the fuck did you say?' Before Gus could repeat his words, she turned and ran from the living room into her bedroom.

CHAPTER 71
Thornbury

The combination of crisp fresh air and warm memories sat well on Anastazy's shoulders; the one outweighing the other, creating a temperate feeling. Being outside like this, the cold nipping his nose and ears, reminded him of being a child back in Poland. They'd never had very much and, especially in the colder months; the meagre food supplies they had never seemed enough to fill his belly. However, the thrill of doing something he shouldn't have, whether it was stealing knickers off a clothes line, watching his neighbour give his dad a blow job or stealing from shops, had always kept him warm. When he'd gotten older, the pleasure of hurting his friends' animals and knowing *he'd* caused their distress when they'd discovered their maimed pets had made him feel powerful... like a hunter. Even now he craved that feeling... there was no drug like it. The feeling of forced ownership and the fear that generated was an aphrodisiac. He thrived on it and, having found the latest subject of his desires, his addiction was intense... he needed his fix... his Serafina fix.

He'd positioned himself on the corner of Serafina's road and was waiting for her to leave the house. Twice now the silver haired woman from the house behind him had knocked on the front room window, telling him to 'sling his hook'. Anastazy had laughed and keeping eye contact with her had pulled himself up on her garden wall. If she knocked again, then he'd pay her a little visit and make sure the old cow didn't bother him next time. But, for now, his focus was on the house further down the street with its blue door, which remained stubbornly closed, giving him time to reminisce about Poland and his early morning activities.

The Old Man had been keen to increase the pressure on both Bazza Green and Shahid Khan and, as far as Anastazy was concerned, the arson attacks had been an inspired choice. An acceleration in pressure and a clear intention of malicious intent. Both men would now be aware that this was very personal. Any lingering doubt would have been replaced by the certainty that they were both under attack from an, as yet, unknown entity.

Anastazy laughed: the idiots would be running scared. As well as the arson attacks, Anastazy had flooded both the Thornbury and the Manningham markets with Eastern European girls with orders to undercut the regulars. Anastazy prided himself on the fact that the girls *he* employed would provide even the most 'unusual' services. His army of men, funded by The Old Man, were more prepared than any of Green's or Khan's thugs. Lack of competition in the past had rendered those two idiots sluggish. Now, they were falling without a safety net. Under this amount of pressure, they would fold. Already Khan was grieving his dead girlfriend and attending his injured brother. He'd taken his eye off the ball, making it easy for Anastazy to slip in and set fire to The Delius.

His Manningham spies told him that, rather than sort out his affairs, Khan was hanging about Oak Lane trying to get that half-sister of his on side. As for Bazza, apparently he'd come squealing out of his flat, a little towel round his skinny waist, leaving the whore he'd been screwing inside, to make her own way out. By all accounts he'd been snivelling like an idiot whilst the fire brigade doused the fire. Ha, neither of those two were worth worrying about now.

So that left him free to concentrate on Serafina... she knew now what would happen if she didn't comply. She was defenceless.

CHAPTER 72
Oak Lane

Alice followed Jessica into the bedroom. The girl was snuggled into the far side of the bed, the duvet pulled right up to her chin, her head was tilted towards the window. Through the dim light that shone through the thin, drawn curtains, Alice could see Jessica's shoulders heaving as she cried. The room smelt stale. Alice presumed the girl had spent most of the last few days holed up in here with her grief. She knew Gus had offered her a FLO and that Jessica had refused. Having met her uncle, Bazza Green, Alice felt sure that he wouldn't have paid his niece a welfare call. She screwed up her mouth. The obnoxious little toad was probably more concerned with getting himself a new pet than with Jessica's mental health.

Alice turned to go and then turned back. Something was niggling at her. She looked first, at the bundle on the bed before casting another glance round the room. Then, it clicked.

'Who sleeps on the other side of the bed, Jessica?'

Jessica's shoulders stilled, then she sat upright glaring at Alice through swollen eyes. 'What are you on about? Nobody sleeps there.'

'Then why are you all bundled up to one side, like you're leaving this side free for someone else?'

Jessica looked at her, her face sullen. 'Fuck right off, okay? Just fuck off!' and she flung herself back under the duvet.

'You got a boyfriend Jess?'

347

Two fingers emerged from beneath the duvet and made a V sign at Alice. *Very touchy,* thought Alice, pursing her lips. *Did Jessica have a mystery boyfriend? Someone capable of killing Trixie, maybe?*

Ignoring Jess' continued sobs, Alice walked to the bedside drawers at the side nearest to the door. 'Why do you need two alarm clocks, Jess?'

Silence, so Alice opened the drawer, 'Nice line in sex toys. Oh and some dog tags on a cheap chain. Very classy' Alice picked it up and looked at the inscription on the back, *With all my love, J xxx.*

She dropped the chain back in the drawer, rolled it shut and said, 'Sweet dreams' before leaving the room, closing the door behind her.

The pair of them exited Jessica's flat as they began to head back up Oak Lane towards The Fort, Gus said, 'What was that all about, Alice?'

Alice grinned at him, 'I'm thinking that maybe Jessica has a boyfriend or…' she cocked her head to one side, 'maybe a girlfriend…'

'What do you mean?'

'Well… the double bed, Jess curled up to one side, two alarm clocks, sex toys and a cheap necklace inscribed from someone called 'J' in the opposite bedside table drawer.'

Gus frowned. Although what Alice said was interesting, he felt there was little substance to it and probably less relevance. 'Hardly conclusive is it?'

Alice shrugged. 'Perhaps not but, I'm sure she is or has recently been in a relationship.'

Gus laughed, 'What are you, Manningham's answer to Cilla Black?'

Laughing, Alice said, 'Just struck me as strange that Jessica was bundled up to one side of the bed if she slept alone, that's all. I've got a double bed and I make *full* use of it, sprawling right over the middle.'

Gus nudged her. 'Yeah, cos you're *so* huge you need a king-size, never mind double bed.'

Alice thumped him and continued, 'Why have two clocks in the bedroom, if only one person sleeps there?'

'Hell, I don't know, do I? Maybe she's got a thing about clocks.'

'Maybe... but what if this person had it in for Trixie for some reason and Jess is covering up for them? Maybe Jess' unknown lover killed Trixie.'

'Hey, hold on a minute Al. You can't go tearing off making assumptions based on a necklace and a double bed.' Gus didn't buy the idea of Jess', as yet unidentified, lover killing Trixie. Who knew how long that necklace had been in the drawer and he still slept on 'his' side of the bed even though Gabriella left months ago. Alice needed to rein in her imagination a bit.

Alice pouted and shoved her hands in her pocket like a naughty schoolgirl. Her sulky expression made Gus want to laugh as she strode a couple of steps ahead of him before stopping abruptly and spinning on her heel to face him. 'Okay, Gus. I get what you're saying but when I think back to the interview Sampson and I did at The Prossie Palace, there was something off. Armani and the girls knew something we didn't about Jessica. I'm going to check it out later. Bet I'm right... bet it's a girl.'

Gus laughed, 'Alice Cooper, sexuality police.'

Alice thumped him again. 'Just cause my gaydar's better than yours.'

Gus grinned. 'Yeah wondered how long it would be before you brought up Gabriella.'

349

Alice bit her lip, 'Shit, Gus, that's not what I meant.'

Gus shook his head, 'Don't be daft, Al. I know my gaydar's well off.'

Alice glanced over the road and nudged Gus, 'Yeah, you can say that again, look over there.'

Gus swing his head round in time to see a car with his sister and ex-wife in it, swing out and up the road towards Duckworth Lane.

Gus felt suddenly exhausted. It had been a long an emotional night and he knew he was in for a tricky afternoon too. 'Come on, Al. There's nothing else we can do now. I'm going home for a shower and a quick kip before the big lunch.'

Alice wiggled her eyebrows. 'God! Can't wait.' She laughed. 'Wonder what overdone atrocity your mum'll serve up today. Mind you, I think you do right to bring the gang… less for us to eat and, besides, Compo'll make short work of whatever's on offer.' She tilted her head to one side. 'Safety in numbers and, with the two witches coming, you'll need all the support you can get.'

As Alice walked towards the stairs leading into The Fort's main reception, Gus called her back. 'What did you think of Shahid Khan, Al?'

'He seemed really upset about Imti,' she shrugged, 'A bit defeated really. Poor sod.'

'Mmm,' said Gus, 'That's what I thought but, now I'm wondering. This is Shahid Khan we're talking about. He's not a bloody pushover. Wouldn't you expect him to be all out to string up the bastard who stabbed Imti? What's he doing approaching Jess who's had nowt to do with either him or Imti for years. It all seems a bit off to me, you know?'

'You might have a point I suppose, but I thought he was quite convincing. He's still reeling after Trixie's death, too.'

Gus nodded. He still wasn't convinced. Shahid Khan was a nasty piece of work and he was sure he wouldn't just lie still and let someone piss on him. Gus would be keeping an eye on Khan.... And Bazza Green, for that matter... for the foreseeable future.

CHAPTER 73
Duckworth Lane

T he building was set back from the road and had no
signs to show its purpose. It looked similar to many
of the larger sand stone buildings dotted around
Bradford that had been converted into Mosques, fast food
outlets or dress shops. Perhaps some of its patrons treated it
with the same religious awe that the devout afforded their
religious buildings.

However, Bazza Green's gym was, unlike its more
'modern' counterparts, a place for serious weight lifting,
boxing and martial arts. Brightly coloured lycra was notably
absent, as was an offer of yoga, pilates or zumba classes.
This was most definitely a *man's* gym – the only two
female regulars were serious weight lifters and had the
sculpted bodies of those seriously committed to their art.
Their only concession to their gender were the sports bras
they wore as they worked out.

At the hospital last night, when he registered where he
knew Serafina from, and heard about her friend and brother,
Shahid became certain that Anastazy was responsible for
attacking Imti too. When news of the dual arson attacks on
his and Bazza's properties had come in, he'd made further
deductions. Then, information about an influx of Eastern
European girls undercutting his stable of girls; and about
cheaper coke and heroin circulating in the clubs and streets
reached him and he understood what was happening. A few
calls outside the district reassured him that neither Johnny
The Gerbil from Oldham nor Colin The Cockroach from
Sheffield were making a bid against him. On the contrary,
Shahid's news had filled them with concern and Shahid was

in the position to pull in a few favours should he need to. And *that* was why he was here, at Bazza's gym.

He'd wanted to talk to Jessica about it first, get information about Bazza's girls, but McGuire and the skinny goth had shown up and he'd not been able too. Jess was too upset anyway, so he'd pretended that all he'd wanted was to tell her about Imti. No point alerting McGuire to his real intentions.

As Shahid and Jai walked into the testosterone-filled lobby where the walls seemed to ooze with the sweat of years of activity, the man behind the reception desk grinned in a way that left Shahid in no doubt that he was unwelcome. Then, he straightened and, before Shahid's eyes, the man's muscles seemed to swell, making the matching lions rampant adorning his upper arms, ripple with a ferocity that Shahid knew was intentional.

He smiled. 'Nice tatts, but I've not come for a show. Bazza around?'

Muscleman glared at him and then repeated the look in Jai's direction, before lifting a phone receiver up in a paw so big Shahid wondered that he didn't break it. 'He growled into the phone and then nodded towards a line of plastic chairs by the door.

Ignoring him, Shahid stayed where he was, with a slight smile on his face.

Hearing a door to the side open, Shahid turned and saw Bazza walk through accompanied by two over-muscled thugs. With an effort, Shahid managed to maintain a neutral expression. The very sight of Bazza Green made him want to throw a punch at the man – but that wasn't why he was there today.

353

He nodded, but made no move to offer a hand to Bazza. Bazza, in turn, looked Shahid up and down, before saying, 'You want to sign up? Looks like you could do with bulking up a bit.'

Ignoring the sheer stupidity of Bazza Green, who weighed all of seven stone, commenting on his physique, Shahid said, 'We need to talk.'

Bazza's face lost its sneer. He gave a single nod and without speaking walked back through the door. His henchmen stood aside for Jai and Shahid to follow.

The room they entered was clearly Bazza's office and Shahid looked round with interest. If he'd been going to set fire to one of Bazza Green's properties this one would have been high up on the list. It was the centre of Green's enterprise. It made Shahid realise that the reason they'd gone for his penthouse flat was purely to frighten Bazza: they were not trying to damage the infrastructure of his business. That figured. Bazza, unlike Shahid, had no emotional ties with anyone, not even his niece Jessica. Bazza himself was the only person he loved.

Like the rest of the gym, Bazza's office was functional. It lacked in the hygiene department. The sour sweat smell replaced by the equally pervasive stink of smoke. Judging by the overflowing ash tray on the Bazza's desk he'd been chain-smoking. Shahid barely refrained from shuddering at the sight. He hated smokers with a vengeance and the smell made him feel nauseous... although, today his olfactory system was probably over-sensitised by the hangover that still throbbed at his temples

Shahid made a point of walking the circumference of the room before speaking. At last he turned to Bazza. 'You've got the place looking nice, Bazz.' Without waiting to be invited, he hooked his foot round an uncomfortable-looking chair arm, and spun it round before straddling it and leaning his arms over the back. Jai folded his arms Mafia style and stood by the door, staring straight ahead.

Bazza, laughed out loud, revealing a mouthful of caries and yellowed teeth. Had the man ever heard of toothpaste, never mind floss? As if in answer, Bazza dropped into a chair behind the desk and, picking up a paperclip, he straightened it with nicotine stained fingers before using it to pick his teeth. Shahid cringed at the sound of metal rasping against tooth enamel. What a truly disgusting creature he was. With difficulty he forced all thoughts of Trixie and what she was forced to do with Bazza to the back of his mind. He'd deal with that in due course but, right now, he had more pressing issues to resolve.

'We've got a problem.'

Bazza pulled the paperclip from his mouth, studied the lump of buttery gunk that was stuck on it then, with gusto, sucked it off, making Shahid's stomach churn. He threw the clip across the room, presumably aiming for the bin but missing by a foot, and nodded. 'We certainly do.'

'So, are we going to sort it or are we going to wait for the oink oinks to do it?'

Bazza laughed, 'Oh, I think we'll have to take matters into our own hands, don't you?'

The two men discussed the information they had until they eventually had a plan they were both happy with. Bazza wiped his hand down the front of his, less than clean, jumper before offering it to Shahid. Shahid took a deep breath and, wishing he'd thought to wear gloves, he took Bazza's hand and they shook.

CHAPTER 74
Shay Lane

With an eagerness that raised Gus' spirits, Compo bounced up and down on the balls of his feet, champing at the bit, ready to be off. As Alice walked into the incident room, her hair still damp, presumably from her shower, Gus said 'Okay, let's do this.'

Sadia had managed to cover her bruise quite well and Gus thought she looked gorgeous, if slightly nervous. He'd managed to shower, change and grab an hour's kip before driving them back to The Fort to collect the rest of the team. Sampson and Compo were driving in one car, while Gus took Sadia and Alice in his. Brighton had texted to say he had another commitment, which suited Gus fine. He was beginning to wonder if the mysterious photographer *had* been Brighton and was glad that he wasn't bringing the obnoxious specimen to his parents' house.

Despite the clenching in his stomach, Gus felt ready for this. After all, he had his friends beside him and Sadia, and, as he kept telling himself, *he'd* done nothing wrong. Gabriella and Katie were the ones who should be anxious, although, knowing Katie she'd brazen it out. She'd always been all front, even as a child.

When they arrived at his parents' old farmhouse, the dogs, Bingo and his parents' two, erupted in rapturous barking. Compo, looking very much like he should also possess a wagging tail, gambolled among them, getting them more and more giddy and submitting himself to licks and hugs, before Gus finally emitted a piercing whistle to calm the dogs and Compo down.

Fergus and Corrine McGuire waited at the front door, his father with one arm draped over his dainty wife's shoulder, huge welcoming grins on their faces. Gus, sensing Sadia's nervousness, took her hand in his and, ignoring Sampson and Compo's less than subtle winks and nudges, he led her over to meet his parents. Fergus stepped forward and engulfed her in a bear hug before bestowing the same greeting on the rest of Gus' team. Corrine raised her cheek for a kiss to each of them in turn before clapping her hands together, 'I'm so pleased to have you all over for Sunday lunch.' And she waved them through to the dining room.

Relieved that Gabriella and Katie hadn't yet arrived, Gus helped his dad sort out drinks whilst, Compo, like a bloodhound, raised his nose and sniffed the air, 'Something smells great, Mrs Mac,' he said.

Gus and Alice exchanged a look and Alice, under her breath said, 'Is there something wrong with that boy's olfactory system?'

Gus grinned, even he could discern the wafts of singed meat that drifted through from the kitchen. Doc McGuire chuckled and in a conspiratorial tone said, 'All the more for the dogs, methinks.' Then as an afterthought added, '…and Compo of course.'

As the doorbell rang, Dr McGuire, eyebrows raised, looked at Gus, 'Must be your sister, though God knows why she's ringing the damn bell. She'd got a bloody key, same as you.'

Gus, slid into his chair between Sadia and Alice and raised his whisky glass to his lips. Under his breath, he muttered, 'Hell, but I need this.'

Alice snorted, 'You don't need Dutch courage, Gus, you've got us.' And underneath the table he felt Sadia take

357

his hand in hers and squeeze. Thank fuck for this lot he thought, as the door opened and his sister, tall with blonde streaks striating her dark hair, entered. Her eyes, like Gus', were carbon copies of their mother's. Feeling like every ounce of oxygen had been sucked from the room, he inclined his head slightly. Keeping his expression neutral, he was determined to stand his ground. 'Katie.'

She reciprocated with a curt nod. Her eyes drifted round the table to the other guests narrowing when they rested on Sadia. Gus smiled when he saw Sadia's chin lift as she met his sister's gaze head on. He could have hugged her there and then. Katie looked away and then stepped to the side so Gabriella could enter. Gus, again raised his glass in the air, feeling much more confident now, and said, 'Gabriella.'

Unlike his sister, Gabriella looked nervous. Her eyes darted round the room never settling on any one thing. Then, when Gus's dad came in and, in his usual bluff manner said her name, she visibly flinched. Despite the residual anger that simmered just beneath the surface, Gus felt sorry for her. He flicked a smile in Gabriella's direction and then when Katie immediately grabbed her hand and glared at him, he grinned. Katie was jealous of him. He felt like laughing aloud. Did she really think he was some sort of competition? Gabriella had made her decision and *he'd* moved on. He wasn't interested in Gabriella in that way. It didn't mean he wasn't hurt. Course he was. No matter how you looked at it he'd been betrayed by both his wife *and* his sister; and the betrayal was still raw.

He turned to his dad and pointed to a large picture that hung, covered by a drape on the chimney breast said, 'What's with that?'

Dr McGuire shrugged and shook his head vigorously from side to side, sending his jowls swinging in a slow pendulum style motion. 'It's your mum.' He pointed to the hidden painting, '*That's* the product of another of your mother's hobbies and, just so you all know, it's there against *my* wishes.' And he prodded his puffed up chest to accentuate his indignation with the situation.

Gus and Katie sensing a bone of contention between their parents, glanced at each other grinning in a shared childhood habit. 'Something wrong with the painting, Dad?' asked Katie, more relaxed now.

Dr McGuire grunted, 'You'll see. All I'm saying is, be prepared.'

The doorbell rang again and Doc McGuire, leaving the room said, 'Ah, that'll be our last guest. Your mother's latest bloody hobby buddy.'

Half an hour later, everyone, including his mum's new friend, Tommy Gilchrist, was ensconced around the sizeable dining table. The atmosphere had thawed and plates were filled with slightly singed lamb, too soggy sprouts and lumpy mash and gravy when Corrine McGuire stood up and clinked her fork on the side of her wine glass.

'It's usually Fergus who delivers the toasts for family meals but today I've decided it's my turn. So, here goes,' she glanced round the room, her brown face creased into a wide all-encompassing smile. 'As a family, I think it's fair to say that we've had quite a challenging year. However, now things have improved and we're in a better place. It's my delight to welcome, Sadia, Gus' partner, to the family,' as Gus and Sadia shared an embarrassed glance, Corrine tilted her glass in their direction and continued, 'and to acknowledge Katie and Gabriella as a couple.'

Gus noted with satisfaction how embarrassed both Katie and Gabriella looked, but also how Gabriella kept sending curious glances in Sadia's direction. Taking the opportunity to deposit some of his meat under the table where the dogs sat, waiting in anticipation, he refocussed on his mother's continuing toast.

'This year, I've looked for another outlet for my creativity and am pleased to announce that, thanks to Tommy here, my painting classes have paid off. It is with great pleasure that I want to reveal a project I've been working on for a number of months now.' She nodded to her husband, who Gus thought looked less than delighted, to remove the drape.

For long moments when the drape came off, there was a stunned silence. Corrine, hands clasped in front of her, looked round the table, a satisfied smile on her face. Gus realised that she'd mistaken everyone's stunned reaction for awe and admiration. He caught sight of his father's thunderous expression and, swallowing the laughter that threatened to bubble from his mouth, he risked a glance at Katie. She met his eye and shook her head slightly, her face a combination of shock and amusement. Feeling Alice's shoulders jiggling against his, he knew she was in danger of laughing aloud as, he noted, were Compo and Sampson. Sadia too, was having difficulty keeping her face straight.

Biting the bullet, Gus stood and raising his glass saluted his mum, 'Well, you certainly hid *your* light under a bushel, Mum.'

Ignoring his father's mumbled, 'Might've been better if Tommy Gilchrist had kept *his* hidden under a damn bushel.'

Gus continued, 'We'd no idea you were doing life drawing, but, I have to say, you've captured the subject perfectly.' It's a very good likeness of Tommy.' He turned and raised his glass in Tommy's direction. 'Well, of course, I can only vouch for the bits I can see at the moment.' He added causing a series of coughing fits to erupt around the table.

Tommy Gilchrist, in his crisp shirt and spotty bow tie with a perfect crease running down the centre of each trouser leg, was the least likely candidate for life modelling that Gus had ever come across. Risking a glance at his dad, who looked very glum, Gus said 'What do you think, Dad?'

Before he had a chance to reply, Gus' mother snorted, 'Silly bloody galoot's got all jealous over it. Your father, Gus, is a philistine, a complete philistine, who can't appreciate the finer points of art.'

His dad snorted, 'Och, I'm not bloody jealous, Corrine. I just don't want to have to see Tommy's bloody gonads when I'm eating my damn tea. Gives black pudding a whole new meaning.'

'Hmmph,' Corrinne folded her arms over her chest as Katie got to her feet and wrapped her arms round her mother's shoulders. 'Look, Mum, why don't we put it at the top of the landing instead. Then, we'll get the full benefit of it as we come up the stairs. It's a bit too close to get its full impact here, isn't it?'

Dr McGuire spluttered, muttering under his breath, for Gus's ears only, 'Benefit? Bloody impact? More like revulsion and despair. In fact, that's what I'm going to call it. Either that or 'Gone to bloody seed'.' But, he got to his feet and walked over to his wife and deposited a big kiss on her cheek before hugging her close. 'You're beautiful when you're angry, you know that?'

'Och, away wi' you, ye bloody old goat' she said, smiling. 'Come on everyone, tuck in. I think I've surpassed myself today' and seemingly oblivious of her guests' dubious glances, she sat down and lifted her cutlery to dig in.

CHAPTER 75
Astor Avenue, Idle

Sampson had struggled during lunch at the McGuires' home. Truth be told, he'd been struggling since his meeting with the Dhosangs the previous afternoon. He hated being so undecided but, seeing Sadia so happy with Gus and knowing how determined she was to find out the truth about Millie Green for Jessica, he'd finally come to a decision. It wasn't one he relished implementing but, it was the right thing to do. So, he'd made his excuses and left the warmth and friendliness of the McGuires' home and made his way here.

He had no idea how this would play out. He knew it could all go horribly wrong and he could find himself out of a job… as for Sadia, he knew he was exposing her, and Gus too, to her father's wrath. He shook his head taking a deep breath. That couldn't be helped. At least this way, if the Dhosang's suspicions amounted to nowt, he'd have saved Sadia that trauma. He *knew* he could have approached Gus for help and he knew Gus would have taken the responsibility on himself, but that wasn't Sampson's way. It was his problem, so he'd sort it out. At one point he'd considered snagging Sadia's hair and getting a sibling DNA comparison done on the DNA from Millie Green's foetus, but that didn't sit right with him. It smacked of dishonesty and, if there was one thing Sampson hated, it was deceit.

So, here he was outside Hannibal Hussain's house, crapping himself. The mere thought of confronting DCS Hussain made him feel like throwing up. He'd suffered humiliation at the DCS's hands before, so he knew exactly what the man could dish out. On the other hand, though,

Sampson didn't very much care what Hussain thought. He didn't respect him whatsoever, so Hussain's opinion of him mattered not one jot. Keeping that thought to the forefront of his mind, Sampson grabbed the door handle and got out of his car.

The air was crisp and the faint smell of burning out bonfires hung in the air. Yesterday would have been twenty years since Millie Green's tragic death so it seemed a fitting way to mark the anniversary by trying to work out what had happened on that fateful night. Wiping his sweating hands down his trouser legs, Sampson flung his shoulders back and walked through the ornate archway onto the crazy paved path that led to the Hussain's front door. The doormat had, what Sampson assumed, was an Arabic welcome painted on it in red. Through the double-glazed porch windows he could see shoes, some female, probably Sadia's, and some male stacked in neat rows on an Ikea shelving unit. He reached out and rung the bell. A silhouette appeared behind the inner door and seconds later, when the door opened, Sampson saw it was DCS Hussain. Contrary to his normal working attire of a black or navy suit, shirt and tie, today the DCS wore traditional Pakistani shalwar kameez and had a pristine white prayer hat on his head.

Hussain frowned when he saw Sampson. He opened the porch door and uttered a single word, 'Yes?' His contempt was clear in the abruptness of his tone.

Sampson thought the other man looked tired. His face had the unhealthy pallor of an exhausted man, but Sampson knew that wouldn't make him any weaker a combatant. Arms folded behind his back, Sampson gripped his hands together, gaining courage from the way his nails bit into his palms. 'I need to talk to you, sir, and I thought it would be better if I approached you away from the office.'

Hussain frowned, then turned to re-enter the house, pointing to the shoe rack, issuing a monosyllabic order, 'Shoes.'

Sampson, in his haste to take his boots off and follow the older man inside, hopped about on one foot trying to pull his boots off without unlacing them fully. Defeated, he bent over and fully aware of Hussain's disapproving glance on his back, he loosened them and finally kicked them off, before, mindful of the stern look on Hussain's face when he'd pointed at the shelves, he picked them up and placed them beside a pair of Sadia's stilettos.

Seeing Hussain looking at his feet, Sampson followed his gaze downwards and flushed when he realised that, not only did he have on one blue and one red sock, but that the red one had a hole in it from which his big toe protruded. He felt heat fill his face as Hussain snorted before leading the way along a carpeted hallway to a room at the end.

Sampson followed, his heart thumping harder with each step further into the lion's den and, when inside the office, he took the seat across from Hussain at the desk. He was immediately aware that his seat was much smaller than the other man's and knew that Hussain had chosen a smaller chair for his guests to keep them at a height disadvantage. Unwilling to let Hussain have it all his own way, Sampson straightened his upper body to minimise the disparity.

Hussain, as if realising Sampson's ploy, snorted, 'Right, this better be good, Sanders.'

Sampson somehow kept his face straight and, despite his blush, he maintained eye contact with Hussain. 'Sampson, my name's Sampson.'

Hussain's lips curled and he wafted one hand as if to say 'I don't care what you're called'.

Sampson cleared his throat, 'I visited Mr and Mrs Dhosang yesterday. Do you remember them? They were your neighbours when you lived next door to Millie Green.'

Hussain, leaned back in his chair and crossed one leg over the other. One hand drifted up to his beard and his fingers ran down it from his chin to the pointed end. His eyes narrowed. 'And why, may I ask, would you do that, Sanders?'

Sampson, knew that using the wrong name was strategy to maintain the upper hand, so he ignored it. Taking a deep breath, he said, 'I wanted to find out what they knew about Millie Green's death.'

Hussain's already thin lips tightened until they disappeared completely beneath his beard, 'I gave very specific instructions that time was *not* to be wasted on the Millie Green case. If my memory serves me well, you, *Sanders* were there when I issued those instructions.'

Sampson nodded, 'I only looked at the Millie Green case in my own time, sir.' And before Hussain could respond he added 'Did you know Millie Green was pregnant at the time of her death?'

If Sampson hadn't been watching closely, he might have missed the flicker in Hussain's eyes. Not wanting to lose his advantage, he continued, 'The Dhosangs knew who the father was.'

Hussain jumped to his feet, a muscle twitching in his cheek. 'Don't be ridiculous. They are an old couple with nothing better to do than make up stories to discredit respectable people.'

Sampson frowned. 'They seemed respectable enough to me. One of their sons is a criminal lawyer and the other a businessman.' Sampson hoped the implied threat of the Dhosangs' lawyer son would push Hussain into being indiscreet but, instead, he moved round the desk and moved to the yank the door open. 'Leave.'

Sampson glared at him as he stood and walked out of the room. Hussain followed and watched as he put his boots back on. As Sampson opened the outer door, Hussain said, 'Have you shared this nonsense with Sadia?'

Sampson looked him straight in the eye, 'Not yet, but I will.' He stepped onto the path, then turned back, 'I'll tell her after work tomorrow.'

Hussain nodded and as Sampson watched he closed the door and then, shoulders hunched, he turned and walked back into his home. Sampson exhaled and, as his body relaxed, he felt muscles he didn't even know he had, begin to throb. He hadn't enjoyed doing what he'd done but he wanted to make it clear to Hussain that this wasn't going to go away. He'd given the man ample time to speak to his daughter about it before he passed the information on.

CHAPTER 76
Killinghall Road

Jai didn't enjoy working with Bazza's thug, but he'd had no choice. Shahid was up at BRI with Imti and, because of the temporary truce between Shahid and Bazza, they had to work in pairs, one from Bazza's crew and one from Shahid's. They'd been sent out, like a swarm of bees to find the honey pot. Not that Anastazy was sweet by anyone's standards. From Serafina, Shahid had ascertained that Anastazy seemed to operate from the Thornbury area, so Jai had opted to target that area. After all, when the Polish bastard had attacked first Imti and then The Delius he'd made it personal. Jai didn't forget personal insults easily.

Bazza's thug, a white guy called Jerome, was high on weed, but Jai reckoned that the guy would be equally idiotic without the enhancement of weed. He'd come across potheads like him in the past and knew not to rely on him. Jai was keeping in close contact with the rest of his men and the favours Shahid had pulled in meant that, should they need it, they could pull in the heavies from Manchester and Sheffield too. Together, they'd decided to pull their girls off the streets. Their dealers and distributers were under strict instructions to keep a low profile.

Jai knew that a coup d'état would be the most effective away to end this. Get to Anastazy and the rest of his crew would fold. Shahid seemed to think that Anastazy wasn't at the top of the tree, but Jai was unsure. He was prepared to hedge his bets, if Shahid said so, but he was determined to deal with Anastazy himself.

The streets were empty and a residual firework bonfire smell hung in the air from the previous night. Jai pounded on a door just down from Habib's restaurant near the Killinghall Road roundabout. From inside he heard shuffling and knew that the door was about to be opened. He stood to the side and as soon as it opened, he inserted his foot between the door and the jamb. Pushing his body against the door, he thrust his arm round, grabbing the man by the throat and bulldozed his way into the hallway. 'How you doing, Dwayne? Alright?'

Dwayne, unable to reply due to the pressure of Jai's fingers against his larynx, tried to nod. Jai backed him up against the wall and smiled when he heard Jerome slam the door closed behind them. 'Check out the rest of this pigsty, Jerome.'

Grinning Jerome bounced along the corridor, checking each downstairs room before progressing to the upstairs ones. When he heard Jerome's '*Clear*', Jai released Dwayne who fell to the floor rubbing his throat and coughing. 'What you do that for, Jai? Thought you and me was mates.'

Jai's mouth turned up. '"Mates" is pushing it, don't you think, Dwayne? To me you're the equivalent of vermin in a mousetrap, you get my drift?'

Dwayne risked a smile. 'Funny, Jai, really funny.'

Walking through to the living room, Jai's nose crinkled at the acrid smell, 'You know what soap is, Dwayne?'

Trailing behind, Dwayne shrugged. Jai rolled his eyes. 'Never mind. What I need from you is information, okay?'

Still rubbing his throat, Dwayne nodded.

'Good.' He slapped Dwayne's cheeks in a friendly warning. 'I need you to think very hard, because if you lie to me right now, Shahid will see that your dismembered body is disposed of in a pig farm near Holmfirth, okay?'

Seeing Dwayne's face pale, he knew his message had hit the mark, 'We're looking for a Polish guy. Bit of a psycho. Name of Anastazy. You can't miss him. He's got teardrop tatts under his eyes and a snake going up his neck. Recognise that description, Dwayney boy?'

Dwayne swallowed and glanced at Jerome, who leaned against the living room door, cleaning under his nails with the tip of a very sharp stiletto blade. Flicking a nervous glance at Jai, he held out his arms out in a pleading gesture, 'Shit Jai, that dude's into some really bad stuff, you get my drift? I tell you owt and I'm dead meat.'

Taking a step forward, Jai reconnected his fingers with Dwayne's neck, 'Looks like you've got a bit of a dilemma to resolve then, Dwayne.' He tightened his grip, 'See. You're dead if you don't tell us. But, the thing is, *you* know and *I* know that Shahid's kind to his friends, so, when all's said and done, there really is no competition is there? You tell us about the Polish bastard and we'll protect you.'

CHAPTER 77
Astor Avenue, Idle

It had taken Gus ages to get away from his parent's house. His mum had insisted he help his dad re-hang the portrait at the top of the stairs. Of course, with all his dad's moaning and groaning, which in all fairness Gus did sympathise with, it took rather a long time. Despite his dexterity in the mortuary, his father, as far as DIY was concerned, appeared to possess two left hands. The result was three separate stoppages caused by injury involving a hammer a screwdriver and a drill. By the end of the process, Gus was more than ready to throttle his dad and, only his mother's smiling gratitude, prevented him from making her a widow.

Sadia, who was exhausted, had bummed a lift back to his house from Compo and Sampson and Gabriella and Katie had sneaked out soon after dessert, which his mum insisted on calling 'Heaton Mess', because, as far as she was concerned, Shay Lane was as much part of Heaton as it was a part of Cottingley. Gus personally thought 'Bloody Inedible Mess' would've been more apt. How could his mother manage to balls up the crumbling of meringue, the whipping of cream and the addition of fruit? But, somehow or other, she had. The cream appeared to have clotted, the meringues were chewy and the juice from the fruit made the whole thing into a scummy liquid. Compo scoffed three bowls of it, which made everyone else's half-hearted attempts go unnoticed.

As promised, Alice had hung on till the bitter end and now they were making their way to Sadia's house to confront her dad. Gus still wasn't entirely sure what he was going to say to Hussain, but at least the passage of time had taken the edge of his anger. He hadn't told Sadia of his intentions either, mainly because he knew she'd insist that she could fight her own battles. The thing was, this was his battle, too, and he wasn't about to let anyone get away with hitting Sadia… far less her bastard father.

He felt more in control of his emotions now and knew he wouldn't lose it completely with the other man, much as he'd like nothing better than to give him a taste of his own medicine.

As he drew up outside the house, his heart pounded in his chest. A sympathetic look from Alice told him she knew how he felt. *Well, at least one of us knows,* thought Gus, not sure if he was nervous about confronting his boss or mad as hell with Sadia's dad. It was as if he had two different men to confront and the reality and complexity of it made him uneasy. He glanced at the front room windows, looking for signs that his superior officer was at home. Despite the dark, the curtains were open and no tell-tale shadows of life passed across the windows. Hussain was probably at the back in his office.

Following Alice out of the car, Gus stood for a minute at the kerb and took a deep breath before walking up the drive to the front door. Alice trailed behind him, a wary look on her face. As he rang the bell, she squeezed his arm and said 'Remember it doesn't matter who he is. He has committed a crime by assaulting Sadia.'

Gus grimaced remembering Sadia's bruised face and haunted eyes. 'You don't need to remind me of that, Al,' he said, pressing his thumb on the doorbell again, this time leaving it there. He could hear the ringing from where they stood, but there was no movement from inside.

'Bet he's gone to the mosque,' muttered Gus. 'praying for forgiveness.'

Alice shook her head. 'Calm down, Gus, he's maybe gone to get milk or something. Let's wait in the car. I'll phone back to the station to make sure he's not there, okay?'

With a curt nod, Gus stepped back from the door, turned towards his car and saw a neighbour watching him curiously from her front doorstep.

Gus smiled at her hoping she hadn't overheard his conversation with Alice. 'Don't suppose you know where DCS Hussain is, do you? We're colleagues of his.' He showed her his warrant card.

The woman returned Gus' smile but didn't answer his question. Instead she said, pointing at Sadia's house, 'Some to-do over there last night.'

Gus raised his eyebrows. 'Really?'

'Oh, God, yes. First a bit of shouting, then Sadia, the daughter, ran out. Looked like she were crying to me. She jumped into her car and screeched off up the road. Seconds later Mr Hussain ran out of the house. He just sort of collapsed onto his knees right there and howled like a bloody werewolf.'

She turned to pull her door closed behind her. 'Then, he stayed perfectly still looking up at the sky with his arms out before him like he was praying or something.' She shook her head, 'From the streetlights, I could see the tears running down his cheeks. You know, I don't even think he noticed them. After ten minutes or so I went over to him. Tried to coax him indoors, but he'd not budge. So I went down to that Mosque on Bannerman Street – there's always lads there hanging around no matter how late it is. Makes some of the white folk a bit nervous like, but not me. I reckon if they're at the mosque, they're not mugging old ladies.'

She laughed and, with a grin, added, 'Unless of course they're making bombs... but I suspect they wouldn't be doing that in the car park.'

Gus, despite himself, smiled at her sardonic humour. He reckoned there were probably very few in this area who shared her liberal views.

'Anyway, I got one of the lads to tell Councillor Majid. Sure enough, he came up and I explained what had happened then he managed to coax him indoors.'

Gus nodded. 'Did you see Councillor Majid leave?

'Oh yes, he left about half an hour later.'

'Don't suppose you know if DCS Hussain's gone out today, do you?'

'I've not seen him out today and I'm sure I would have. He's had two visitors though... a Pakistani bloke and one of yours.'

Gus frowned. 'One of ours?'

'Yes, a tall skinny officer, seemed nervous like, but you can tell by the walk he was a copper. Then later on the Pakistani lad came.'

Gus exchanged a look with Alice, and turned back to the house. Something made him feel a bit uneasy, but he couldn't put his finger on it. From the neighbour's description it sounded like Sampson had visited Sadia's dad earlier. What the hell for, though? As for the Pakistani bloke, well, that could have been someone from the mosque, he supposed. Still, it didn't explain why Hannibal Hussain wasn't answering his door – unless of course he was asleep. 'Just try that door will you, Al?' but Alice had already stretched out her hand to press the handle.

The porch door opened and they looked at each other. Gus grinned and said, 'Okay, I'll try the inner door, shall I?'

Alice shrugged. 'Why not? If we're resorting to entering a senior officer's home uninvited, then I'd much rather *you* were the one to do it.'

Gus tried the inner door and it, too, was unlocked. He sighed: his concerns had just increased tenfold. DCS Hussain did not strike him as the sort of man to leave his front doors unlocked at any time of the day and far less so, after dark.

Gus sighed and looked at Alice. 'I don't like this. Hope he's not gone and had a bloody heart attack. That's all Sadia would need. As if she doesn't feel guilty enough.'

Alice followed him through the door as he shouted, 'DCS Hussain, it's DI Gus McGuire. Your door was open, so we came in. We're worried about you, as you didn't answer your bell. Where are you, sir?'

When there was no reply, Gus gestured towards a door further down the hallway that was only half shut and seemed to have a light on. Brushing his knuckles against the door he knocked and called out again, but still no response. He pushed the door open and stuck his head through the gap, 'Aw, fuck, Alice. Call it in, please, paramedics and scene of crime.'

CHAPTER 78
The Delius

Dwayney boy had come up with the goods and Jai had him holed up in the office at the Delius now. Little bastard had moaned about the smoke smell but as far as Jai was concerned he was damn lucky not to have been left to rot in his manky house in Killinghall. Little bastard had been doing the dirty on Shahid, getting drugs from Anastazy at a better profit margin and selling them at a discount on the streets. Undercutting them. Well, maybe when all this was done, Dwayne would be the one being cut. For now, though, Shahid had ordered Jai to lock him up in The Delius.

He'd given them some useful information. Turned out Jerome could be quite persuasive with his knife and, as Jai found was often the case, Dwayne was a coward. Not brave enough to play with the big boys... disposable probably in the long term. Now, it was all systems go. Shahid and Bazza were pulling in favours left right and centre... building up their armies, so to speak. Amassing their power force, whilst allowing their enemies to expose themselves. The more drugs and women Anastazy and his crew put on the streets, the easier they were to trace.

The one thing Dwayney boy couldn't give them was the Pole's storage facility, but that didn't matter. They were rounding up the lowlife that had betrayed them on the streets and sooner or later something would pop. Someone would know more than they should and Shahid was out to send a message now. He didn't care how they got the information... he was past that. He'd turned the corner.

The minute Anastazy Dolinski had spilled Imti's blood he'd signed a death warrant, not just for himself but, for anyone who crossed Shahid. Shahid had nearly lost everything and Jai knew what that could do to a man. He loved the Khan brothers like family and he would do whatever Shahid wanted. The pig farm in Holmfirth hadn't been utilised since Shahid's dad's time... Tonight, once more though, the pigs would eat well.

CHAPTER 79
Astor Avenue, Idle

From the doorway, Gus could see that it was too late to do anything. The motionless figure, tongue protruding and black, hung from a rope that had been looped through a metal ring in the ceiling. On the floor nearby lay a hanging chair, its chain still attached. It had been removed from the ring to accommodate a rope. The steady drip of urine from the bottom of DCS Hussain's trousers onto the laminate flooring was the only sound in the whole house.

'Fucking selfish bastard just couldn't let her be happy. He had to go and pile on more guilt. How the hell am I going to tell her, Al?'

Alice rubbed his arm, but said nothing. Gus knew that this may be too big a hurdle for him and Sadia to overcome. Deep in his own thoughts, he was startled when he heard a panicked 'Oh dear!' from behind them. He and Alice spun round just in time to save the next door neighbour, who had followed them, from falling to the floor.

Guiding her through to the front room away from the swinging body of DCS Hussain, Alice sat her on a sofa. Gus kneeled before her and ascertained that her name was Mrs Appleby. 'What made you follow us inside?'

She shook her head and with a shaking hand brushed a strand of hair from her forehead. As she took a couple of deep breathes, he noticed that the colour was beginning to return to her cheeks. He held her hand and waited till she was ready.

With a grateful smile she said, 'Well, I thought you should know what the young Asian lad said. It was clear you were worried, you know?'

'What did he say, Mrs Appleby?'

'Well, I hadn't actually seen him before but he came knocking on the door about 4 o'clock. Not long after that young officer left. He really hammered and hammered and then went round the back and hammered there too. Then he came back to the front and Mr Hussain opened the door. Mr Hussain clearly knew the lad. They were very angry with each other, but the only thing I heard was the young lad shouting "You bleep, bleep, bleep. You know you did it and you've let her think it was me all these years. So much for our boys in blue upholding the law.' Then, Mr Hussain saw me and opened the door wider to let the young man in.'

'Did you hear anything else?' asked Alice

Mrs Appleby shook her head. 'I never even heard the young lad leave, so I presume things had quietened down by then.'

'Can you describe him by any chance?'

'Not really. Mid to late twenties, I suppose. Good looking, nice haircut. Huge gold bracelet and chain. Very effeminate, I thought, considering the rest of his clothes were sporty.'

At the mention of gold jewellery, Gus raised an eyebrow. 'We'll, get you to look at a few photos, see if you can pick him out, Mrs Appleby. Now, let's get you back to your own house before the circus arrives.'

Mrs Appleby waved Gus' courteous hand away saying, 'I got myself here, I can get myself home. You've got a crime scene grid to cover. I'll be okay on my own.'

As Mrs Appleby exited the front door Alice looked at Gus, 'Crime scene grid, huh? The wonders of CSI.'

'Hm.' Gus headed back to the other room and, surveying the scene from the door, said, 'Might not be a suicide, Al.'

Alice joined him. 'You're thinking that was Shahid Khan, aren't you?'

Gus shrugged. 'Fucked if I know, Al. The description fits, but then it fits umpteen others, too.'

He craned his neck standing on tiptoe, 'Can't see a note on the table. You'd think he'd leave one. Maybe we'll find something on his computer. Looks like there might have been a scuffle. The chairs knocked over, papers on the floor, pictures broken and ornaments knocked over.'

'You think the Asian lad, maybe Shahid Khan, killed him?'

Gus jingled his car keys in his pockets, 'Bloody hope not. But we won't know owt for sure till Hissing Sid and his lot appear.'

With a last look at Hussain hanging from the ceiling, Gus said, 'He's a big man isn't he, Al? I know Shahid's built, but I'm not sure he'd manage to rope him up there.'

She shrugged. 'Don't suppose so, but here are the boys to put us right.'

Whilst the scene of crime team worked, Gus sat in his car, a cup of coffee, supplied by Mrs Appleby, in his hand and tried to work out how to break the news to Sadia. He didn't want to be the one to break her heart like this, but he knew there was no way out of it. No way he wanted anyone else to tell her. No way she'd want anyone else to see her broken. He didn't feel anything for the dead man who'd just been taken to the morgue. He'd never liked him. Always found him too stern, too judgemental and, especially with all this business with Sadia, he'd grown to intensely dislike him. But he'd still need to get to the bottom of it and he wanted as much info as possible before he reported back to Sadia.

He'd already got them looking for Shahid Khan, who was probably at BRI with Imti. He'd still got to make time to see Sampson who had already admitted to paying a visit to DCS Hussain earlier. He pushed his way out of the car and deposited his empty mug on the tray Mrs Appleby had left on the wall between the two gardens. The scene had just been cleared by Hissing Sid, and Sampson, who'd arrived with Brighton half an hour earlier, was sifting through the papers on the floor, looking for anything resembling a suicide note.

'Anything?' asked Gus, opening a drawer and sifting through it.

'Nah. Don't reckon there is one,' said Sampson, stretching his back.

Gus turned towards him. 'Come on, let's get some air and you can tell me what you have. Sounded pretty urgent when you arrived.'

Sampson eyes down followed Gus outside, then recounted his earlier visit to the DCS and the purpose of it. Gus listened nodding every so often and when Sampson had finished he frowned, 'So you're telling me Hussain all but admitted that he was the father of Millie Green's unborn baby.' This put a whole new perspective on Millie Green's death and it explained why Hussain hadn't wanted them reopening the case. Shit, he'd have to tread very carefully when speaking to Sadia. This was a complete mess.

Sampson nodded. 'Yeah, when I told him I was going to tell Sadia by close of play tomorrow, I thought he was going to take the opportunity to tell her himself first. Looks like he decided to do this instead. It's all my fault. I shouldn't have confronted him. I should've handled it differently. I blame myself for knocking him over the edge. Sadia will never forgive me.'

'Look Sampson, what you did was brave. Hussain wasn't the easiest to work with, so I think you did well to confront him. I think that between your visit and Shahid's – if it was Shahid – he realised the game was up. He decided to take the easy way out.'

Sampson looked up at Gus 'So you think he killed Millie Green too?'

Gus nodded 'Looks very much like it, Sampson. We'll have to investigate that much more fully now all this has come to light.'

'Poor Sadia,' said Sampson, looking distraught.

CHAPTER 80
Astor Avenue, Idle

Brighton had just finished a nice curry when the call came in from Alice. The cow had said it was urgent, that all hands were needed on deck so he'd jumped to it... well actually, he'd taken another chapatti and used it to wipe up the last of his tikka masala sauce, tidied the containers away, wiped the work surfaces down, washed his hands and *then*, with a last glance round his house, he'd headed over to Astor Avenue.

The address had been unfamiliar to him and it wasn't till he'd arrived that he'd learned who'd topped themselves. No denying it, it had been a bloody shock. Not that he felt anything for DCS Hussain but, rather because that was his meal ticket off down the fucking Swanee. What was he supposed to do now? Cursing under his breath he followed the stupid cow's instructions to hold the crowd back and to be on the alert for the media. Meanwhile, every time he glanced over he saw McGuire with a coffee cup in his hand chatting up the neighbours or Sampson. It made his blood boil at the best of times but tonight Brighton had other things to consider.

What was he going to do? He was sure the photos he'd taken would be found and he was equally sure that it wouldn't take a mastermind to trace them back to him. When that happened, he'd be in real trouble and with Hussain gone he had no safety net to protect him. He'd relied on Hussain to watch out for him. He'd been his last hope of being able to dodge away the next few years till his pension kicked in, secure in the knowledge that he had something on Hussain. For a nanosecond he wondered if McGuire might be amenable to turning a blind eye to the photos to keep them from being public knowledge… then he caught himself and laughed aloud. No way would McGuire countenance a cover up of any description. Not even to keep his private life secret. No, he was too much of a bloody goody two shoes. He'd make sure Brighton paid for his indiscretion with the camera, regardless of any personal embarrassment to himself.

Which brought Brighton onto plan B. He hadn't wanted to go down this route. He was happy with his job and the prospect of a pension but, needs must. He'd have to go cap in hand to his brother and beg for that security job he'd offered last time Brighton had gotten into a bit of trouble at work. He didn't want to work security for his brother's building site. He hated the cold and he hated being on his own overnight but, what other option did he have? Fucking Hussain! It was all his fault. Ungrateful bastard paid him back by topping himself. Arsehole!

Brighton edged closer to where McGuire and Sampson were chatting. Little bit of ear-wigging was in order. After all, how else would he find out if they'd found the photos yet?

Sampson was banging on about that Millie Green whore… the one who'd burned to death years ago… Bazza Green's sister.

Brighton, shuffled further into the shadows by the gate and continued to listen. When he heard them talking about how upset Sadia was going to be, he smiled. Served the bitch right. She'd hassled him enough, rollicking him for no damn reason in front of those uniformed officers. Maybe she'd be so upset she'd off herself too. Seemed like no-one had informed the bitch yet. McGuire wanted to do it himself... stupid bleeding heart idiot.

Brighton sidled back down the lane, shoulders hunched. He felt dejected. There was no other way to describe it. He'd worked hard to curry favour with Hussain and now it'd all backfired and before long he'd be out on his proverbial arse. He shook his head and had taken out his phone, planning to make the uncomfortable begging call to his brother, when a thought struck him. What if he allowed himself one final act of defiance before he went? He deserved it after all. He nodded and after a quick glance round to make sure no-one was watching, he headed to his car.

CHAPTER 81

They'd nearly finished in DCS Hussain's home and Gus felt done in. His head throbbed and his eyes felt gritty. His lack of sleep and the emotions of the day were beginning to take their toll on him but, he had one more job to do. The worst one imaginable and he'd give anything not to have to be the one to do it. That, however, was *not* an option. This was a job he couldn't delegate. He took his bottle of Wee Bru from his pocket, grimaced at the lukewarm dregs that remained and, fumbling for his pills, he popped his anti-depressants from their packaging. He'd only just swallowed them and was stepping towards the door when it flew open, bringing in a breeze of autumn leaves and Sadia, her hair tangled about her head and her coat flying open revealing a hastily fastened cardigan, buttoned wrongly.

Her eyes darted around the hallway of her home which was lit by crime scene lights, before resting on Gus, 'When the fuck were you going to tell me my father was dead, Gus?' She threw herself at him, her fists pummelling his chest. 'Too busy to come yourself, so you had to send that fucking creep, Brighton? How *could* you?'

Momentarily paralysed, Gus stood open mouthed as she hit him, then frowning he gripped her upper arms and gently shook her. 'Stop it, Sadia. Look at me. Stop it.' What the hell was going on? Had Brighton told Sadia about her father, against his express instructions? Surely even he wouldn't be that stupid. Seeing that Alice and Sampson had rushed into the hallway, he nodded at them over the top of her head telling them to leave them alone. No wonder she was upset.

The last place she should be is here in the middle of all this. He was thankful though, that, at least, her dad had been removed from the scene.

Heaving grating breaths, Sadia rubbed her sleeve over her face and sighed, half falling against him. 'Aw, honey,' he said, kissing her hair, 'I was on my way to you now. The CSI's have only just gone, sweetheart. But I don't get it. What the hell was that about Brighton?'

Sadia hiccupped and pushing agitated fingers through her hair said, 'He came to the house and told me.'

'He fuckin' what?' said Gus, 'I specifically said I would break the news to you.' If Brighton had been there right at that moment, he was sure he'd have torn the man limb from limb

Sadia extricated herself from Gus, her eyes refusing to meet his as she peered along the hallway. 'Where is he? My Dad? Where is he?'

'They've taken him, Sadia. I'll bring you to see him tomorrow.'

Her eyes hardened as she looked at him. With a glance laced with hatred, she shook her head, 'No Gus, no. I'm going to Shamila's tonight. I don't want to see you just now.' Turning, she walked back out the door. He ran after her but, she pulled away from him and got into the passenger side of Shamila's car. Shamila shrugged and drove away, leaving him on the pavement.

Closing his eyes, his mouth set in a thin line, Gus exhaled. 'What a difference a fucking day makes.' The phrase had never seemed so apt. Deep down inside him, he knew that, whatever happened next, Sadia would always associate their relationship with her father's death. He suspected that what they had wouldn't prove strong enough to withstand her guilt. He really wanted to kick something, punch something, so he shoved his hands into his pockets and took deep breaths. He was aware of the few people milling around behind him doing their jobs and casting curious looks in his direction. He wished he was on his own. Right now, all he wanted to do was stand under a scalding hot shower and then collapse into his bed for a week... or maybe a month.

The sharp bubbles of panic lapped at his chest. Fuck, the last thing he needed was to have an attack now. He'd too much to do. Ignoring everyone, he stumbled out of the house into the street and forced himself to focus on the yellow street light. Slowing his breathing, he waited for the tightness to ease. From somewhere far away, he heard Alice ask if he was okay but, he maintained his focus, ignoring her until the light-headedness left him and he was shaken but in control. He felt as if his heart had been ripped from his chest. It felt nearly as bad as when he'd lost Billy. He shook his head. No, this wasn't *that* bad... nothing could ever be that bad again. This was painful but he could cope. He knew he would.

Turning, he saw Alice and Sampson standing by the car, their expressions concerned. He smiled a tight smile and then his eyes narrowed as he saw a figure walking along the pavement towards them. Gus saw the cigarette in his hand and the supercilious sneer on his face. A wave of rage overtook him and, without stopping to think, he marched over to meet Brighton.

'Did you do the death notification for DCS Hussain?' Each word seemed to tremble in the air as Gus clenched and unclenched his fists.

Brighton smiled. 'Thought I'd save you a job... *sir*. I could see you were busy here.'

'You know the protocol, Brighton. A senior officer designates that role and I certainly did not ask you.'

Brighton shrugged. 'Needed doing. Thought I'd use my initiative. Thought you might be too close to the DS, *sir.*'

Seeing the self-satisfied look on the other man's face, a rush of anger hit Gus and without thinking, he raised his hand, clenched his fist and rammed it, with force, straight into Brighton's face. The resultant squelching sound as his nose burst, sending a spurt of blood onto the pavement, made Gus smile. Brighton cupped his hand under his nose to catch the blood. Turning to Alice and Sampson who'd rushed over, Gus grinned. 'That felt good, Al.'

He thought that maybe in the morning he'd regret his actions but, right then, he just didn't care. Brighton deserved that – and more.

Alice, concern making her face taut, frowned at him, as Brighton said, 'You'll really wish you hadn't done that, McGuire. Especially in front of witnesses.'

Before Gus could react, Alice had spun towards Brighton looking, Gus thought, like a gothic avenging angel, as she glared at him. Her tone menacing, she turned in a slow circle to encompass those who stood nearby. Holding her hands out palm upwards in query she said, 'What witnesses? Any of you lot see owt?'

Sampson and two of Hissing Sid's team shook their heads and Gus grinned. He knew Brighton had rubbed too many people up the wrong way and this was his reward… one he richly deserved.

Alice, smiling now, turned back to the bleeding man. 'Bit careless of you to walk into a door, isn't it?'

Brighton glared at her then at Gus before sidling off back to his car leaving a dripping trail of blood in his wake.

'You didn't need to do that, Al. I'd have taken whatever was coming.'

Alice turned round and thumped him hard on the arm. 'Yes. I bloody did. What. Were You. Thinking?' each word was punctuated by an additional thump that Gus knew would bruise, but seeing the tears glistening in Alice's eyes he accepted his punishment, saying only, 'I'm sorry, Al. It's been a long day.'

She nodded. 'Yeah, but at least we know which dickhead took those photos of you and Sadia.' And she nodded to the red Vectra pulling away from the kerb further up the road with Brighton at the wheel.

CHAPTER 82
The Fort

The interview with the Assistant Chief Constable had been difficult. Gus had outlined DCS Hussain's death as a probable suicide and updated her on Hussain's tacit admission of being Millie Green's unborn child's father. Her parting words 'cluster fuck' still rang in Gus' ears and although there was no blame attached to Gus he knew that for the department this was a huge issue. A senior officer committing suicide was bad enough, but the additional aspect of said officer's possible involvement in a police cover-up, combined with his subsequent implication in his mistress' murder and what could have been a mild headache, quickly swept under the carpet of 'personal issues', now became a mega brain tumour ready to haemorrhage, causing untold damage to the force's reputation. Of course, as expected Assistant Chief Constable Gracie Kielty had issued a press blackout, which Gus had duly passed onto his team. Not that he or any of his colleagues were ever keen to talk to the press. Deciding to be partially honest with the ACC, Gus had requested Brighton's removal from the team citing his direct flouting of orders regarding the death notification to Sadia and she had acquiesced, no doubt having enough on her plate without bothering about the petty internal politics of Gus' team. He would deal with Brighton's photography later. ACC Keilty had also directed the investigation into DCS Hussain's death and the Millie Green case to a team from North Yorkshire as per protocol. Gus was glad about that as he had more than enough to deal with already with the prostitute murders, the arson attacks and the rogue Polish thug.

Now, he needed to focus. Shahid Khan had been brought in and, although the interview was pertinent to Khan's visit to Hussain, Gus was reluctant to pass him off to the North Yorkshire team without first having a go with him. After all, it appeared that Khan was linked heavily to both investigations.

Grabbing a coffee, he headed down to interview room one with Alice. Khan was pacing the floor and practically growling by the time they entered.

'What the fuck's this about, McGuire? You got no respect? They've just taken Imti back into surgery and you've dragged me back here. I've no fucking time for this.'

He hadn't known Imti had been taken back into surgery. He fleetingly wondered if Sadia knew. He hoped not. She had enough on her plate as it was. Sitting down, he said, 'I'm sorry about Imti, but we need to ask you a few more questions.'

Shahid flung himself into the plastic chair opposite Gus, 'You couldn't have just come to the hospital to ask your stupid questions? That's where I've been since that bastard knifed Imti.'

Gus leaned back, folded his arms and raised an eyebrow at Alice. Alice pulled out a chair and sitting down said, 'Well, Shahid. We know that's not strictly true, don't we?'

'Eh?' Shahid glared at her.

Alice smiled. 'Well we've got a witness who places you at the scene of a possible murder earlier on today.'

Shahid sprung to his feet, 'What fucking murder? You're not fitting me up for some murder now!'

Alice took out her notebook and flicked the pages over. 'Ah here we are, 4:45 this afternoon. Our witness places you at our crime scene.'

Gus watched as Shahid made the mental computations. A frown appeared across the ridge of his nose. His eyes flashed and then he leaned forward elbows on the table, 'You telling me old man Hussain's dead?'

Gus nodded. 'So, you were there at his house?'

Shahid nodded. 'But I didn't kill him.'

'You were heard shouting at him,' said Alice.

Shahid turned to her, 'You never shout at anyone, Little Miss Perfect? Bet you do; but you don't go around offing them, do you? And neither do I. The old bastard was still standing when I left him.' He turned to Gus with a grin, 'Anyway, seems to me you've got as much of a motive as anyone, Gussy boy.'

Gus nodded slowly. 'Ah, so *you* removed the photos did you? Wondered where they'd gone.'

Shahid grinned. 'Course I did. I was after owt I could get on that old bastard. Always thought he'd had summat to do with Millie's death and when the Dhosangs told me she were up the duff, I knew exactly who'd done it. Mr "'holier than thou" Hussain, that's who.'

Gus exchanged a glance with Alice. Shahid had seemed genuinely surprised to hear about Hussain's death and Gus knew that he'd be more likely to use a gun or a knife than to go to the bother of hanging the man. Besides, the absence of a suicide note didn't necessarily mean murder. Gus looked at Shahid, 'Where's the photos then?'

Shahid didn't even pretend not to know what Gus was talking about. 'If I hand them over, you'll let me go back to the hospital?'

Gus considered for a moment, then, 'Okay, as long as you stay available. Other officers will want to interview you too.'

Shahid snorted. Then he stood up and unzipped his designer hoodie and lifted his T-shirt revealing a tan envelope tucked into his jeans. He pulled it out and threw it on the table, 'Screwing the boss' daughter, McGuire, not a good idea. Maybe you've got more of a motive for killing the old bastard than me.'

CHAPTER 83

The wind had picked up and the streetlights below cast amber hues over the dusting of leaves that skittered down Lilycroft Road, like a herd of marauding rats following an invisible Pied Piper. Gus shivered, despite the heat that made the incident room feel like a sauna. At least the rain had eased off for now. Compo worked in the corner of the room, headphones on, oblivious to Gus' presence and with a stack of chocolate biscuits and a pile of crumbs beside him on his desk. He smiled as Compo's head bobbed to a beat he was thankful not to be able to hear.

He wished Sadia was here but, despite numerous texts and calls she refused to speak to him. All he wanted to do was comfort her but he guessed his presence was too much for her to bear. He could only hope that, with time, she'd be able to see things more clearly and overcome whatever guilt was making her push him away. He knew that it was becoming more and more likely that, even in the absence of a suicide note, the North Yorkshire team would cite suicide as cause of death. Sadia would be sure to blame herself for driving him to it and Gus wasn't sure if any subsequent discoveries regarding Millie Green would alleviate that.

Unable to bear another solicitous look from Alice, he'd despatched her and Sampson to the BRI to check up on Charlotte who, it seems was coming slowly out of her induced coma. Gus wanted a friendly face there when she fully wakened up and you couldn't get more friendly than Alice.

Things were falling into place. He had officers on the ground looking for Anastazy; Compo was close to getting a photographic ID of Jankowski's 'The Old Man'; and all he could do now was wait. He moved away from the window and had just sat down when his phone rang. A quick glance told him it was Alice. 'What's up, Al?'

'It appears that Shahid lied when he said Imti was back in surgery, Gus. I just asked the nurse on duty and she knew nothing about it. Serafina's mum, who's been here all afternoon with Jacob said that almost as soon as Shahid got back to the hospital, Jai arrived and they high-tailed it out of here without even saying bye to Imti. What's made her even more anxious is that her other two sons, Thomas and Luka, went with Shahid. She thinks they've found Anastazy. She'd also worried sick about Serafina. She's not seen her since this morning. She'd scared Anastazy's got her.'

'Shit!' said Gus. 'I'm on my way.' Dragging his coat on, Gus yelled over to Compo, who, blinking like a myopic owl, looked up, pulling his head phones off. 'I need you to pull up CCTV from BRI, pronto. Start with the main entrance camera and pan out from there. Make it from 10pm tonight. We're looking for Jai and Shahid.'

Hanging over Compo's shoulder as he worked, Gus identified Jai going into BRI at 22:05. 'Isolate that shot there and zoom in. I want to see who's with Jai.'

Compo, zoomed in on the man walking with an unmistakeable bounce, next to Jai.

Gus prodded the screen, 'That's one of Bazza Green's thugs, Jerome. Looks like they've teamed up. This is not going to end well, Compo. Track the footage and follow it so we know where they're headed and keep me updated. I'll get the armed response unit on standby. I'm going to meet up with Alice and Sampson at BRI. Keep us updated.'

Gus was nearly at the lifts when Compo ran after him, 'This just came through from Jankowski. It's the image of we've been waiting for of The Old Man. It's a bit grainy and a few years old but it's the best Jankowski could get.'

Gus grabbed it and glanced at it. It was of a man at his daughter's birthday party. 'Shit, I've seen this man, Compo. Thanks.' And after jabbing the lift button once more to no avail, he spun round and took the stairs two at a time.

CHAPTER 84
Off Ingleby Road

Bazza Green hadn't accompanied them to the deserted warehouse off Ingleby Road and, to be honest, Shahid was pleased. Bazza was too old for this game, as well as being too much of a coward and he'd only be in the way. He'd insisted on sending his men, though, and Shahid respected that. He'd have done the same. No point in trusting someone else if you could have your own men on the job. To be fair, they'd probably come in handy. Shahid had no idea what Anastazy's capabilities were, or the extent of his network, so they'd agreed to stake the place out for a bit before going in guns blazing.

The warehouse had once housed a halal supermarket, but after a fire a few years previously it had never reopened. From Ingleby road the building looked deceptively small but, from the back, where Shahid had stationed himself and some of his men, it was huge and sprawling. It had two floors and jutted out into a huge rectangle that spanned, at least, the length of a football field. Its windows were covered with corrugated metal, but still, the occasional chink of light could be seen. Shahid wondered what exactly Anastazy kept inside. Jerome had seen him entering the warehouse from a shuttered back door earlier in the evening accompanied by an older man. According to Jai's source the older man was the boss and Anastazy was his deputy.

Shahid didn't much care about the hierarchy. As far as he was concerned, Anastazy was his, although he knew that Jai was keen to score him for himself too. His boss would get what was coming to him afterwards. After all, apart from what they'd done to Imti and Trixie, they'd seriously affected his business. Bastards had tried to implement a takeover bid. Tried to disturb the status quo and neither Shahid nor Bazza could tolerate that. They'd rubbed along fine for years, respecting each other's territory and no fucking immigrant was going to disturb that. No fucking chance.

Shahid glanced at Jai who sat beside him in the car. He wondered how Jai managed to appear so contained, so emotionless. Shahid's blood was boiling. The interview with McGuire had wound him up. The fact that Hussain had taken the easy way out had pissed him off. After all this was over, he'd planned on handing him to Jess on a plate, preferably with his balls rammed down his throat. Now, it seemed he'd have to rely on the oink oinks to expose him for what he was. Hmph, and that was as bloody likely as him scoring the winning wicket for Pakistan at Lords. They'd probably cover it all up like they did last time. Well, not if he had his way. No, he'd see to it that they squirmed. He'd make sure the papers learned all about DCS Hussain's other life.

Jai nudged him. 'Ready to go in, then?'

Shahid pointed to the cameras dotted around the building. 'You managed to disable them? Don't want to give them a heads-up, do we?'

Jai smiled in a rare display of humour. 'I was thinking more along the lines of a heads off.' And he pulled a pistol from his pocket.

Although his heart thumped, Shahid's mind was crystal clear. He lifted his pistol from his lap and grinned. 'Right then, we're ready. Give the signal.'

CHAPTER 85
Bradford Royal Infirmary heading to Ingleby Road

'Compo, you're sure of their location?'

Compo's voice excited and high came over the airways, 'Yes, dead sure. It's the old Pakeezah warehouse. There's no cameras round the back of the warehouse but, I managed to get GPS on Shahid's phone and that's where he is. ACC Kielty has authorised helicopters and they're on their way, as are armed response. Her instructions are for you to get eyes on but to wait for back-up.'

Holding onto the dashboard for dear life as Alice took a right from Thornton Road onto Ingleby Road at the Morrison's traffic lights, narrowly missing an oncoming truck, Gus cursed under his breath. Sampson squashed in the back of Alice's mini gasped and Gus imagined that the other man had closed his eyes and was praying. If he wasn't so bloody scared he'd have done the same.

'Grow some balls,' said Alice, as she straightened the wheel and sped down Ingleby Road. 'We're nearly there.'

Seeing a gap in the traffic, she swerved out, accelerated and pulled back in, just in time to make the opening into the road where the warehouse back entrance was situated. Gus reached over and flicked her headlights off. As Alice edged forwards, Gus and Sampson checked the cars lined up on the roadside. 'All empty,' said Sampson.

She pulled into the warehouse car park and Gus, hoping they weren't too late, scanned the windows, 'I can see lights from inside, faint but they're there. He flung open his door and, in a crouch, ran towards the building. A sudden gunshot

399

made him duck and run for cover, then as his eyes accustomed themselves to the dimness he saw a group of men huddled in the shadows near the door. One of them was just withdrawing his gun from the door and a taller man, kicked it open before they all filed through.

They'd clearly not opted for stealth thought Gus realising the gunshot was them firing at the lock. Not waiting to see if Alice and Sampson were behind him Gus counted to twenty then followed the men through the door and into a spacious but empty room with a staircase in the right-hand corner. Above him he could hear the other men's feet thudding on the stairs. They were clearly making no secret of their approach. Never a good strategy.

Throwing a quick glance over his shoulder he saw Sampson just behind him and Alice slightly further back, talking into her phone. Good, she was calling it in. He put one finger to his lip and began to climb the stairs, keeping his back to the wall and making no noise. At the top of the stairs, he stopped and listened, but all he could hear was his elevated breathing and Sampson's heavier pants behind him. He poked his head round and saw that a series of large metal doors lined the walls which, no doubt, accounted for the absence of sound. Creeping closer, he saw that all but the first one had padlocks on. He put his ear close to the door and could hear the faint sound of angry voices. Hopefully they were too busy arguing to hear anything.

Holding his breath, he reached out and depressed the handle, waiting for a sign that he'd alerted those inside. As soon as he pushed the door open the voices became clearer. The door had indeed been heavily soundproofed. Fine as long as your other security systems hadn't been disabled… not so good if they had.

As he pushed it open wide enough to see what was happening inside, there was a tumultuous explosion, followed by the rap of automatic gun fire. Puffs of concrete dust drifted through the open door and Gus realised that someone inside the room had fired repeatedly into the ceiling. He heard coughing, followed by laughter and then a voice he recognised as being Shahid's, 'I'll kill you for what you did, Anastazy, but shooting you will be too quick.'

Gus poked his head through the door. The dust was beginning to settle and he could see Shahid pointing his gun towards a metal pillar. Behind the pillar, Gus could just make out Anastazy. A trio of men, one of whom appeared to have been hit either by a ricocheting bullet or some debris, stood, guns drawn at the ready. On closer inspection, Gus recognised the one who was bleeding as Jerome. Nearer to the door, Jai held his gun to the head of an older man. Shahid stood just in front of him. In the corner, Serafina sat on a chair, her eyes wide. 'Please don't hurt my dad,' she said, but Jai ignored her.

Shahid, turned to her. 'You still don't get it, do you?'

Gus could see her shaking her head, tears rolling down her cheek as Shahid continued, 'This is all because of your dad. He set this monster loose on the streets of Bradford and look what he's done. Your fucking dad couldn't control him and look what he's done. He's hurt your brother, and your friend, he's stabbed Imti, he's killed Trixie and some other girls'

Anastazy laughed, 'I didn't kill your whore, Shahid. Someone else did that but, yes I killed the others… or rather I had them killed… all so your dad, Serafina, could be the boss again, like he was in Poland.'

Serafina glanced from Shahid to her father. 'Dad?'

Her father looked at her. 'Where did you think all your fine clothes and everything came from in Poland, Serafina? I worked hard for us, for our family. I did what I had to do.'

Anastazy laughed again, 'Tell her, Old Man, what you did to get your money. How many people you ordered killed. How many people you stole from. How much money you took from people's investment accounts leaving them destitute. How, when the authorities began to link you to all these activities, you had to flee Poland with nothing but your snivelling family.'

The Old Man, fire in his eyes, took his opportunity and lifting his leg, he kicked Jai in the balls. Jai's gun clattered to the floor. The Old Man grabbed it and before anyone could react, he shot Jai in the head. Shahid, hand shaking, aimed his gun at The Old Man. Anastazy immediately ducked from behind the pillar and fired a shot, hitting Shahid in the leg. He fell to the one knee. The other three men, raised their guns, but were too slow, as Anastazy with three separate pops floored them. Blood pooled under their bodies leaving Gus in no doubt they were dead.

Serafina jumped to her feet and, hands over her mouth, she glared at her father, who now had his gun trained on Shahid. Anastazy approached her from behind and grabbed her, 'You're coming with me. That was the deal.'

Her father flinched, but nodded once at Serafina.

She cried out, 'You sold me? To this monster? Even after what he did to Jacob and Mum? How could you do this. Say you didn't do all these things?'

Her father's lips curled and he shouted something in Polish that made Serafina flinch. She pulled her arm away from Anastazy, 'I won't go with you. You'll have to kill me.'

Anastazy put one arm around her waist and lifted her off her feet. As she began screaming he raised his gun and pressed it to her forehead as he walked across the room.

Gus poked his head through the door and when he was certain Shahid had seen him he yelled as loudly as he could and using all his upper body strength he pushed the door so that it crashed into Serafina and Anastazy. Seeing the Old Man whirl towards him, Gus yelled 'Shoot, Shahid!'

From the corner of his eye, he saw The Old Man fall to the ground and he scrabbled across the floor to claim Anastazy's gun. As he felt the metal of the gun, Anastazy delivered a scissor kick to Gus' thigh that made him yelp. The gun slipped from his fingers and skittered across the floor. He rolled away and onto his back and, pulling both legs up to his chest, he forcefully propelled his heels down onto Anastazy's head, thankful that today, he'd worn his boots.

Undeterred, Anastazy shook his head and, blood streaming from his skull, he crawled towards the gun as Sampson and Alice barrelled into the room. Lifting it with shaking hands, Anastazy his face a manic grin, extended his hand. Gus on his knees, yelled a guttural cry and lunged for the man as the gun exploded.

For shocked seconds Gus stared at Anastazy as his eyes rolled back in his head and he fell to the concrete, unconscious as if the final firing of the gun had been all he'd remained conscious for. Gus' eyes flitted round the room assessing the damage. The old Man lay sprawled in a heap, Serafina, screaming, was in Shahid's arms. Sampson was crouched over a bundled up pile of dark rags. Gus could see his mouth move but couldn't hear what he was saying. A cold sweat broke out over his body and without knowing how, he was there beside Sampson looking down at Alice's small frame lying in a dark puddle.

Dragging Sampson back, Gus knelt beside her and for an instant he was back with Billy. His heart hammered and his breathing accelerated. Then a sudden clarity took hold and he yanked up her clothes looking for the wound. This wasn't Billy. This was Alice and he wasn't going to lose her. As he worked, his hands became slick with blood, but he wouldn't give up. Pressing down on her stomach, he yelled at Sampson to find something to compress her wound.

Pushing down on Sampson's rolled up jumper, he spoke to her. Begging her... cajoling her... ordering her, to stay with him. Then, when she stopped breathing he made Sampson take over applying pressure and he moved up to her chest, alternating between compressions and mouth to mouth until finally the paramedics arrived and took over.

Unaware of the blood streaking his hands or the tears streaming down his face, Gus stood up and looked round at the carnage. The paramedics were working on The Old Man. The bullet appeared to have hit his shoulder and Jai appeared to have suffered a flesh wound to the head. Strangely detached from the scene, the sounds reached his ears as if through a muffler. He saw Serafina stand up and wobble over to her father. The paramedics moved to allow her to kneel beside him. She whispered something in Polish in his ear and then got back to her feet. Before the paramedics could react, the girl turned and raising her leg, kicked him in the kidneys, 'That is for Jacob and...' she kicked him again, 'That is for my mother.'

Gus knew he should feel a sense of satisfaction at Serafina's actions but, all he felt was numbness. He walked over to Shahid who was applying pressure to his own wound, 'You know you're under arrest, don't you?'

Shahid nodded. 'Yeah, you always play it by the book, McGuire.'

Gus turned and looked around him, 'Luckily for you, Shahid, not always. Otherwise you'd be dead.' He walked away, signalling to a uniformed officer to read him his rights, but was halted when Shahid spoke again.

'Just promise me one thing, Gus?'

Gus tilted his head to one side. He was tired and the last thing he wanted was to do deals with Shahid Khan. He wanted to get off to the hospital to find out how Alice was. Actually, that wasn't strictly true. He didn't want to go anywhere near the hospital. He felt he was cursed and the last thing he wanted was to jinx Alice's recovery. Deep down he knew he was being a coward. He was scared to go in case Alice was dead. He looked at Khan, 'Depends?'

'Make sure Jessica knows the truth about Millie's death. Don't let them cover it up.'

Gus' lips thinned. 'You should know by now that I won't let that happen, Shahid. Millie Green's murderer will be exposed and that's a promise.'

Hissing Sid arrived to process the scene as Gus was about to go downstairs where Sampson waited to take him to the hospital. 'Well thank God, no one has to tell your parents you're in hospital this time.'

Gus shook his head and continued walking. 'No, it's much worse this time, Sid. It's Alice who's injured.'

CHAPTER 86
Marriner's Drive to the Fort

Gus hadn't slept well. A combination of residual adrenalin, a throbbing thigh where Anastazy had kicked him and thoughts of Sadia and Alice had kept him tossing and turning for most of the night. Bingo, sensing Gus' low mood had tried his best to be endearing, licking his face and wiggling his bottom in a way that normally had him laughing but, today he felt flat. He let Bingo out the back, fed him and made coffee on automatic pilot. Finally, knowing he had to do something he packed his rucksack with work clothes and donned his joggers and trainers and set off jogging to The Fort.

He knew he should go to the hospital to see how Alice was doing but he couldn't bear it. The sight of her parents, bruised and fragile, keeping a silent watch over their daughter had sent a knife through his heart. This was all his fault. He should have waited for the armed response team instead of bulldozing in and risking his officers' lives for a bunch of scumbags. If he'd stayed out, with any luck, they'd have killed each other, saved the taxpayer a shed load of money and Alice would be alright.

Entering Lister Park by the bottom entrance, he began a slow circuit of the park, heading round the bottom end of the pond as his warm up, before hitting the hill that would take him behind the imposing art gallery, Cartwright Hall. The Hare and Minotaur Bull were gone. Apparently, they were on loan elsewhere and Gus missed them. He took a detour and jogged slowly through the Moghul Gardens, his feet pounding Imran Qureshi's artwork commemorating the fallen of World War One. Normally, he appreciated the richness of this beautiful city, but today his heart wasn't in it. Bradford's diversity gave the city a heart and soul that Gus usually found warming. Today, he barely felt lukewarm. He continued on, doing two more laps of the park, trailing through the autumn leaves, with squirrels snagging conkers from the ground keeping him company. The slight fog that made trees appear suddenly before him, like floating Dementors. The eeriness of leaves illuminated by white LED lights and falling like engorged raindrops matched his mood.

Sweating and breathing hard, Gus left the park by the top entrance on North Park Road and wound a circuitous route towards The Fort. Heading up Victor Road past The Church of God of Prophecy, its spire protruding like a witch's finger whilst next door, on Victor Street, was the Jamiyat Tabligh-ul Islam Masjid. Behind these two religious edifices, Lister's Mill dominated the skyline; a giant's turret floating off the ground in a cloud of fog.

By the time he reached the Fort he was drenched by the early morning mist as much as by his sweat. His dreads held droplets of moisture which, like a dog, he shook before entering the station. Feeling the need to cool down after his run, he took the stairs, slowing his pace to normalise his breathing. A mere six months previously he would have struggled to cover even half the distance he 'd done today. But, his thigh muscles were stronger and his shoulder had recovered enough for him to carry a rucksack when he jogged. He shrugged. At least some things were improving for him… if only he could say the same about everything else.

The incident room was empty and Gus' entry stimulated the light sensors. He took a swig from his water bottle and set up the coffee machine before heading through to the male toilets where he showered and changed into his work trousers, T-shirt and his usual crew-neck jumper. Applying moisturiser to his face he realised he looked wan. He always felt that his complexion paled into a jaundiced hue when he was off colour. Sadia had told him he was talking shite. That even when he was paler than usual, his skin was like cappuccino. Studying himself now he wondered if she meant the pale froth on top or the rich coffee underneath. Thinking about Sadia whilst Alice lay in a hospital bed made him feel disloyal. So, shoving his damp clothes into his bag, he wandered through, poured himself a coffee and settled down behind his computer to answer his emails.

As usual he had loads of emails, some of which he immediately deleted: even Police Yorkshire seemed to get its fair share of spam. Flicking down in order, he came to one dated Sunday at 16:35. Hesitating, with his finger on the cursor Gus frowned. This was completely unexpected. Why the hell would Sadia's dad have emailed him?

CHAPTER 87
The Fort

Gus hadn't been surprised to get the phone call this morning. After the email from Sadia's dad, he doubted he'd ever feel surprised by anything again. He'd suspected it would only be a matter of time before guilt made Jessica come clean. She looked waiflike, sitting in the stark interview room, her clothes baggy and less than clean. Her hair fell in rats' tails, reminding Gus of how her friend Trixie had looked when they'd arrived at her crime scene. The only difference was that Trixie's hair was wet whereas, Jessica's was greasy.

He'd taken one look at her through the one-way mirror and ordered one of the uniforms to get her a bacon butty from The Chaat café. Now, with the interview about to start, he wished that Sadia could be here for the girl. He knew she'd want to but maybe it would be easier for her without Sadia. He would have brought Alice in with him but, hell… she was fighting for her life in BRI. He'd been reluctant to bring Sampson in with him, knowing that both the incident with Sadia's dad and Alice's injury had hit him hard. However, Sampson had turned up for work and between the two of them and Compo they were trying to make headway with their workloads. Anastazy and The Old Man were being dealt with by North Yorkshire as a favour to ACC Kielty, who knew Gus' team was overstretched.

Jessica hadn't met Sampson in an official capacity, so he hoped it would help her to relax. Sampson had a way about him that relaxed people and made them open up.

The air carried the lingering aroma of Jessica's meal when they'd entered and the empty wrapper on the table top told Gus she'd been hungry. He pushed a cup of sugary tea across the table and said, 'It's good you've opted to come in, Jessica. It'll make it easier for you, you know?'

Jessica nodded and using the cuff of her jumper wiped a tear from the corner of her eye. Gus nodded at Sampson who went to the door and requested a tissue box. With the tissue box in the middle of the table, the tape recorder on and the initial introductions made, Gus read Jessica her rights and offered her a solicitor.

Shaking her head, Jessica sniffed and rubbed her nose with a bunched up tissue. 'No need for that.'

Gus nodded. 'You can start when you're ready, Jessica, okay?'

Jessica swallowed and then, hands clasped in her lap, she stared to the left of Gus shoulder as she began to talk.

'It was dark, you know, and raining. It felt like it'd been raining for weeks. I knew Trixie was up to something. She'd changed, you see. Didn't spend as much time with me. Oh, I knew she was Bazza's pet but it weren't that. No, there was summat else going on. I wondered if she were using again.' Jess looked at Gus, her face earnest, 'I'd worked so hard to get her off the drugs. I'd stayed with her for weeks at The Prossie Palace and we'd done it together.' She sniffed, 'I were so proud of her. She was so strong. I never blamed her for using drugs.' Jessica yanked her fingers through her hair pulling out long greasy strands in her anguish.

Gus waited and in due course she continued. 'Her bastard of a step-dad raped her you know? She were only ten and he kept on doing it. Then, when her brother were old enough, he made him do it to her too. Then, his friends and then folk down the pub and punters and strangers. When she finally

410

got away and came to Bradford she was broken. Not surprising she got hooked. That's what the likes of Bazza does. They get them hooked and then put them out to work. Fucking animals, the lot of them.'

She lifted her fingers to her mouth and began gnawing at her cuticles. Speckles of blood oozed around the nail, but she kept on nibbling, as if she couldn't feel it. Gus wanted to put his hand over hers and stop her but, he knew that if he did, if he showed any sympathy she might not be able to go through with it.

At last she pulled the sleeves of her jumper down and covered her hands completely. Gus wondered if this was a technique she'd taught herself.

'When I met her she were hooked. She was so young and I was angry. Bazza swore he hadn't got her hooked but, you can't trust him. Trixie said it weren't him either. Said it was some Scottish bloke from Leeds. Anyway, I took her in and I got her clean. We made plans, me and Trix. We were going to get away from all this. Go to Spain or somewhere hot, but not Italy. Not with all them earthquakes.'

'Did you know her real name, Jessica?'

Jess glared at him, 'Why? So that bastard can come to her funeral? Don't fucking think so.'

'No, so that *bastard* can be locked up once and for all. So he can't do what he did to Trixie, to other girls. That's why.'

Jessica looked at Gus, then her mouth curled downwards, 'Don't fuckin trust ya.'

Gus shrugged, but said nothing. Jessica hadn't had much cause to trust the men in her life.

She leaned back in her chair and Gus mimicked her. He knew mimicking other's body language struck a chord with them. Made them more likely to trust you.

'Anyway, we were best mates me and Trix.' She grinned. 'We had such a laugh. She was so funny, so alive so real.'

She started to sob. Gus plucked a tissue from the box and placed it in her hand. He lowered his voice, 'You were more than friends, though, weren't you, Jess?'

The girl's shoulders stilled and for a moment she remained silent then she sat up and rubbed her face dry, Gus sat up too and held her gaze. At last her shoulders fell and she said, 'Yeah, she were my girlfriend. We didn't tell the other girls. Didn't want them calling us dirty lesbos or owt. It was our secret.'

Gus nodded. 'So, what went wrong, Jess?'

She closed her eyes and stayed silent for a long time. When she spoke again her words erupted from her like cold shards of ice, 'Shahid! That's what fuckin went wrong.'

Her hands clenched and unclenched in her lap and her eyes blazed. 'He took her away from me. He bought her things, made her promises I couldn't make and he took her away from me!'

Tears flooded her face but Gus didn't think she even noticed.

'I knew summat was up so I followed her. She *should've* been with Bazza. It was his night but I heard her telling him she were on the rag. I knew she weren't so I followed her. I thought she were meeting a dealer or summat. I only wanted to stop her doing drugs again.'

She looked at Gus so beseechingly that he smiled and said, 'I know that, Jess. I know you only wanted to help Trixie. You loved her.'

She nodded. 'Yeah, I loved her. All I wanted was to help her. But, when I got to the allotments, she were with a punter. Well, that's what I thought at first. I could hear them you see. I thought she were trying to make some extra money for us to escape, you know. Behind Bazza's back like. But then, after they'd finished, I heard them talking. I walked closer and I could see it were Shahid. I listened. They were planning to get married. She said they were having a baby. She said she loved him and that she'd sort it out with me. But how could she ever sort that out with me? He killed my mum and now he were taking Trixie away from me too.'

Gus and Sampson exchanged a glance as she went on, 'I waited till he'd gone and then I went over to her. She weren't expecting to see me, she kept glancing round like she were nervous or summat. I don't know what happened. Next minute she was on the floor and I was on top of her my scarf round her neck and I were pulling and pulling so tight her eyes were bulging. Then, I stopped. But, she wouldn't move. She were all floppy and I didn't know what to do. I panicked so, I stood up and there, by the bushes, was an empty wine bottle. I broke it against the fence and then I shoved it up her fanny like what happened to them other girls and then I grabbed her phone and smashed it and then I phoned you lot with my phone.'

Gus felt as exhausted as Jessica looked. It must have been sheer hell for her to carry the guilt of what she'd done to Trixie on her own. He knew what it was like to carry the burden of guilt. He leaned across the table and squeezed Jessica's hand, 'You did good Jessica, you did good.'

Then, standing up he walked round and knelt beside her. 'You know I have to charge you now, Jessica?'

She nodded. Gus formally recited the charges. Then, with one last look at her he turned to leave the room. As he reached the door, Jessica said, 'Wait!'

He turned and met his eye. 'Dawn Jones.'

413

Gus nodded. 'Thanks, Jessica. You did the right thing. I won't let you or Trixie down on this one.'

As soon as he was out of the room he got Compo to run the name through missing persons. He maybe couldn't do anything for Alice or Sadia right now but, maybe he could do something for Dawn 'Trixie' Jones.

CHAPTER 88

This was proving to be the longest morning in all of history. The lack of news from the hospital was wearing the team down. Even Compo was more subdued than usual and Sampson, though professional as always, looked wan. They hadn't seen Brighton and that seemed to suit them all. Gus' parents had taken over Alice's parents' vigil for a few hours that morning and, although they knew he was busy, he could tell they were disappointed that he hadn't made the time to visit Alice. As soon as he'd dealt with Shahid Khan and the email from DCS Hussain, Gus was going to take Compo and Sampson with him to see Alice. He put the thought that he was using them for moral support to the back of his mind.

He hadn't intended for Shahid Khan and Jessica's paths to cross but, a delay with the duty solicitor resulted in Jessica being moved back to the cells at the same time as her half-brother was being escorted to interview room two. Gus felt Shahid tense when he saw Jessica, head down shuffling along the corridor. The panic in his voice was obvious, when he called out to her. 'Jess, what are you doing here? You hear me? Don't you say owt to them. Keep schtum.' He pulled against the uniformed officer trying to squirm round to yell after Jessica, 'Jess, I mean it! Keep quiet, okay?'

Watching the interplay with interest, Gus saw Jessica's eyes dart to her brother and then away again. Her shoulders seemed to slump even more as she walked on in silence. Gus felt sorry for the girl. She'd had a shit awful life and now her future didn't look too rosy either. He knew Sadia would be

415

gutted when she heard what had happened but, for now, he was more interested in Shahid's reaction.

Shahid had been cautioned on various weapons charges and on breaking and entering. As the damage inflicted by Shahid had been done in self-defence and as Serafina was pressing charges against both Anastazy and her father, it looked like Shahid would get off with a caution. So far none of the weapons could be linked to Shahid and, in his first statement, he'd said that he, Jai and Bazza's men had entered the building unarmed and had picked up the weapons inside the building. Serafina corroborated their story and Gus and Sampson had arrived too late to refute that. Gus had decided to 'forget' the gunshot used to gain entry to the building in the first place. After all, he did owe Shahid Khan his life and maybe there was something to be said about 'better the devil you know'. Besides, he couldn't see which of the men had actually used the gun and there had been enough residue flying about to make it an academic question anyway.

Khan had also hired a hot-shot lawyer who, as Gus knew from past experience, could wangle his way out of most things. He didn't hold out much hope of getting Shahid banged up but, then again, he was more than happy to have so many testimonies against Anastazy and Mathias Nadratowski, AKA The Old Man. At least there'd be some justice for the Camilla and Starlight's families even if they were extradited back to Poland for their crimes there. He knew they'd be spending a long time in prison.

Shahid's lawyer was waiting for him in the interview room so Gus went into the observation suite and watched with interest. Although there was no sound, Gus could see that Shahid was agitated. He stalked up and down the enclosed space, running his hands through his hair and was clearly disagreeing with his solicitor about something. Gus had a sneaky feeling it was to do with Jessica, rather than the current charges against him.

He turned to Sampson, who was also watching the scene in the interview room. 'Brace yourself. This is going to be interesting.'

The pair of them walked round to the room. As soon as they entered Shahid whirled round, eyes flashing. 'What the fuck's Jess doing here?'

His solicitor reached out to touch his arm but Shahid pulled away: 'Leave me alone, for fuck's sake, okay?'

Raising his eyebrow, Gus pulled out a chair and sat down without replying. Leaning back, he folded his arms across his chest and studied Shahid who paced the room like a caged animal. Sampson followed Gus' lead and took the chair beside him. Shahid's lawyer darted glances between Gus and Shahid, whose breathing was growing heavier as he paced.

Without warning, Shahid spun on his heel and slammed both palms down on the table, making the lawyer's bottled water shake precariously then fall onto its side and roll off the table, landing on the floor with a bump. Shahid towered over Gus, his eyes flashing. 'You fucking going to tell me what's going on with Jess?'

Gus without flinching, maintained eye contact with Shahid, whilst the solicitor scrabbled on the floor for the bottle. 'You need to sit down, Shahid,' said Gus.

Shahid glared at him for a moment more and then pushed himself away from the table, flopping into the chair opposite Gus. His solicitor, looking flushed and with a sheen of sweat along his top lip sat next to Shahid. Gus noticed with amusement that the solicitor angled his chair away from Shahid, as if to avoid being in the line of fire.

417

Gus nodded to Sampson, who started the recording and introduced those present. He looked at Shahid, who now sat shoulders hunched over, his elbows resting on his thighs his hands tightly linked. Gus could feel the tension radiating from him and wondered how best to capitalise on it. Keeping his voice low and calm, he said, 'You seem upset, Shahid? Care to share what's bothering you?'

Shahid's head jerked up and he began wringing his hands. 'I've told you what's up. I want to know what Jess is doing here.'

Gus bit his lip and shrugged, ''Fraid I can't talk to you about Jessica, Shahid. Confidentiality, you know? Anyway, we're not here to talk about your half-sister. We're here to talk about what happened at the Pakeezah warehouse.'

Shahid slammed his hand on the table again. 'Fuck that!'

Gus, head on one side, studied Shahid. 'You know, if you don't calm down, I could add "threatening behaviour towards a police officer" to the charges against you.'

His solicitor, finally manning up, cleared his throat, 'No, no, Inspector McGuire, my client is understandably concerned about the welfare of his sister. It's been a very stressful few days with extenuating circumstances. After all, he's recently lost his fiancée, his brother is still in hospital after a vicious knifing and his business premises were the subject of an arson attack. On top of this, he had the trauma of rescuing Serafina Nadratowski only last night. I'd say these circumstances are enough for you to cut my client some slack.'

Gus nodded and smiled. 'Okay, I'll do that providing Shahid allows me to continue with this interview with no more aggressive outbursts.'

Hearing Shahid's sharp intake of breath, Gus turned to him, 'Okay, Shahid?'

As his solicitor began to speak, Shahid waved him to silence. 'Shut up! Let me think, for fuck's sake.' Resting his head in his hands, he sat immobile for a few minutes and then, lifting his head, he looked at Gus. 'I want to confess to Trixie's murder.'

Lips pursed, Gus nodded, but before he could reply, Shahid's solicitor interjected, 'I want to speak to my client in private.'

This was a turn-up for the books. Two confessions for the same murder in one day. Could things get any more complicated? Gus pushed his chair back, but Shahid turned to his solicitor, 'I don't want your advice, okay? Just sit there and shut up. Don't worry, you'll still get paid for your time but I want to confess.'

The solicitor started to argue but, at Shahid's glare the man subsided in his chair with his notepad before him, 'As you wish,' he muttered, under his breath.

Gus sat back down with an exaggerated sigh, 'So, you killed your fiancé and, in so doing, also your unborn child?'

Shahid flinched, but held Gus' stare, stating in a firm voice, 'Yes, that's right.'

Gus nodded and rubbed his chin. He needed to be very careful here. If he ballsed this up, he could be looking at weeks of delay in sorting out Trixie's murder. Finally, happy with his plan of action, he said, 'Okay, Shahid, but what I don't get is why you folded her tights up and placed them so carefully on her chest after you strangled her.'

Shahid swallowed. 'Just did, that's all.'

Gus leaned back, placing his hands behind his head and sighed. 'So, you admit to killing Trixie by strangling her with her tights.'

Shahid frowned and glanced at Sampson, who maintained a neutral expression, 'Yes! Fuck! I've already told you that, haven't I?'

Gus propelled his chair back till he was balancing on the back legs. He knew exactly what Shahid was doing and he admired him for it. In his own way, Shahid had tried to look out for his sister over the years, despite her hatred of him. 'Didn't you think that biting her neck and thighs was just overkill, Shahid? Especially after you rammed that broken bottle inside her, ripping her to shreds.'

Jumping up, Shahid grabbed the bin from the corner of the room and retched into it.

Gus went over to him, handing him a tissue and waited till the other man had finished before taking the bin and handing it to the officer waiting outside the room. 'You no more killed Trixie than I did, Shahid.'

Shahid, tears streaming down his face, allowed Gus to guide him back to his chair. When he was sitting down, Gus said, 'Look, I know you want to watch out for Jessica. I know you feel she's your responsibility but, you can't do this, Shahid. You just can't, okay?'

Shahid sniffed and then wiping his cheeks dry, he looked at Gus, 'Did Jess do those things to her?'

Gus shook his head, 'No, Shahid. She didn't bite her, nor did she rip her to shreds, but she did kill her.'

Shahid sniffed, 'Because of me... because of us.'

Gus nodded.

'I thought she'd come round, you know? Thought she'd get used to it and maybe even move in with us. She were Trixie's best mate you know? They were so close. Trixie didn't want to hurt her. That's why we kept it secret.' He shrugged. 'Jess could never accept that I didn't kill her mum... and now it's too fucking late. That bastard Hussain, he did it, and now he's beyond justice and we're all still here suffering.'

Gus leaned across the table, 'Look Shahid, I know right now it doesn't seem like much, but, at least, now, Jess knows you weren't responsible for her mum's death. Who knows, maybe in time you'll be able to see her. Do you think you'll be able to forgive her, maybe not now, but sometime in the future?'

'Maybe… but not right now.'

Gus looked at Shahid's solicitor. 'We'll suspend this interview for today. I think your client needs some time to come to terms with everything.'

CHAPTER 89
Bradford Royal Infirmary

If he never had to see a hospital again it would be too bloody soon. Gus was grateful to be there with Compo and Sampson but he was also as guilty as hell. As they climbed the stairs, Gus was aware that their steps had slowed to a near crawl. They hadn't spoken about what had happened to Alice... not really. They were too scared to put their fears into words, Gus reckoned. He knew he was, anyway. She'd survived the emergency surgery the previous night and was holding her own. The next twenty-four hours would be critical.

Being here, yet again, in the critical care unit was torture for Gus and the emotional pain was worse because it was Alice in there now fighting for her life. As he approached her room, Gus could easily have run away. In fact, had Sampson and Compo not been with him, he probably would have. They held back, allowing him to approach the small window first. As he looked inside, all he could think was that Alice appeared to have shrunk. Under the sheet with monitors all around she looked tiny. Her parents sat, one on either side of the bed, their hands touching her arm as if they couldn't bear to let her go.

Gus felt his throat clog up as he watched them. The Professors Cooper were exactly as Alice had once described them to him. They were other-worldly. The nastiness and viciousness Alice dealt with on a day to day basis were anathema to them... and yet, here they were, dragged from their world of academia and plunged into the sordid reality of policing in 2016 and he was responsible for it.

Last night they'd clung to his hand, peering myopically up at him, seeking reassurances he felt obliged to give but, knew deep down inside were not based on anything more than hope. They were scientists through and through and had no religion to see them through this frightening time. Gus knew that they'd have spoken to the surgeon and would know, like he did, how unlikely they were to get Alice back.

As he watched, Alice's dad rose and walked round to his wife's side. Gus realised that she was sobbing, her head bowed in her grief. She put her hand over Alice's and he put one arm round his wife and placed the other hand on top of his wife's as if the three of them were making a pact, like he had done with his friends in childhood. Wiping his tears away with the back of his hand, Gus turned and patting Compo and then Sampson on the back, he left.

CHAPTER 90
Myrtle Park, Bingley

Myrtle Park was resplendent with shades of autumn but Gus couldn't have cared less. His thoughts were still with Alice and her parents, yet he knew he had to get this over with. He'd phoned Shamila and insisted that she make Sadia meet up with him on neutral territory. He needed to talk to her and he hoped that this outdoor venue would be suitable for what he had to say. When she'd agreed, he'd dropped back home to collect Bingo. If nothing else, Bingo might prove a distraction for both of them. Besides which, Bingo deserved a decent walk with Gus. He'd relied too heavily on his mum to take the dog out over the past few weeks.

Partly to spend time playing with Bingo and partly to try to compose himself for what he knew would be a difficult meeting with Sadia, he'd arrived early. The park was within walking distance of Bingley so Gus had parked up and he and Bingo had skirted the children's play area and gone to the huge field where the remnants of bonfire night still scarred the ground.

He and Sadia had spent many happy hours strolling through the park over the past few months... young lovers savouring their closeness, arms wrapped round each other, hips brushing together as they walked in synch. Finally, tossing Bingo a bone, he hooked the leash over his foot and slouched on the bench where they'd agreed to meet.

He'd wanted to give her the opportunity for a quick and un-embarrassing getaway, should the need arise, so had opted to avoid Tarquin's café and gone for the safe outdoor option.

Alerted to her approach by Bingo's low growl, he turned his head. Loping easily towards him, her hips swinging, she wore her leather jacket with a glittery blue scarf wrapped round her neck, matching gloves and a hat with a grey fur bobble on her head. As she neared, Gus could see the worry lines across her forehead. Her mouth was tight and her eyes avoided meeting his gaze. He felt his heart sink when she opted to sit at the far end of the bench as far away from him as she possibly could. Earlier, he'd decided not to burden her with Alice's condition, so it seemed the only thing they had to talk about was her father.

Nudging Bingo with his toe to make him stop growling, Gus cleared his throat and tried to remember what he'd planned to say but, his mind was a blank. Swallowing, he turned slightly to her. She held herself rigid and, he suspected that one slight push would have her toppling backwards off the seat, so determined was she to distance herself from him. He sighed, knowing that what he was about to reveal wouldn't ease the situation between them. Hmph, that was probably exactly what her old man had been aiming for when he sent Gus that email. Even from beyond the grave the old bastard was manipulating her.

Clenching his hands in his jean pockets Gus took a deep breath and began, 'I'm really sorry about your father, Sadia.'

She snorted and in his peripheral vision Gus could see her shaking her head from side to side, 'Are you though, Gus? Are you really sorry or do you think that his death clears the way for you and me?' she glared at him and then without waiting for a response she continued, 'Well, if that's what you think you can forget it, okay? You and me are the last thing on my mind.'

Their relationship, or indeed, lack thereof, was the last thing on Gus' mind, too, but he couldn't reveal that to her. Instead he nodded, 'Yeah Sad, I understand that. I don't expect anything from you. That's *not* why I insisted we meet.'

She waved her gloved hand at him, 'Well, in case you don't know, I've already been notified of...' she swallowed and despite her obvious effort a tear rolled down her cheek. 'They told me about his involvement in Millie Green's death. I know what he did to Millie,' She rubbed her glove over her cheek, 'and to me ... and to my mum. Thank God, she at least knew nowt about it all. Thank God, she died before this all came to light.'

Gus swivelled round so he was facing her. 'Look, Sadia, I need you to listen to me.'

She laughed, the sound hollow and incredulous. 'Why should I listen to *you,* Gus? What makes you so worthy of my attention. For fuck's sake all you were to me was a quick shag... a bit of a novelty, that's all. Now, I've more important things to think about, like burying my dad, convincing Councillor Majid to bury him in the Muslim cemetery, despite the fact he committed suicide... Fuck, I almost wish he'd been murdered. Why the fuck couldn't he leave a suicide note like normal people?'

Gus jumped to his feet and moved closer to her. He knew that the venom streaming from her mouth was caused by grief but, he felt each barb like a bullet piercing his skin. It wasn't like he was on top of the world right now either. Still, what he felt wasn't what was important right now. He had to be the one to tell her this, even if she was making it as difficult as hell.

'Look, Sadia, I need to tell you something and you need to listen. This is important.'

Just when he thought she was going to jump up and flounce off, she capitulated. Her shoulders relaxed and she turned and leaned back. 'Okay, Gus, you win, but make it quick.'

Gus sat back down and plunged right in. 'I got an email from your father dated yesterday at 16:35.'

Sadia lurched to her feet, her eyes wide. 'What?'

Gus ignored her question and continued, 'I reckon that was after Shahid Khan's visit. It was your father's suicide note. I've had to pass it onto the relevant officers but, I asked them to let me tell you in person. I couldn't let anyone else tell you.'

Sadia exhaled. 'What did he say, Gus?'

Gus pulled a folded piece of paper from his pocket and handed it to her. 'I printed it out, Sadia.'

Pulling her gloves off, Sadia took the paper and looked Gus straight in the eye before opening it. 'Thank you, Gus.'

With a shrug, he waited as she unfolded it. As her eyes scanned each word, Gus recited them in his own head. Her father's last communication was seared in his brain and he knew that it would be seared in her heart forever.

DI McGuire,

I have decided that I am too cowardly to face my beautiful daughter Sadia with the truth. I have proved to be unworthy of her love and, despite my intentions to protect her over the years, I now realise I have, in fact, failed her. I am entrusting you with this communication and am sure you will deliver it in whichever way you feel best.

In recent years, in commune with Allah, I have realised that my actions surrounding the death of Millie Green have had consequences from which I can no longer escape. I now wish to reveal the truth and trust that my punishment will be meted out on the other side by my God.

Sadia's mother was unable to have children after Sadia and that left her despondent. She became extremely depressed and for long periods withdrew from both me and Sadia. Thankfully, the full impact of that was lost to Sadia in her early years. However, this lack of comfort at home, led me to embark on an affair with Millie Green. I make no excuses for that. I have prayed for forgiveness and stand before Allah to be judged on this.

I truly loved Millie. She was a remarkable woman; loving, caring and honest. When she became pregnant with my child, I decided that I would leave Amina and take Sadia with me. I was sure that Millie would be a much better mother to Sadia than Amina. However, what I didn't realise was that Amina had discovered mine and Millie's affair.

Sadia's mother was not in her right mind when she did what she did to Millie Green. I also believe that if she had known Millie was pregnant, she would have taken a different course of action. I was in a unique positon to misdirect the investigation. I falsified interviews and drip-fed lies about Millie's state of mind and about her relationship with Arshad Khan. I disposed of Amina's clothes and, ultimately, I moved us away from that area and protected Sadia in the only way I could.

I have made my peace with Allah and trust my sins will be expunged. Suicide is against the will of Allah but I can no longer continue in this life. I give my life and soul to my God and accept his decision for me.

I love Sadia more than I can say. I am proud of her fierce independence and her resolve. She has been the one true joy of my life and I pray she can forgive me.

Please accept this as my confession of obstructing the course of justice
Yours sincerely
DCS Khalid M Hussain.

When she had finished reading Sadia folded the paper up, put it in her pocket and with her gloves in one hand, she walked away. Feeling as if his heart had been yanked from his chest, Gus watched her retrace her steps to the car park.

He stood, picking up Bingo's leash, then leaned over to traced his finger over the inscription on the back of the bench,

'In memory of Janet and Robert Dingle, who for fifty years shared their lives lovingly with each other.'

Sadia and I didn't even make fifty weeks, thought Gus and, whistling to Bingo, he too made his way back to his car.

CHAPTER 91
Three weeks later,
Marriner's Drive

L istening to soppy songs had never been Gus' thing but, since Sadia had asked for and been approved a transfer to Scotland, he'd been more susceptible to love songs on the radio, tearing up and getting all emotional. When he'd confided this to Sampson, he'd told him to get a grip and take a leaf out of Little Mix's book with their 'Shout Out To My Ex' song.

Truth was that although he missed Sadia he knew that the circumstances surrounding her father's death were too much to overcome and he wasn't sure he was strong enough to help her anyway. They'd been working flat-out at The Fort in the preceding weeks, what with being four officers down since Sadia had left and Brighton's enforced transfer – hopefully to outer Siberia – and of course the absence of their DCS. Alice was still in a coma and with each day that passed Gus grew more despondent. Her parents had authorised that, later on today, she be taken off the life support machines. Gus was dreading the outcome of that.

However, on Friday in a flurry of Chanel and chiffon, DCI Nancy Chalmers had drifted in bringing joy, laughter and a much-needed bottle of whisky. The team were overjoyed to have her back and Gus was thrilled. She'd lost weight since The Matchmaker case, but the old glint was back in her eye and she seemed ready to dig in. Her return was the one bright light in an otherwise dark future.

A burst of ecstatic barking from Bingo seconds before the doorbell rang, told Gus that his parents were at the door. He pulled himself from the couch where he'd been watching the

430

football and, barefoot, wandered through to open the door, Bingo bouncing beside him.

At first, he wasn't entirely sure what he was seeing on his doorstep, but then his mothers' head poked over the rather large box she was carrying and his father's voice boomed from behind her saying, 'In you go, Corrine,'

Puzzled, Gus stepped back from the door as his parent's trooped through to the living room. Following them, his heart sinking in trepidation, Gus wondered what they were up to. Much as he loved them, he'd found them quite unbearable these past weeks. He felt like they'd put him on suicide watch. Every time he turned they seemed to be there, eyes anxious, watching him as if they thought he was going to break down. No matter how often he told them he was fine and that he was taking his meds and that he'd re-enrolled with the dynamic counselling, they flapped. He dreaded to think what they were doing here today.

Seeing his father's balloon face grinning at him, with a striking similarity to Bingo when he thought he'd been particularly clever, Gus shook his head, knowing that no matter what idiocy they were about to subject him to, he'd submit.

His mum was practically hopping from foot to foot. 'Quick, Fergus show him.'

Holding his breath, Gus watched as his father swept the phone book and a vase from the sideboard and placed them on the floor before bending down to rummage in the box, talking all the while in a baby voice to whatever was inside.

Shit, thought Gus, *please not another bloody dog.* Much as he loved Bingo, another dog was not what he wanted. Finally, his father, face jubilant stood upright with a birdcage in his hand. His mum, unable to maintain her silence

431

anymore said, 'Look, it's a wee canary, Angus. Do you see its wee Beatle-style fringe... well, it's called Ringo!' She turned to the small yellow bird with its distinctive brown head feathers that, did indeed, make it look like a Beatle and began talking to it as if it were a parrot, 'Who's a pretty boy, who's a pretty boy.'

Speechless Gus could only watch as his dad looked at his mum. 'It's not a parrot, Corinne darling. It's a wee canary birdie.'

Gus rolled his eyes and then, as Bingo, paws up to investigate the new addition to their family, gave an approving bark, said 'Bloody hell, you two will be the end of me. What am I going to end up with next time a relationship of mine goes down the pan? A bloody goldfish called Pingu?'

Looking sheepish, his dad flung a big arm round Gus' shoulders. 'It'll be company for Bingo when you're at work.'

Gus watched the small yellow bird jump from rung to rung, its head nodding from side to side. Smiling, he turned and gave his dad a hug before lifting his mum up and swinging her round, making her squeal. 'You're the best parents in the world, you know?' and he deposited a kiss on their cheeks before heading to the kitchen to turn on the kettle.

Just as it boiled he heard his phone ring, followed seconds later by his mum's 'phone' voice. 'Who is it, Mum?'

She walked into the kitchen, tears streaming down her face. Reaching out her arms to Gus she said, 'It's Alice...'

ACKNOWLEDGEMENTS

There are always so many people to thank for getting a book through to publication and *Uncoiled Lies* is no exception.

I have been lucky to have had such expert advice and support from my Leeds Trinity Tutor, Martyn Bedford as well as my fellow students, who fed back at critical times in the production of the book. They know who they are. My family has, as always, been a source of support and encouragement throughout the writing process. I couldn't do it without them.

As ever, *Uncoiled Lies* is a work of fiction and any errors are all down to me.

Writing is a lonely profession and I delight in reading the reviews so many of you fabulous readers write. Reviews are an author's lifeblood and really help with getting an author noticed. So, if you liked DI Gus McGuire and his team, please consider leaving a review on Amazon or Goodreads. It needn't be long, a few words are all that's necessary and they really do help.

Here's till next time, Best Wishes

Liz Mistry

If you want to connect with Liz, you can do so on:

Twitter: @LizMistryAuthor
Facebook: LizMistryBooks
Amazon: https://amzn.to/2xhdOgG
Website :   https://www.lizmistry.com/

Printed in Great Britain
by Amazon